ABIDING FAITH, HIDDEN TREASURE

Abiding Faith, Hidden Treasure

Helen Gumienny Glowacki

This book was printed in the United States of America.

To order additional copies of this book:

Visit the author's website at:
www.helenglowacki.com

For wholesale or multiple copy information:

Send inquiry to helen@helenglowacki.com

Contents

Novels by Helen Gumienny Glowacki

When God Broke Grandma's Heart
When God Took Grandma Home
When Grandma Chased the Spirits
The Granddaughter and the Monkey Swing
Grandma's Little Book of Poetry: The Story of God's Plan of Salvation
Abiding Faith, Hidden Treasure
And Then They Asked God

Why God Why Series by Helen Glowacki

To What Purpose?
Why God Why?
Why Trust Scripture?
What Should I Know About Life after Death And The
Coming Tribulation?
What Does God Want Me To Do *RIGHT NOW*?
Do The Little Sins REALLY Count?
What Do Angels Do?

Other non-fiction Books by Helen Glowacki

Politically Incorrect: The Get Some Gumption Handbook
When Enough is Enough
What No One Is Telling You about Addictions
Overcoming Depression: How to be Happy

****

Authors Website: www.Helenglowacki.com

Face book: http://www.facebook.com/pages/The-Grandmother-Series/155300907853909?ref=ts

Book Reviews

From Dallas, Texas:

I've just read one of the most inspiring books I have read in a long time! The story and characters reveal real life situations in a remarkable and inviting form. I am certain that such a riveting story can also serve as an effective supportive tool for pastoral and mental health counselors. Ms. Glowacki described the stages of grief and God's comforting plan in an extraordinary way and through characters that really grab the heart. She is an author I expect to see on the bestseller list very soon and for many years to come. I look forward to the next books in her wonderful, inspiring series. A pleasure to read, a masterful idea, *When God Took Grandma Home* by Helen Gumienny Glowacki is filled with the most beautiful insight into God's plan for us!

> **—Reverend Fred Krueger, retired Lutheran minister of twelve years and clinical social worker for twenty-six years**

From Sea Cliff, New York:

Helen Gumienny Glowacki is a magnificent writer, who is truly able to weave a story that will make the reader become emotionally involved in the character's lives. It was a joy to read this book, and the reader will appreciate the strong Christian values portrayed therein. This book will certainly whet the appetite for the other books in the series. *When God Broke Grandma's Heart* by Helen Gumienny Glowacki is a certain bet to be a best seller.

> **—Reverend Richard C. Freund, president, New Apostolic Church USA**

Once again, Helen Gumienny Glowacki enthusiastically presents a scenario, which will delight readers and bring comfort to anyone who is grieving. This book, *When God Took Grandma Home*, will inspire all readers and give them a deeper insight into the after-life. This book is a masterful portrayal of young people searching for the truth. It is sure to be a great success.

> **—Reverend Richard C. Freund, president, New Apostolic Church USA**

From Port St. Lucie, Florida:

When Grandma Chased The Spirits: One Star . . . Star of Bethlehem . . . Rating! Helen Gumienny Glowacki's novel, *When Grandma Chased the Spirits,* serves the reader in a similar manner as the Star of Bethlehem served earlier seekers . . . . it leads the reader to a beautiful spiritual experience. It shows us the gifts God offers that leads us to inner peace and understanding. Helen's work is so special that I believe it will become a shining navigational tool for many who search for understanding just as the Star of Bethlehem once served as a navigational tool for those who searched for the Christ child. Helen Gumienny Glowacki has, with extraordinary skill, created characters who express their love for others in a beautiful way and have the desire to go the extra mile to help those struggling with doubt and those who have been misguided. Through the manuscripts and journals created by "grandma" and discovered by the various characters in Helen's stories, one can actually see into the caring nature and loving heart of the author. Her stories eloquently reveal her love for God and her diligent search for truth. Five star rating? This work is worthy of more . . . the one star rating mentioned above . . . . The single Star of Bethlehem rating. God bless you "GiGi," and thank you for sharing your *magnificent* gift with us.

—**Frank Geores**

From Odenton, Maryland:

As a counselor to many who struggle with challenging circumstances in their lives, I found *When God Broke Grandma's Heart* an inspirational story of hope. Despite cruelty and betrayal from those she trusted and the multiple adversities Grandma endured, she was able to find strength and understanding through her faith in and love of God. Helen Gumienny Glowacki beautifully portrays the phases that individuals move through and the transformation that can occur when one is able to let go of negative events in their past and strive toward the understanding that regardless of how unjust, none of the pain was for naught.

—**Tammera L. Shelton, MS Psychology**

From Clifton, New Jersey:

I am the wife of a retired minister. Many times during my husband's ministry, I was aware of a parishioner living through a difficult circumstance, but because of my husband's responsibilities to provide assistance and counseling, I was not always able to help in the matter. Helen Gumienny Glowacki's The Grandma Series are a wonderful way to provide help and support to someone in need when other avenues of communication are closed. These books are inspiring, uplifting, educational, and heartwarming. Every story ends with a beautiful example of how God explains our pain, renews our hope, shows us the way out of our situation, and creates a miracle for our lives. I love this series.

—**Edith Stier, thirty-two years as the wife of a minister**

From Brookfield, Wisconsin:

Wow! I've just finished reading the third book in this series of wonderful novels and can't find words great enough to describe them. At a time when there are so many troubles in the world and so many people who suffer, these books are a real eye opener about God's plan of salvation and why bad things happen to good people. They remind me of Jim LaHaye and Jerry B. Jenkins's Left Behind Series. These books are a MUST READ!

—Ben Lodwick, avid reader

From North Palm Beach, Florida:

Grandma's Little Book of Poetry: The Story of God's Plan of Salvation is a wonderful book about the successes and failures of real life and the story of the Good News of God's love for us. All of Helen's novels are wonderful to read, but more importantly, they are a balm for the soul and an education to the seeker.

—Dr. Walter Forman

From Boca Raton, Florida:

To Ms. Glowacki, author of The Grandma Series: So grateful to have found your books. I think it is refreshing to find a Christian author who sees the *difference* between religion and spirituality AND that the two can be, and should be, used in the same sentence.

—Luke Jansen, senior vice president, Medical Connections

Reader Reviews From Online Bookstore Web Sites

Five-star rating. *When God Broke Grandma's Heart:* (February 03, 2009) WHEN LIFE GETS YOU DOWN, PICK THIS BOOK UP. I didn't have any expectations before reading Helen's first book, but as I got into the story more and more, it literally pulled me in and wrapped its arms around me. I wasn't ready for that. What a wonderful read. Congratulations on an inspiring work.

—Anonymous

Five-star rating. *When God Broke Grandma's Heart:* (A) well-written, heartwarming story of Grandma's struggle to overcome heartbreak and tragedy through her belief in God. This story will touch your heart. A worthwhile read for all generations. I look forward to reading more from this author.

—A reviewer, a reader in Kentucky

Five-star rating. *When God Took Grandma Home:* Remarkable for someone looking for answers! Found it extremely inspirational and deeply moving. A fascinating storyteller with a real message.

—Fred D'Alauro

Five-star rating. *When God Broke Grandma's Heart:* This book is written from the heart with such thoughtfulness and grace. The author provides the reader with a meaningful experience. The messages are gentle yet powerful to the soul even though experiencing grandma's struggles and grief throughout the novel. The author shares the ideas of strong beliefs in ourselves, carries our faith, and shelters us in times of need and guides us home. Transformation and courage are profound themes of this novel to find truth and faith within all of us. The reader will be captivated at the books end and will want to read what comes next. Thank you, Grandma.

—Debra Forman

Five-star rating. *When God Took Grandma Home*. HEARTWARMING! This book touched my heart. It is both heartwarming and very spiritual.

—Debbie Espeland

Five-star rating. *When God Broke Grandma's Heart*. What an outstanding writer! I chose this book because throughout my life, [my] Grandma was always there for me making things become rosy. This book kept me riveted—there are many valuable lessons. Helen is an angel sent to help us through our trying days. I am now reading her second book. Thank you for helping me find some peace in this world.

—Robert W. Rothe, USMC 1970-1976, a reviewer

Five-star rating. *When God Broke Grandma's Heart*. WONDERFUL INSPIRATIONAL NOVEL. I enjoyed reading this book. It is well written with stories of disappointments and pleasant experiences too. Guidance is given through a loving "grandma" who shows through her example the kind of positive attitudes we could have in our lives. The Bible references throughout the book are helpful. The list of ways to achieve peace of mind and soul written by "grandma" are very good for facing what happens in our lives.

—Patricia Robinson

Five-star rating. *When God Broke Grandma's Heart*. Fantastic ! A must read for all generations.

—A reader

Five-star rating. *When God Took Grandma Home*. Must read! Touching story of life's tragedies and heartaches and how lessons learned from these heartbreaking events can turn into blessings.

—A reviewer, a Kentucky reader

Five-star rating. *When God Took Grandma Home*. A very captivating book, keeps you moved from the beginning.

—A reviewer

For Crystal

a courageous young woman who trusted God through a difficult
circumstance, became a role model to others,
and thus demonstrated how the word of God teaches us
that Satan loses his power when we pray, wait, and trust.

Note To The Reader

The King James Version (KJV) of the Bible, which is public domain in the United States, is used throughout the novels written to date by Helen Gumienny Glowacki. However, for further study, the author recommends the New King James Version (NKJV) of the Bible for easier reading and less usage of the old-world language while remaining true to the original text.

This book contains a scriptural index. Instead of assembling this index according to *The Chicago Manual of Style*, I have put it together in a format I believe might be more useful to the reader. I have chosen key words that may highlight the reader's specific concern or interest, and under those words, I have listed the scriptures that address those concerns. I believe that this index style may also better support a teaching program based on this book.

Acknowledgments

To my husband, Wally, who graciously accepted my many hours with computer,
Bible, and concordance and made my computer behave;
to my loving children and grandchildren for their support;
to Richard Levinson whose kindness can never be repaid;
to Jim whose penchant for pithy rejoinders inspired the dialogue

to Master Chief Thomas Eldridge
for sharing his extensive knowledge about Iraq;
to Bill O'Reilly whose books and interviews tell the truth
about the invasion of Iraq
and who would enjoy both knowing "Jim," the fictitious character in this book,
and listening to the resplendency of his aphoristic rhetoric;

to new friends and old friends who pray for me, keep me striving, never doubt,
and in so many wonderful ways give me the greatest friendships
I could ever ask for;
to my sisters-in-law for loving and encouraging me;
to Kethly who is always first in line to buy and read my novels;
to all those at Xlibris who have supported this effort;

to the ministers and deacons of the New Apostolic Church
who diligently look after my spiritual life
and keep me in their hearts and in their prayers;
and most of all, to my Heavenly Father who guides my life, gives so much,
loves so much, and made all this possible,

MY HEARTFELT AND HUMBLE THANKS!

Message From The Author

This novel is about a young man who has spurned God because he mistakenly believes that God is indifferent to the cruelties and injustices in the world. His story speaks to the struggle of the soul to move the heart toward an understanding of God despite the power that pushes toward complacency. It is a story of how faith is challenged by the hatred, greed, jealousy, and lack of accountability in those given the responsibility to protect what is good.

The young man in this novel has personal values very much like those God acclaims throughout scripture, yet categorizes himself as nonreligious and concludes with good reason that religion does not appear to produce a change for the better in man or society. He finds himself caught between two worlds, one where his anger at God for allowing evil to exist is a governing force and another where the hunger that lives in his heart to find goodness in the world overwhelms him. He hardens his heart toward all things relating to God to allow him to ignore his hunger and fuel his anger. Unconsciously however, he is challenging God to step up to the plate and fix what is wrong and to prove Himself all-powerful and loving.

What this young man eventually learns is that a perfect and all-encompassing plan for every person who was ever born, conceived, or died has been placed into the physics of our world and will overcome the evil that exists. He learns that evil is far more painful than a cruel action, far more powerful than hypocrisy, far more subtle than mankind realizes, and that it must prevent God's plan from being completed or die. But what he does not recognize is that it is evil that endorses his complacency about religious matters and provides the boost to his ego that his denigrating and sarcastic rejoinders give him and which allows him to retreat from any accountability to God.

As he witnesses the harm people do to one another he feels that love no longer exists. However, God's love for him does exist and continues despite his thoughts and brings him into the embrace of an entire family who speak often of God's plan of salvation and His love for mankind. Through this special gift, the young man begins to learn of God and learn that love can be understood through the sacrifice Christ made for mankind when He gave His life for them. Christ exemplified perfect love in His willingness to suffer so others could be free.

His family understands that while they strive to develop their ability to love unconditionally and sacrificially, they often fall short of the example Christ provided. They view God's love as a precious and undeserved gift and appreciate as another precious gift the love they find in one another. They discuss how every act of kindness and every commitment of time and effort given to nurturing the love they receive can cause that love to last throughout a lifetime and reach into eternity. Love that is nourished, flourishes even in the worst of times. But they sadly acknowledge that many in the world do not know how to love or how to appreciate or sustain the love they are given.

The importance of love is described in Matthew 22:37-39 when Christ answered the Pharisee who asked Him which of all the commandments was the greatest commandment. *"Jesus said unto him, Thou shalt love the Lord thy God with all thy heart, and with all thy soul, and with all thy mind. This is the first and great commandment. And the second is like unto it, Thou shalt love thy neighbor as thyself."*

The first part of what Christ said clearly explains that one must love God with *all* their heart, soul, and mind. But to truly fulfill what Christ says, one must seek to understand the meaning of love as Christ practices love. The family shows this young man how they turn to scripture to help them learn how to behave in ways that will promote the growth of love in their hearts so they can truly love and trust God, and one another. They find that to help them gauge the success or failure of their efforts to do this, it is key to understand that truly loving and trusting God requires more than a superficial love; it requires that they are passionately attached (Revelation 3:15, 16 *"because thou art lukewarm . . . I will spue thee out of my mouth."*), intimately associated (Matthew 25:12: *"Verily, verily I say unto you, I know ye not"*), and actively learning about the one they love (*Matthew 11:29: "Take my yoke upon you and learn of me."*).

But this young man, while listening carefully to the family discussions, cannot accept that perfecting love should be the goal of mankind and balks at any commitment believing might require. But he does read that if he considers Gods words, God promises to provide a greater understanding of all things. 2 Timothy 2:7:, *"Consider what I say and the Lord give thee understanding in all things."* But then God also tells him to continue in what he has learned so he can be perfected in all things. 2 Timothy 3:14-16: *"But continue thou in the things which thou hast learned . . . the holy scriptures . . . make thee wise unto salvation . . . all scripture is given by inspiration of God . . . for instruction . . . That the man of God may be perfect."*

These passages are excellent indicators of what God means when He asks us to love Him. They are also excellent indicators of our ability to love others and they guide us to successful relationships. In a nutshell, what scripture tells us is that when we offer passion, intimacy, active attention, a desire to learn what pleases the one we love, and are stedfast and continuing in our love, we are giving to that relationship the very things that will make *us* happy in that relationship as well.

This young man's journey toward an understanding of God's plan of salvation and man's part in and responsibility to that plan addresses the inertia caused by being confused about God. He is caught between two worlds; one that inspires hope but demands he give more than he does, and the other that allows him the comfort of complacency. The journey discloses how creation and evolution can co-exist, why evil works to destroy our faith by causing us to harm one another, and how God comforts us through scripture when we are heartbroken.

This story also addresses the failure of mankind to follow the latter part of Christ's admonition to the Pharisee found in Matthew 22:37-39, *"And the second is like unto it, Thou shalt love thy neighbor as thyself"*, and what God says in Isaiah 29:13-15 about failing to do this: *" " . . . . Forasmuch as this people draw near me with their mouth . . . but have removed their heart . . . . behold I do a marvelous work . . . Woe unto them that seek to hide their counsel from the Lord, and their works are in the dark, and they say 'Who seeth us? . . . "*

The young man in this story however, has already adopted a code of honor that practices love toward his neighbor and thus he does fulfill the second part of the commandment Christ left. He follows what God asks in Proverbs 3:29, *"Devise not evil against thy neighbor, seeing he dwelleth securely by thee"*. And in Proverbs 11:12, *"He that is void of wisdom despiseth his neighbor; but a man of understanding holdeth his peace."* And even more so in Zechariah 8:17, *"And let none of you imagine evil in your hearts against his neighbor; and love no false oath; for all these are things that I hate, saith the Lord."* But he is also comforted to know that God will deal with those who harm others. Malachi 2:8:, *"But ye are departed out of the way; ye have caused many to stumble at the law; ye have corrupted the covenant of Levi, saith the Lord of Hosts."* When he reads the words of Matthew 25:40, *" . . . Inasmuch as ye have done it unto one of the least of these my brethren, ye have done it unto me"*, he is able to control the anger he feels toward those who bring harm to others through the comfort he gleans from knowing God will deal sternly with them.

Despite what he learns, he is not ready to give his heart to God. He believes that he is already the overcomer God speaks of in Revelation 2:7, *" . . . To him that overcometh will I give to eat of the tree of life, which is in the midst of the paradise of God."* He feels that he already lives a life of integrity and doesn't see why this is not enough. He cannot give his heart or make a commitment to God and therefore continues to be embroiled in defending his position. Thus he struggles to justify his actions by employing the use of sarcasm and by pulling back whenever he feels himself drawn to God as he listens to the family's approach to problem solving through scripture. But, finally as he recognizes his responsibility to acknowledge what he has been offered and what he has learned, and after reading in Revelation 4:20, *"Behold, I stand at the door, and knock; if any man hear my voice, and open the door, I will come in to him, and will sup with him, and he with me"* he secretly asks God for help. His journey reaches its end as he learns what is written in four letters that arrive many years after the death of their author and show him the miracles God can provide through faith.

It is my hope that this story demonstrates that we cannot profess a faith in God, nor profess to truly love God when we put no effort into knowing what God says, what His plan of salvation is, what He asks of us, or why He must battle evil on our behalf. This novel examines many of the heartaches life brings us and many of the mistakes we make, but ultimately demonstrates how God continues to love us by stepping in to comfort us and to re-direct our path. This is not to say we will not have problems, but it does say that we will always be brought through our problems and refined in the process and that we need not fear the outcome. I hope this story will warm your heart and that the magnitude of God's love is reflected in this young man's journey back to God.

Christ did not teach by accusation or complaint, but by speaking with loving kindness, and by offering information about how to love one another and love God. By His example He taught us to trust God to protect us when we strive to do God's will. But He also recognized the spirits that governed the actions of his tormentors and understands that we too are attacked by the spirits of evil. He warns us to be aware of the dangers that these spirits represent, the subtlety of their attack and how we can lose God's protection through complacency. Our enemy is a lover of our complacency and is not only clever and falsely unobtrusive, but also seductive, tempting, and as dangerous as he was when he presented the innocent looking fruit in the Garden of Eden.

It is easy to forget that this powerful enemy still lurks today, more potent than ever, still the sly and enticing stalker of the children of God and one who revels in the chaos of our daily lives. Satan rarely takes the obvious path, in fact through simple complacency about God's words he believes he can win his battle to destroy mankind and prevent God from gaining the last soul to be a part of the bride of Christ. God gives us all we need to secure our future, but we have to know God's words to claim this prize. We also need to recognize and thus avoid the ease of complacency and the danger this brings to our lives and our future.

I hope you enjoy this story and wish for you God's richest blessings. May He grant you the wisdom to understand His ways, His words, and the wonderful future He so freely offers all of us. May your heart be filled with the beautiful promise He gives us:

Blessed is the man that walketh not in the counsel of the ungodly,
nor standeth in the way of sinners, nor sitteth in the seat of the scornful.
But his delight is in the law of the Lord; and in his law
doth he meditate day and night.
And he shall be like a tree planted by the rivers of water,
that bringeth forth his fruit in his season;
his leaf also shall not wither, and whatsoever he doeth shall prosper.

Psalm 1:1-3

Helen Gumienny Glowacki

Synopsis Of Prior Novels By Helen Gumienny Glowacki

When God Broke Grandma's Heart, is a story about the legacy of love and faith that a grandmother instills into her granddaughter and which the granddaughter uses to help others. The grandmother tells her heartbreaking story of the pain of betrayal, of sibling rivalry, and of spousal abuse through which God taught her to forgive, restored everything she lost, and brings happiness into her life. It also addresses God's support of our leaving situations where we are unequally yoked before those situations destroy us.

When God Took Grandma Home, is a story about drug addiction, about a child innocently trapped by an unscrupulous adult, and about righteous anger. It is a story of death yet uplifts the reader through its description of the incredible plan God has for those who were unjustly treated, for those who die too young or under unfair circumstances. It is a story that explains why and when it is good to be angry, why we should retain the memory of injustice, and why we should pray for those who have died.

When Grandma Chased the Spirits, is a novel about the subtle temptation to follow other gods, its unseen and dangerous force, and its lure of practical application. Employing the ancient art of feng shui to decorate their home, a young couple falls under the power of a vicious enemy but are helped by their budding friendship with Matt and Sarah and a manuscript written by Sarah's grandmother which addresses feng shui. God brings them an incredible miracle that ends a heartache they thought impossible to resolve.

The Granddaughter and the Monkey Swing is Helen Gumienny Glowacki's fourth novel and a story about friendship and its impact on our lives. The story culminates in a beautiful wedding, the revelation of a secret Matt has kept from Sarah, how Caleb helps mend a broken relationship, and a friends wisdom about the heartbreak and fear of a serious illness. The story also offers surprising information about how to gain God's blessing on our homes by how and why we choose our furnishings and explains why divine proportion provides perfect balance.

Grandma's Little Book of Poetry: The Story of God's Plan of Salvation, is a novel that explains the process of life, what we are here to learn, why we have an enemy, and what the outcome of life's struggle will be. A manuscript found in an antique desk brings back memories of a whimsical fairytale about the angels who live in the verdant land of heaven and who watch the inhabitants of the cold, bleak planet below them wrestle with good and evil to learn of God.

Abiding Faith, Hidden Treasure, is the story of a young man who is burdened by a cynical view of God, politics, and his fellow man. His life experiences have led him to believe that most people who profess to be religious are hypocrites who do not live by the tenets of their faith. He questions the apparent conflict between the story of creation and the science of carbon dating and why a god of love would allow such incredible heartache to exist. It is a story of how unwavering faith and the adherence to walking the walk can touch even the most cynical heart.

Description Of Characters

Grandma

Grandma's life story is filled with the debilitating pain of sibling betrayal and marital abuse and is told in *When God Broke Grandma's Heart*. Grandma's suffering allows her to develop a special relationship with God that becomes a legacy of faith for her grandchildren and a constant source of incredible inspiration and wisdom. Her interest in alternative medicine and interior design, her love of chiming clocks, her empathy and ability to love and forgive is a treasure her grandchildren share with others.

Sarah

Sarah, the granddaughter, helps Grandma write her journal and through this learns about the power of God, His unwavering love, and His desire to help mankind. Sarah also learns about a powerful, subtle enemy and how to fight him as she struggles through a period of grief and the discovery of a suppressed anger she must acknowledge. She and Matt marry when they complete the renovations to their home. But when they publish *Grandma's Little Book of Poetry: The Story of God's Plan of Salvation*, they begin to face many heartaches and challenges of faith.

Matt

Matt, whom Sarah marries, has a rocklike faith in God and the ability to see problems with "the glass half full" rather than half empty. He suffers through the loss of a loved one and overcomes his anger at God for the injustices he witnesses. But in this process, Matt learns about God's incredible plan of salvation and the role God wants him to take in that plan. Matt loves their new home and enjoys the renovation process through which he makes a new friend and proves his worth as a wonderful role model.

Paul

Paul is Matt's older brother. He earned a captain's license to operate a seagoing tugboat. Paul married and had two children, Becky and Christina, and suffered their loss when his wife took the children and ran off with another man when Paul was out to sea. Paul's story in *When God Took Grandma Home* demonstrates his extraordinary faith in God and how it sustains him through heartbreaking circumstances. The terrible injustices that Paul lives through cause his brother to question God's decisions. But God brings Paul's family a miracle from eternity.

Mary

Mary and Kevin's story is told in *When Grandma Chased the Spirits*. Mary and Kevin are Matt and Sarah's neighbors, and the two couples have become close friends. After struggling through a dangerous need to obtain good luck through any means, Mary and Kevin learn about Matt and Sarah's faith in God. Mary struggles with the pain of a childhood trauma and the panic attacks these memories induce. When she ventures into the world of feng shui, Matt and Sarah show her something that forever changes their life.

Kevin

Kevin, Mary's husband, is delighted to have Matt as a friend and neighbor and wants to learn from him how to be the kind of husband who can lead by example. Matt has shown him what God asks of him and teaches him about an unscrupulous enemy longing to harm his family and how to thwart those efforts. He is happy with Mary's plans to renovate the carriage house and delighted by the changes that have come into their life as a result of their friendship with Matt and Sarah and their family.

Elizabeth

Elizabeth becomes a friend to Mary and Kevin and their growing family. She adopted a child when she was in her late forties and lost her husband when the child, Rebecca, was twelve years old. Elizabeth is concerned about a potentially deadly illness. She brings a wealth of wisdom into their circle and a happy spot in the life of John. Because of her unselfish, loving, and down-to-earth nature, everyone who meets Elizabeth comes to admire and respect her for her strength and her unwavering faith in God.

Rebecca

Rebecca is the child Elizabeth adopted. She is struggling to accept the many changes that have and are now occurring in her life. The incredible love that Elizabeth has given her and the example she has been to her has given her a maturity far beyond her years. Her friend Jayden draws her into a relationship with God and helps her finally acknowledge her anger at God for what her mother must endure. Rebecca and Jayden form a friendship that blossoms under the teaching of those around them who become their role models.

John

John is Elizabeth's new friend, and he is also Jayden's grandfather. Many years ago, John lost his wife to a debilitating illness and has worked to help others through similar ordeals. He enjoys spending time with Elizabeth and her newfound family. His faith in God comes from a lifetime of service as a deacon in his church, and he uses the wisdom he gained in this capacity to help his daughter and grandson cross the rock-strewn bridge from the devastation of divorce to the joy of God's love and to help Elizabeth find hope.

Jayden

Jayden is John's grandson and becomes a friend to Rebecca. Jayden has grown up in the church and knows a great deal about approaching God with personal problems. He has learned from listening to his elders speak of their own difficulties and seeing those problems solved through prayer. He is active in the youth group at church and invites Rebecca to join him. Their friendship blossoms, and they share their tales of the heartaches they have experienced. Jayden longs for his mother to find happiness.

Ruth

Ruth is Jayden's mother and John's daughter. She went through a difficult divorce and struggles under a financial burden when her ex-husband does not meet his obligations. She is shy and sweet, but her past experiences have left their mark as has the loneliness that past trauma can inflict. She harbours a secret anger at God for allowing her to go through what she has but finally learns to let go of the past when love once again comes into her life. She is delighted to be included in Matt and Sarah's family circle.

Joshua

Joshua is Sarah's younger brother. Joshua expects too much of others, which makes him demanding and judgmental and affects his relationship with his fiancée, Debbie. The story of his engagement to Debbie in *The Granddaughter and the Monkey Swing*, describes the many serious issues they need to resolve in order to save their relationship. Josh thinks it's unmanly to show his pain or to give in to Debbie, and only Caleb can finally reach him. But as he recognizes what it means to be a husband, he begins to grow into the man Debbie can love.

Debbie

Debbie, Joshua's fiancée, thrilled to be a part of Matt and Sarah's wedding, has grown up without a good role model and looks happily to Joshua's family to fill that void in her life. She learns quickly and gladly but needs to learn how to curb her impulsiveness. The insecurities she developed during her childhood and her inability to communicate well under pressure bring her into a situation that may ruin her relationships. She finally sees that with God's help she will grow into the person she wants to be.

Caleb and Ann

Caleb is Sarah and Josh's older brother and has been a source of strength and protection to them since their mother died when Sarah was only eighteen years old. The family turned to their grandmother for help and guidance, and through her love and faith in God, they learned to accept what happened and continue the education that their mother wanted for them. Caleb has grown so much in spirit over the years that the family now looks to him as they did to Grandma. Ann, Caleb's wife, is always willing to lend a helping hand. Often unacknowledged except by God and Caleb, Ann gives incredible spiritual gifts to this family she loves through her fervent prayers for them day and night. She is a rock providing strength to those she loves, but there is a secret sadness in her heart that needs to be addressed. They have two children, Andrew and Lorraine.

Barbara and Jim

Barbara is Matt's sister and a close friend of Sarah's. She has excellent communication skills in addition to being talented, down-to-earth, a good seamstress, creative in craft projects, and an excellent gardener. She gladly takes efficient charge of family gatherings and has the ability to do this without anyone feeling left out. Her husband, Jim, had never been willing to join the church everyone else attends but listens carefully to their discussions of faith. He is family oriented, hardworking, smart, and up-to-date on political issues. He loves to play devil's advocate when the family gets into the debates they love to share. Jim has fun playing matchmaker for his best friend Wade, and together they venture from the exhilarating debates of politics to the awesome evidence of a loving God.

Wade

Wade is Jim's boss and best friend with whom he forged a close relationship of mutual respect when they worked together in Iraq under extreme difficulty and danger. Wade's story in *Abiding Faith, Hidden Treasure* introduces the reader to this new character who is a great big bear of a man with a huge and loving heart. While in Iraq, Wade and Jim try to rescue a pregnant woman and her small son after a terrorist attack but later learn that the mother dies as her child is born. Wade is deeply concerned for the well-being of these children and seeks to find a way to help them.

Heza and Bara

Heza and Bara are the children from Iraq whom Jim and Wade meet following a terrorist attack outside a busy food market. Bara is just one year old when the attack occurs and sustains a serious, permanent, and debilitating injury. Heza is born as her mother, their only relative, dies from wounds incurred during that attack. Both Jim and Wade follow the children's recovery and their subsequent transfer from the hospital to an orphanage. Wade and Bara form a strong bond with each other, and Wade commiserates over what the future holds for these children. Eventually, Wade makes a decision that impacts his life and the lives of the children.

Chapter One

JIM, IRAQ,

J im was angry with himself. He'd made so many mistakes and now had to live with the results of what he himself had caused. He'd been arrogant in thinking he'd accomplish so much professionally while he was in Iraq. He'd been completely blindsided by his unfounded and romantic perception of what Iraq would be like. It wasn't the Lawrence of Arabia's desert that he'd envisioned it to be. And suddenly he laughed at himself, at how he'd imagined himself standing with his back against the triangular flap of the canvas door of a tent that he'd folded to an open position against its side wall. He'd seen himself, dressed in Khaki's, sweating from the heat of the desert. He'd never imagined that before noon the temperature could reach as high as one hundred and twenty degrees Fahrenheit.

He'd actually daydreamed of gazing toward the rising sun, noticing the shadows of deep gold and brown undulating across the sea of sand, cast by the height of the dunes blocking out the light as the sun made its climb into the sky. The nighttime wind would have created ripples across the surface of the sand that appeared so even they looked as if a rake had been drawn across the entire face of the desert as far as the eye could see. It was beautiful in his imagination. The best word to describe the way it appeared to him was "ethereal." He'd been so sure that the huge expanse of the desert held so much promise, and had envisioned what he could have built here, what he could have accomplished.

But he'd been wrong about so many things and he had acted impulsively, hadn't done his usual and thorough research. The sand he'd thought would be so ethereal was really a dry yellow soil with the consistency of crushed putty. It turned into a mud so thick when it rained that it could suck the boots right off his feet. His boss had warned him not to stir up particles of the sand because it contained microbes that could be harmful to his health. And instead of the beautiful oasis' he'd imagined, the vegetation was a sparse and unattractive flat scrub except along the straight, narrow waterways lined with trees. Evenings created a dull pewter colored sky and not the spectacular sunsets he'd envisioned.

He'd also been wrong in his romantic notion that he'd be sleeping in a large tent where he'd be lulled to sleep by the sound of the wind that worked to create magical ripples across the surface of the sand. Instead, he found ugly temporary trailers, three to a unit, all raised on cinderblocks. Each trailer contained a door, a window and an air conditioner. An eight or nine foot wall lined with sandbags protected the huge compound of hideous compartments.

Working with female Army engineers and other females who were just as expert in their various duties was commonplace for him, so he'd been surprised by the reaction of the Iraqi's to these women. The Iraqi's were uncomfortable with what they considered too much intimacy in the camaraderie between men and women as they worked together. Barbara would have put an end to that!

As Jim stood outside his trailer with these thoughts swirling through his head, he realized that it would only ruin his day to think about the mistakes he'd made. It made him wish that Barbara was here to help him get his thoughts in order and rein in his anger.

His anger wasn't only limited to his own mistakes. His anger rose like a blinding fire when he was reminded of the ineptitude of those decision makers who stood in the way, those whose shortsightedness prevented the contractors from completing the many projects they'd been sent here to oversee. The people of Iraq needed to get their lives back and had been willing to support the United States until they realized that their lives were not improving; their lives were, in fact, getting worse. *For crying out loud,* Jim's thoughts raged, *many of these people no longer have running water or electricity! No wonder they are losing their initial joy of being free of Saddam Hussein's dictatorship!*

Jim believed that the decision to go to war was made with the right heart's attitude, that his president had fully believed the intelligence he'd received about weapons of mass destruction and how this could impact the United States. He had also recognized the Iraqi people's plight of living under a dictator who ordered the mass murders of those with differing viewpoints.

Jim believed that the decision to invade Iraq came from a genuine desire to create a democracy in the Middle East. *Creating a democracy here would have been such a wonderful example to other countries here in the Middle East who refuse their women equal rights and don't allow freedom of religion or freedom of speech.* But Jim now realized that not enough planning had gone into its aftermath.

When U.S. forces first arrived, the people of Iraq viewed the United States of America as a bright star of efficiency and power and democracy; but now, that great star was losing its brightness, falling in stature, crumbling. The people of Iraq saw that nothing was being accomplished, that nothing was changing for the better, and this caused their hope to disintegrate. As time marched on, the people of Iraq began to ask themselves whether or not the United States really cared about their plight. Later, they asked if they were simply inept. Being inept brought the greater horror.

Jim was embarrassed for his country. He understood the Iraqi's anger with the United States, but those in Washington with the power to bring change to Iraq relied on the intelligence and the advice they received from others and, sadly, that advice had not been good advice.

Jim's head dropped from the weight of the emotion his thoughts brought him and he looked toward his feet at his heavy dust laden boots. Suddenly he felt tired. He felt like a failure . . . both professionally and personally. *We could have accomplished so much,* he thought. *We had the idealism, we had the contractors, we had many of the supplies, the money had been appropriated for rebuilding, we'd even found skilled Iraqis who could have helped us, but we couldn't get approval to begin our projects because of the bureaucracy in Washington because of those few who brought back the wrong advice.*

Jim knew he and his team could have accomplished miracles here in Iraq. They could have won the hearts of the people by engaging them in building their democracy and in developing their self-sufficiency. These gains would have encouraged them to work toward the goals that the United States offered for creating an independent and prosperous country.

We could have trained so many Iraqis in a viable future skill, we could have utilized Iraqi engineers, teachers, builders, and given the people the pride in their accomplishments that would have made them champion the cause of democracy and put a stop to anything that tried to come against it, Jim thought. *But we needed to prove ourselves by first providing the basics such as water, electricity, living quarters, and security.*

Jim could feel his anger rising like bile in his throat. *Could have . . .* The key words were "could have." *It is such a shame that we can't say "have accomplished" because we had been ready and we had been willing. All those who were here in Iraq, those who worked on the ground, who moved with the people of the country agreed on what to do. But not the few who made the decisions that affected so many.* Jim fumed, knowing that many of those who advised the president hadn't even been to Iraq nor had they even attempted to consult with those who lived among the people and saw what needed to be done.

Jim, like many others, could hardly believe that what they had worked for all this time, what they'd fought for and believed in could be wiped away by the recommendation of a few shortsighted politicians. He was being kind by using the word *shortsighted*. He wanted to scream the words he *really* felt about these men: that they were liars, they were pompous, arrogant, self-aggrandizing, ignorant, envious, greedy men who lusted for personal power and were willing to destroy what others had worked for, had sacrificed for. They just wanted to get their names in the papers or their pompous little faces on TV. They were shortsighted, ignorant of the needs of the people, and worse, impervious to the sacrifice made by every member of the armed forces who laid down their lives and impervious to the needs of those who supported democracy in this country!

If only Jim could get to the president himself. *The president would listen,* Jim thought. *But so often a president's hands are tied because the advice he receives isn't the right advice! A president can't do it all alone. He has to rely on the advice of others, . . . and when that advice is wrong or hides a personal agenda, . . . it's the president . . . and the project . . . that suffers.*

Jim's jaws were clenched so hard that his teeth hurt. Suddenly, he noticed that his hands were clenched so tightly that his fingernails were cutting into the skin of his palms. At that moment, he understood the power that could move a man to lose control of his anger. It was when the self-centeredness, self-interests, and irresponsibility of a few men hurt so many.

With great effort of will, Jim unclenched his teeth and then, unclenching his fists, rubbed away the soreness in his jaw, lifted his head again, and wondered for the thousandth time whether he should quit, leave Iraq, or keep banging his head against the wall of bad judgment and inaction he'd encountered. He could probably resolve his concerns about Barbara if he left Iraq.

Even the very basics of approving the installation of water pipes and electricity cables and the replacement of housing destroyed years earlier when the war began were held up by these few people and the so-called diplomatic red tape they claimed had to be resolved. In Jim's world, this wouldn't be tolerated. People in the construction business were held accountable for meeting completion schedules and the benchmarks that demonstrated their timely progress toward that completion. He smiled as he thought of Barbara in hard hat, fists on her hips, marching right up to the politicians and generals and giving them a piece of her mind about their ineptitude and what that ineptitude was costing others!

And the projected costs were astronomical! Sometimes Jim couldn't believe the figures he saw. Where did anyone get the nerve to overcharge so much? If Jim could have bypassed these guys, he would have had these necessities completed by now and would have had them up and running for 10 percent of the costs they were *now* trying to process. It was outright thievery. Getting these basics done immediately would have won the people to their side easily! And getting them done for a fair price would have helped the United States continue to invest in this country. *What was the matter with the politicians who made these decisions and provided this advice in the States?*

Jim's thoughts ran from what they could have accomplished by now and how effective it would have been if they had created some manufacturing plants right here in Iraq. This would have put the people to work, put money in their pockets, fed families, and given them dignity, a sense of purpose, and the desire to continue to help rebuild their country. The Iraqis would have rejoiced over the American presence; they would have applauded our fortitude against all odds, our organizational skills, and our desire to help them establish a better life.

The Iraqis had been so willing to love us, to emulate us, to learn from us. At least in the beginning they were. Now it was different. Now it would be an uphill battle to win back their trust. Jim, frustrated, thought, *all because of a handful—yeah, a handful—of aristocratic bumbling fools, the incredible opportunity we had as a country, the opportunity that everyone else had seen so clearly, an opportunity to show the world what we were made of and how much we were willing to do to help others had been lost.*

Jim was an engineer who had gone back to school to add architecture to his many achievements. He was talented, really talented. He was so well organized that he could run ten jobs at once and still produce the result and quality his high standards demanded for each project. His workmen respected and admired him and gladly followed his lead. Suppliers gave him great deals, trusted his word, and the people of this country liked his straight talk and had believed that he could get the job done—and done quickly and efficiently. And if it wasn't for the bureaucrats back home, he could have.

Jim felt that he'd let the Iraqi people down. He was furious with the powers that be that had thwarted such a great effort, a great ideology. Instead of working to make things better, many spent their time attacking President Bush.

Jim didn't have many heroes, but Bill O'Reilly of *The O'Reilly Factor* television show on Fox News was one of them. He'd set the record straight in some of his television interviews, pointing out that both President Clinton and Prime Minister Tony Blair had seen the same intelligence that President Bush had seen and these two men had, based on that intelligence, fully backed President Bush's decision to invade Iraq.

Further, during an interview with Bill O'Reilly, CIA director George Tenet stated that he was the one who presented President Bush with the intelligence that confirmed the existence of Iraqi WMD. This intelligence had turned out to be incorrect; but Bill, in his unique understanding that a mistake was different than a lie, supported President Bush against those who would not acknowledge that the President had done his best to keep the country safe. Now was the time to make everything right again, not just dwell on an honest mistake. *Get off your duffs,* Jim wanted to scream, *and fix things while they can be fixed!*

When Jim had worked with the Corps of Engineers before the contract had been awarded to Wade's company, he had such great hopes for the restoration of this country and had wanted to help the people realize their desire for independence and their desire to establish a democracy. Becoming the first democracy in the Middle East should have brought the people a great sense of pride. They would have thrived under a democratic government and a capitalist economy! But living in squalor with no water, no electricity, with the ugliness of bombed-out buildings and pockmarked roads *never changing*, with suicide bombers seeming to come out of the woodwork, their hope was soon destroyed and their dreams were replaced by disappointment. Democracy wasn't as important as survival, simple survival. And so the anger of the Iraqi people followed the failure to provide them with the basics they needed. That anger had nowhere to go except toward the United States.

Didn't those who sat on committees, who gave the president advice, who decided what to do understand these principles? Didn't they see how important it was to move swiftly, decisively, and with strength? Couldn't they even agree on rebuilding one city, one town, one development to show what they were capable of, what they wanted for the people of this country? Couldn't they stop the blame game and instead understand that they were making themselves the enemy by default?

Often Jim wondered why a decision hadn't been made to send every troop they had into Iraq just until law and order could be established. Just to help the Iraqi people recognize that the Americans were there to help them rebuild, help them toward the democracy they longed for. *If we'd started out right, we could even have gotten away with later mistakes. But we'd bungled it right from the beginning. It was so frustrating, and it put the morale of everyone there on a downward spiral.*

But now, two years later, still with little accomplished because of the ineptitude of the governmental advisors, the insurgents who were entering Iraq by the droves were growing in wisdom and strength. The people who once had so much faith in the Americans were losing that faith. Some were joining the insurgents, thinking that this was the only way they could help their country move forward and the only way they could develop the services they so desperately needed. Jim was angry at what they had lost, and he was ready to give up.

No wonder he lived for the letters he received from Barbara. Thank goodness, he had something to provide him with respite from the agony of each day when he could make no headway on the approvals he needed to get his projects started. His stress level because of his frustration had already been in full swing for two years, and stress was supposed to be worse than any illness for the toll it took on the body.

Barbara was just a friend. That's all. In Jim's conscious mind, Barbara was someone who enjoyed writing to a guy she knew was in Iraq, in danger, someone whom she thought needed a kind word from home. That was all there was to their relationship. After all, she was just a kid. She was almost ten years younger than he was, and that seemed like a hundred years when one compared her lack of worldly wisdom to his jaded wisdom, or her innocent trust to his cynicism. He'd seen it all, and she'd been protected all her life. For these reasons alone, they'd never be compatible.

He'd met Barbara two years ago, just before he'd left for Iraq. He'd been twenty-nine, and she had just turned nineteen. He'd returned home for a short visit ten months later, had seen her again and been stunned by how she had matured and by how beautiful she was. But most of all, he'd been stunned by how smart she was, how incredibly fast and accurate her mind was, and how good her powers of observation were. Barbara was attending college when they met and trying to decide whether she wanted to go to law school or to become a writer/journalist. She seemed to be good at everything she did. She was always quick to grasp his point, understand his way of thinking.

He liked that in her, although at first, thinking she was just good at understanding the nuances in his conversations, he'd greatly underestimated her. And she'd called him on it! He'd said something about the costs of something he'd been estimating and had thrown out a figure that she quickly said was incorrect. She said it was closer to another figure. He'd balked because math was one of his best subjects. So she'd explained that she'd rounded his item cost up to the nearest ten, then multiplied the number of items required, then deducted something or other . . . and had come up with her ballpark figure . . . in her head . . . immediately. He'd pulled out his pen to show her she was wrong and, well, he'd had to swallow his words; his figure had been wrong. *How had she done that so quickly in her head?*

He'd responded by telling her it was a lucky guess on her part and she'd responded by telling him in no uncertain terms that his remarks were those of a chauvinist who dared to assume men were more capable than women in math, in fact, in all things! He retorted by telling her that men were definitely stronger than women, and she'd replied indignantly that women could accomplish what a man could in terms of strength because they used their head and could, for instance, simply employ a lever and fulcrum and never even work up a sweat! Her quips always made him laugh.

She spotted the sarcasm that many missed, spotted the important parts of what he'd said under the guise of his cutting humor. When he was being sarcastic, she would raise an eyebrow and give him a look that seemed to say, *That's not the* real *Jim speaking, is it?* It made him more careful when choosing his words, but it made him chuckle to know that she caught what others missed. It was as if they shared a private joke. She also let him know when she thought he'd been condescending, and she surprised him with the fight she had in her to make him admit it! As young as she was, she wasn't the least bit intimidated by him. It was almost impossible to outwit her. This kept him on his toes.

Barbara had an uncanny ability to draw him out, make him speak seriously, make him lay down his barbs and say what he really meant and felt. She called him on his so-called pithy comments, especially when they were deprecating, by making him explain why he'd made a particular remark. But she also encouraged him . . . well, actually she challenged him . . . to look into his heart and speak about what was there, not just about what his anger created. She'd called his form of response *a cop-out that allows your fears to force you into sarcasm, because perhaps you can't sustain a debate on the issue!* She'd said that while she understood his frustration, she wanted him to be honest about his feelings on any given subject, not couch them in an unapproachable sarcasm to scare others away.

He was surprised when she told him that she felt he hid behind his sarcasm, that he used sarcasm to keep others at a distance. He'd never asked himself why he spoke the way he did, so this was definitely food for thought. She wanted him to discuss what he wanted, what he felt, and said that if his thoughts were important enough for him to express in sarcasm, then they were too important for him to do so. That was profound, and at first he'd been hurt by what she said. *Him? Hurt? Nah.* But then as he thought about it, he smiled and thought that maybe she'd hit the nail on the head.

Convoluted, but probably true, he'd thought. *Maybe I am afraid to say what I mean unless it's in the "protective" form of my sarcasm. If someone is angered by what I say, I can retreat on the basis that I am always sarcastic or by saying that I was only teasing.* No one had ever challenged Jim to look inside himself before and analyze why he might do or think as he did. It was disconcerting. *Maybe this is a cop-out on my part.*

But Barbara also saw good things in him that he wasn't sure were really there. And the more he got to know her, the more he desired her good opinion of him. In fact, the more he saw the quality of her responses to how he viewed the world, the more he sought her input about what bothered him and what was important to him. She made him wonder if maybe he'd met his equal in arguing an issue, in searching for answers. In fact, sometimes he said things just to test how she'd respond, what she'd say, then watch her face become animated with the passion of her response while listening carefully to every word she said.

She was very religious but never pushed him about her religion. Even when they had conversations about various philosophies outside her belief system, he found her willing to listen and discuss different ideas. But when those philosophies dictated a behavior that differed from what her faith dictated, she seemed able to come back at him to prove her point of view and disprove some of the stuff he'd said. Well, maybe not disprove them always, but at least cast reasonable doubt on what he'd said. He was intrigued by the way her mind worked. *How did she get that way, how does she know so much?* he wondered. *How did she stay so calm even when he saw she was outraged by something?*

But she was so young and innocent, and Jim decided that he needed to make plans that the next time he went home, he would break off the constancy of their correspondence. He felt it was unfair of him to take so much of her time when he had no plans for a future with her. Barbara was only twenty-one now and had her whole life ahead of her. He was in Iraq and would be here for a few more years, and while he loved her letters, he knew he couldn't expect them to go on forever.

She was just trying to be kind to someone who wanted to help his country by working in Iraq, and it wouldn't be right for him to take advantage of that kindness. But then, he'd think that he was being arrogant, presumptuous to think that she had given him time because she cared for him in any special way. Maybe she *was* dating someone, and maybe she *was* just doing a good deed by writing him.

As Jim's leg cramped, he realized he'd been standing in the same position, back against the side of his trailer for at least an hour. His muscles ached, and he could feel the sun now fully on his face, the sun that was just beginning to rise when he'd first left his bed. He'd been thinking all that time and standing in pretty much one position. He walked from one end of the three joined trailers to the other end, then decided to circle the three completely, lifting his legs high off the ground with each step so he could stretch as many muscles as possible. When he reached the doorway of his own trailer once again, he went inside to dress for the day. He was hungry now too.

As he was about to leave the trailer, he glanced at the picture of Barbara that he had placed on his nightstand, and wondered why she was so constantly on his mind. He was looking forward to mail call, realizing that he hadn't received a letter from her in a week. *What happened?* he wondered. *I usually get a letter every three or four days. Maybe she's met someone her own age and begun dating seriously.* Then of course, eventually there would be no time for him. He knew how that worked; he'd been there, done that! Well, she deserved a nice, smart young college kid, up-and-coming in a career and crazy about her.

Since Jim was far from their main facility, he had to jump into his jeep and drive to the mess hall where he enjoyed eating with the other guys working with the corps of engineers. As he drove, he realized suddenly that he was in a rotten mood and decided that he didn't want to think of Barbara anymore; suddenly, he hated the fact that she was always on his mind. *It's gonna be a bad day.* He tried to stop the pictures that came into his mind that were about Barbara. But he couldn't, and his thoughts jumped again to the tall athletic-looking college kid who, in Jim's imagination, wanted to date Barbara and had been the reason Jim hadn't had a letter from her.

I have to purge these thoughts because they are a distraction from what is really bothering me, he thought. *What I am really concerned about is the runaround I'm going to get again today about the work we want to start. The work to rebuild that had been scheduled for immediate attention.* The work that when completed would have provided water and electricity and apartments for the people. He knew that he'd get put on the back burner again when he asked for some specific dates for starting their project. And at that moment, Jim decided that if he got the same old runaround, the same old "maybe we'll know more tomorrow," he'd ask for leave and go home for a few weeks.

I really need to check out this guy that Barbara is dating. Maybe this guy isn't someone deserving of her; maybe he'll break her heart or be a bad influence on her. Maybe he is a ladies' man and will destroy her trust. Maybe I'd better go home and check him out. As Jim's thoughts moved back to Barbara, he told himself that he owed it to her to be the kind of a friend who would look after her, a sort of big brother. He wondered if he'd get a letter today. He wondered if she'd cut her hair or kept it long as he'd suggested. He'd check out this guy and make sure that he is the right kind of guy for her and let him know that he'd better walk away now if he isn't.

Breakfast was hearty, and Jim ate with healthy appetite. Three cups of coffee gave him time to listen to the many different pieces of information making their way around the camp. After breakfast and a challenging round of conversation about whether or not they'd get word on the start of the massive project they had come to Iraq to execute, Jim hopped into his jeep once again and drove to the main building that housed the contractor's offices. His boss was there already, on the phone with someone and obviously in a heated argument. He was raising his voice and telling whoever he was speaking with that his contractors were going to pack up and leave and they could take their plans and projects and burn them for all he cared. He told them that he'd come here to get the job done, not sit on his duff, and then he abruptly hung up. Jim could see that Wade was very upset.

As he turned away from his desk to walk to the coffeepot in the corner of the room, he saw Jim and bellowed, "Jim, whadda ya say you and I go back Stateside and see if we can ruffle some feathers in Washington. If not, if we can't get them moving on this project, I'm pulling out."

"Well, good morning to you too, Wade. The day is not going too well, I presume? It was great to hear you exercising such diplomacy with whomever you were speaking on the telephone. But I agree with you, Wade. I came here hoping to exercise every skill I had to bring about something wonderful, something the people here would appreciate. But if we can't get it moving very soon, it will be too late and we'll end up with these great people who were once willing to work with us hating us . . . and blaming us for every problem they now face and will ever face."

"Jim, how can I get to the president and bypass some of these guys who must not be giving him the right advice? What can I say that would explain the situation clearly? Do you think that what we say will even reach the president?"

"I don't know, Wade. That's the problem. We can't know. But we can try. We'll go back home . . . that's a great idea. We'll see if we can't get to talk to someone who will listen and understand. All we can do is hope it makes it to the president, to whoever can really make the decision, and hope they see the validity in what we say."

"Carrottop!" Wade bellowed. "Get me and Jim on the next transport outta here and Stateside. Andrews. Now!"

"Jim, I'm disgusted with the red tape, with the politicians back home who stand in our way. Why don't they listen to the generals, the soldiers, the people who are here, or even to us contractors who see what's needed? Why don't they talk to the *people* here who want to live and work right here? Why listen to some idiot who only comes to Iraq for a photo shoot, who doesn't have a clue about Iraq, *and worse yet*, who doesn't really give a darn about the country or her people and *then* as he's on his way home . . . asks an aide for advice about Iraq . . . and brings *that* idiotic advice back home?"

"I was just thinking this morning about asking for leave, Wade. I'm fed up too. I'm sick to death of the horrors I see. Horrors caused by situations that could have been avoided. Like the insurgents for instance! The powers that be who think they know how to run things here didn't have the brains to make use of the Iraqi police force and the Iraqi army to help keep the insurgents out. Disbanding the police force and the army with no pay, no other jobs available, no way to feed their families almost forced these guys toward the insurgent force. What an irresponsible decision! What a waste! And if I had the guys who made these unproductive, irresponsible decisions here now, they wouldn't leave this room unscathed . . . at least by some pretty strong language!"

"Jim, you wouldn't be nearly as vociferous as I would. I mean, well, let me give you some interesting facts! You know that there are forty-five thousand American contractors here and that all are paid a doggone pretty good wage. But the only ones that are really accomplishing anything are the ones who are trucking supplies. They are busy round the clock even when they require escorts to keep their cargo . . . and them . . . safe. Just think what would have happened if these guys who made the decisions had sent just half that number of contractors here *and* hired the Iraqis at a slightly higher wage than they'd been earning before we got here. The people would *love* us, the work would be well under way if not *completed*, and the costs would be so much *less* to our own government. And *everybody* would have a sense of accomplishment and pride."

"Sir, I can get you and Jim on a C-30 to Kuwait that leaves in three hours . . . that okay?"

"Yeah, Carrottop. Perfect. Thanks. Okay, Jim, anything you need to do to clean up your desk before we go? Anything you need from the corporate office in Kuwait while we are there?"

"Nope! Unfortunately, we've not done enough work or have enough planned to worry about. I'll just let Karl and Mickey know I'll be going so they'll take care of my things and alert anyone looking for me. How long will we stay at home?"

"Carrottop?"

"Sir, you just have to call the base, any base, to find a flight when you want one. They are bringing supplies here all the time, so getting a spot to fly back here shouldn't be a problem."

"Yeah . . . bringing supplies . . . hah! Not the right supplies though! You know, only one in every eight Humvees was equipped with armour last year? Instead of sitting on our duffs, we could have changed course and tried to do something to help alleviate that disaster. Instead of waiting for changes to be made Stateside and wait forever while our guys remained unprotected, we could have built a manufacturing plant right here and made everything they need as armour for their vehicles, right here. But nooooo . . . has to go through channels . . . has to be discussed . . . there is that good ole red tape . . . authorization is needed . . . union regulations have to be met . . . appropriations approved . . . I don't know what else! And in the meanwhile, our boys are being maimed for life because they have no armour, no defense against the suicide bombers, and car bombs! Unbelievable!"

"It is frustrating, Wade, and I am pretty disgusted because we haven't gotten the authorization to get on with our projects. It also leaves me with a lot of time on my hands. If I don't keep busy, my anger boils over at the stupidity we see. My stress level is way too high, so sometimes I visit the hospitals to see some of these boys before they are shipped back home. The first time I did this, I had nightmares thinking about the severity of their injuries. My anger at the people who perpetrate such terror boils over. And then I think about something my mother once told me that comes from Psalm 15:3. There, David asks God who will abide in His tabernacle and God answered, *'He that backbiteth not with his tongue, nor doeth evil to his neighbour, nor taketh up reproach against his neighbour.'* Those terrorists who attack women and children and the elderly so indiscriminately sure won't abide there, and that's some comfort. But I still keep imagining the life these people and these soldiers face in the future because of the extent of their burns, because of the loss of their limbs, because of the many ways the attack leaves its mark on them.

"One guy's face was gone, Wade, and his hands and fingers were curled, and these guys are going to live. They will keep on living and not only have to remember the horror of what happened but also see the results of the maiming every day of their lives! Our soldiers will always ask themselves if it was worth it and why our government didn't jump to provide them with the protection they needed. I wonder too how the families will react, how much support these guys will get at home not only from their families, but later from the government as they continue their struggle to be productive, to work, to support their families. They also have to deal with their memories of what happened and the reality of an impairment that might affect their productivity and their happiness for the rest of their lives. It's a nightmare that never ends . . . It's heartbreaking."

"Jim, do you remember when we were told that the U.S. had allocated eighteen billion dollars for reconstruction in October of '03? Well, let me give you some surprising figures: in '04, only one billion of that money was actually spent. One billion out of eighteen billion! The money is there, it's been appropriated, but we can't get the approval to start our projects! This is what is fueling the insurgency. If everyone was back to work, earning money, seeing progress being made in their country, they wouldn't *let* these insurgents bomb it out again. But this progress is being held back . . . and the insurgency grows because Washington argues . . . and blames . . . and talks and talks . . . of corruption and fraud and whose fault what is . . . to sound important . . . and doesn't *do* anything. What a mess!"

"It sure is, and I'm tired of it too, Wade. That's why I want to go home. I'll help you in DC, but then I want to go home and reassess what I'm doing here and whether or not it's worth it. Hey, Wade, I'm thirty-one years old, and I need a couple of big jobs under my belt . . . completed . . . on my resume . . . so I can go where I want to go with my career. Someday, I want a wife and kids, a house, all that stuff. I have just so many years to accomplish my goals. I had wanted to do something worthwhile here, give something somewhere before I settled down. I also wanted to prove myself, prove that I can get the job done. I'm not so sure I'll get the chance here . . . on either front."

"You're right, Jim, but as your boss, I can tell you . . . I don't want to lose you . . . so let's fight as hard as we can to see the decision makers when we get to DC . . . and let's get something going . . . and then I'll let you *run* the show and give you as many men as you need to get the job done."

"Thanks, Wade, I appreciate your confidence in me. I can do this job . . . if only the powers that be would let me . . . Okay then, let's get moving and let's head out to DC. I'd better get to finishing up some loose ends here and then pack. See you in a couple of hours."

"Carrottop! What field, what plane, what captain, what time, and all that stuff . . . got it yet?"

"Yes, sir, here's your script. It has all the info you need. You're both all set to go. And you'll need this one to get back here."

"So long, Wade, see you soon. So long, Carrottop. Make sure you hold down the fort while we're gone."

Jim phoned Barbara as soon as he could to let her know that he was coming home. She offered to pick him up from the airport, and at first he said no, thinking it would be difficult for her and easier for him to get a cab. But the thought of her standing at the gate when he arrived, watching for him, was so strong and so pleasant that he accepted her offer and thanked her. Then he wondered if that guy, that college kid, would be with her; and his mood plummeted again.

Jim forced his thoughts from Barbara back to Wade and the concerns he had for his friend. Wade was a guy everyone learned to respect. He was a straight shooter who said what he meant and meant what he said—a man of his word. He was trying so hard to create something good here in Iraq, but he just couldn't get the authorization he needed despite their readiness to start the reconstruction. Jim worried that Wade would have a heart attack or a stroke because of the anger and frustration he carried day in and day out for two years already!

Wade was a great guy, honest, caring, smart, a tough taskmaster, a good businessman. He knew his stuff, knew how to get a job done, knew how to do it right and make his crew take pride in their work. He took pride in producing a well-made product and having a workforce that did too. That was rare in today's world, and this is why Jim first came to respect and admire him. Now Jim considered Wade a valued friend.

Wade had lost his wife a year before he came to Iraq. Breast cancer. He'd been devastated. And he'd needed to work hard to put the bad thoughts aside about how much she had suffered and how young she was to have to die, of how little time she had had to do the things they'd planned for their life and how much he missed her. He needed to work hard so he could put the pain behind him. He was still struggling to accept that she was gone . . . forever. This job would have been good for him if he could have gotten it going. It would have helped him over the pain. It would have given him purpose again. But here he was two years later and still nowhere on the project.

Wade was a big guy. Six feet two inches tall, slightly overweight, mostly in the belly. He had a large florid face, a full head of graying hair, piercing intelligent blue eyes, and was thirty-seven years old to Jim's thirty-one. He had large hands and thick wrists indicative of his large frame. It was a surprise that when he entered a room, people didn't hear him coming. It was because he walked so gracefully, stealthily like a large lion silently moving through the brush. Wade bellowed when he talked, his face became animated with whatever emotion best fit his topic, and his laugh was infectious.

He was serious about his work and cared deeply for the people who worked for him and for the people of this country. He took responsibility for everything, and he protected his men and fought for their good. Jim looked up to Wade. He respected him. And he wanted to do everything he could to help him. Now especially, Jim was determined to do everything he could to help Wade make his point to the idiots in Washington and get this job under way. Time was running out, and their chance to do some good in Iraq would end soon and end forever if they didn't do something now.

The trip back to the States was terrible. They didn't have great accommodations on the aircraft since it was a C-17 transport plane. It was cold, cramped, uncomfortable, and noisy. The plane was designed to carry cargo and once underway, many passengers simply threw sleeping bags on the floor hoping that by falling asleep, the long hours of travel would pass quickly. Nevertheless time seemed to stand still and the trip seemed unending. Wade and Jim had to yell to converse, so noisy was their environment; but nevertheless, they discussed Iraq, the job, and the future they foresaw in Iraq.

Jim told Wade about Barbara, making sure he understood that they were just friends because she was just a kid. But Wade saw something in Jim's demeanor and heard something in the way he spoke that made him wonder if Jim was fooling himself about Barbara just being a friend. There was something in Jim that reminded him of himself when he was dating his wife. And suddenly Wade felt sad again, and their conversation dwindled. This made the travel seem longer still.

But finally they were home and landed at Andrews Air Force Base. They decided to walk for a few minutes near the hangars to get their circulation going again and then decided to get something to eat before going to the Hill. Over a hearty breakfast, they talked about what they would say to the powers that be and what strategy they could use to be sure that they could get the results they wanted; but first, they needed the opportunity to talk with the right people.

Finally breakfast completed, and strong coffee fueling their energy, they went into the city and up to Capitol Hill to present the letter they'd obtained from their superior in Iraq. Despite their letter, they hit a brick wall. No one seemed to have the authority to make these appointments for them, let alone allow them to speak with anyone that day without an appointment! Finally, both Wade and Jim decided to go to their respective state representatives and see if they'd help. Wade bellowed and threatened to no avail.

Jim and Wade sat on a bench in one of the hallways, wondering what they could do to force an appointment with someone in authority. Jim repeated something he'd heard Bill O'Reilly say, "When the bastards pound you, fight back" and suggested that perhaps they could fight back by Wade threatening to go to the newspapers with the story if they were not heard. Wade loved Jim's idea and stood and briskly walked back to the very offices they'd just left.

Wade began his conversation by telling the aide with whom he spoke that the United States was never going to make headway in Iraq if they didn't do something quickly and therefore they were going to the newspapers with this story *and name this aide and who he worked for* if they couldn't speak with someone in authority, immediately. The aide seemed surprised by the threat and quickly backed down. Bill O'Reilly had been right—fight! And when they did, they finally got help. They were given an appointment to see someone at the Pentagon who would be able to bring the information directly to Donald Rumsfeld's office. But because he was not available at this time, an appointment was made to see him the following week. They hadn't expected to have to wait so long, but at least they had an appointment.

Jim clapped Wade on the back, proud that he'd stood his ground. "Yup Wade, even big ole Bill O'Reilly would be proud of you! When he's spoken about unfair situations, he's said 'You can ignore them, confront them directly, or deal with them later using a well-thought out strategy' and he was right, Wade, strategy worked."

Exhausted from the emotional toll created by their non-productive hours on Capitol Hill, they made their way by taxi to National Airport and booked their trips home. Jim's plane was leaving shortly, but Wade had to wait another hour and a half. So they said their goodbyes, and Wade said he would phone Jim when he confirmed their appointment and made a hotel reservation for them, planning to meet back in DC the night before their scheduled meeting at the Pentagon. With high hopes that they would soon be talking with a decision maker, they went home. Maybe they'd finally get some action.

Just before Jim boarded his plane at National Airport, he phoned Barbara to give her his estimated time of arrival. When he thought again of Barbara, he suddenly felt nervous about how he looked and what she would think of him. His clothes were rumpled, he hadn't shaved, he looked tired from the long trip from Iraq, and he thought that he'd better try to clean himself up a bit aboard the plane.

He couldn't get the thought out of his head of this big, gawky, football-playing, nerdy, well dressed college kid who was from a wealthy family, went to church regularly, and had asked Barbara to marry him. He envisioned this guy at the airport with Barbara, all clean and Ivy League looking, and thought of the comparison Barbara could then make between them. Jim would probably come out the loser. But anyway, the guy had better be worthy of Barbara.

Once the aircraft leveled off and the seat belt sign was turned off, Jim decided to shave in the tiny restroom because in order to "protect" Barbara from this guy, if that was necessary, he'd need to make the right impression on this guy; that Jim was someone in authority. He wasn't cleaning up because of Barbara; he was cleaning up because this guy's first impression was important if Jim wanted some clout. Women didn't always know this, but men sized each other up maybe even more than women assessed one another.

So Jim decided to wear his fatigue jacket over his shirt and tie when he left the plane because its cut added to the breadth of his shoulders. Maybe if he looked bigger, tougher than this college kid, he'd scare the guy a little. Suddenly, he felt somewhat nauseous and wondered if all the air travel was getting to him.

When Jim finished shaving and was also losing his cool because of the incredible lack of space in the tiny bathroom, he managed to splash on some aftershave cologne. Well, actually, he'd splashed it over his clothing because the plane lurched and he'd spilled it, missing his face and neck entirely. He returned to his seat, having completed his ablutions as best he could.

When the plane finally pulled up to the gate, he plastered a happy and what he thought nonchalant grin on his face and disembarked the plane to look for Barbara. When he saw her, once again he was stunned by her looks and by her composure. How could anybody be that gorgeous, be that smart, look so elegantly dressed, and still be so easy to be with? *Whoops, better not let Barbara hear me say that or I'll be mincemeat.* "Male chauvinist" would be her choice words for him! Then she would ask why he thought it was possible for a man to be handsome, smart, and be elegantly dressed all at once if a woman could not.

Speaking of handsome, smart, and elegant guys, where was the college computer geek? No geek? Jim's narrowed eyes roamed the area around Barbara. But he could see no tall, handsome college kid closing in to hold her arm in an effort to show Jim that he'd staked a claim as if he owned her.

Barbara acted as if they'd never been apart. She looped her hand into the crook of his arm and began to stride alongside him toward the luggage area. "Wait a minute, young lady, doesn't this old man, serving in dangerous Iraq, whom you haven't seen for a year, at least get a hug and a kiss before you whisk him into the blue of the night somewhere?"

"Well, *old* man, I didn't want to embarrass you. The truth is . . . in fact . . . I worried about this . . . that it might be too much for your *old* heart . . . you know . . . the *old* heart in an *old* man . . . to receive a hug or a kiss . . . so I waited until you asked so a heart attack wouldn't be on my conscience!"

Gosh, she was quick! Jim thought. Then she turned to him laughing and threw herself into his arms by leaping off the ground and encircling his neck with her arms, forcing him to hold her body off the ground. He was so pleased. The game was on. He could kiss her now; *there was no geek,* and in fun, she could kiss him . . . in fun . . . and there was no commitment being made. *Wasn't this what he wanted? Well, maybe not exactly. After all, hadn't he been thinking of at least one moment, one look, one kiss that was serious, one action or word that let him know that she had missed him not as a friend but as something more?*

When they finished exchanging their *friendly* hug and kiss, Jim gently lowered her to the ground. But then something made him hold her, not let her go, and look into her eyes, her beautiful, expressive shining eyes. Then he leaned toward her and gently touched her lips with his. Her eyes widened, and she returned his kiss, gently too. But then she closed her eyes and sighed, and Jim's heart lurched and pounded and suddenly he did not want the moment to end. Barbara smiled again, slowly, pleased, and then to break the mood, she grabbed his hand and turned toward the escalator, causing him to turn abruptly to walk beside her and match her pace.

The moment had been there. It had been good. Very good! And Jim thought, *Wow, maybe she isn't a kid after all!* They both hoped there would be another moment like it.

Chapter Two

BARBARA

Barbara had been so pleased when Jim phoned and told her that he was coming home for a visit. She loved his letters, his conversations, and the tender heart that he tried so hard to hide from everyone. She'd seen the pain he felt not only for those he loved but also for others who had been hurt. She had learned to recognize his cynicism for what it was. It was his heartbreak turned into something he could live with.

She'd always had the gift of seeing the real person inside the facade they portrayed on the outside. Sometimes she would look at someone and a picture would come into her mind of a heart that was green from jealousy. In others she would picture a heart that was wrinkled and shriveled from its inability to love others, or she would see a heart that was distorted by spots of ugly colours because of the hatred it harboured. Sometimes she wondered if the people whose hearts these were recognized how unhappy and how shallow they were, what they were missing by being unable to know the love God speaks of, and the danger they were in when they let Satan dictate their actions and emotions.

But with Jim's cynicism, it was different. His heart was huge and tender. He just didn't want anyone to see this. He had to look like Mr. Tough Guy! He was so smart that he easily covered his tenderness with his cynicism, with the sarcastic humor that could sometimes be so cutting. Barbara also noted that Jim could use his humor to force someone to back away when they were getting too close or their views or actions were making him too angry. Barbara saw that what Jim said—or more correctly, how he said it—was often a defense mechanism and he used this well.

She wondered if he was afraid that if he expressed the anger he really felt rather than the sarcasm he could throw out as a part of his personality, he might do harm. He was adamant about not harming anyone. Well, maybe not a child molester or a rapist or terrorist killer. But again, following the rules of society as Jim did, in most cases, he felt that unless someone's life was being threatened, he didn't have the right to harm anyone. *Perhaps*, she thought, *he had to work to rein in his anger, and perhaps sarcasm was the way he did this. Sarcasm might be his tool for controlling the expression of his anger.*

But Barbara recognized that Jim followed a strict set of rules that encompassed a deep personal integrity. His honesty, his willingness to work hard, his empathy for others was also unfailing. She wished that the whole world could see these traits in Jim because they were so strong, so true, so good. She wished that everyone could see that his sarcasm was the way he expressed his disappointment with society, his anger at how badly many people behaved. And perhaps not too kindly, he used his sarcasm toward those with whom he lost patience, those whose opinion differed from his, especially when it came to politics. He hated injustice.

Jim was ten years older than Barbara, and their age difference really bothered him. He would always mention it in some way whenever they were together, often referring to himself as an old man. But their age difference didn't bother her at all. In fact, she liked the wisdom that came with his years and the maturity and strength that she knew he would use to protect her if necessary. She'd always wanted someone she could think of as a defender, a protector, a partner who would always have her back, never letting anyone harm her.

She also loved the way his mind worked and the debates they often had and how he pursed his lips when he was bested in an argument of words although that rarely occurred. She observed that Jim retained an incredible number of facts about religion and politics, about health care and alternative medicine, about people who impacted the lives of others.

He loved his country and was deeply appreciative of the freedoms and equal opportunity this country offered, but he also intensely disliked those who were lazy and unwilling to work hard and honestly to make a better life for themselves. He did not have respect for people who looked for a handout or those who wouldn't carry their own weight when they could. He also had an excellent memory, and he chose his reading materials carefully, comparing the conclusions of a number of authorities and then developing his own with acuity.

He wasn't or didn't think of himself as religious, but there was a deeply religious side of him. Well, maybe she'd be more accurate if she defined it as spiritual rather than religious. She could sense the spiritual side of him and the hunger in him to find something he could believe in, something that wouldn't let him down, something he could trust. But he was so wary about religion that he looked for ways to impugn what any doctrine or system declared. Yet he loved his fellowman enough to help whenever and wherever he was needed.

His knowledge was so widespread that it was difficult to debate him unless one really knew the subject and understood where Jim might attack what he saw as its weaknesses or what he felt was an injustice. Barbara had to resist the temptation to get angry with him when he moved to sarcastic humor as a way to make his opponent back away. He did this when he felt that the substance of their argument was no longer valid, when he felt that his opponent would not listen to his point of view or when he felt he'd won his point. But even so, Jim tried to be fair. He always told the truth as he knew it, and he usually had statistics of some kind to back up his statements.

Barbara wanted Jim to know God the way she knew Him. But with Jim, she knew that this would take time. He'd been hurt once too often. And he'd been badly hurt. However, on her side was the fact that she knew God and she knew God's plan for mankind, and Jim would never be able to withstand that debate. She hoped to engage Jim in that conversation someday. It would be interesting. But first, she would watch to learn when his heart was open and when he might be willing to learn.

Barbara understood that a hardened heart could not accept God and remembered Hebrews 3:7-8 where they were told, *"Wherefore (as the Holy Ghost saith, To day if ye will hear his voice, Harden not your hearts, as in the provocation, in the day of temptation in the wilderness . . . . . .)"*

One day, Barbara asked Jim point-blank what had happened to make him cynical about religion. After a moment of silence, he'd told her. When his father had died, his mother had gone to their church to make the necessary arrangements for the funeral service. His mother spoke with a crusty old minister with whom his father had once had an altercation. Remembering that altercation, he adamantly stated that Jim's father had been a terrible sinner because he had been absent from church. Thus, the minister would only grant the funeral service his mother requested for her husband if she made restitution for what that minister considered his father's failures.

Jim had always been one to accept and follow the rules of society especially when they were clearly stated. When he heard what had been said to his mother, his first question was to ask what the rules of the church were in regard to this situation. His mother didn't know, so he accompanied his mother to the church to ask this of the minister and was met with an argument that resulted in Jim being told that this minister had the sole authority to make this call.

Jim's father had been a man who earlier in his life had gone to church fairly regularly but after a disagreement with this minister rarely attended the church again. But Jim's father was a man with integrity. He loved his family and worked hard to provide for them. He was honest, followed the rules of society, and lived trying not to bring harm to anyone. He was also a man who believed in God, loved Him, and thanked Him often, though privately, for the blessings He had provided to him and his family. He believed in the sacrifice Christ had made so men could be forgiven their sins, and he believed that forgiveness was freely given if one truly repented.

But Jim's father was also stubborn, and when pushed, he pushed back. One day, when he'd gone to church after a long period of not attending services, this old-school, brusque, and crusty minister loudly and publicly proclaimed to his father that because of his sporadic attendance, God would punish him and he would not be allowed into heaven. In anger and rebellion, his father never went back. And Jim didn't blame him.

Thus this minister, still smarting from Jim's father's anger toward him, told Jim's mother that she would have to make restitution for her husband's errors if she wanted a funeral service in "his" church. He told her that he could grant her permission for the funeral only if she would make a number of sacrifices on her husband's behalf. She readily agreed to do whatever he asked of her. She was happy with this news, but when she spoke with Jim and told him what had been said, Jim was livid. He felt anger then disbelief that such a thing could happen in today's world and was disgusted by a faith, a god, who allowed a minister's personal and egotistical grudge deny a faithful widow access to the comfort she needed.

As his mother fulfilled what was asked of her, Jim phoned this minister and asked him where in the Bible Christ taught his apostles to require payment for any sacrament or any act provided by those apostles to God's children. The minister hung up on him. The entire episode left Jim terribly embittered and forever wary of those proclaiming to be God's emissaries. *This was the behavior of a man of God?* Jim thought. *This is the behavior God wants in His representatives, this is what Christ would have advocated His disciples say and do?*

Jim told Barbara that he could not wrap his heart around a god who would ask this of his mother in her time of grief or who would condone the insensitivity of that minister. There was no sense to it. Maybe he could understand requiring some charitable work in the name of his father, he could also understand the requirement of prayers offered on behalf of his father, but he could not understand what had been said to his mother or why she had been denied the ministerial assurance of God's love in her time of grief. Nor could he understand how performing the acts this minister required could "buy" his father immediate access to heaven. Wasn't whether or not his father went to heaven God's call?

Anger filled Jim's heart toward the man who should have been a comfort to his mother while she still grieved and toward the church that allowed their ministers to behave so heartlessly. He felt terrible to know that his mother was now worried about him because this same minister was now questioning Jim's right to God's forgiveness because Jim challenged the minister's actions. Jim was disillusioned by a system that allowed this. It wasn't right to do this to his mother in her time of grief. And it wasn't right to "sell" the forgiveness of sin. These feelings came together to form an aversion to the organized religion that Jim believed was in direct opposition to what a loving God would ask of His people.

Unbeknownst to Jim, these bitter disappointments embedded themselves into his heart and caused the destruction of the precious faith that had once meant so much to him. Thus, Jim closed his heart so he would never again experience such disappointment. It wasn't until much later that Jim would understand that one minister, even one evil or misguided minister, did not a religion make. But nevertheless, that incident lost a young man forever to his church and filled his mother's heart with fear for her son's future.

When Barbara heard this story and understood even those things Jim did not mention, she felt sad. She understood the incredible hurt that Jim felt by what this minister had done to his mother. Jim had seen his mother's tears, and he had seen her struggle to fulfill what was asked of her. He had also seen the size of the check she'd written. He did not begrudge the church any donation, nor did he begrudge any offering, but he did begrudge a *required* payment.

Barbara understood the frustration Jim felt at being unable to help his mother in her grief. She understood how both must have had their faith sorely tested by what that minister had said and had required. She saw that Jim's trust had been broken and understood how this robbed him of his faith. Yet she also understood that it was his trust that had been broken, not his desire to find a way to restore his faith. She knew that to draw Jim back to God, he would first have to learn to trust again. She'd recognized how closed his heart was, but now she understood why.

Barbara's faith taught that Christ freely gave His gift of forgiveness to both the living and the dead and that Christ instructed His apostles to give this gift freely to those who would accept it. Christ taught the apostles not to be concerned about where their next meal would come from or where they would sleep that night as they traveled to bring the Gospel to others. Christ promised that God would care for their needs.

Matthew 10:8 speaks of God's instruction to freely offer His gifts: *"Heal the sick, cleanse the lepers, raise the dead, cast out devils: freely ye have received, freely give."* In Matthew 10:9-10, Christ told His apostles that they need not worry about money or clothing, lodging or food: *"Provide neither gold, nor silver, nor brass in your purses, Nor scrip for your journey."* And then in Matthew 10:29, 31, Christ reminds them, *"Are not two sparrows sold for a farthing? and one . . . shall not fall on the ground without your Father . . . . Fear ye not therefore, ye are of more value than many sparrows."*

Barbara also remembered a verse in Matthew 23:28 where Christ spoke about the Pharisees, who were priests in the time of Jesus, saying, *"Even so ye also outwardly appear righteous unto men, but within ye are full of hypocrisy and iniquity."* And she comforted Jim by reminding him that his father had believed in God and in the sacrifice of Christ. She also reminded Jim that in Acts 15:11, the early apostles had said, *"But we believe that through the grace of the LORD Jesus Christ we shall be saved."*

As Jim shared his experience with Barbara, she knew she loved him. She wasn't sure it was the kind of love that meant marriage because she'd had no experience with being in love, but she did know how much he meant to her. She wanted to be instrumental in bringing him back to God.

But Barbara was also practical and recognized as she thought along these lines that she needed to be careful. For her, it was important to marry someone with whom she could share her faith and who, together with her, would bring the love of and for God into their home, not only for them as a couple, but also for the benefit of their children. She wanted her life to be filled with the striving to learn God's words, to incorporate them into their lives, and to remain faithful until they died. She didn't yet know if Jim could ever fit that mold.

Barbara knew that she had been blessed because she had always had ministers who were honest, who taught her well, and who loved her no matter what. The members of her congregation did their best to treat one another as if they were truly brothers and sisters in the family of God.

Because she'd had such a positive experience with her ministers, when Jim first told her the story of his father's death and his mother's difficulties, she'd thought of the scripture in Matthew 23:23-25 that said, *"Woe unto you, scribes and Pharisees, hypocrites! for ye pay tithe of mint and anise and cummin, and have omitted the weightier matters of the law, judgment, mercy, and faith: these ought ye to have done, and not to leave the other undone. Ye blind guides, which strain at a gnat, and swallow a camel. Woe unto you, scribes and Pharisees, hypocrites! for ye make clean the outside of the cup and of the platter, but within they are full of extortion and excess."*

Barbara felt badly that Jim and his mother—his father too—had not had ministers who simply loved them and patiently taught them how to come under God's freely offered gifts. But the damage had been done to Jim and his family, and the wound had festered and burned for many years. Jim knew that his mother had worried over his father's experience with the church and after he died she also had the burden of worrying about her son's spiritual life. Jim felt guilty knowing that his mother had died with that worry. It appeared to be a wound that had left a permanent scar on Jim's heart.

Nevertheless, Barbara was sure that God could do all things. She knew that God loved Jim and believed with all her heart that God would create the circumstances in Jim's life that would allow him to learn how much he was loved and, in time, love and trust God once again. So she prayed for Jim every day, and little by little, in her letters and her conversations, in her phone calls and e-mails, Barbara brought her sweet, quiet testimony to Jim, even though it sometimes seemed to fall upon rocky ground.

Barbara was also wise enough to understand that souls are won to God by the *actions* of others more so than their words. She hoped that over time, Jim would learn that not everyone would disappoint him, that there were many who sought God's words and tried their best to do as He asked. Jim needed exposure to these people who were always growing in strength, character, and faith because they were striving to live up to godly standards and the example Christ had been to them.

Jim was terribly cynical about religion. Sadly, he had many tales to tell Barbara of people who went to church and spoke of God but thought nothing of taking cruel action against their neighbors and of the vindictive ways they acted that caused emotional harm as well. He'd even told Barbara the story of his mother's experience with a neighbor living next door to her. As Jim told this story, Barbara could hear the bitterness that still remained in his heart over this incident.

His mother had moved into a condo after Jim's father died because the house had been more than she could care for. A few years later, a new neighbor moved into the apartment next to his mother. They shared a common outside hallway. The neighbor was a woman who had been divorced for many, many years and who seemed very much alone. Jim's mother made an effort to be kind to her, buying her a small Christmas present each year, moving her newspaper from the walkway to her door, phoning from time to time to make sure she was okay, arranging for the installation of a storm shutter across their walkway and a new carpet in their joint entryway. But this woman never acknowledged anything his mother did.

Jim believed that this neighbor was jealous of his mother's gentle heart and of her acts of kindness and her faith in God. He knew that his mother was very popular with the other condo residents and often received e-mail and phone calls and cards from them especially as they began to hear the unkind things the neighbor said about his mother. They never heard a word of complaint from his mother; they heard only the gossip this neighbor spread, which God used to indict the neighbor, not his mother.

Nevertheless, this neighbor continued in her cruelties. One year, she removed *and discarded* the Christmas decorations he and his mother had placed in the elevator lobby on her floor. Another year, she entered his mother's apartment with a friend to make foolish and unfounded accusations.

What angered Jim the most was when this woman complained about a small seat, a very pretty little bench he had placed outside his mother's door on which his mother could lay her packages while she located her keys and unlocked her door. Jim had placed the bench there because his mother suffered from a heart condition that made her truly need this little bench.

Jim was enraged by this woman's constant acts of cruelty and recognized her need for power and the driving force of her jealousy. But his mother did not respond in a negative manner to what this woman did; rather, she sweetly pointed out that this woman acted this way, not only with her, but also with many others and made a myriad of complaints to and about everyone. His mother told Jim that their job was to pray for this woman because she must be very unhappy to behave in such a manner toward so many.

However, when this woman could not make an impact on his mother, she finally contacted the board of directors and the fire marshall, demanding that the bench be taken from the hall way. Again, his mother would not let Jim have a talk, a stern talk, with this vindictive person. Jim told Barbara that his mother prayed about the incident and told God that she would gladly remove the bench if this was what He too wanted, but if it was His will that she could keep the bench, which was of so much benefit to her, she would be very pleased. And so his mother left the matter in God's hands and would not think ill of her neighbor. When Barbara heard this story, the first thing she did was rejoice in the love and beauty that lived in the heart of Jim's mother. She had trusted God and accepted whatever He allowed to come her way. She did not hate her neighbor but felt sorry for this woman's need to behave in a way that was contrary to what God asked of her.

Nevertheless, Barbara, feeling a sudden spout of loyalty toward Jim's mother, envisioned the neighbor as a person with a cold and shriveled heart that could only feel when bringing harm to others. And she remembered that God spoke of people who acted as this neighbor had in Romans 3:11 and 18: *"There is none that understandeth, there is none that seeketh after God. There is no fear of God before their eyes."*

Barbara wished for a moment that Jim's mother was still alive. If she had been and if that neighbor was still there, Barbara would certainly have given that person a good lesson in scripture! This woman *purported* to go to church and *purported* to believe in Christ! Yet Barbara also knew that the truly righteous were always persecuted and that Satan used other people to harm those God loved. Satan especially liked to use other so-called believers to harm the children of God. She knew that it was through these difficulties that the righteous were tried and would come through with flying colours to be elevated to become a part of the bride of Christ.

And Barbara thought, *When someone realizes that the book of life does not contain their name and they find themselves being one of the goats cast into the lake of fire with Satan, they might be terribly shocked. Sadly for these people, Satan succeeded in fooling and using them to obtain his objectives.* She wished that everyone could discern the spirits of Satan. Perhaps then, some would try to rectify their behavior.

But for now, Jim was Barbara's main concern. He was someone worth reaching out to, someone worth knowing and supporting. And Barbara wanted to do just that. She wanted Jim to know God and to know of the incredible love that He had for mankind and of the plan he developed that was so perfect that every soul would have the opportunity to spend eternity with Him. Little by little, she planned to tell him of this wonderful plan so he could understand that God, like Christ, was truly love and that love was kindness, trust, integrity, unfailing, long-suffering, and perfect in its ways.

But Barbara knew that she would have to move slowly in terms of talking to Jim about God. Jim was due to arrive home today for a leave from Iraq, and she could hardly wait for the hours to pass until his arrival. She would be leaving for the airport in just a few more hours and already had butterflies in her stomach. She planned to wash her hair and use her new conditioner so her hair would be soft and smell like almonds! She had wanted to cut her hair, but Jim had said that he liked it long so she'd just gotten a trim.

What should I wear to the airport? Casual, but classy, she thought, *definitely with an aura of "grown-up,"* . . . *not college student* . . . *since Jim always worried about our ten-year age difference.* After trying on a dozen combinations, Barbara decided to wear her black trousers with a tailored white satin blouse and a black-and-yellow floral cardigan sweater over the blouse. She hoped she didn't look like a honeybee. *What if he teased me about that?* She giggled. *Ahh* . . . *to be safe and to eliminate a first strike, I'll change the sweater to the pink cardigan with the black trim along the edges of the sleeves, across the hemline, and down the front placket where the white pearl buttons are sewn.*

She applied pink rouge to her cheeks and bright pink lipstick to her lips. She brushed her hair until it gleamed. She added a thin gold belt, lightweight black trouser socks, and black loafers. Then she took up her black shoulder strap purse with gold trim and was ready to go. She wished that she wasn't still living at the college dormitory so she and Jim could have a place to sit and talk, but decided a restaurant would have to do. During Jim's stay, they'd probably visit her brother's apartment and maybe even Sarah's spacious apartment filled with her grandmother's beautiful antiques. Barbara's brother Matt had been engaged to Sarah . . . well . . . forever!

She loved Sarah. From the first day they'd met, they had been best friends. They thought alike, they both wanted to serve God, they liked having family around, and when Sarah had introduced Barbara to Grandma, well, the same thing had happened—friends for life, family! When Sarah's grandmother had moved from a house to a condo, she had given Sarah lots of wonderful things from her home.

Sarah and Matt didn't plan to marry until they finished their master's degrees and maybe not until they were well into their doctorate degrees. They also hoped to purchase a house before they married so when they did marry, they could move right in. Barbara knew that Jim would love Matt and Sarah and that they would love him too. They would wonder how serious Barbara was about Jim because she'd never brought a "date" home to meet them before.

Maybe she *was* serious about Jim. She could picture Jim as a husband and as a father, she could also picture him with her family, but she couldn't picture Jim in church . . . *yet.* And that was an important part of her life and an important aspect of what she wanted to impart to the children she might have one day. And since it was also such an important part of what her whole family did, well, it would be awkward with Jim's cynicism toward religion. This is why she'd have to think carefully about Jim in terms of a really serious relationship.

Well, I am going to enjoy this time with Jim anyway and see how it goes and see if I feel any different when he goes back to Iraq. She would try to get a better handle on whether or not she felt Jim could ever have a change of heart about living a life where practicing their faith was integrated into everything they did. These thoughts filled Barbara's mind as she drove to the airport. Time went by so quickly that suddenly, here she was, ready to enter the vast complex of parking lots, walkways, and terminals.

Barbara arrived at the airport about forty-five minutes before Jim's flight was scheduled to arrive. After parking the car, she made a concerted effort to remember *exactly* where she parked. She didn't want Jim to tease her about losing the car. She walked as far as she was allowed toward the exit where Jim would emerge to retrieve his luggage. She sat in a little open section that was used as a waiting area until she knew his flight had arrived. Then she walked toward the narrowed area of the walkway where he would pass into the nonrestricted zone. She had butterflies in her stomach again. *Nonsense*, she thought.

When she saw Jim, her heart flip-flopped, and she knew that her feelings for him might be serious after all. *Go slow*, she told herself. *Give it lots of time.* Then suddenly, he was beside her and she was slipping her arm into the crook of his arm and smiling up at him, then walking alongside him, matching his stride. When he stopped walking, grinned, and asked for a hug, she reacted impulsively and literally threw herself into his arms, at first embarrassed by what she had done. But he was so receptive to what she had done so impulsively, lifting her off the ground to hug her, that she felt okay about it.

Then after their silly bear hug, after he allowed her feet to touch the ground once more, he placed his hands on the sides of her face and bent down to kiss her so tenderly, so thoughtfully that she was glad she had acted impulsively. *Now,* she reminded herself again, *take it slowly!*

As they walked toward her car, she chatted about her hope that Jim would meet her brother Matt and Sarah, his fiancée. She told him all about Sarah's wonderful apartment and that the apartment was located in an old stone building on a street lined with tall oak trees whose branches reached entirely across the road to blend with the branches of similar trees on the other side.

Barbara used her hands to describe how the branches met to form a gorgeous canopy of green in the spring, summer, and fall. She told him of the tall arched windows with mullions set into them, which held glass rectangles that were slightly curved to catch the light, and of the thick chestnut moldings and dark-stained wood floors that went so well with Sarah's grandmother's beautiful antiques.

He marveled at her elaborate descriptions and her definitions of the various styles of furniture in the apartment. He loved listening to her and marveled at how expertly she wove vibrant images through her descriptions and explanations. Her interest in these things drew him in, and he became interested too. He loved her voice, and he loved the inflections she introduced into certain words as she tried to make her points more emphatic, and he loved to watch the expression on her face.

Sometimes he had to concentrate on what she was saying because being so enthralled with her face as she talked, his mind wandered from what she was saying. He was so busy defining what he saw in her animated facial expressions and gestures that sometimes he almost lost the gist of what she was telling him. He noticed her slim curved body and admired how she looked in her black slacks and bright pink sweater trimmed in black. *Chic,* he thought. *Why isn't she wearing the jeans that college kids usually wear?*

They separated for a moment as he walked to the revolving baggage station to wait for his large duffel bag to make its appearance. When he had retrieved the bag and walked back to where she was standing, he shifted the bag to his other arm so they could walk arm in arm to her car. He didn't want to go right home and then not be with her. He wanted to spend more time with her, not just drive directly home. So he said, "Let's go out to dinner . . . I'm starved . . . have you eaten yet?"

"No, I haven't. I figured by the time your flight was scheduled to leave Washington that you probably would not have eaten dinner, so I was going to suggest we do just that! We can sit awhile and talk, so I can catch up on all that is going on in Iraq! I want to hear about everything, work, play, worries, the people, your experiences! What would you like to eat, Jim?"

"Okay! Well, I'm not so sure I have anything interesting to tell you, but to go out for dinner together, that will be great . . . uhh, what do they say . . . uhhh, that great minds think alike? Do you have anything special you'd like to eat or a place you especially enjoy?"

"Well, I thought that after being in Iraq for so long, you may not have had a great big juicy steak in a while and thought that it might be something you'd really like to have! What do you think?"

"I'm salivating already, so just drive away. I am at your mercy. I will follow you anywhere, especially when bribed with a huge steak—ohh, and even more so by the simple fact that you are driving so therefore, I have no control over where I am taken. Thus, I am indeed ready, willing, and able to go where you lead . . . I am at your mercy!"

Barbara laughed. "Yeah, like I didn't ask you first where *you* wanted to go, what *you* wanted to eat!" Secretly, she was pleased that he was pleased, and he was delighted that she had put so much thought into her suggestion about what he might like to eat. They both enjoyed their easy camaraderie, and they both had the fleeting but pleasant thought that maybe at the end of the evening they would exchange another kiss. But both had also decided that *they* would not be the one to initiate it! Each would wait for the other to make the first move.

Jim felt like a kid, and he didn't like feeling that way. It was, well, unsettling. He was a grown man after all, and it was just that he wasn't quite sure what to do with a sweet, innocent college kid. He didn't feel that he could talk of the horrors of Iraq and wondered if she'd be interested in the disgusting dynamics of the politics hampering their attempts to get anything done. On the other hand, while he was worried about what they'd talk about, she seemed so composed. He wondered if being in Iraq for so long had shaken his self-confidence.

Barbara sensed his unease and smiled and was content to see where the conversation would lead. She truly wanted to understand what he lived through in Iraq, but she wanted him to move into his conversation easily and she didn't want him to talk about anything that wouldn't contribute to him relaxing. She wanted the friendship to be the most important issue tonight, and she looked forward to a few hours of light conversation and friendly interaction rather than the troubles she knew he faced. She could see that he was tired from his long trip and thought that she'd try to get him home at a decent hour and try to make their conversation light and cheery so he could relax.

He'd asked her to call the woman who checked out and cleaned his apartment once a month while he was gone. He'd wanted her to arrange for this woman to go to his apartment and make sure that everything was in order and that fresh sheets and towels were ready for him too. Barbara phoned her and made the arrangements he'd asked her to make. She also arranged to bring some groceries to his apartment. Barbara told the woman that she would drop off some groceries while the woman was there to clean. She wanted his refrigerator and pantry stocked with healthy things to eat for at least a few days.

The waiter appeared to take their order. First, as an appetizer, they ordered the restaurant's famous fried onion with a spicy sauce for dipping. They enjoyed every morsel of it. When their steaks arrived, they attacked them with vigor, both grinning from ear to ear at the other's enthusiasm for the food. As their appetites waned, they slowed their attack on the food and Jim began to speak about his experiences in Iraq. He told her of the terrible loss to the country of their artifacts and literature when the museum and the library in Baghdad were looted.

"It was one of the first big and terrible mistakes made on the part of the Americans," he said. "We should have placed guards around these historical sites to protect them and preserve the heritage that the people were so proud of. Barbara, these places contained artifacts that were *thousands* of years old and which cannot be replaced and probably will never be recovered. I can't believe that so little insight went into planning the aftermath of ridding the country of Saddam Hussein."

Barbara asked him if he thought that in time the Iraqis would blame the United States for this loss. "Yes, absolutely, they *already* do . . . and rightfully so. We should have at least stopped it after it began, but no orders were issued other than not to interfere with the civilians at all, and so our soldiers just watched as the looting took place. And once the looters saw they could get away with it, more came. And finally, after all the good stuff was gone, they even chipped away at the concrete to get at the rebar so they could sell them! It was awful!"

"That was a big mistake . . . and even if some of these items could be recovered, they would probably have to pay quite a bit for them because the price would escalate every time they were sold. Every country is proud of its heritage, of its artists and writers, and of what their ancestors centuries ago created. It must be an awful feeling to think you've lost that . . . forever."

"Didn't anyone think about the cultural assets of the country, Jim? I mean, even about the fact that they might add something that would commemorate the day of their liberation? Their first opportunity for democracy could have been commemorated by a plaque, declaration, artistic rendition . . . something . . . and added to their museum. I mean, this was their library and their museum! I wonder how people would feel if every library and museum in Washington DC was looted of every artifact that spoke of our history and our greatest achievements. Jim, did any politician or military leader address any of this either before the attack or right afterward?"

"Well, as far as I know, only after the looting had taken place . . . and even then, no action was taken to recover anything. Yeah, our government should have been better prepared, and our generals and soldiers should have had more authority to make split-second decisions so they could have stepped in to stop what was happening. If the soldiers felt that they would have been supported in their decision to act even without direct orders, maybe it could have been avoided. Maybe they could have stopped the looting as soon as it started and been able to preserve many of the artifacts."

"Jim, what is the most disturbing to you now in Iraq?"

"Probably the lack of security. And our inability to stop the suicide bombers who kill civilians . . . women, children, the elderly . . . and of course, our young soldiers. I can't tell you how many people I have carried to ambulances, people without arms or legs, babies that are bleeding. I've also carried young soldiers to the hospital after a bomb went off . . . soldiers who were willing to give their life for democracy, who have now given their legs. The injuries are horrendous because there is so much shrapnel. It travels long distances and penetrates even the vehicles. Naturally, it does terrible damage to any physical body it hits. Brain damage is also prevalent in these victims and often is the cause of seizures and blackouts, loss of vision and loss of hearing . . . even the loss of memory and cognitive ability. And then there are the horrible burns."

"From what you are telling me, Jim, you are much closer to danger than I realized. Do these suicide bombers come into the area where *you* work and where you sleep? Is there no protection for you?"

"Well, most of the compounds where we sleep now have thick walls around them, so we are pretty safe. The hospitals are located inside these walls as well. But whenever we travel from one place to another, we risk running into one of these crazy misled people who think nothing of killing and maiming innocent people. And of course, sometimes we move into more desolate areas or into areas where the insurgents hide so we can make our assessments, create our blueprints, discuss our plans for the projects we need to complete, and we *are* in danger there and, of course, as we drive to and from these locations. But you know, Barb, it's seeing the aftermath of an attack that is so devastating . . . it's seeing the children and the young soldiers and the elderly that are severely and permanently injured or can no longer work. And it's the wondering about how they will survive, what they will have to face in life that I can't shake. It really hurts to think about it."

"What happens in terms of medical care to those who are so severely hurt, . . . is your hospital equipped to handle such horrific injuries?"

"They do an amazing job. I've been there, I've watched, I've even helped when they were so inundated with patients that the medical personnel couldn't handle the influx. In fact, I think I'm getting some training as a paramedic. But seriously, the answer to your question is no. The severely injured don't stay there.

They are stabilized, bleeding is stopped, dressings are applied, IVs started, that kind of stuff. But usually, they are taken to Balad Field Hospital, which is sixty miles north of Baghdad . . . and if they are more traumatically injured, they are then flown 2,140 miles to our largest military hospital outside the U.S. It's called Landstuhl Regional Medical Center and is located in Landstuhl, Germany, right near the Ramstein Air Base in Landstuhl. They get great care there, but nevertheless so many injuries are traumatic, the damage so permanent that many of these guys suffer for a very long time."

"Jim, do you pray? Praying for those who have been injured does help. God can perform miracles . . . Sometimes they are miracles of healing, but more often they are miracles of *strength*. They are miracles that send the right people into our lives to make the bearing of it a little bit easier. With help from God, we can carry a lot of heartache, and the blessing is that what we suffer can perfect us. If we can forgive those who harmed us, we have started the process of becoming a part of the bride of Christ. Do you ever ask God to look after you, to protect you, to protect those who strive to do good? Do you ever ask Him to stop those who want to bring harm to others?"

"No, not usually, Barb. I'm angry . . . and it just doesn't seem right to pray when you're really angry and can't find any forgiveness in your heart. I don't understand a god who allows this stuff to happen in the first place. Wouldn't it be better for these people to die quickly and immediately rather than have to suffer all their lives? Wouldn't it be better just to zap the bad guys out of existence? I'd think that an all-powerful God could do all of that. It just doesn't make any sense that He'd allow so much heartache to exist."

"Yeah, God could change all that. But there *is* an evil force at work here on earth, and it has been given the right to play itself out because of man's sin. It seeks to destroy mankind. Yet God has engineered that in our suffering, we can learn how to overcome that evil and in the process be drawn closer to God. It is in winning the struggle to forgive those who want to harm us and bearing our heartache that we are perfected. It is finally being able to pray for those who hurt us that God can bless us and that Satan is broken by the love God has been able to perfect in us. Satan is the one to be angry with, not God. Satan is the one who wants to bring us so much agony that we begin to hate and lose the love God wants for us. Satan is fighting for his life by bringing us harm . . . He is hoping to break us so we won't become God's children or fulfill the number that God wants as the bride for His Son. And sadly, I think that sometimes it is inherited or generational sin that allows these calamities into our lives. Maybe it's what allows Satan the opening to do such harm."

"I'm not sure I can accept that. Why would God go through all this just so we know good and evil? And also, I'm not so sure that there is an entity such as Satan who exercises that kind of control over us. I mean, why is Satan so important that God would give him that much power? And by the way, how do you know all this stuff? What makes you say what you do about this Satan character with such conviction? I mean, well, . . . I guess I can believe that there is a Satan, but I only know him as the serpent in Eden who tempted Eve and as the bad angel who sits on the opposite shoulder as our good angel and whispers in our ear to get us to do what we shouldn't. But that's *all* I've ever heard. And I don't think I understand what you mean when you say inherited or generational sin. What's that?"

"Well, it's complex, but just to give you some understanding about what I mean—and we'll talk about it again another time because it's too complicated not to give it a lot of explanation . . . but let's say that you had an ancestor who was in a position of incredible power and was a great and unrepentant sinner because he enjoyed killing people who disagreed with him. The actions of that ancestor may have opened the door to allowing that same evil, those same spirits to affect his children, grandchildren and great-grandchildren. That open door could allow the evil to affect future generations by either opening a channel by which they can become the *targets* of other killers or by which they can inherit the same tendency to *be* a killer themselves."

"Whoa, . . . this is heavy stuff. Slow down. Wait a minute. I've *never* heard of that before. That's pretty terrible to think about. Are you saying that if I had an ancestor who sinned, I can either become the same kind of sinner myself or become a *target* of that kind of a sinner? That's absolutely ridiculous, Barbara."

"No, it isn't and yes, I meant exactly what you thought I meant. Like the woman who wanted to hurt your mother . . . she could be opening the door for the tendency to rest upon her grandchildren to cause or receive harm from others. Whether she knows it or not! God speaks many times in scripture about the sins of the forefathers being visited upon the third and fourth generations. This woman's actions could be laying down that tendency . . . opening the door for her grandchildren or great-grandchildren to become extremely cruel people or be harmed by them.

"Jim, you know the story of Adam and Eve. Well, in some ways, this story warns us about this phenomena. God explained that through the sin of Adam and Eve, all future generations have to pay the price for the sin of disobedience they committed. For instance, nowadays, they consider drug addiction and alcoholism either an inherited tendency or an illness. But those who read the Bible see these weaknesses in a slightly different way. We believe it is an *influence* rather than an illness. It is an influence that may have gained access to certain people because of their ancestor's sins. These sins may have given Satan the right *to lay claim* to certain areas of their lives, just as Adam and Eve's sin allowed Satan the right to introduce evil to all mankind."

"Wow. I am stunned. But I don't buy it. Honestly, I've never heard this before. I don't know what to say, and it's sort of unbelievable. Maybe it's because it's simply such a new concept to me, but it's sort of way out there, Barb. But if God loves mankind as you say, then why doesn't He prevent these later generations from having to pay the price of the sins of their forefathers? I mean, it sure seems unfair to me."

"Well, it's because of the battle between good and evil that we are living through. The sin of Adam and Eve resulted in the *requirement* that mankind learn of good *and* evil. God warned them, and they did not listen. That single act of sin now allows Satan to work with sin and use it against mankind, but only for a certain amount of time. God, because of His righteousness, *cannot* interfere unless man asks for His help. And believe me, God *has* provided us with all kinds of help to get through it—even overcome it. It's complex but all a part of an incredible plan to perfect love, which is an environment in which evil cannot exist, and thus eventually will allow God to create an untainted new world."

"This is all new to me. I will accept what you say on faith *for now* because I have a lot of respect for the way you think, Barb. But *believe* me, I'm gonna check this out. It's interesting, but I think you've got it wrong. I want to know where I can read up, learn more about this. I've got to be able to challenge you on this one . . . but I need more information, more information to even try!"

"Well, it will take more time than we have tonight. I'd sure love to talk about it some more . . . It is fascinating. But you know, you should talk to my brother Matt. Jim, you will love my brother. He is the *best* storyteller ever, and he can tell you the story of inherited sin and of the work of Satan so well that every question you could possibly have will be answered. What's your schedule? How long will you be with us? Would it be okay with you if I call Matt and Sarah and set up a date for us to spend an evening with them? I think you would enjoy being with them and really enjoy Matt's great gift for knowing the Bible and telling it like it is."

"Yeah, I would enjoy that kind of a discussion. That would be great. But you'd better expect a challenge! I think that I will be home for a total of three weeks. I'll be here this week. Next week, I have to go to DC for a couple of days to help Wade talk with someone at the Pentagon about the mistakes they are making in Iraq. Once we do that, then perhaps I'll have another week back here. Then we might have to testify before a congressional hearing or something, . . . that is, if they care . . . if they really want the facts. Altogether, I'm expecting that we'll be here for three weeks or so except for a couple of days in DC. See if you can set something up within the next five days and perhaps we can get another few visits in when I get back from DC."

"Okay, Jim. It seems that your schedule will work for us getting together for a good talk! And now, we'd better get home. I have to be in school tomorrow morning, and you have to get some rest after that gruesome trip. I want you healthy, bright, and rarin' to go when you talk to the DC bigwigs . . . and for when you might have to debate Matt . . . or you'll *lose* that debate for sure!"

Jim laughed out loud at Barbara's remark about debating her brother. She was challenging him! Yeah sure, . . . start off on the wrong foot with her protective brother? No way. Jim could see how her brother might adore her as much as he did. She was funny and audacious, and she was sharp. Very sharp. Then again, he sure would love that argument.

Jim finished paying the bill just as Barbara returned from powdering her nose or whatever women called their trip to the restroom, and they walked out of the restaurant hand in hand. When they got to the car, Jim turned toward Barbara; and looking down into her pretty face, he leaned in to kiss her as she lifted her face to his. And without the other knowing, both hearts soared.

Barbara thought, *He's been through so much. He could be such an asset where he is in Iraq to help those embittered by what they live through. He has such a beautiful heart and so much tenderness and concern for others.* Her heart filled with a request to God that He look after Jim and that He draw Jim to Him.

Jim had similar thoughts about Barbara. *She is compassionate, she listens well, and she understands what the Iraqi people go through,* he thought. *She didn't talk about herself. Instead, she listened to me. She is concerned. She is worried about my safety. I hope she never has to suffer.* Then he thought, *I'd like to meet her brother. But they'd better be prepared for me to defuse some of their enthusiasm for what they believe . . . I can shoot a lot of holes into such a crazy theory as soon as I gather some facts!*

When they'd first met, Jim had explained to Barbara that he'd recently been offered the opportunity to go to Iraq for his company and that they had offered to pay his expenses for the apartment while he was in Iraq. Jim had been pleased by that offer and happy to have a place to stay when he came home. So Barbara drove him back to his apartment and then drove to her dorm with thoughts of the danger Jim faced in Iraq. She would ask her family to pray for him, especially when he went back to Iraq. She'd call Matt in the morning and set a date for the four of them to get together, and maybe it would fall nicely into place for Matt to tell Jim about the terrible enemy that would do anything to thwart God's plan and timetable. *Jim will never be able to win a debate with Matt,* she thought.

Chapter Three

THE FAMILY

Matt, Barbara's brother, was engaged to be married to Sarah. Last July, Sarah had moved into her own apartment from her college dorm after graduating with a bachelor's degree in psychology. When her Grandmother decided to move into a condo and sell her house, she'd offered Sarah her extra furniture because Sarah was to move from her college dorm directly into her own apartment. Because Sarah loved the things her grandmother had in her home she was delighted. Sarah would be working, as a requirement of her master's degree program, to train as a special education teacher/psychologist while she earned her advanced degree.

Sarah and Matt planned to marry but not until they completed their master's degrees and had established their studies toward their doctorate degrees. They also wanted to purchase an old house to renovate so when they married, it would be ready for them to move into. Matt helped Sarah move her possessions from her college dormitory room and also the furnishings Grandma was giving to Sarah and the possessions Sarah had left at Grandma's when she was living there before going off to college. He too loved the old-world charm and the elegance of Grandma's furnishings and how well they complemented the style of the apartment Sarah had chosen.

According to Grandma, many years ago Grandma's grandmother had purchased traditional-style furnishings and passed some of these on to her daughter who then passed them along to Grandma. Now Sarah would join this line of succession because she too loved the old-world charm and elegance of the more traditional styles. Sarah, like Grandma, had excellent taste and, with the help of the beautiful antiques handed down to her, had decorated her apartment beautifully.

Grandma taught Sarah that it was the sense of balance through placement, colour, and style that gave everything its legitimacy, made everything seem to blend even when many different styles were used together. She'd said that balance produced a feeling of harmony and a sense of well-being and told Sarah that she had often watched her mother move furniture and accessories around the room until everything seemed to fit each area perfectly. This enabled Grandma to develop her own knack for decorating. Grandma also learned from her mother of the influences of different cultures on the various furniture designs.

Whether the item was influenced by the pagodas of China, by the curves found in many French furnishings, or influenced by the solid mahogany used in much of the English designs, the dark stained woods, the substance of the pieces, and the elegance of their lines needed to combine properly to create balance. It was the balance that produced a sense of harmony in the room, and that harmony was what provided Sarah with a sense of stability and peace. The same peace she'd always experienced when she was with Grandma was what she wanted for the home that she and Matt would have someday.

Sarah felt blessed that Matt too liked the old-world look and that he too loved the furniture that her grandmother had given her. He'd also been delighted by the practical aspect of stained and varnished doors and woodwork when he'd painted Sarah's apartment. The job was done so quickly because there was nothing to paint except the walls and ceiling surface. They were both grateful that they were compatible in so many areas of their lives.

Both Matt and Sarah were the middle children in their families. Each family had two boys and one girl. Both Matt and Sarah had an older and a younger sibling, and each set of siblings were five years apart in age. When they first met and learned this, they were amazed by the similarities in their families. Matt's sister Barbara was five years younger than Matt, and his brother Paul was five years older. Sarah had two brothers, Caleb who was five years older and Josh who was five years younger.

Barbara telephoned Matt and asked him to arrange a date and time when everyone could meet Jim, explaining that he was only home for a three-week leave from Iraq. As soon as Matt hung up the phone, he phoned Sarah to set up a date for when they could all meet. They wondered if Jim was special to Barbara because she'd never brought anyone home to them before. They were curious and looked forward to meeting him. Barbara was strong-minded and should have a husband who could match her in wit, intellect, and faith. This was a tall order, big shoes to fill, but it was because Barbara herself was so special!

Just the day before, Grandma had reminded everyone of her expectations that the family would come to her house for Thanksgiving dinner, so it was decided that Barbara should bring Jim along. This way, everyone would get to meet him. Barbara worried about so many of them suddenly besieging Jim with questions but then thought that it might be a good opportunity for her to see how he reacted under fire! She grinned with the thought of Jim giving them all quite a run for their money! *This should be fun*, Barbara thought.

There would be eight for dinner: Grandma and Paul; Caleb and his wife, Ann; Sarah and Matt; and Barbara and Jim. Josh was in college and in need of some disciplined time to hit the books for his upcoming exams, so he had decided not to attend but use the time to study. Caleb and Ann planned to drive to Grandma's early in the morning to bring her the turkey they purchased. Grandma would make her famous stuffing the day before, and Ann and Caleb would help her get the turkey stuffed and in the oven before they went to church.

Naturally, Grandma would already have set the table for dinner and naturally it would look wonderful! Caleb had said that he would bring apple cider and some hors d'oeuvres and maybe even a bottle or two of Asti Spumante as a toast with which they would begin the meal.

Paul also said that he would arrive at Grandma's early so he could deliver the huge lattice-crust apple pie that he planned to buy at Costco along with an equally large, sinfully spicy and aromatic pumpkin pie and some whipping cream. He would accompany Grandma, Caleb, and Ann to church and leave his car at Grandma's. Grandma teased by telling everyone that she had a "date" with a tall, handsome, smart, and very young man and that he would be bringing her to church and then dining with her! Everyone knew that she was talking about Paul but pretended to be shocked by what she said and asked with pretended consternation just who this mystery man could be.

Just a few days earlier, Paul had learned that his wife had run off with another man and he was suffering from what she had done. The agony he felt was written all over his face not only because she left but also because she had taken the children with her and did not plan to tell him where they were. The family had been aware that Paul's wife had brought him pain over the years and had in fact been unfaithful to him on numerous occasions when he was away at sea.

They were delighted that Paul would be coming to church and then to Thanksgiving dinner at Grandma's. Paul's wife had never wanted him to come to church or spend time with his family and friends and so the family looked forward to sharing the church service and Thanksgiving dinner with him. They knew that now more than ever, Paul needed God's help and needed his family to rally around him.

Sarah wanted to make a green bean casserole and a marshmallow-topped squash dish that the family preferred over sweet potatoes. She and Matt planned to run back to her apartment after church to retrieve these items from her oven and pack them in an insulated bag to bring them to Grandma's while they were still hot.

At Grandma's house, they would all gather in her kitchen and work together to boil and mash the potatoes. They all loved Grandma's special way of preparing mashed potatoes and also loved Grandma's incredible gravy. She would sauté onions in butter, allowing them to caramelize so they would be sweet. She would add all kinds of herbs and spices to them, and she would use this mixture as an additive to the gravy she would create from the turkey drippings. Grandma might have some packaged biscuits too to pop into the oven.

When Barbara invited Jim to join them for Thanksgiving Day, and told him of the wonderful foods everyone would be making, he gladly accepted her invitation and suggested they also bring something to eat. They decided upon a tossed green salad and a fresh fruit salad, which they would create together in Jim's apartment. Jim told her that she would be impressed by his culinary skills and how much at ease he was in the kitchen. She smiled, liking what he'd said. Barbara hadn't yet asked Jim about coming to church with her, but thought they could run back to Jim's apartment after church to toss together those things they would have previously washed, chopped, and chilled so the salads would still be crisp when they brought them to Grandmas.

Barbara began reminiscing about her family, sharing her thoughts with Jim. Grandma was eighty-eight years old and still as active as ever, still as feisty as ever. They all loved being with her and teasing her. She was just a little thing, not even five feet tall, and she always wore black slacks and a chic flowing blouse over the slacks while at home and a tailored jacket over the blouse if she went out. She always pinned a unique broach on the lapel of her jacket. She wore her hair pulled up into a bun on the top of her head while wisps of her curly white hair formed little ringlets around her still pretty face.

Grandma made Ann and Barbara, Matt and Paul feel as if they were her grandchildren too. Just recently, knowing that Sarah cherished the words Grandma had always used only with her, *my dearest darling sweetheart love*, Grandma winked at everyone then said these words to Paul.

Sarah admitted that she was surprised the first time she'd heard Grandma use those words with Paul; she'd even felt a momentary pang of jealousy, but then she'd laughed and realized that she had just been caught by surprise and was happy to share them with Paul. Paul hugged Sarah and called her his big little sister then quickly looked over to Barbara, suddenly aware that maybe Barbara had been offended, but no. They all loved one another and were happy to share these little endearments, and they especially liked to tease one another with them.

Not to be outdone, Matt asked if he was the only one in the family that couldn't lay claim to some special words of endearment, then Ann caught on to Matt's playful idea and she too asked for some special words of her own, accusing Grandma of playing favorites. Then Caleb complained that it wasn't fair to leave him out and also asked for his own set of words. And the game was on with silly words flying from person to person.

And Barbara remembered that Grandma had said, "Okay Matt, I will address you as 'dearest, wonderful, courageous warrior.' And, Caleb, how about 'incredible man of rocklike faith.'" And Matt chirped in with "or immovable role model of excellence!" Then Caleb said, "And, Ann, hmmmm, well, what about 'my lovely, sweet supporter' or—ohhhh, I know, 'the inexorable, sweet power behind the throne!'"

Grandma giggled, enjoying the unexpected game immensely. Everyone joined in to add their own two cents' worth of new and different words such as "wondrous" and "spectacular." Finally, everyone ended up with a silly nickname and not one that they particularly liked, names like "rocky rock" and "puffy power puff" and "windy warrior."

Grandma loved games. So as this game moved forward, Grandma soon had the idea that each of them should write their name on a slip of paper. That paper was passed to the others, and each person in turn wrote two or three descriptive words best fitting the person whose name was at the top of the paper. Grandma said that every word they used had to start with the same letter as the person's first name. When they finished, they collected the papers, one per person and redistributed them for reading aloud . . . except that you could not read your own.

Barbara remembered some of the words used for each of them. Sarah's had been "silly and serene Sarah," "sassy and saucy Sarah," "salient sushi Sarah," and "sophisticated, supercalifragilistic Sarah." Grandma's list included such words as "grand and garrulous Grandma," "gorgeous and gaudy Grandma," and "Grandma of geniuses, geeks, and grunts." Grandma was happy because her wish had come true to simply "make memories" for each of them of the good times they shared. They would have these always in their hearts and remember them when it was important to do so.

Making memories was very important to Grandma. She'd endured so much pain in her life and worried that someday, those she loved might also have to endure pain as they were "tried in the fire" and so she always wanted them to have good and happy memories to sustain them in times of duress. Grandma felt that many people became spoiled and didn't appreciate what they had and what others did for them. She'd tell them that sometimes they had to lose what was important to them in order to appreciate what they had. She also told them that sometimes they needed to learn that God was more important than anything that this earth could offer them.

She felt that making memories helped people recognize their blessings and then to remember and finally appreciate them. She said that it would also inspire each of them to create good memories for their own families, memories of love and trust and good clean fun. She was right. Having memories of their good times together, of the love they had for one another, and more importantly, of the love God had for them helped them through the difficult times.

This was the atmosphere into which Barbara would be bringing Jim. She truly felt that he would enjoy being with her family. They were looking forward to meeting him on Thursday. Barbara also knew that everyone simply *expected* that Jim would accompany Barbara to church. But Barbara hadn't yet mentioned church to him. She wasn't sure how he would react.

She and Jim had made plans to go shopping together for the food they needed for the salads. They would go together on Wednesday evening after Barbara finished her classes and after they went out for dinner together. Barbara hoped to broach the subject of church over dinner. They chose a little place where they could get everything from pizza to hamburgers and from sandwiches to fish-and-chips, then after they ate, they planned to drive to the food market.

Barbara drove to Jim's apartment to pick him up for dinner. When she arrived, he beckoned her inside because he was on the phone with Wade and hadn't even had time to put on his socks and shoes. When he finished his conversation with Wade and explained that they'd made plans to meet in DC the following week, Jim asked Barbara to describe her family to him as he quickly donned socks and shoes and combed his hair.

She started with a description of Grandma and then of each of the other five people Jim would meet, explaining that they often saw one another three times a week. He was intrigued by the fact that her family got together so often and on such a regular basis and asked why they did that and how everyone fit it into the kind of busy lifestyles that most people had. "Well, we, well, most of us . . . uhh . . . see one another twice a week at church, in addition to having a fellowship every week or so," Barbara began.

"Church? . . . *Twice* a week . . . *Every* week?" Jim replied with eyebrows raised. "*Twice? Why not just move in?*"

Barbara ignored his last remark. She choked back her desire to tell him that Bill O'Reilly would say his last remark was "rapaciously pietistic and pithy in its raillery". *That would show him,* she thought, but replied instead, "Yeah, it's about one hour on Sundays and often we go out for brunch afterward. And on Wednesdays, the service lasts for about forty-five minutes except for once a month when the congregation shares in a huge birthday cake for the members who celebrated their birthday that month. It's fun. Can you imagine . . . Grandma stills sings in the choir, and her voice is still okay to do it!"

"Do *you?* Do *you* sing in the choir?"

"Yes. I love it! I feel that it's just another small way that I can show God that I love Him and appreciate what He's done for me. And, Jim, I want you to know that Matt and Sarah and I have made the commitment for our lives that we will *always* hold one truth in our hearts and help one another hold on to it. Our commitment can be summed up by a few verses from the Bible, out of Joshua 24:15, which says, '*As for me and my house, we will serve the LORD.*' But anyway, I know that you will enjoy the choir immensely . . . the choir sounds really great."

He caught her words "*you* will enjoy" but decided not to respond to the word *you* because he wasn't quite sure how she meant that. So instead Jim asked, "Does *everyone* in your family think this way, you know . . . sing in the choir, do this twice-a-week church stuff?" He was suddenly wary, afraid that maybe here was a family who really *did* pray together and stick together and believe together. On the one hand, he felt a familiar surge of hope that there *was* real goodness and commitment in the world, but then he felt his mind kick in with the cynicism that reminded him about human nature and whispered to him, *Yeah, but just wait until they fight with one another or their minister begins a campaign for large amounts of money or a member of their congregation commits some horrendous act against another member . . . what then?*

But Barbara didn't know what Jim was thinking. She'd only heard a drop in his tone and a sudden wariness in his voice when he asked if they all went to church. So she turned to him, lifting her perfect face to kiss his cheek, twining her hand over his, and said sweetly, "Well, Matt and Sarah and Caleb and Ann sing in the choir. Paul doesn't because he is not a member of the church . . . *yet.* He is a mariner who's out to sea a lot and would have to miss rehearsals, but actually it was his wife that didn't want him to come. That's why we are so glad that he is coming now. Oh, and Josh doesn't come right now because he's away at college and . . . well, he's also into his rebellion stage right now too."

"Sooooo . . . basically . . . *all* of you go to church."

"Yes."

"Great . . . Well . . . that lets me off the hook about going with you because I'd have no one to sit with, and being the nonreligious rebel that I am, I wouldn't know what to do! Haa!" Jim said, quite satisfied with himself for having an excuse to bow out.

"Honnnnneyyyyy, . . . not so fast . . . I can sit with you anytime I want. I can skip choir. And I will sit with you if you'll come."

Jim was surprised by what Barbara said. Actually, he was even more surprised by what *he'd* said. She hadn't even asked him to come to church, and he'd already intimated he'd come "if." What an idiot! He shouldn't have acted as if he'd considered coming to church first of all, and second, when he figured he was off the hook, he'd led her to believe that he would come under certain conditions and he hadn't really meant that. He'd not responded truthfully, and now he was stuck. Third, she'd outwitted him by saying she could and would sit with him. And fourth . . . had she called him "honey"?

Jim looked at Barbara. He knew that she did not realize that he'd spoken about going to church with her before she'd asked. She also didn't realize that he regretted making her think he would come. She was watching him now, carefully, waiting for his response about whether or not he would join them. He also thought of the logistics of how much easier it would be for them all to be together.

Her smile was so sweet and genuine; hope was written all over her, and what was killing him was the trust she seemed to have in him that he would do the right thing. It made him feel guilty. What had he gotten himself into? Why had he glibly led her to believe he would go to church if it weren't for the fact that she couldn't sit with him? *I'm lost. Lost. And it is my own fault. Well, even though I'm caught for the moment by my own stupidity, I'll set Barbara straight as soon as I can. I'll set them all straight.*

Her faith in him almost made him angry. She seemed to have no clue that he disliked organized religion, that he considered it hogwash, total hypocrisy. But her innocence was written all over her, so he said the only thing he could. He said yes and immediately regretted it. He felt that by his response, he had misled her. He was not a church kinda guy, and she needed to know this. She just didn't understand that he would never believe, never join an organized religion. Never.

He'd gotten himself caught doubly because as soon as he had said yes and stood up, having put on his socks and shoes, she grabbed his shoulders, leaped into his arms, and kissed him on the cheek, all the while saying, "Thank you! Thank you!" He'd been so surprised that he dropped the comb he'd just grabbed so he could run it through his hair before they left for the restaurant. *Oh boy*, he thought. *What have I done?* He had to explain; he had to tell her how it was with him before she got the wrong idea.

"Look, Barbara, I'm only going to go this *once* because of the logistics of the dinner and all the people gathering for it. I won't go again. I have had my fill of disappointments with so-called Christians who can't wait to feed their envy, and because of that envy, they harm others any way they can. They think they can treat people any way they want . . . because . . . after all . . . they *believe*, and that's all they have to do . . . I don't buy that . . . Hah! That way of thinking can't be the way any God would want people to behave. I'm sure that God requires *some* standards to be met! That's how I feel, and you need to understand this. I won't be coming to your church again . . . It's just this once, and it's for the sake of expediency."

"Okay, Jim, that's okay. I am so happy that you are coming this once. I appreciate your being so considerate, and I understand perfectly." And she sent a silent prayer to God, saying, *Thank You, Father, for engineering this. Thank You for giving Jim the opportunity to hear what You want to tell him.*

Jim was surprised that she hadn't gotten angry, that she'd been . . . well, okay with what he'd said about never going to church with her again. She'd even seemed to back away from the subject. He thought she'd push and she didn't. She had caught him off guard with her response. He was relieved, yet wary. Was she trying to lull him into thinking she wouldn't push him again but she would? Well, at least he had let her know how he felt, and this way, she wouldn't be disappointed by any future refusal. He was as he was, and that was all there was to it! Period.

But Jim's heart softened toward Barbara when she had been so sweet about his response. His respect for her soared. She was strong, and she wasn't looking for someone to lean on in her life or her faith. She handled it by herself. She was so . . . interesting.

And so they left Jim's apartment hand in hand for dinner, first for a good meal, then to the supermarket. Barbara wisely did not mention church again. Jim kept wondering why he'd agreed to go to church and wasn't happy that he'd apparently trapped himself, but his anger was at himself, not at Barbara. What she'd said and what she'd expected was natural for her. But it had been his reaction, his response that had messed everything up.

Jim had no idea that Barbara knew beyond the shadow of a doubt that it was heavenly intervention that made him agree to come to church and that only Jim thought it had occurred because of his own stupidity!

Barbara chatted about Matt and Sarah and about Grandma. She told Jim about Grandma's clocks and Sarah's stories about how Grandma had taught her when she was just a little girl, to listen for the silence in the house and, when she could hear the silence, listen for the ticking of the clocks. And then when she could clearly discern these, wait and listen for the chimes.

Jim was intrigued, curious about this little old lady who seemed so faithful to God and so involved with her family and their friends, who taught her grandchildren to listen for the silence. *Silence?* Jim's imagination was caught. *Not a bad idea,* he thought. And out loud Jim said, "I can't wait to meet Grandma . . . sounds like I'm going to have a good time sparring with her!" And Barbara laughed, thinking, *More like Grandma having a good time sparring with you!*

When they began to wash the fruits and vegetables they had purchased and located the bowls and the covers they would use for them and then made the salad dressing, Jim asked Barbara to tell him more about her family. She decided to tell him about her older brother Paul. She told him about her parents enrolling Paul in a military academy when he was seven years old and about the coach Paul met whom he'd adored. She sobbed for a moment when she described the "vitamin" pills the coach gave to the boys on the football team, and she could see Jim's face darken with rage as she spoke.

Barbara described Paul's struggle every day of his life to stay clean, to fight the addiction that once crippled him, the addiction caused by the coach whom so many innocent children adored. She described the love Paul had for God, which helped him through the countless failures, and how much he loved his wife and children despite her being unfaithful, cruel, and coldhearted. Then Barbara told him that Paul's wife had taken the children and run off, and Jim's fists clenched in anger.

He thought of Jezebel and how she had been devoured by wild dogs and felt that this should be the end for Paul's selfish wife as well. But then he thought that it was Paul's coach that should be thrown to wild dogs and devoured piece by piece. Unkind thoughts, yes. But what Paul had been put through because of these two people was pretty terrible, unconscionable.

Barbara told Jim that Paul enjoyed helping everyone and how he was the handyman of the family and did so much for all of them when he was home. She told him that he was working his way up through Mariners School to obtain his captain's license and described the way Paul spoke of the sea and of his awe of the majesty of it.

She explained that Paul saw the sea as a part of the magnificent Creation made by God and saw God's awesome power in it. Paul always said that few people can imagine the extent of the ocean's fury or its beauty. They'd have to be in the middle of the ocean during a storm and then again after the storm passed to be able to witness it. *Paul seems to have quite a loving and poetic nature,* Jim thought and knew he would like him.

Jim made a promise to himself that he would be Paul's friend if Paul would let him. He already had a lot of respect for him. Just to survive all he'd been through from such a young age showed strength . . . and character too. Jim asked Barbara if she thought that Paul would find his kids, and she explained that he'd hired a detective but the expenses might add up to more than his paychecks. Paul's daughter Becky was eleven years old now, and Christina was ten years old.

How does a guy stand this kind of pain? Jim wondered. He was starting to feel so badly about Paul and knew that Barbara was too, so he changed the subject and asked Barbara to clue him in a little bit about that inherited-sin-of-the-forefathers stuff she'd mentioned earlier. He said that he didn't want to appear clueless in case her family discussed it on Thanksgiving Day.

He told Barbara that he had a Bible at the apartment that had belonged to his mother and wanted to look a few things up so he wouldn't sound totally ignorant. "Barbara, where in the Bible does it mention the forefather-sins bit, you know, that third-and-fourth-generation stuff you mentioned, and what words are actually used to say this?"

"Well, when something is very important and God wants us to particularly take note of and learn about something, it is often mentioned in almost every book of the Bible, sometimes even using the same words. So for this subject . . . well, let me just look it up on my BlackBerry . . . It contains a concordance. I'll look up the word, uhhh . . . how about *iniquities* . . . and we'll see what we get. Okay, here we go. For example, in Jeremiah 11:10, it says, '*They are turned back to the iniquities of their forefathers, which refused to hear my words*' and in Exodus 20:5, '*Visiting the iniquity of the fathers upon the children unto the third and fourth generation.*' And in Numbers 14:18, '*And by no means clearing the guilty, visiting the iniquity of the fathers upon the children unto the third and fourth generation.*' That should be enough for a start. There are many other scriptural references that are similar to these, and they can all be found by using the concordance."

Jim scrambled to write these three verses down so he could look them up later, and Barbara went on to say, "In one place in the Bible, God even says that the children of these certain sinners, if they were allowed to live, would rain down even greater sin than their forefathers. This is heavy stuff, I know . . . but think about the other end of the spectrum. The blessings! Have you ever looked upon a certain family who has never had a broken marriage and all spouses have really loved one another and stayed in love? Or one generation owned a successful business and all the children eventually create their own successful business and know no financial problems? And what about the United States as a country? We had God written in our constitution, on our currency, carved in stone on our memorials and state buildings, and we had prayer in our schools. We sent food and water, medicines and doctors, teachers and ministers to poorer countries too. And we have been blessed as a country for doing it because in God's plan, in the physics He laid into our world, the blessings from our forebears also continue from one generation to the next."

"Well yes, I can accept that this country has been blessed and probably agree that it's because we have always come to the aid of others. That's true. Even after a war, after being attacked, we as a country have always stepped up to help rebuild and reestablish that country. And yes, I can name some families who for generations have been what I'd called lucky in a particular area of their life and others that have been . . . well, it's as if they are cursed in a particular area. I've watched people try so hard and never have things go their way. But you are saying that this is because of what you are calling generational sin. Is that right?"

"Yeah, exactly."

"If so, then that's quite a concept, Barbara. You would think that it would make people pause when contemplating any wrongdoing if they knew that what they did would impact their children. But I'm sorry. As interesting as this is, I don't buy it. If what you are saying was true, wouldn't every religion, every news reporter be talking about it? Wouldn't everyone want to know everyone else's background and stuff? I mean, if this were true, it could open a can of worms for every relationship that ever tried to get off the ground!"

"You made a good point, Jim, and I guess it would be smart to do that. But then it would negate what God does for those who love him. It's no concept . . . it's real. God says He will bless those who follow Him and curse those who sin or harm His children by their sins. It seems that we bring a curse on ourselves by our sinful conduct and have to fight that curse all our lives and more so if the conduct of our forebears was also sinful. God explains this in many areas of the Bible, but this is beautifully stated in Deuteronomy 30:19, where God says, '*I call heaven and earth to record this day against you, that I have set before you life and death, blessing and cursing: therefore choose life, that both thou and thy seed may live.*' What God is telling us in this verse is that we have a choice. He very clearly says *we must choose*, and then tells us just as clearly that the choice we make will impact not only us but our seed, meaning of course, our children.

"That's why it's so important for us to keep God in our lives, our homes, our work, our fellowship, our country. And if our forebears *were* sinful and we truly desire to break that pattern so it cannot affect us, God will help us and protect us. That's what Baptism is for . . . . the strength to overcome our past. And the absolution, a part of Holy Communion, is . . . the forgiveness of sins . . . for us . . . and forgiveness for those in eternity who also repent. Holy Sealing provides us with the Holy Ghost that allows us to discern the spirits and teaches us to fight against the spirits that tempt us. The Holy Spirit also comforts us when we struggle with our problems.

"We can see how the world is changing, Jim, and we can see in people's behavior the loss of our faith as a nation. I fear we are losing the blessing we once had on our country. We have allowed prayer, worship, and praising God to be removed from our schools and our government because of the actions of just a few atheists. God's blessing is important for the safety and even the productivity of our country. But it is even more important for our families. This is why it is so important that people who marry, those who will become the fathers and mothers of our next generation of children be willing to do good, to learn God's words, and teach them to their children. We need to recognize Satan and what he does so we can keep our family safe, put aside the temptations Satan brings, and teach these things to our children. I wouldn't want my kids to get bogged down by my sins and surely would want to show them how to break the patterns of the sins of past generations!"

"Gee, Barbara, . . . I'm seldom at a loss for words. But this is a little mind-boggling . . . I mean, what you are saying says that the responsibility of having children is *huge*. I can't really disagree with you because kids *do* learn by what their parents do. I think we all try to justify our wrongdoing by telling ourselves that what we did was 'legal,' or we were 'harmed' by something or someone, and that's why we did what we did. We do justify our actions even when we know we're wrong. I realize that kids see right through justifications . . . they have an uncanny way of knowing right from wrong when they are very young . . . and they know what kindness is and when there isn't any. But I also know that when kids hear and see wrongdoing for too long, they can become immune to what's right and will start to adopt the wrong things they have seen or experienced. I agree that things *are* getting worse for our country and I agree that our country has been blessed in the past, so maybe there *is* something to your theory. But again, I ask, why isn't this stuff taught in schools and churches if generational sin exists and causes so much harm? And if God is so powerful, why doesn't He work something out that will cause people to understand this stuff and make things right? This is why I still can't buy your theory. And another question is, why would God allow a kid to be saddled with that kind of parent or grandparent then?"

"It's because of sin. God arranged an out for people caught in the generational stuff. If we as a people allow a few atheists to prevent prayer in our schools, then surely we have allowed these same atheists, by our complacency, to block the teaching of these biblical truths. If the "theory" of evolution can be taught, why not the "theory" of creation? No one wants to fight for what is right anymore. . . they want the easy way of life. . . even in their own personal lives. This is right up Satan's alley because if people don't know something, they can't fix it. This is why God admonishes parents to teach their children His words and to live them as an example to others. I'm not saying we can't make mistakes, Jim. God wouldn't have had to send Christ to us if we never made a mistake. But it's the heart that matters. When we know what God asks of us and make a mistake, the question is, are we truly repentant or not? Would we be willing to make restitution for what we did if we could?

As one small example, that woman who plagued your mom appears to have justified her cruelty, and she was *not* repentant. If this is true, then do you think God would accept her as a bride for His Son? I don't think so . . . at least not in the state of sin she was in when she hurt your mom. I mean, if you stole from someone and then years later . . . got religion and were sorry, repentant, . . . then sent the money you stole to those you stole it from, then God can bless you again. Do you know what I'm trying to say about being truly repentant? Christ taught us in the Lord's Prayer that we can only gain forgiveness *as* we forgive those who trespass against us. He doesn't mention those who did the trespassing, except to tell us that He will deal with them. But all through the Bible, God teaches us about repentance and restitution and loving your neighbor as you love yourself . . . and learning and teaching His words!"

"Barb, some of the things you've said are true, and I can agree with them. In fact, I think that many people would agree with you, but some of it, obviously—that is, if what you say is correct—is not taught at all. If it really is in the Bible and to be interpreted as you interpret it and if teaching or learning it seems to slip through the cracks and no one is taught about this stuff, then what should be done about it? Why does God allow that so few learn it, understand it? How could something so important slip through the cracks like that? It doesn't make sense. While I agree that it is amazing and makes me want to learn more about it even though I will never be a church kinda guy, why does God give so much power to the bad guys? Look, this is enough for now. I can't debate this issue, but it's because I don't know enough to debate it. I'm changing the subject.

"Why Jim, are you being a quakebuttock?" And Jim burst out laughing at her statement recognizing the word she used as one Bill O'Reilly had recently featured as his word for the day and one that Jim hadn't even been able to find in his dictionary. When they both finished laughing and Jim admitted that Barbara had indeed "gotten" him, he couldn't wipe the grin off his face. She'd been so clever to use his own mechanisms on him.

"Thanksgiving should be an interesting day. I can't wait to meet your family. I'll also listen carefully at church because now I am very curious . . . but don't get any ideas. I am *not* a person who will ever be a churchgoer. I may find religion—well, philosophy anyway—very interesting, but I do not trust one single minister, priest, prophet, or religious founder. Money, glory, fame, importance, narrow-mindedness, their way or no way, no love in their hearts . . . that's how I see them. And these concepts, well, they are hard to believe . . . I can't conceive of God sitting back and just letting all this bad stuff in the world happen . . . Sorry. In fact, thinking about it makes me angry with God."

"Jim, I've never been cross with you before, but right now, I do have to say something. *You* are the one being narrow-minded, and *you* are saying my way or no way. What God wants of all of us is an open heart, a willing heart, a hunger for truth and decency, a desire to learn what He asks of us. That's all. So don't condemn what you haven't yet experienced. Go ahead and condemn what wrong you have seen done, but remember also that until you have walked in someone's shoes, you don't know how rough their path has been . . . or why they might have done what they did. This is why God says only He can judge others. And this is why He tells us to study His words. And whether you accept it or not Satan is alive and well and this is why God helps us. I hope I haven't offended you, but I have to speak up if I think you've gone overboard. God is bound by His righteousness and has a plan. An incredible plan. There is a reason that He allows these things to happen, and until you learn about Him and His plan, don't condemn it. You haven't the right to do that! Condemn the wrong that is done, but don't condemn God unless you know His plan and what He says."

"Sorry, Barb. You're right. I just know so many who have done—and still do—wrong. And you're right, I don't know the so-called plan that God has. I guess I'd better learn from you what it is. I am properly chastised. I will really make an effort to keep my mind open. I do want to learn and shouldn't judge God by the actions of a few. In fact, tomorrow at church and later with your family, if they talk about religion, I will listen carefully without making judgments, but . . . but . . . I have to tell you that I will retain the right to close my mind to something that I find wrong. And when with your family, I will speak up if I disagree . . . and I am sure that I will. I like to work with facts, not conjecture. Okay? Now can we have a truce?"

"Okeydoke, Jim, we can call a truce since you've agreed to *learn* God's plan before you *judge* God's actions! And you know, we may not even talk very much about religion or God. It just depends on what comes up . . . Often we just tease one another . . . and we play games that Grandma devises . . . sometimes silly games, sometimes Bible quizzes extraordinaire, sometimes we talk about health remedies . . . you know, alternative medicine. And we may discuss Christmas because Grandma creates the most beautiful arrangements at Christmas it takes your breath away. Did you guys do a lot of decorating for Christmas?"

"Yeah, my mom would always say that she would just do a 'little' bit of decorating, but then as the days moved closer to Christmas and she did just a little bit *more* each day, our pile of stocking stuffers grew, hidden from us of course. And the house filled with more and more Christmas decorations, and the cookie tin exploded too."

"I love Christmas. So much to do, but so much fun doing it! Well, I'd better get going, Jim. We have a long day tomorrow with lots of family, fun, and foolery! Would it be okay if I swing by to pick you up at about nine forty-five tomorrow morning?"

"Okay, that's good. I'll be ready, and I promise to make you proud! I remembered my instructions . . . shirt and trousers that can be comfortable at Grandma's when the tie comes off and jacket just for church. Right?"

"Right!"

"Now for the good part . . ."

Jim put his arms around Barbara and kissed her lightly then held her, letting the perfume of her hair . . . mmmm almonds . . . take him with its loveliness. She leaned into him and put her arms around his neck and on her toes kissed him back. He walked her to her car and off she went, leaving him with all kinds of thoughts about her and about tomorrow, about her faith and family, and about how he felt about her. He'd better let her know that their relationship just couldn't work. He could never believe as she did, and he could never accept some of the crazy concepts she'd talked about. He'd need proof.

Chapter Four

THANKSGIVING

Whenever a holiday approached that might bring the family together, everyone thought of Grandma and all the wonderful things she did to make the gathering a special memory. She made every occasion fun. Whether through her conversation, her Bible quizzes extraordinaire, her discussions about alternative medicine and natural remedies, or playing one of her unique games, she created magical memories. Sometimes those memories came from her talent for decorating. The ticking of her clocks and the sweet sounds of their chimes were soothing. And we all had learned to listen for and appreciate the sound of silence as we prepared to listen for the ticking and the chimes of her clocks

Grandma's house always looked beautiful. Sometimes she'd make exquisite centerpieces for the dinner table that took your breath away or she would fashion napkin rings from something that suggested the theme of her gathering. She knew what everyone's favorite dish was and would draw us into the kitchen, delegating little jobs that brought us together where we would all share the experience. Through these activities, she created a day where we would, as she liked to say, make family memories.

We all wanted to visit Grandma's during these special days in anticipation of what she would create and what pleasant experiences would be gained. We would talk about the children we hoped to have someday and how we wanted the children to grow up under these same experiences of family interaction. Grandma said that while life would not provide the fairyland she wished we could have, a godly family life could help us endure the reality and hardships of what we would face in life.

She always reminded us that we would have to endure some tough times, that life was a battleground between good and evil, but that perfection could be achieved if we remained faithful to God until Christ came again. Grandma would say, "Perfection is what God made heaven for, and striving for that perfection is what He made earth for." She warned us that if troubles did *not* come our way, it might mean that Satan had us where he wanted us—either complacent or sinning!

Barbara told Jim about the open house that Grandma always held when she completed her Christmas decorations and invited the entire congregation, her neighbors, and of course, the whole family to join her. Everyone looked forward to being with her, seeing the magic of what she'd created, and enjoying her famous glogg and Christmas cookies. And she explained that when Grandma was just a young woman, her aunt had given her a recipe for glogg that had been handed down for generations from her uncle's family in Norway.

Glogg was a hot drink made from port wine and whiskey and heated in a big pot that contained a mesh bag filled with cloves, cinnamon, cardamom seeds, ginger, and orange zest. Grandma would add a thin curl of orange peel, a few raisins, and some almond slivers to each cup and pour her mixture over these as she served it. As it warmed on the stove, its aroma alone was festive.

Sometimes, if the weather was cold or the day was especially dreary, Grandma would make the glogg for Thanksgiving too but usually substituted orange juice for half the whiskey. This allowed us to enjoy its aroma and taste without worrying about its potency. Much of the alcohol content evaporated in the heating also.

Heated slowly on the stove, the warm glogg filled the house with the aroma of cloves and cinnamon, ginger and cardamom, oranges and wine, which was caught by the air ducts and circulated from room to room. The aroma contributed to that warm and fuzzy loving feeling of a holiday at Grandma's. When first arriving, everyone noticed the wonderful aroma and was immediately transported into the spirit of Christmas. They would breathe deeply to draw in the savory smells associated with all the beautiful and precious memories that family holidays wrought. Sarah had copied Grandma's recipe into her computer and had changed its font to a beautiful script to create an old-world look and printed it onto a special paper edged with delicate flowers intertwined with ivy. She had given each family member a copy.

As a Thanksgiving gift, Barbara made a copy of the glogg recipe for Jim and purchased the cinnamon, cloves, ginger, cardamom, orange zest, and steeping bag made of gauze. She found a box exactly the right size for containing everything she'd purchased and planned to give it to him when they left Grandma's after their Thanksgiving dinner with the family. She hoped he would bring it back to Iraq so he could make the glogg for his friends on a special day when they needed to "make their own happy memories." It would also serve to remind him of the special day they had spent together.

As Barbara packed the items for the glogg, she looked again at the recipe and smiled as she imagined its aroma and how much Jim would enjoy it. The recipe read:

For one quart of glogg,
pour 1 pint of port wine into a pot,
add ½ cup raisins, ½ cup skinless almond slivers, 4 cloves,
½ cup sugar, 3 figs cut into pieces, 2 four-inch-long cinnamon sticks,
6 cardamom seeds, 1 small piece of ginger about the size of a nickel,
and the peeled skin from one orange (wash first). Soak for 15 minutes.
Slowly heat until hot. Do not boil. Add 1 pint of your favorite whiskey.
Heat until hot, still not letting the mixture boil. Let cool.
Store in a tightly sealed, wide-mouthed container until ready to serve.
Pour through a strainer, reheat, not allowing the mixture to boil.
When heated, pour into clear glass cups preferably with a handle,
containing a few fresh raisins, slivers of almonds,
and a small piece of fresh orange peel.
Serve and enjoy!

Thanksgiving Day dawned, and Barbara dressed but not for choir because she planned to sit with Jim instead of singing. When it was time, she drove to Jim's apartment. He was waiting for her and looked wonderful in a navy sports jacket, gray slacks, and a red tie arranged against a soft yellow dress shirt. "Well, do I pass the test? Will I be approved by the family?" he asked with a big grin, fully aware of how good he looked.

"Yeah, I guess so, I mean, you could have dressed *up* a little more, but I guess you'll do," she quipped. He pretended to look crestfallen so Barbara said, "Okay, okay, you are one handsome guy, and you do look perfect, yep, totally spiffy!" He smiled, satisfied, almost cocky, and pranced like a rooster before he climbed into the car, unable to resist saying, "Handsome meaning having qualities that delight the eye; spiffy meaning fine looking, and perfect meaning flawless, impeccable, ideal". And then he smiled at her, happy to be with her

When they arrived at the church, Barbara explained, while they were still in the car, what the procedure was for Holy Communion so if he chose to accept the sacrament, he would know what to do. Smiling, he sarcastically asked her when he should get his money out so he would be ready when they "passed the plate," and she explained that they never passed a plate.

"We have an offertory box in the back of the church that we will walk past as we enter the sanctuary. Those who want to give and those who regularly tithe just drop the money into the box as they pass it before they sit down. But no one is ever asked for money, and no plates are ever passed around. What the church gives their members is freely given to everyone. If what God offers mankind is freely given, how can the church do otherwise? And also, what man gives back to God is private."

Jim seemed surprised by what Barbara said, and as he thought about her words and did not actually respond to her words, he was, nevertheless deeply affected. *What kind of a church never asks for money?*

Grandma, Paul, Caleb, Ann, Sarah, and Matt were waiting for them at the front door and greeted Jim with a hearty welcome—a hug and a kiss from the women and a handshake from the men. Then the five who were in the choir ran for their choir seats. Paul walked in with Barbara and Jim to locate seats. Soon thereafter, the choir began to sing and Jim had to admit, just as Barbara had said, they sounded like angels. The songs were wonderful and, as Jim realized afterward, they had been chosen to support the words of the scripture that was read at the start of the service.

Fifteen minutes later, the ministers entered from the sacristy and walked toward the altar as the congregation sang the opening hymn. After the opening prayer, the scripture that was the basis of the sermon was read, and the service began. The scripture read that day was from Revelation 3:15-16 and read, *"I know thy works, that thou art neither cold nor hot: I would thou wert cold or hot. So then because thou art lukewarm, and neither cold nor hot, I will spue thee out of my mouth."*

The lead minister began with a story of a young couple who had dated for many years and were very much in love with one another. Each cared so much for the other that they devised all sorts of little ways to show their love. They might place a note into the briefcase of the other so it would be found sometime during their hectic day. They might bring home a special treat for the other. They might telephone during the day with an endearing word. At home they would offer a touch or a hug when they passed one another as they moved from room to room.

He also spoke of how intimately this couple communicated with one another, sharing their concerns, the good and the bad parts of each day, asking one another how they might handle a particular problem. They often reminded one another of how much they were loved. They discussed the purchases they wished to make and the state of their finances. In other words, they were like one entity. They were entwined in heart and mind and spirit. They were like-minded. They appreciated one another and expressed that appreciation. This is what kept them close.

The minister spoke of the way they looked at one another and the feelings each experienced in their heart from these special looks and endearments and how much their hearts soared to hear and see these expressions of love. Then he spoke of the child they had and how that child learned how to love from the way the parents acted with one another, from how they responded to people who hurt them, from how they appreciated those who supported them and from how they prayed aloud with one another.

The congregation began to form a picture in their mind of a happy family and why they were happy. They were not lukewarm with one another. They were warm and loving and openly giving to one another. They articulated their love to one another and shared their triumphs and their burdens.

Then the minister addressed the congregation, asking them if they would be happy in a relationship where they were treated with indifference, where the person they loved was uncommunicative, acted neither hot nor cold, neither caring nor uncaring. "Would we feel loved, would we feel that we were important to that person, would we feel that they cared? Would our love for them then also become cool and become lukewarm?" he asked.

The minister asked if the relationship each person had with God was like the relationship between the young couple he first described. "Do we converse with God as they did with one another ? Do we speak to God each day of our difficulties and our triumphs as they did with one another ? Do we trust God and ask His advice as they did with one another ? Do we seek to do little things each day to show God how much we love him as they did with one another ? Do we try to learn what pleases God as they learned to please one another ?" he asked.

He went on to say that if we did not know or do these things, the things all good relationships require, we hadn't yet developed the kind of relationship with God that would allow Him entry into our hearts and minds, our spirit and our future. And if we hadn't yet developed that kind of a relationship, we really didn't know Him.

He said that if we fit this description, then we would be classified as being lukewarm toward God, and this is a state that God warns us about. God wants to develop a bride for His Son, and inhabitants for His new heaven and new earth who will be capable of giving and showing love, and He will not accept those who are not willing to work for the kind of a relationship that existed between the couple he'd described. God will, as the scripture says, "spue thee out of my mouth" and say "I know ye not."

The minister concluded with the words, "Only we can answer the question about what kind of relationship we have fostered with God. Only we can answer this for ourselves." Jim noticed that the minister had spoken extemporaneously and used no notes or script or teleprompter, and it did not appear that he had memorized a sermon he'd written earlier. He'd read only the scripture from the Bible and then spoke from the heart.

The choir sang once again, and another minister spoke for a few minutes about the need for each member of the congregation to love, help, and encourage one another. He said that these actions are actions of love. He went on to explain that unless we learn how to love and how to express that love to others, we would be unable to be the kind of bride God wants for His Son.

Then the first minister came back to the altar to administer Holy Communion and Jim got up to walk to the altar for the sacrament. He'd thought to himself, *Oh, what the heck, I know I need it, so I might as well take it and hope it does some good.* But, of course, Jim didn't share these thoughts with Barbara. Barbara, however, was surprised and delighted that Jim had participated.

When the service was over, Barbara greeted the other members of the congregation and introduced Jim. As they left the church, Barbara also greeted the ministers who stood near the door to shake hands with their parishioners and, once again, introduced Jim. Everyone welcomed him and said that they hoped to see him again, and wished him a blessed Thanksgiving.

As Jim and Barbara walked toward the car, a man about Jim's age ran toward them, calling to Barbara. He was dressed in a camel-coloured jacket (the type with the patches at the elbows and the brown leather buttons), brown slacks, and a white dress shirt with a gaudy tie of brown, gold, and green. He was tall and well built and had a perfect smile, one that only braces could have produced. He took Barbara by the arm and told her he'd looked for her at the meeting they usually attended together at the university. Barbara greeted him warmly, explaining that she'd had to go to the airport, then turned to Jim and introduced the two men.

They were civil to one another; they shook hands and spoke the appropriate inanities without meaning them. They sized one another up, not really liking what they saw. Jim could see that Barbara's friend was educated, and as he spoke, Jim deduced that he was a professor at the university Barbara attended. *Yeah,* Jim thought, *he is old enough!* Jim could see that the professor was just about as old as Jim was and that he was possessive of Barbara and felt a sudden and unexpected wave of jealousy hit him in the chest like a ton of bricks.

Barbara chatted with him as Jim simply listened and observed and was unaware that he had clenched his teeth and locked his jaw. Barbara promised to be at next month's meeting and then said her goodbyes to the professor. Barbara and Jim left to finish making the salads and head to Grandma's.

Jim wanted to ask Barbara what her relationship was with the guy he now deemed "the professor." But he bit his tongue, feeling like a jealous fool. So instead he talked about the church and what he'd just heard. He surprised himself by beginning with the words "Okay, . . . go ahead and say it. I know you're thinking that based on what the minister said, I don't have a close relationship with God and that I'm one of those lukewarm people."

"No, I'm not, Jim. That's between you and God. I don't know the depth of your relationship with Him. For all I know, you pray and talk with Him and have a *very* close relationship with God . . . that's not *my* call, it's yours."

"I'm sorry, Barb, I guess I'm feeling a little guilty . . . Dag nab it but that minister hit hard, and I didn't like it one bit."

"No, Jim, he only pointed out what we *all* need to examine. He wanted *each* of us to take a good look at ourselves so we can do the best we know how . . . *if* we want to. That's all. God gave us free will you know, and since we can't do what we don't know we need to do, the minister told us what that was. Now of course, we've all heard what we need to do so there is no longer any excuse. Now we *have* to look at ourselves carefully! And if we don't, we are consciously spurning God's advice. That's the tough part, Jim. Now *you* know what He asks, and *you* have to decide what to do about it."

"So you're saying to me, 'How do you like them apples, Jim?' And you're right, I don't like them apples. I guess because I don't want to have to answer those questions, maybe I'm even afraid of the answer, so I'm feeling like a kid who got caught with his hand in the cookie jar, and it makes me angry. I'm not happy with the idea that I am supposed to know something now and act on it even though I'm not a believer like you are. That's not fair, I mean, it sure doesn't *feel* fair. I feel as if I've been blindsided. Sorry, but I'm just telling it like it is."

"Jim, all of us had to start somewhere to develop our faith, and all of us have made mistakes, some of commission and others of omission, maybe even over and over again. But God *is* fair. In fact, he's so fair—*just* is a better word—that He goes out of His way to bring things to our attention when it's time for us to know them and perhaps begin to think about them, or when it's the right time for us to begin making some adjustments in our lives. Once we've heard or read what He asks of us, the rest is up to us. We have free will."

Jim didn't reply. She was right. But thankfully at that moment, they arrived at his apartment and he was off the hook. That service had shaken him, and he didn't like it one bit. *This stuff could turn your life upside down, and right now, I'd like to forget it.*

As they pulled in front of Jim's apartment, Barbara said, "Well, here we are. Let's just run inside, cut up the last of the salad stuff, freshen up, grab the food, and *go!* Okay?" Jim was surprised that Barbara seemed okay with what they had been talking about. She didn't even seem to want to know more about how he felt about the content of the service or about what she'd said or what he was going to do about what he'd heard. She hadn't been the least bit judgmental or critical of him and he was relieved. *But then, why do I feel bad about this stuff?*

They arrived at Grandma's to find the house filled with the aroma of turkey and something akin to oranges or cinnamon and it made them salivate. And Grandma had made glogg! Jim was glad that Barbara had filled him in on what glogg was, and he looked forward to tasting it. She'd been right about its magnificent aromatic quality. It filled the house and made it smell like paradise! Everyone greeted Jim once again. They handed him a glass cup filled with glogg, showed him the food they'd put out to nibble on, and then began asking all kinds of questions about Iraq. Jim relaxed right away, glad to find that they did not talk about what they heard in church that morning.

Jim told them why he and Wade had come home. He explained why they felt it was incredibly dangerous not to get the reconstruction in Iraq under way. He explained that he and Wade hoped to talk to someone in authority to explain why the rebuilding and the restoration of services should be a priority and how they were losing the loyalty of the people by what they were *not* doing.

Matt asked if there was anything they could do to help, and Jim told them that they could write their senators and congressmen, and ask them to allow the servicemen, the contractors, the generals, and the other officers who were in Iraq *every day* to tell them what they felt was needed and make sure it was done. All these people, the ones who were actually there, all agreed on what was needed, yet the powers that be in DC would *not* listen! Jim said it was so frustrating when no one would listen and that the bad decisions they made would come back to bite them.

"I guess with this lesson from Iraq, we can all see how frustrated God must get when we won't listen and our bad decisions come back to bite us," said Grandma with a grin. "And Grandma gets frustrated when no one takes the turkey out of the oven so it can 'rest' and keep its juices when we slice it! Git hoppin', fellas!"

They all laughed, and Caleb jumped up and donned the oven gloves while Ann cleared a place on the counter for the turkey's "resting" place. Paul put the electric carving knife together and plugged it in, then placed it next to the huge platter and fork that Grandma had put out for the slicing project. Paul winked at Jim, as if to say "We gotta hop when Grandma says so or we won't eat!"

"Ahh, it looks delicious," they all exclaimed as the crisply browned skin gleamed and crackled when they took the turkey from the oven and gave it its special spot. "Who's going to mash the potatoes?" Grandma had already placed some chicken broth, salt, cream, and butter into a small bowl so she could heat this mixture in the microwave before adding the mixture to the potatoes as they were being mashed. She had also added cornstarch to the chicken broth she had poured into a pot into which she had asked Caleb to pour some of the turkey drippings before putting the turkey on the counter to rest. She'd bring this to a boil on the stove to obtain the right consistency before adding the caramelized onions. "Mmmmmm, good," they exclaimed, wanting to dip a spoon into the gravy for a sample but holding back because of their "company."

In no time, they were seated around the table, and Caleb led them in their Thanksgiving prayer. Caleb also thanked God for bringing Jim into their fold and asked Him to help Jim with his Iraq project and to keep him safe. Then they dove into the food, and silence reigned for a few minutes as they savored the taste of everything they'd placed on their plate. Jim couldn't remember eating anything so wonderful ever before in his life and said so. Grandma beamed! Sarah chirped, "Beware, Jim, Grandma uses real butter and cream in everything, and that's why it's so good! If we weren't careful, we'd all be known as 'the Chubb Family'!"

Grandma had turned the chandelier lights down just enough to give the room a soft glow and had lit candles to complete the festive look. Caleb had filled small glasses with the Asti Spumante he'd brought, and they toasted Grandma for all she meant to them and all she'd taught them. Now they could sit back and relax while enjoying one another's company, the warmth of the setting, and the atmosphere of togetherness. Jim was touched by what he saw and what he felt.

They asked Paul where he'd been on his latest trip out on the "tiny," 200-foot-long oceangoing tugboat he worked on and asked him when he was going to purchase and captain the 254-foot-long *Zwarte Zee IV* he admired so much. He laughed, knowing they understood how much he loved that sleek, magnificently beautiful workboat. "You guys don't have a clue about the *Zwarte Zee IV's* incredible 73-ton bollard pull, her sail space of 6.90 meters, her draft of 5.75 meters, but let me tell you she's huge and she's powerful and she's absolutely beautiful. Jim, you might be interested in the fact that this ship, this wonderful workboat, even has its own welding plant and diving gear. It also carries pipe patching and sealing materials along with powered drills and saws . . . and . . . she can distill 7 tons of water every day! In my opinion, she's the most beautiful workboat ever built!"

"Wow, that's really some list of statistics. I seem to get the impression that you really like this workboat, Paul!" Jim teased. "I sure would like to see something that big that can do so much."

"Well, my boat is fifty-four feet shorter and not as efficiently equipped, but come down to the port anytime we're in, and I'll take you aboard. I'll show you the stuff these guys can't understand. I mean, you're a contractor, right? An engineer or something . . . so you'd understand?"

"Yeah, I think I would understand what you'd be showing me and would love to see it. Thanks, I'm gonna do that. And as an architect too, I appreciate sleek lines and efficiently used space so would sure love to see the *Zwarte Zee* as well."

"Ahhh, me too, but she usually works across the sea. Her proportions are beautiful, so as an architect, you'd appreciate that. She's great to look at, but she's also a real workhorse. She's tough, strong, efficient, and well equipped. Check her out on the Internet. There's a picture and some really interesting facts about her and about some fascinating jobs she's tackled."

"I'll do that, thanks. I sure would like to see your boat, Paul, and have you fill me in on what kind of work your boat can do and what the crew does to support that work. I've always been fascinated by the sea and the people that brave those powerful elements."

"When you are alone in the vastness of the ocean, Jim, no matter how big your boat is, you learn how essentially powerless you are under the strength and force of the wind and the waves. During a storm, it's mind-boggling to watch the ferocity of the ocean. It's humbling, and it shows you the incredible engineering feat, the physics, the architecture, the foresight, and the power of God. I think that few people can spend a lot of time on the sea and not come to know God."

"I know the sense of awe you are talking about, Paul. When I'm out in the field in Iraq and I get up at dawn, often before anyone else is up, I think about the potential of that great country, but then I think about the terrorists and wonder how God feels about His creation today and the failures of the people he placed in it. It does make you wish you could meet the architect of all this and ask Him to answer all our questions. It is a humbling experience and shows us how small and inconsequential we are in comparison to the wonders and awesome power around us."

"You know, Jim, sometimes it's hard to think that we could mean anything to God when you see the enormity of what He has created. And for me, when I communicate with God, I try to let Him know that I appreciate what He's given us, how through the beauty and diversity and power of nature, I know that He's tried to show me who He is and the sensitivity of His makeup. I know what you mean about having questions. I might ask why Satan was allowed such power over us, but then I see what God's given us and know He must have an awfully good reason for everything."

Grandma spoke then, saying, "Boys, it is a wonderful thing that you recognize the talent and beauty in the Creation and that when you think of God, you recognize not only His power but also the love He has in His heart for us to give us these wonders. Paul, like you, I truly believe that God uses this beauty to catch our attention, to get us to speak to Him, to recognize Him. I believe that God longs to open a conversation with us that can lead to a relationship with Him, sometimes doing it in the most unusual way. He longs for the kind of relationship that the minister spoke of this morning . . . from each and every one of us. God can do so much for us within the kind of relationship that exists between people who truly love one another and with people willing to work at nurturing that love. He gives us an incredible amount of loving care and in time, when we are ready, he does answer our questions. But do we give Him our love and our trust?" Then, abruptly Grandma turned to Jim and asked "Jim, do you go to church?"

"Well, Grandma, I did as a kid, but I saw so much corruption in so-called religion and so much cruelty in people who called themselves religious, even in ministers who are supposed to be teachers and role models, that I've lost my faith. I've lost my trust. Not in an overall God but in what we are offered on this earth in the name of religion . . . and I must admit that I can't reconcile what is happening in the world with a loving God."

"That's *exactly* what Satan wants you to believe and do, Jim. Satan, not God, influenced the ministers and the people who hurt you, who betrayed you, who broke the faith you had in them so he could prevent you from becoming a child of God. Don't let him win, Jim, fight back! Remember, in Acts 28:27, God said, '*For the heart of this people is waxed gross, and their ears are dull of hearing, and their eyes have they closed.*' Let those who hurt you be those people God speaks of, but don't let them be you. Don't be one of them! Remember too what will happen to those who harm you, for God also said in Mark 9:42, '*And whosoever shall offend one of these little ones that believe in me, it is better for him that a millstone were hanged about his neck, and he were cast into the sea.*'"

"Ahh, that last part makes me feel better about those scoundrels. I don't want those people to have power over my final decisions, Grandma, but I'm not sure I know who or what Satan is or why he even exists. I haven't found my answers and haven't found many true hearts where it comes to religion. In fact, I haven't found many people who actually do what Christ asks them to do even in that one commandment . . . ten simple words that He left—love God above all things and your neighbor as yourself. I don't even see *religious* people practice this, so how can I believe what they tell me? It galls me to see people who claim to be religious, claim to be Christians, even go to church, yet find it perfectly justifiable to harm others. I don't understand religions where people remain unforgiving, vindictive, hurtful. I guess that I just have too many unanswered questions and see so many things that don't gel to accept what I was once taught."

"Like what?"

"Well, there's quite a lot. Even Barbara and I have been butting heads over some of her theories. It's hard for me to think of one off the top of my head. Some of my questions would probably take weeks to explain, not just a few hours. But . . . hmmm. Well . . ."

"Jim, can you think of a huge question you'd like answered, something unique that the average person might not know?"

"Now Grandma it looks to me as if you are challenging me to a debate and that sure sounds like fun! Okay, okay, if you want just one example. Well, . . . how about . . . well, let's not get into what Barbara and I were discussing. Let's start with a clean slate . . . So how about me starting with this one . . . Okay, what about evolution? Carbon dating makes a case for evolution. It has a scientific basis, tests that can be repeated to prove their accuracy, tests which supposedly prove the age of artifacts derived from organic matter such as bone, cloth, or even wood. These dates negate the Bible's account of creation since the Bible says that our world was created in only seven days. Thus, from those seven days to today, the Bible accounts for less than seven thousand years. The two don't gel. What science proves through artifacts and what the Bible says about when the Creation occurred simply do not agree. Which concept is correct and why?"

"Hmmmm," Grandma said with a smile. "Okay, so you'd like to see if they do gel, if there is a way the two accounts could coexist."

"Well, I hadn't thought they could coexist at all. I was just asking which one was correct."

"Okay . . . just that one *little* question, huh. Well, you young whippersnapper . . . I think that *you* think *we* can't answer that one . . . and . . . you're about to get a *very* interesting account of how these two *can* coexist . . . in fact . . . do coexist. Ready, Jim?" And Grandma grinned from ear to ear, cocked her head to one side as she looked at Jim.

Jim grinned back at Grandma, recognizing the challenge in her eyes and that she was playing with him and feeling pretty sure that she would win this debate. He would have to be on his toes! Jim stood, faced Grandma, bent forward slightly with upper arms and elbows tight to his body, lifted his hands to waist level palms up, and curled his fingers back and forth, saying with a smile, "Bring it on, Grandma, . . . bring it on . . . I'll debate you . . . and win! And just so no one thinks I'm taking advantage of a sweet little grandma, how about the rest of you guys jumping in? Matt? Caleb? Paul? . . . Come on, bring it on. Oh boy, wait a minute. I'm gonna be accused of being a male chauvinist, won't I? So let me change that and add . . . Sarah? Ann? Barbara? . . . You jump right in too!"

They all laughed, and the game was on! Paul pretended to roll up his sleeves to do some hard work and said, "First, before we begin, let me ask you a question, Jim. Would that be okay?"

"Sure, fire away, ask any question you want. Lemmee have it!"

"Jim, tell me what you think creates our twenty-four-hour day?"

Jim thought a moment and then answered by telling Paul that it was the time and manner in which the earth rotated around the sun.

Then Paul asked, "Okay, just a few more questions. What precisely provides us with twenty-four hours to each day? What causes the night and the day within that twenty-four-hour period? And what creates our seasons?"

Jim answered by saying that he believed that when the earth faced the sun, it was day and when it faced away from the sun it was night. The twenty-four hours it took the earth to make one turn on its axis determined how long one day and one night was. He said, "When the part of the planet we personally occupy is facing the sun, it is daylight, and when the earth rotates so we are not facing the sun, it is nighttime. And to answer the second part of your question, I think that the earth moves on a sort of egg-shaped or elliptic rotation around the sun, yet its axis always remains pointing in the same direction. Therefore, it's the angle that the sun's rays hit the earth that causes the seasons. For instance, when the Northern Hemisphere is tilted toward the sun, it is summer in that hemisphere, and when the Southern Hemisphere is tilted toward the sun, it is summer in that hemisphere. In between these two positions, the earth is still tilted but not in respect to changing the angle that the sun's rays hit the earth. In other words, the greater the variation in the angle of the sun as it hits earth, the greater the variation in the surface heating of the earth."

"Wow, you sure remember some heavy-duty astronomy! That was an incredible explanation. Okay then. From all you've said, would I be correct if I summed up what you've said by stating that you believe that it's the sun that creates our days and nights and our seasons. Is that right? In other words, you believe that it is the earth's position, how close or far the earth is from the sun, and what areas of the earth face the sun that dictates our days and nights, our time and our seasons. Is that right?"

"Yeah, that's exactly right."

"Okay then, believing this, do you believe that without the sun, and the earth's rotation around the sun as they are now, things might be different? For us, the time it takes the earth to rotate is twenty-four hours and that comprises one day for us. But, if things were different, we could have a twenty-eight hour day, or we might always be cold or always be warm, all depending on the angle of the earth to the sun, how far we are from the sun, and what direction the earth faces toward or away from the sun?"

And Jim said, "Yes. I do. Absolutely. It all boils down to the how the earth and the sun interact."

Sarah jumped in with "Let me tell him, Paul. Let me—" And Paul smiled and bowed to Sarah, saying, "In the interest of avoiding any accusation of male chauvinism, I bow to you, Sarah, so you, on behalf of all the gals present herewith, can show us guys what you gals know and prove to any who might be chauvinistic that you gals know just as much, maybe even more than us guys! Go for it! And watch out, Jim, these gals *do* know their Bible! They love these debates, so hold on to your hat!"

Sarah began by saying, "Well, the first book of the Bible, Genesis, tells the story of how the world was created. It is commonly accepted that it took seven days to create the world as we know it. Well, actually it took six days to create because on the seventh day, God rested. But if we look carefully at the word *days*, the Bible gives us an incredible clue about how carbon dating along with some parts of evolution, can be compatible with creation. In other words, how both theories, creation and evolution, can be compatible. Days, as we know it, are made up of a period of twenty-four hours and exist, *as you yourself just stated*, only because of the sun and its interaction with the earth.

"When we read the first verse in Genesis and then follow this accounting in Genesis from the first verse to the nineteenth verse, we find that the sun and moon and the 'seasons, days, and years' were not created until the *evening* of the *fourth* day. Therefore, since by your own admission about what is needed to create time and the seasons, we can conclude that it wasn't until the end of this fourth day that we could have entered into time as we know it."

Matt had Grandma's Bible in his hand and took up the conversation, explaining, "Therefore, the days preceding that fourth day are not necessarily days as we know them since we all just agreed that time, as we know it, was not yet introduced into the Creation. The Bible gives us a hint about these first days and what they might mean in terms of time. In Psalm 90:4, God says, '*For a thousand years in thy sight are but as yesterday when it is past, and as a watch in the night.*'"

Barbara, holding the most battered of Grandma's many Bibles, held it up and added, "It says it even better in 2 Peter 3:8 where it states, '*But, beloved, be not ignorant of this one thing, that one day is with the Lord as a thousand years, and a thousand years as one day.*'"

"So," Caleb continued, "if the passages of the first through the thirteenth verses of Genesis chapter 1, which describes the Creation doesn't correspond to time as *we* know it, it could be that the many years you mentioned in relation to carbon dating falls into this period before the evening of the fourth day. These verses 1 through 13 speak of the form, the darkness, the waters, light and darkness, the firmament, and finally the division between dry land and the seas. In Genesis 1:9 and 10, it says, '*And God said, Let the waters under the heaven be gathered together unto one place, and let the dry land appear: and it was so. And God called the dry land Earth; and the gathering together of the waters called he Seas: and God saw that it was good.'* This occurred on the third day, one day *before* the sun and moon and seasons were established."

"Wait a minute. You are telling me that thousands of years could have gone into the making of everything up to the end of the fourth day when God made the sun and moon, which then created the seasons, days, and years as we know it? Wait a minute. You have me at a disadvantage here because I've never heard this before."

"You wait a minute. There's no disadvantage. Don't cop out on this debate, Jim. Here, read it and tell us what you get out of what you read. Have we stated the case accurately according to what the Bible says?"

Jim skimmed the first chapter of Genesis in just a few minutes and then was handed another Bible that Barbara had opened and marked to Psalm 90:4 and to 2 Peter 3:8, and he read those two passages. And he was stunned; he was speechless. He sat back in his chair and looked around the table and slowly nodded his head, agreeing that what they said was possible based on what the Bible said. From what he'd just read, from what the Bible appeared to be saying, and from what they said, creation and evolution could possibly be compatible. Perhaps it could not be proven empirically, but what they said *was* possible, and that could make the Bible compatible with carbon dating and with all parts of evolution *except* the leap from ape to man . . . and that connection had never been found to satisfy science anyway. Incredible!

"With just a little more supporting information, you could almost use carbon dating to *'prove'* the Bible rather than disprove it. Wow. You know, I'm never tongue-tied," Jim exclaimed, "but I am now and you can bet that tonight, when I get home, I'm gonna read this stuff carefully and see if I can still accept your premise after a little study. After really looking it over a few times, I'll bet I can find where you are wrong because this is mind-boggling . . . unbelievable! I just can't believe it. I'm at a loss for words. If this is true, then why doesn't anyone talk about this? Why wasn't I ever taught this stuff in Sunday school or anywhere else in the church or classroom? Why isn't this news on TV? How can scientists say that carbon dating negates the Creation then? Why don't biblical scholars study this more and then openly debate the evolutionists with this stuff?"

Then Grandma spoke, saying, "Sadly Jim, I have to respond sarcastically by saying . . . What? . . . Do you imagine the *devil* is going to let everyone think that what the Bible says is *true?* Are the people who are *not* believers going to explain that creation and most parts of the theory of evolution might be able to *coexist?* Fat chance because then they might *have* to believe in God . . . or worse yet, might have to admit they are wrong. Or maybe they'd have to make a commitment to serve God as He asks them to do. Uhhhh, uhhhh, we don't live in the kind of a world where we learn and do. We live in a world where we learn then rationalize, then justify *not* doing! And, Jim, let me tell you that some arguments can get so ugly that they are not worth the engagement. Christ pointedly did not engage those who wanted to harm Him when they were looking to crucify Him. That was a lesson to us. It just gets ugly, and as Christians, we need to stay away from that. We just have to keep the faith that God will provide the understanding we need when we need it and we must choose our fights carefully. God miraculously finds a way to bring to our attention what He wants us to learn and when. Then we can ask Him to open our understanding to help us believe. We must trust that He will show us what He wants us to know and help us share what we learn with others whom God also wants as a part of the bride he's developing for His Son."

Matt added, "Let me just mention another three verses in the Bible that we do not fully understand yet they refer to time and to days being different, unusual. In Mark 13:19, God tells us, '*For in those days shall be affliction, such as was not from the beginning of the creation which God created unto this time, neither shall be. And except that the Lord had shortened those days, no flesh should be saved: but for the elect's sake, whom he hath chosen, he hath shortened the days.*'

"Here we are told that God had or would shorten the days. It's interesting to consider the words 'hath shortened.' If we interpreted this to mean that He *already* shortened the days and that He did this when He created our sun and moon on that fourth day, this would give even more credence to the possibility that days, before the sun and moon existed, were much longer."

Paul added that in Revelation 10:6, it says, "'*And I sware by him that liveth for ever and ever, who created heaven, and the things that therein are, and the earth, and the things that therein are, and the sea, and the things which are therein, that there should be time no longer.*' The words 'there should be time no longer' indicates that we will live without the confinement of time as we know it when God creates the new heaven and the new earth. This supports the fact that God can control time and that time might have been created just for us and just for a specific *span* of time."

"And," Sarah added, "in Joshua 10:13-14, we are told, '*And the sun stood still, and the moon stayed, until the people had avenged themselves upon their enemies. Is not this written in the book of Jasher? So the sun stood still in the midst of heaven, and hasted not to go down about a whole day. And there was no day like that before it or after it.*' So here too is an indication that God controls time."

"Interestingly, there are many accounts in history of a missing day," added Paul. "Ancient Chinese writings during the reign of Emperor Yeo, Egyptian priests, ancient Indian writings, the Aztecs of Mexico, the Incas of Peru, the Babylonians, Persians, and Polynesians have all written accounts of time seeming to stand still for one day. Professor Pickering of the Harvard Observatory, then

Mauder of Greenwich, and Totten of Yale said that they traced a missing day through astronomical calculations."

Then Grandma jumped into the conversation, adding, "I love to read, and when I find something wonderful, I usually tell the others so we can discuss what I've found. And, there is a lot of information regarding the interpretation of Joshua's account of the sun standing still. The consensus of many theologians and scholars, as an example in the work of Gleason Archer who wrote the *Encyclopedia of Bible Difficulties* in 1982, seems to be that a retardation of the movement of the earth, a slowing down of its rotation from twenty-four hours to somewhere around thirty-six to forty-eight hours is what occurred in the biblical account of Joshua. But, Jim, if you are looking to read some fascinating works, read one of the sixty books or six thousand articles written by Johnson C. Philip. He is a Christian apologist who was born in 1954 and has seven degrees, which include physics and theology. He founded the first seminary in the world that offered a master and a doctoral program in Christian apologetics through distant education. His writings have been published in six languages."

"But you know, Jim," Paul added, "it doesn't really matter to us whether there is absolute proof of this or not. We all trust the Bible because we trust God. We have seen the power of God firsthand and experienced His love and His all-encompassing wisdom. Sometimes when we try to *prove* everything, we can get bogged down and lose our real focus. And it's faith that we need to have. As Grandma said, Christ teaches us that there are some arguments not worth fighting. While we thoroughly enjoy the engagement of a great discussion, the bottom line is our faith, and the bottom line is that we trust God and want to learn what He asks of us so we can serve Him. We hope that by doing so we will please Him. We want to please Him because we love Him."

"I came here today thinking that you'd be spouting Bible verses, Paul, but never expecting to have what I can say is an intellectual awakening and such an incredible challenge to my mind and my entire way of thinking. I'm still shaken. In fact, to speak as Bill O'Reilly might, I feel like a blunderbuss rather than my normal perspicacious self! Seriously though, I am in awe of how you learned all this. Is it mainly from reading the Bible?"

"Partly. But it's also from the sermons we receive when we go to church, it's from our question-and-answer evenings at church when we can ask any question that we have about our faith, and it is from Sunday school classes, confirmation classes, Bible study . . . everything combined. And because we are really interested in the Bible, we also read different books that we share with one another, those similar to the ones Grandma just mentioned. Our faith is so important to us that we actually enjoy having lively discussions when we get together. We all want to know more. But whatever we learn, whatever someone shows us that might not jive, might not seem to be interpreted correctly, would not change our faith."

"Well, that's a strong statement. I don't want to offend anyone, but isn't a statement like that also a little bit, . . . well, . . . fanatical . . . Well, maybe that's too strong a word but, you know, isn't that foolish? Even Bill O'Reilly condemns what he calls the 'Kool-Aid' drinkers, meaning people who follow something or someone in blind faith using no common sense. I mean, what if someone finally disproved the Bible and you found out that you'd been wrong all along? I do respect your views and I respect the wisdom you bring to the table, and I really do want to learn more, so I hope none of you are angry with my own views, my own inability . . . or desire . . . to believe in an organized *man-made* religion. Isn't it better to have an open mind in case your interpretation is wrong?"

"No. You reference Bill O'Reilly, and I think he'd be the *first* one to tell you that God is real, that the way we conduct ourselves is important, that teaching our children, especially about God is important, and he is adamantly opposed to injustice and even fights for the rights of unborn babies that must endure a late-term abortion. While we might not know *why* Mr. O'Reilly believes, we do know that *we* believe because we have all had so many beautiful and incredible experiences of faith. In our quest to learn of God we have become sure of what we believe. God has shown us, just as He will show all who seek Him. But your heart has to be ready for Him. He gladly comes to everyone who has the desire to know Him."

"Well, I'm not ready to ask for anything like that. In fact, I doubt that I ever will be. But I still want to say thanks for all you gave me today—the welcome, the friendship, the wonderful food, the intimacy of your conversation, and the acceptance of who I am with no appearance of condemnation, especially about how little I seem to know about religion."

"Jim, everyone has to start somewhere; and religion, believing, trusting is a very personal thing. It may begin with something someone says or even what you read, but it's what you personally want in terms of your relationship with God that moves you toward a trust in Him and in the future He has planned for you. Some people fulfill a calling God gave them and do so well with it that they have no need to learn every nuance of the Bible. In fact, you mentioned Bill O'Reilly before, and he's someone who champions God and the teaching of right from wrong. We have no idea what Mr. O'Reilly does or doesn't know about the Bible, but by his very actions and what he writes in his books, you can see his underlying faith. Even his television programs reflect his strong personal virtues and demonstrate how he works for God by championing the cause of others. While for us it's a great adventure to research the Bible, we understand that everyone is different and finds and practices their convictions differently and we understand that people serve God in different ways too."

"Well put. I guess you're right, no one can make someone believe . . . It does have to come from inside. And it certainly is true that what we *don't* know can be very detrimental. I guess I should be thinking about what I can learn so I can make better decisions, but right now I still carry a lot of bitterness from what I've seen so-called people of faith do that brings so much harm to others."

"Jim, just try to keep an open mind and let God bring you what He wants. In time, you'll have your answers and be better able to know where you want to go. It will be your heart that will guide you, not your mind.", Grandma added.

"I surely appreciate that you've shared so much with me, and I think that you are all pretty super people . . . thanks. I'd sure like to get together again . . . I mean . . . I'd like to learn some more of this stuff. I would love to study some of these premises. I can see how they apply to our lives . . . I mean, it's sort of helpful. Well, I don't know what I mean, but I'd like to talk about this again and even about the inheriting of or generational sin Barbara told me about. But I also have to provide you with a caveat. I am *not* a believer. Well, that's probably not true because I do believe in God, I mean I do believe that there *is* a god, a supreme being. But I don't think I believe in any engineered plan. In fact, I am pretty sure that for every so-called fact you have given me today from the Bible, I will be able to find another that negates it. So if you don't mind us having another discussion where I can challenge what you've said, I'd really enjoy the debate."

"You are quite welcome, thanks for all your kind words," Sarah interjected, "and we'd love to talk again. Bring on your challenges, and we will see what we can tell you. How about now though, we clean up for Grandma, stretch our legs, and then we can relax in the living room and talk some more."

Jim was pleased by their openness and by their lack of condemnation. They didn't appear the least bit concerned by his challenge. He hated to see their conversation end and said so. Then they all got up to clear the dinner dishes and lay the table for dessert. As they rinsed and loaded the dinner dishes into the dishwasher so the dishwasher would be ready to empty after dessert, Paul began to speak once again about what they'd discussed about Genesis and the Creation.

"You know, Jim, scientists claim that our universe is made up of dark matter that contains a kind of web that connects multitudes of superclusters, which are themselves made up of about one hundred billion galaxies. We live in the Mergo cluster in the relatively small Milky Way galaxy, which contains one hundred billion stars, one of which is our sun. Interestingly, in the beginning of Genesis, *before* God created our sun and moon and thus provided time as we know it, the words *firmament, void, waters, darkness,* and *light* are used. I once looked these words up in *Webster's* dictionary and found that *firmament* means the vault or arch of the sky and also means a 'support.' After reading this, I realized that the word *void* could be the dark matter itself, and that the word *firmament* could be referring to the webs within the dark matter that support or hold together the superclusters of galaxies.

"Darkness—meaning, according to the dictionary, devoid of light, not reflecting, receiving, transmitting, or radiating light—could be what existed before the stars were created. The word *light* has one of its definitions state that it is an electromagnetic radiation in the wavelength range including infrared, visible, ultraviolet, and X-rays traveling in a vacuum with a speed of about 186,281 miles per second. This could refer to the stars, so I believe that there may even be another correlation here, one that allows for the big bang theory. Of course, believing in God and believing what He tells us in the Bible, we'd believe that it would be a 'big bang' *that was a controlled event with an engineered result,* not a haphazard event with an unpredictable result. I just thought you'd be interested in that information too."

"Paul, that's amazing. It's beyond my scope of knowledge, but I sure will think about all this. I really enjoy talking about this. Thanks for sharing. But I'm still sure that you've got it wrong as it pertains to a religion we should practice, I just can't wrap myself around a plan God put into place that seems so complex."

Barbara heard Jim's words and knew him well enough to put them into the context of Jim's heart and realized that she had never seen Jim so engaged, so surprised, so tongue-tied over some of the things they'd told him. Whatever his words, he'd been completely stunned by what he'd heard. Even his usual sarcasm hadn't reared its head. That was good. But she was concerned by his adamant desire to prove them wrong. He was a little bit too cocky.

As they ate dessert, they talked some more but not about their faith. They shared their hopes and dreams and wishes and some of their everyday concerns. Soon it was time to go, and with everything in perfect order at Grandma's, they said their goodbyes. Caleb prayed for their safety on the way home, that they would always be protected from Satan and would remain faithful to the end and also asked God to open Jim's understanding.

Once in the car, Jim told Barbara that he was still excited about the dinner conversation and wanted to know if they could all get together again. He had also secretly thought of the "professor" and wondered if he too had been privy to these kinds of conversations with Barbara's family. That thought made him incredibly jealous; for some reason, he didn't like the idea that the professor had also had these conversations with them. He wanted so badly to ask Barbara about this guy, but he bit his tongue, not feeling good about his unkind thoughts nor about why he was jealous.

He was happy when Barbara suggested they meet the next night when Jim would be able to give her the details about his plans for going to DC to meet Wade. Jim kissed her good night in the car, and again, his heart was moved. He knew that he'd have a lot to think about tonight. He really liked this family, every one of them. But he didn't like the fact that he felt guilty about his lack of faith. But what really boggled his mind what that he, someone who took pride in knowing about important things, had not ever heard some the information he'd been given today. *How was that possible,* he thought. *How could I have gone through life, gone through Sunday school classes, read some of the Bible, even attended church when I was younger, yet never heard this stuff before? Why not? And it was interesting that Grandma had said that it was because Satan . . . who I am not even sure exists . . . can have been the cause of me not ever learning any of this. Where did Satan come from and why in the world would God let him exist if he did so much harm to God's work? It didn't make any sense.* Jim's thoughts exhausted him. He was frustrated by his inability to answer any of these questions and so he forced his mind to something more to his liking . . . Barbara! *Not only is she a gem, but her whole family is terrific too.* He really hoped to see them all again soon.

Chapter Five

JIM, WADE, HEZA, AND BARA,

After all this time in Iraq, he was finally going home. This time, he was going home to stay and Wade was coming with him. As they reflected on their years in Iraq, it was hard to believe that the invasion of Iraq had begun on March 20, 2002. They had arrived soon after with great expectations, Now it was time to leave. They had both done what they could, but for them, it wasn't enough. They had wanted to accomplish so much more.

As they looked at Iraqi society, what they saw saddened them. Most of the engineers, teachers, scientists, musicians, economists—in fact, most of the well-educated people—many with children in universities in the United States, had left Iraq, immigrated to other countries, safe countries. Some planned to return if and when the country stabilized, but others felt it would always be too dangerous and had left permanently. The loss of this segment of society, many of whom had become their friends, saddened them and fueled the fire of their anger against the petty politics that had harmed the generous intentions of the reconstruction effort.

What a waste, Jim thought. Wade felt the same way. But now, they had the opportunity to work Stateside and had accepted that opportunity. Jim was delighted that he and Wade would continue to work together. Their new jobs would be challenging. They would be developing and building a huge complex that would include high-rise office buildings, condos, parking garages, restaurants, and retail shops and they would oversee everything from water lines to power lines, everything structural to architectural, even the landscaping. Jim looked forward to the change and had written Barbara to tell her his good news.

He'd last been home in November of 2004, and so much had happened in these last fifteen months in Iraq. Barbara had written him sad news about Paul, describing the terrible attack he'd endured aboard his workboat a year ago, and of the friendship between Paul and the captain of his workboat and how that captain had saved Paul's life. She told him that after Jim had gone back to Iraq, Paul had been coming to church with them whenever he was home. He was also still looking for his children.

She also told him that Ann and Caleb were expecting their first child in August and were overjoyed and frantically looking for just the right house to buy so they could move before the baby arrived. She devoted an entire letter to telling him about the journal Grandma was writing about her life, and that Grandma had enlisted Sarah's help to put it together. Sarah had at first resisted but was now enjoying every moment of the experience as she learned more about Grandma's early life and the circumstances that had brought her so close to God.

Jim was anxious to get home. The guy he'd nicknamed the professor when he'd last been home had done his best to capture Barbara's heart. Probably seeing Barbara with Jim had galvanized him into action, and he'd begun calling her as soon as Jim left for Iraq. He and Barbara apparently went out to dinner and to a movie together quite often. Jim could make no complaint because before he'd left, he'd told Barbara that she should find a nice guy her own age and qualified his statement only by saying she should be sure to check with "Uncle" Jim before she did anything foolish, like marrying someone before Jim checked him out.

He meant these words when he said them, but nevertheless, Jim was shocked when she'd smiled and accepted calmly what he'd told her. He had hinted that there was no future for them because of their age difference and her need for a guy more religious than he was. After he'd said what he did, he wished he hadn't. In fact, he wasn't even sure why he'd said what he did. He wanted to be fair to Barbara. Barbara had calmly replied that she and Jim would always be friends. . . . and then, to Jim's chagrin, seemed to begin dating the professor. But she continued writing him, and when he asked, she told him about her "evenings out on the town" as she called them.

Jim, without realizing it, lived for her letters. He felt happy when a description of a date with the professor sounded boring, and he was upset when it appeared that she had a really good time. Sometimes Jim was so jealous he would be in a bad mood for days. Here he was in Iraq, and there the professor was parked right on Barbara's doorstep. They were on some kind of a committee together too, so they had that in common to talk about and another reason to get together.

Jim was glad that she wrote to him about this guy because if she hadn't said anything about him, he would have worried even more. He still had the hope that she'd dump the professor, not for him of course but for someone who would be more suitable for her. Jim hated to admit that the professor was a pretty good candidate for a husband. Despite what Jim told Barbara, he was not ready to let her go.

Jim and Wade struggled at times to keep a positive attitude. Wade was still hurting from the loss of his wife, and time wasn't healing for him mainly because they didn't have enough meaningful work to keep them busy. They both recognized that the time had come for them to move out of Iraq and into a career Stateside and were delighted that they'd be working together at home. They genuinely liked and respected one another and shared similar moral and political views.

Jim had invited Wade to move into the apartment Jim had maintained back home until Wade decided on a place of his own. Wade wanted to buy a house, not rent an apartment, so he had agreed to Jim's offer, immediately realizing that it would give him time to decide in what area he wanted to live and what type of house he wanted. He was delighted with Jim's offer not only because it fit his plans but also because he looked forward to spending the time with Jim. Jim's companionship in Iraq had helped fill the void left by his wife's death.

Jim told Wade about many of the conversations he'd had with Barbara's family and the biblical information they shared with him. He told Wade how he had marveled about what they said in regard to the sins of the forefathers and how evolution could possibly be compatible with the biblical account of creation.

Afraid that he sounded too enthusiastic about what they'd told him of the Bible, Jim quickly apprised Wade that he was sure that Barbara's family "had it wrong" and that he wanted to find some way to negate what they'd said. "Facts, Wade. We need some facts," he'd said, imitating his favorite TV personality. Wade too had been astonished by the information Jim shared with him, and he also wanted to see what backed up some of these crazy ideas Jim had related.

Jim explained that the family carefully pointed out that there was no empirical evidence for what they'd found and that they were not biblical scholars. He also told Wade that they'd explained that the original language of the books of the Bible contained words that could have changed meaning as they were translated into the various languages. They explained that they took their King James translation at face value trusting that God would help them unveil any mystery in what they read. "Nevertheless", Jim said, "what they did show me was impressive and certainly food for thought, and they even said that God says we can test Him.

"They insist that the Bible inspires them, gives them an even greater understanding of the size and scope of what God has done for them. When they find words in the Bible that they can apply to their life or that explains why God allows certain things, it is comforting to them." Wade heard the wistfulness in Jim's voice and could see that while Jim wasn't yet aware of this, Jim admired the strength of conviction, and the openmindedness Barbara and her family had about their faith that allowed them to search, even test, and then follow what the Bible said. But Wade had also recognized the challenge in Jim's words and knew that another part of Jim wanted to find a way to negate what they had said.

Wade thought to himself, *I think Jim wants to find faith, but he's afraid of it . . . Is he afraid of the commitment it would take if he believed, or is he afraid of being disappointed again?*

What Jim told Wade made him curious about the Bible, and this gave Jim someone with whom he could share his newfound quest. From that day forward, they sat together for hours in one of the nearby open cafés, discussing how the Bible seemed to support many of the statements that science dictated. They searched for certain words in the concordance Jim had purchased before he came back to Iraq so he could locate what they wanted in the Bible.

Jim wanted to find statements that would not support what Genesis said about the time span that carbon dating seemed to require. But he could not. They wondered if what Barbara said about a plan, a sculpted all-inclusive plan that had been engineered into the physics of the world, was indeed possible.

They wondered if the dinosaurs might have existed before God removed the waters from above the firmament. These waters may have created a greenhouse effect that could have supported such an era. They wondered if the Ice Age occurred when God removed those waters, because if the greenhouse effect was removed, and there was no sun to warm the planet, these conditions might have supported an Ice Age.

They also discussed the passage in Genesis 1:9: "*And God said, Let the waters under the heaven be gathered together unto one place, and let dry land appear: and it was so.*" They felt that this supported the physical evidence of sea life found embedded in rocks high on the top of mountain peaks since those passages indicated that for a time, water covered everything. And if a natural evolution was indeed taking place, this would allow for the primitive sea life found by the archeologists. Wade pointed out that the dry land mentioned in Genesis 1:9 occurred on the third day because as he read further, Genesis 1:13 ended that segment of occurrences by saying, "*.....were the third day.*"

As Jim and Wade read this scripture, they understood that this apparently indicated that the tides, the gravitational pull of the moon on the waters, also had not yet occurred. The lack of tides, thus the lack of wearing away caused by moving water, further supported why there was an abundance of sea life on mountains. They wished they had other books, other resources they could study on this subject. Even apart from any religious belief, this stuff was *interesting!*

Despite what they read that appeared to allow the biblical account of creation and the scientific parts of evolution to coexist, Jim could not accept even the possibility that the Bible could be taken literally. As he and Wade talked, Jim also told Wade that Barbara had explained that if someone wanted to develop their faith, it was dangerous and narrow-minded to live only through one's head or mind or science.

She told him that faith had to originate in the heart and that if one only looked to believe with the head he would never be able to *really* converse with God. Wade felt that what Barbara said held much truth and wisdom. But Jim stuck to the Kool-Aid admonition to make sure this stuff wasn't potentially dangerous. If he were ever to believe it would have to be with his head, not just his heart!

When Jim shared Barbara's words with him, Wade saw some part of Jim shut down. He felt that Jim had hunkered himself into a stubborn refusal to accept the god that Barbara followed, and realized that Jim was simply not ready to accept anything that would change his view of religion. He was not ready to allow *any* concept or *any* biblical statement upset his way of life. Currently, Jim found himself content to live within the guidelines he'd created for his life. It would be too upsetting to change course now. What he had now was safe and allowed him the freedom he wanted.

But Wade knew that Jim's personality carried an "all or nothing" aspect so that when he did something, he did it with all his heart and worked hard to do it. This in itself would present Jim with a dilemma. If he ever capitulated and came to believe, it would indeed mean a lot of work on Jim's part to give his life to it. It would indeed change many things in Jim's life.

So subconsciously, Jim really did not *want* to believe. He *wanted* to find the family wrong in their biblical interpretations. Wade wondered if subconsciously Jim pushed Barbara away as another means of avoiding the dilemma that believing would bring to his life.

Jim wrote to Barbara and told her that he and Wade had been discussing Genesis and its account of creation. Her letter in reply to his suggested that he look up Proverbs 3:5 which said, *"Trust in the LORD with all thine heart; and lean not unto thine own understanding,"* and Proverbs 23:26 which said, *"My son, give me thine heart, and let thine eyes observe my ways."* Jim noted that these verses stated that one should not just seek their own understanding, but seek a better understanding through their trust in God. *Ahh Barbara, you may be pertinacious, but I have the greater pertinacity!"*

The next letter that Jim received from Barbara mentioned another verse. It was Ephesians 3:17 and said, *"That Christ may dwell in your hearts by faith; that ye, being rooted and grounded in love."* According to Barbara, having faith and trust and using one's heart seemed to be the key to believing. When Jim shared this with Wade, Wade admitted that he wanted to believe if he could. Jim, on the other hand, said that he wanted to keep his belief system as it was. But Wade and Barbara saw a part of Jim that was drawn to a god he could trust.

Then something happened that shook the hard-earned faith that had been building in their hearts. Jim and Wade were walking toward one of the outdoor cafes when a young woman entered an area filled with little shops and outdoor stalls where many were purchasing food and other necessities. The young woman's burqa hid a bomb that was detonated when she reached a busy area of the market. He and Wade were just a half a block away when the explosion occurred. They'd ducked and instinctively sought cover, not knowing what had happened.

Only seconds later they understood and began running to the people who were lying on the ground to see who needed help. They witnessed firsthand the death or injuries to children and adults, young and old. Many were killed outright; others were dying or maimed for life.

Wade scooped up a one-year-old child who was bleeding profusely and, with him in his arms, began to run to the hospital just a few blocks away. Jim struggled to lift and carry a woman to the hospital who was pregnant and also bleeding profusely. Others ran to help. As he and Wade reached the emergency entrance, they could see and hear ambulances responding to the call to attend to the injured.

When Jim ran into the hospital, a nurse pointed to the bed where he could lay the woman, and a swarm of medical personnel came to help. Before he could leave her side, the woman grabbed his shirt, pointed to the child Wade carried, and then pointed to her womb, saying in Farsi, "My children, care for them, they have no one else."

The child Wade carried recognized his mother's voice and cried out to his mother, reaching his thin arms toward her. Jim heard Wade gasp and turned to look. As Wade laid the little one-year-old child on the gurney, he saw that the boy had lost his foot. As the mother turned back toward her son, she saw too and screamed, and with that last effort she died.

One team of physicians cleaned and dressed the boy's leg and began an IV to prevent infection, avoid shock, and help with the pain. They arranged to transport the boy to Ramstein Air Base and Landstuhl Regional Medical Center. Another team of physicians performed a caesarean section on the mother and delivered a baby girl from the dead woman's womb.

The hospital records team asked Wade and Jim some questions to help them locate the relatives of the mother and her children. But Wade and Jim knew that there were now two children without relatives, now alone in the world, and one no longer had a foot. And they were both wondering why God would let such things happen to children. The children didn't deserve what had happened. In those few minutes, all Barbara had tried to instill in Jim's heart and all the striving that Wade and Jim had put into learning God's words seemed to fall away, impotent, lost, meaningless, in a world of unexplained cruelty.

Wade and Jim visited the hospital every day. They held the baby, and they named her Heza. They fed her, played with her, cooed to her, and read to her, feeling responsible for her. They put in for two days' leave and flew to Ramstein Air Base and visited the little boy who, when the nurses asked them for his name, repeated what they thought they heard the mother call him and said, "Bara". Later, they learned from the hospital nursing staff that what the mother had said was correct; there were no other relatives. The children would be sent to an orphanage.

Wade and Jim would have liked to get their hands on the people who had planned the terrible attack that had killed the mother and killed or injured so many other innocent people. Jim thought of the inherited sins of the forefathers that Barbara had mentioned, but he was too angry to let those thoughts remain. It was easier and took less effort to blame God.

Every day, Wade and Jim walked back to their quarters after visiting Heza, still discussing how they could find no answers to how God would care for these children and why He allowed their mother to die. One day, they decided to visit a local orphanage to see if they could help in any way and learn what these children might need, how they lived, who cared for them. To their surprise, there were American soldiers with minor injuries there on crutches, in wheelchairs, holding on to walkers, and they were busy telling the children fairy tales in English or passing out candy bars or giving the children toys that they had either purchased or made. It touched their hearts.

Wade and Jim felt pride in these young men who, despite their personal injuries, reached out to help others. It was heartwarming to see that others cared, that conditions at the orphanage were not as bad as they'd feared. Nevertheless, Jim's cynicism peaked as a protective measure so he would not feel the pain of these people, of injured parents, of children without limbs, of soldiers helping others who needed so much help themselves. Jim's tender heart couldn't bear the pain he felt, and his upbringing would not allow him to express his anger, so his cynicism and sarcasm had to take over to protect him. It camouflaged the hurt and gave him an acceptable way to express his anger.

By the first of July, Heza had been moved from the hospital to the orphanage, and Wade and Jim continued to visit her whenever they could. As the months passed, a bond grew between them; and suddenly, Bara, who recovered enough to leave Landstuhl Medical Center, was there too to be reunited with his sister. Such a strong bond formed among the four of them that Jim and Wade worried it would cause even greater pain when they left Iraq for good in February.

A few weeks later, Wade asked Jim if they could talk privately. When they sat together with a cup of the strong boiled tea of Iraq, Wade told Jim that he had decided to adopt Bara and had turned in all the application papers necessary to make it happen. Bara's name for Wade was "Poppa." Bara would be twenty months old when Wade went back home. Wade, just under forty years old with no wife to help him if he adopted Bara, would be taking on this responsibility by himself. Bara was just learning to walk with the use of a prosthesis strapped to his calf and over his knee and would require medical attention for many years.

Jim didn't think Wade should adopt Bara, but he admired Wade for doing it. Wade filed the papers, then spent hours with Jim commiserating about Heza. Wade did not want to leave her behind and did not want to separate her from Bara. After all, Bara and Heza were brother and sister. But how could he handle a baby? She would only be seven or eight months old when Wade left Iraq.

Jim told Barbara about Wade's decision, and she was happy for Wade and for Bara. She told Jim that God would bless Wade for what he was doing, explaining that God asked them to look after widows and orphans and keep them under their roofs. Jim hadn't expected that reaction from Barbara.

Deep in the recesses of his heart, Jim worried that adopting a disabled child from Iraq would prevent Wade from ever having a wife and children of his own. He didn't understand why he worried about that. But it was because Jim was thinking of how much Wade sacrificed for others and how little he asked for himself. *On the other hand,* Jim thought, *Bara and Heza, being brother and sister, shouldn't be separated and deserved a better break in life.* Jim even wondered if he himself should adopt Heza.

Jim then thought about his relationship with Barbara. They had no commitment to one another. In fact, he had always pushed her away. Well, sort of. He didn't know if she would even have him. How could he ever ask Barbara about helping him raise Heza? Then Jim realized that he didn't have the right to ask such a question of her. Not only of Barbara but of himself. He was not prepared for a child and would not be doing the right thing to adopt a child or think of marrying a woman for the wrong reasons.

And so in February, Jim and Wade went home with the question of Heza's future unresolved—Wade facing the red tape of an adoption process for Bara and Jim worrying about Heza and Wade. But Wade worried about Heza too.

Suddenly, they were back in the States, this time for good. Wade and Jim settled into Jim's apartment and into their new jobs. Wade devoted many of his evenings and weekends to the task of finding a house, wanting one with all the rooms on one level so Bara could get around easily. He'd have to find a housekeeper or a nanny so there would be someone to look after Bara while he was at work.

Jim admired Wade for what he was doing. Wade had solved his battle against the sadness in his heart by doing something for someone else. But what had Jim done? What was he going to do? Jim too was battling the concerns he had about his feelings for Barbara, the obligation he felt for Heza, and his desire to find peace in a heart filled with doubt and turmoil.

Barbara saw that Jim was in turmoil. She recognized his anguish and his feelings of responsibility toward the child they'd left in Iraq. Her own mind raged with possibilities as she searched for how to help Jim. She knew that at twenty-three years of age, a college graduate, and happy in her career on the staff of a good newspaper, she was ready to consider the prospect of settling down. She wasn't sure she'd like to take on the responsibility of an Iraqi child less than a year old, but she knew that she would do it if Jim wanted it, assuming of course that he asked her to marry him.

But Barbara could sense Wade's concern for Heza and had a feeling that Wade was thinking of adopting Heza because she was Bara's sister and they belonged together. When she mentioned this to Jim, his eyes lit up as if this solution had never occurred to him. Evidently, Jim and Wade had never discussed this as a solution to their concern for Heza.

By May, Wade found a house to purchase and had negotiated a good deal because he planned to make the purchase without the need for a mortgage. He moved in within the month and announced that the agency said that Bara's adoption would be finalized in a few months. He planned to fly back to Iraq to get Bara. Wade kept busy by making improvements to the house, furnishing a bedroom and play area for Bara while easily building his reputation with his company.

He seemed content, but because he and Jim were close, Jim could tell that Wade was still lonely. He would not accept invitations to Barbara's family get-togethers nor from anyone at the office. Other than Barbara and Jim, he did not interact socially with anyone. Barbara began to pray that God would send Wade the perfect helpmate, the perfect wife.

A series of circumstances began in July that kept Jim hopping and distracted from his worries about Wade. On July 7, Grandma died. She had been ninety years old. Sarah had completed the journal that Grandma had wanted her to write. Grandma's death left a terrible void in the lives of her family and friends, and it seemed that no one picked up the gauntlet to run with the fellowships that always brought the family together.

Caleb asked Sarah and Matt if they would be willing to tackle the job of getting everyone together to go through Grandma's personal effects, pick out what they wanted, and throw out what needed throwing out. Sarah gladly took the furnishings and accessories the others did not want and put them into storage for the home that she and Matt planned to have one day. *One with old-world charm, one that would provide a beautiful backdrop for Grandma's furnishings,* she thought. But Sarah struggled with her loss, feeling lethargic and moving through the stages of grief that came unbidden into her body and mind.

As the family gathered at Grandma's to begin sorting and packing or deciding what each person wanted to take as a remembrance of Grandma, they reminisced about Grandma's Christmases and the joy her fellowships had brought to everyone. Jim and Wade were asked to join them at Grandma's under the pretense that they were needed to help. The family knew that they would not turn down a plea for help and when Jim and Wade said they would come, the family was glad. They all liked Wade and Jim so much and knew that Wade had been feeling lonely. Wade hadn't wanted to come, but was glad he did. He enjoyed their company and when they described a typical Christmas with Grandma, Wade was enthralled and decided that he wanted to give Bara the same kind of experiences that Grandma had given her family.

Wade was fascinated as they reminisced about Grandma's tree filled with tinsel, lights, and garlands so thick you could hardly see the tree itself. The lights and garlands and tinsel were interspersed with her collection of vintage-looking Santa faces and miniature teddy bears, with large hand-painted ornaments in between. Grandma created a sea of poinsettias under the tree to hide the tree stand, and electric trains ran through the little village nestled in snow that graced the perimeter of the tree skirt. The leaves of the poinsettias looked like a primordial forest behind the uphill slope of the tiny village.

Two forty-eight-inch shelves in Grandma's bookcases were used to create a village of taller ceramic houses and shops. There were sidewalks made of miniature bricks that were filled with people and gates and fences that surrounded a miniature park with a skating pond and skaters. Pine trees loomed lush above snow-covered streets that held tiny old-fashioned automobiles and a horse and carriage. Chestnut vendors and fresh flower vendors further enticed villagers carrying gifts home to their families. Puppies sat at the feet of old men on benches under ornate lanterns.

Recreating this lovely village each year, each time a little differently, Grandma seemed like a little girl again. Her eyes were alight with the innocence of a child seeing a fairy tale come alive. Watching her with her village always reminded everyone of how she must have played with the little paper dolls she said she cherished as a child.

When Grandma was a young bride preparing for her first Christmas in her own home, she created a sled and four reindeers out of wood she cut to shape with a saber saw. Years later, she refinished the sled by placing thin sheets of gold leaf over a burgundy base colour, then staining the gold leaf and varnishing the entire surface. She had hand painted old-world curlicues along the edges of the sled. It was elegant. She painted the reindeer white and rolled them in silver and white sequins and added coloured sequins for eyes and nostrils and brightly colored red beads for the reins that traveled from reindeer to reindeer and then to the sled for Santa to grasp when he was ready for his long journey.

She'd purchased a uniquely dressed Santa outfitted in bow tie and shirtsleeves, lush burgundy velvet pants, and black leather boots, seated on a bench playing a fiddle. He was in perfect proportion to the sled and reindeer. She'd found tiny Christmas elves that were also perfectly proportioned to the setting she created and placed them on ladders and pathways or atop the sled where they appeared to be loading gifts onto the sled for Santa's long trip.

Tiny packages, teddy bears, sleds, and rocking horses lay on the snow, awaiting careful placement by the elves onto the waiting sled, and a snowman sang his Christmas song in the background when the key in his back was wound. A row of miniature Christmas trees formed a backdrop for the sled and reindeer. Little children visiting Grandma's house during the Christmas holiday couldn't help reaching for the tiny rocking horses and sleds on which the elves were working.

They recalled how Paul, with his long reach, had hung Grandma's gold angels with billowing sleeves and flowing hair from the edges of the huge mirror over her couch and how the angels were reflected in the mirror, their lights and their ribbons doubling.

Grandma said with a smile that the angels were watching over her house and her guests and had been assigned the duty to make sure everyone was safe and happy. Their skirts, long and full, were elegant. The ribbons they held in their hands complemented the colour scheme of Grandma's room and flowed gracefully, being held in place by the wire along their edges. The angels were perfectly placed to balance the Christmas tree on the opposite side of the room.

Her largest display, the most important in her eyes, was her nativity scene. The papier-mâché figures were two feet tall and wore exquisite robes in the jewel-tone colours of green and burgundy and gold and blue. They, like the angels, had deep sleeves and full skirts. The three wise men wore shapely crown hats with gold trim and carried shining gifts, one of which was a chest filled with precious pearls and gold chains, which spilled over its edges and cascaded to the feet of the Christ child.

A manger held the Christ child as he lay in a bed of greens ringed with pinecones that were intertwined with delicate gold ribbons and tiny silk rosebuds. His arms were lifted toward His mother, His beautiful crocheted, wide-sleeved gown slipping down one of His outstretched arms. Grandpa always hung a spotlight on the ceiling above the nativity scene and directed it at the Child and His mother, and later, Paul actually installed a spotlight into the ceiling and put a dimmer switch on it. The light showcased the beauty and importance of the nativity scene, which became the focal point of all the rooms.

Everyone loved Grandma's Christmas decorations and would have liked all or any part of them. But they agreed that the decorations should go to Sarah and not be divided between them, provided she set them up for all to see each year. Interspersed among the furniture once belonging to Grandma, they knew that visiting Sarah at Christmas would bring back the memories of each wonderful holiday they spent with Grandma. Sarah gladly agreed and said, "In a few years, Matt and I will have a light like that installed in our home for when we place Grandma's lovely nativity set in our own special niche for Christmas! How wonderful that will be!"

So a sad time was nonetheless filled with memories of happy times and wonderful examples of faith and fellowship. Wade began to love and respect this amazing family and was so glad that he had agreed to join them. He began to see the effects that their faith had on their lives and it moved his heart with longing.

On August 30, Ann and Caleb had their first child, a boy. They named him Andrew. Just a few days earlier, they had moved into their own home and needed as much help as they could get since the settlement date came later than they had expected. The whole family pitched in to help with the move, Wade too. The move was so efficiently conducted that the house was already in excellent order when the baby arrived.

Everyone knew that Ann and Caleb would pick up where Grandma had left off. They knew that Ann and Caleb would often invite all of them for a fellowship with one another now that the baby had arrived and now that they had a home that could so easily accommodate everyone. Little by little, they would all be getting married and creating a home that they could use for fellowship!

Jim and Barbara had dinner together often. They talked on the phone. They visited Matt and Sarah and Caleb and Ann, and they saw Paul when he was home from the high seas and of course, they saw Wade quite often. But Jim never said anything of permanence about their relationship, and Barbara seemed content for them to be just friends. But suddenly, in just one day everything changed. A few days after baby Andrew was born, one early, balmy September evening, Jim and Wade decided to go out to dinner together after work. Unbeknownst to them, Barbara and the professor had also made plans to go to dinner together. Thus, they were surprised to find one another in the same local restaurant.

Jim and Wade had left work that evening and, with business decisions still not completed, decided to have dinner at an Italian restaurant not far from where they lived. As they entered the restaurant, they noticed Barbara at a table with the professor but followed the waitress to a table of their own without addressing them. Neither Barbara nor the professor seemed to have seen Jim and Wade enter the restaurant. When Wade and Jim sat down, Wade saw that Jim kept looking to the other side of the restaurant where Barbara and the professor sat. Jim was seething.

Wade noted Jim's reddened face, the extension of his neck tendons, his clenched jaw. He began to tease Jim about letting the best woman in the world get away and being the biggest fool he'd seen in a long time. Jim's anger grew as he watched the other table and listened to Wade's words, and Wade saw something formidable in him.

Suddenly, Jim, terribly angry, leaned into Wade's face, and slowly, quietly announced that they were going to join Barbara and her friend for dinner. He rose from their table and began to walk to Barbara's table. Wade clumsily rose to his feet as well, laid his napkin on the table, and followed where Jim led. Slowly, a huge grin spread across Wade's face, and his heart sang as he realized that Jim was jealous. *Finally!* he thought.

As Jim loomed beside Barbara, she appeared surprised but delighted to see him. The professor also appeared surprised and certainly not delighted. As Jim stood next to Barbara, he brazenly asked if he and Wade could sit and join them for dinner. Barbara readily agreed. The professor looked pained but played the polite card.

Neither noticed how angry Jim was, neither saw his effort to stay calm, neither observed the tenseness in his fists and jaw and in the set of his mouth. Wade and Jim sat, opened their napkins, and placed them on their laps, and Barbara began to chatter about what a coincidence it was that they'd all chosen the same restaurant.

When the four of them had ordered, the professor began to talk, telling them of a recent award he'd received. Barbara praised him for his achievement, which pleased him enormously. Then he turned to Wade and began to explain that he had just proposed to Barbara and pointed to a beautiful blue velvet ring box on the table.

Wade glanced quickly at Jim and could see that he was startled and saw the fiery colour of anger rise again in Jim's face. The professor, as Jim called him, ignored Jim and, turning to Barbara, said, "Well, what do you say? Can we set a date?"

Wade, looking at Jim, could hardly contain himself. He wanted to laugh out loud at the expression on Jim's face, at the colour of his skin, at his clenched fists, at his tightened jawline. Jim got the professor's attention by saying "Now just a minute," and Wade surreptitiously looked at Barbara, fearful that she would end up hurt by Jim's anger. But incredibly Barbara winked at him. Wade's grin filled his face, and he thought, *She understands! She knows he loves her, and . . . she loves Jim! Oh, this is gonna be good! This is one they are gonna tell their grandkids. This is great!*

Because of the exchange between Jim and the professor and because they understood Jim so well, Wade and Barbara looked at their plates. They did not want to make eye contact with Jim or the professor because they did not want to be drawn into their conversation. And they could not look at each other or they would burst out laughing. *Go to it, Jim,* they were both thinking. *Go get him!*

For Jim, it seemed as if time stood still. He was no longer even aware of Wade or Barbara; he was focused only on the professor. Jim knew he was terribly angry. His anger galvanized him into action; but as he acted, Jim shocked himself, not only by his behavior, but also by the way he felt and certainly by what he said. His voice—deep, slow, intense, loud—came out of his chest, and both the sound and the words he spoke were a surprise even to him.

The professor was looking at him now, so Jim leaned forward with eyes narrowed, neck extended, lips grimacing, and when he was eye to eye with the professor said calmly, "Professor, how foolish of you. You see, *I* am going to marry Barbara, and it's going to be this week. So I'd suggest you pick up your ring so you do not embarrass yourself any further, and you *leave! Now.*"

The silence that followed was a noise unto itself while Jim glared at the professor. The professor stared, mouth agape at Jim. Barbara and Wade continued to deliberately keep their heads down and looked only at the plates laying against the tablecloth. The professor continued to stare at Jim, his mouth open, so shocked by the tone of Jim's voice that Jim's words seemed to take more time than necessary to register. The words hadn't yet made sense to him. The silence hung heavy for another minute, and slowly the professor's eyes filled with the comprehension of what Jim had said. He was still speechless, so shocked was he by Jim's words that he did not know what to say.

Jim was also silent but kept glaring, leaning forward. Wade waited for a moment, then unable to bear the silence any longer and worried that Jim's anger would explode even further if something didn't happen, raised his head, leaned toward the professor, and said quietly, "It would probably be best if you go now, young man. We'll take care of the check."

The professor looked at Barbara, and seeing her disinclination to get involved and certainly no inclination that she would take his part, he grabbed the ring box off the table, muttered the word *barbarians* under his breath, and stood up. He turned toward Barbara and said loudly and indignantly to the air above her head, "Good night, Barbara." And then he turned his back to them and left.

They sat in silence. Jim too was now staring at the table. He was still in shock, not understanding why he'd reacted so vehemently. Thoughts that Barbara would be furious with him passed through his head. Wade knew that something had to be said, so when he saw that the professor had left the restaurant and would not hear what he said, he pounded Jim on the back, loudly acclaiming, "Congratulations, Jim, best thing you ever did, best lady you could ever marry, when's the wedding?"

Jim looked at Wade, at his beaming face, at the laughter he was holding back, and he too started to grin, saying "Yeah, that *was* the best . . . and smartest thing I ever did, wasn't it?" as if Barbara wasn't even present. Wade, still grinning, looked at Barbara, and his heart lurched as he realized that she deserved so much more from Jim. What had just happened wasn't fair to Barbara. He wondered how she would handle this. Jim needed to say something, do something. *Now.*

But true to form, always thinking of others, Barbara quipped, "Yeah, Jim, it *is* the best thing you ever did. I thought for a minute you were gonna do something silly like act impulsively!" The ice was broken. Wade thought, *That Barbara is a trouper, she's one in a million!* Both Jim and Wade relaxed, and miracle of miracles, they all burst out laughing. They laughed so hard and for so long that their ribs hurt, they had tears in their eyes, and their jaw muscles felt tired.

It looked to Wade as if Jim had hit the jackpot and that he and Barbara had just struck a deal! Wade guffawed with glee. He was so pleased! His cheeks hurt from smiling so much! Wade looked at Jim, hoping he'd speak. He was relieved to see that Jim realized that he needed to say something to Barbara; and Wade crossed his fingers under the table and, for good measure, sent a prayer to heaven asking God to make it right between Jim and Barbara.

Jim leaned toward Barbara, looked at her face, and took her hand. He was quiet for a moment, trying to put his thoughts in proper form. Then he said, "Barbara, I'm sorry that I just blurted that out, . . . but it did take almost losing you for me to realize just how much you mean to me. Will you marry me? Can we elope this weekend? I will do everything in my power to make you happy and to make up for this crazy stuff I just pulled tonight. I love you, Barb. I think I've been head over heels in love with you ever since we met and too dumb to know it. Please forgive me for doing this so clumsily."

Barbara knew that she had to take a leap of faith at that very moment. She hadn't expected this. She had never thought a proposal would come in this manner and didn't quite know what to do. Yet she knew that this was a moment that was important to her and Jim's future. She understood that right now, right this minute, Jim was more fragile than he'd ever admit because even he was stunned by what had happened.

He hadn't expected this either, she realized. He wasn't prepared. In fact, he was probably frightened by this new and unexpected commitment. She struggled to find what felt right to her and sent a quick prayer to God, asking Him to put the right words into her mouth and help her do what He wanted for her, what was also best for Jim. God was to answer her prayer through the next words that Jim spoke.

Jim noticed Barbara's hesitation and felt a pang of fear. A wave of adrenaline washed through his body, bringing with it the most terrible fear he'd ever experienced. *Barbara is going to refuse. She just considers me a friend. What have I done? I've lost her. I've turned her away so adamantly for so long that she can never trust me. Oh God, please help me, don't let me lose her.*

Jim knew now that he loved her, had loved her for a very long time. He realized that he'd been hiding from his feelings. He hated to admit it, but he'd been afraid—of what he wasn't really sure. He wasn't even sure whether or not she loved him! Quickly, right this minute, he needed to do something, say something, tell her how he felt, hope that what he said would let her know that he loved her with all his heart. But what should he say, how would he explain, what could justify how badly he'd acted?

His fear mounted and was so great that his mouth was dry while his hands were clammy with sweat, and his heart pounded in his chest, matching the throbbing of a vein in his neck. *Please, God, put the right words in my mouth. Please, God, help me, don't let me lose her.*

So Jim took the plunge, followed his impulse, and the words flew unchecked by his mind, created from his heart. "Barb, I know that church, your faith, and God mean everything to you. I respect and admire that. I want to make you happy, give you everything I can. I can't promise you that I will believe. In fact, I probably never will. But I do promise you that I will *always* go to church with you and support you in your faith. I promise that we will be a united family that way. All I ask is that you accept that I cannot make a personal commitment to believing unless something changes in me in the future. But I will try my best and will always accompany you to church and to church functions. I promise you. I realize now how dumb I've been, how much you mean to me . . . Please say yes . . . Please give me a chance to make everything up to you . . . Please let me prove to you that I will do everything in my power to make you happy. Please marry me."

Barbara knew that Jim had given her all he could, and she thanked God for helping him make the decision to attend church with her. She knew that with his promise to attend church, God would be able to work on Jim's heart. Being in church would give him the opportunity to learn about God. He would listen to what came from the altar so he could support Barbara in her faith as he promised. This would open the door for God to touch his heart.

Barbara had her answer. She understood that God had provided an answer to her prayer through Jim's words about church and so she too followed her heart, content in the knowledge that she would have God's blessing, and said, "Yes, Jim, I will marry you. And if you really want to elope, I'd like it if Wade will come with us and be our best man . . . If he will agree to this, then I will elope with you this weekend!"

When Barbara accepted Jim's proposal, Wade recognized the sacrifice Barbara was making for Jim. Because of Grandma's death and the birth of Andrew just weeks ago, Barbara knew that if Jim wanted to marry right away, she could not have the large wedding she had always dreamed of. Not only was it not fitting given what was happening with the family, but there was also no time. Sarah, Caleb and Josh were still hurting from Grandma's death, and so were the rest of them. Barbara also understood Jim; knew he was surprised by this turn of events even though he was sincere in wanting to marry her. So, in that moment, just on the faith she had in how God had inspired Jim to tell her that he would always attend church with her, Barbara turned everything over to her Heavenly Father, knowing that He could have engineered things differently, but for some reason, this was what He brought to them and she was going to be thankful.

Wade could also see that Barbara understood Jim and understood how skittish he was about her faith, her youth, and the commitment Jim would feel this required of him. It was as if Wade could see into Barbara's heart and could see her relinquish all the youthful hopes and dreams she'd had for a wonderful family wedding—and did so for Jim's sake.

Wade also saw that Barbara had recognized that Jim was still surprised by what had happened, and that for some reason, it was important that their marriage take place now. Barbara loved him enough to recognize his need and give up her own. Wade could only think, *Jim, you better well appreciate what this gal is giving you.*

Because Barbara had asked, Wade went with them, intending only to stay for the ceremony, more to give the bride away than to be Jim's best man. After the ceremony, they insisted he stay and joked about it being a much better story for their grandkids if he stayed. So Wade did, and they had a wonderful time together. Barbara told them that they were making memories!

They were married on September 6. When they returned from a four-day honeymoon, Wade was still with them! Barbara gave notice to vacate from her tiny studio apartment and moved into Jim's apartment until they too could find a house to purchase.

Jim was happier than he'd ever been in his life. He was fully aware of the incredible gift he'd been given to have Barbara as his wife, and he wanted to make her happy. He wanted to be all she deserved, all she seemed to think he was. He also knew what a special friend he had in Wade and that Wade had recognized the love that existed between Jim and Barbara and had had the courage to act upon it. Who else had such a good friend that even his wife wanted that friend to join them on their honeymoon? Ohh, he'd never live this one down.

Barbara and Jim broke the news to their family by telephone right after they were married. Matt was concerned that Jim had not given him the courtesy of first talking to him as Barbara's brother and sort of everyday guardian. But like everyone else, he liked Jim, knew he was settled in a good career, and had certainly noticed the way he and Barbara looked at each other. They obviously loved each other, so the whole family gave them their blessing and could hardly wait for their return so they could get the details about what had precipitated the elopement, and learn why Wade went with them! That should be a good story!

When the family saw that Jim accompanied Barbara to church, even though he sat in the back of the church while she was in choir and even though he didn't actively participate, they were thrilled. Jim had come, and it made their hearts glad. Barbara and Jim invited the family to join them in the sacristy after church so they could all pray with the ministers and receive the wedding blessing.

Barbara was overjoyed with the scripture the minister provided for their blessing. It was a verse found in the Apocrypha section of the Bible in Song of the Three Holy Children verse 17 that said, *"Like as in the burnt offerings of rams and bullocks, and like as in ten thousands of fat lambs: so let our sacrifice be in thy sight this day, and grant that we may wholly go after thee: for they shall not be confounded that put their trust in thee."*

Barbara was especially delighted with the verse because it addressed Jim's commitment to go to church with her. She was touched with the words in that verse that asked that they go "wholly" after God, for this was her wish for them as a family. It brought to mind another verse she loved from Psalm 5:11 which said, *"But let all those that put their trust in thee rejoice: let them ever shout for joy, because thou defendest them: let them also that love thy name be joyful in thee."*

The minister told them that those whose faith revolves around scripture believe that the Bible not only records the historical words and deeds of God but also provides them with helpful advice. He also said that God speaks through scripture of the many blessings he gladly offers and how to become a part of the bride of Christ. God intends that the Bible be the help manual the children of God rely on when they have important decisions to make or problems to solve. It also teaches them that good spirits (the Holy Spirit and God's angels) and bad spirits (Satan and his helpers) have a tremendous impact on our world and on our lives as they battle for our souls. The Bible also clearly warns to carefully discern what is good for us and what is harmful, and much of this wisdom would develop from studying God's words and from the services at church.

Barbara realized that because Jim was now committed to attending church, he would begin to hear God's words and begin to learn. Soon she hoped, these words would begin to take root in his heart and begin the transformation that would bring him the great joy she wanted for him. Barbara decided to place a special offering in the offertory and to pray diligently, not only to thank God for bringing Jim into her life, but also to ask that He work to bring forth a beautiful and bountiful harvest of faith from Jim's heart.

Chapter Six

BARBARA AND PAUL

Barbara and Jim were happy together. Being married seemed natural to them. The friendship that they had shared for so many years was one that now enhanced their union as husband and wife. The past ten months had whizzed by for them. They marveled that the timing for everything they did had been so perfect. Wade had moved out of Jim's apartment about five months before Jim proposed because he had purchased a home of his own.

During that time, Jim and Barbara spent much of their free time helping Wade repair, repaint, and furnish his new home. Therefore, it was only fitting that after Jim's surprising proposal and their sudden elopement Wade helped them redecorate Jim's apartment to Barbara's taste. All three of them felt that their efforts had paid off, and even more importantly, Wade was ready for Bara's arrival.

When Wade returned from Iraq with Bara, Bara slipped into the family's heart as if he'd always been there. He was a wonderful boy, happy, well adjusted, and miracle of miracles, able to run and climb and play just like all the other children his age. Wade not only brought Bara back from Iraq but also brought the news that he'd filled out all the applications necessary to adopt Heza. He was told that the adoption process would take approximately six months and was walking on clouds. Wade's joy dominated his expression.

He lost twenty pounds from all the activity required to keep up with Bara, and his energy level soared. He couldn't wait to get home at night to spend time with Bara. He'd proudly bring Bara for visits to everyone in the family to show them something new that Bara had learned to do. Thus, ultimately everyone bonded with Bara and he became another member of the family, as had Wade.

Wade also found a housekeeper. She'd arrive at the house at seven in the morning and leave at seven in the evening. Sometimes she brought Bara to her own home when she had to catch up on some personal duties; but otherwise, she spent her days at Wade's, taking care of food shopping, cooking, cleaning, laundry, and of course, Bara. She was a grandmother herself, but when her family moved out of state, she found herself with too much time on her hands. She loved being needed again and with her family gone was even available to stay overnight whenever Wade had to travel for business.

Hildegard didn't coddle Bara. She made him do things for himself and patiently taught him how to load the dishwasher, pull the covers on the bed tautly when making it, and to say "thank you" and "please" and "may I." Wade was proud of his learning prowess, just as any other poppa would be, and Wade was also delighted with the loving care provided by Hildegard.

When Sarah learned the name of Wade's housekeeper, she clutched her ribs and bent over from the force of her laughter. Sarah was reminded of the story Grandma used to tell about a young family with a housekeeper named Hildegard. She and Caleb (and Josh by phone when Sarah called to tell him) laughed with the memory of how Grandma used that story to make them better appreciate their mother and also teach them to look into someone's heart rather than just respond to their words. Grandma was always telling stories that contained a lesson for them, but they'd particularly remembered this story because at first they'd been afraid of Hildegard.

As Grandma told the story, her voice became gruff and guttural by her use of a strong German accent, and it had taken a while before they could get past the almost frightening tone to recognize the loving, caring heart of the Hildegard in Grandma's story. And that was *just exactly* what Grandma wanted them to learn, along with the premise of the story that taught them to appreciate and help their mom.

Everything seemed to be going well for all of them when tragedy struck with a vengeance. Paul died suddenly and without warning. They were all devastated. Matt was distraught and shocked by how angry he was with God. He couldn't understand why God would take Paul when things were finally going his way, especially after all the heartache that Paul's life had brought him. Matt knew life was unfair, but this seemed too much to bear. Unable to accept what had happened to Paul, Matt blamed God. The tragedy also reawakened Sarah's grief over Grandma's death. She no longer had the energy to plan their wedding, and this angered Matt even further.

Barbara too was devastated. Paul was her brother, her gentle, loving older brother who was always there to help others. How could this be? How was she to reconcile this event? Was she just supposed to accept what happened, have faith, and trust that God had a purpose for this? *There had to be something to learn from this, something important.* Barbara buried herself with work and with plans for the house that she and Jim hoped to purchase. But still, she felt helpless and hopeless. And sometimes she wondered what would happen to all of them, to the faith of the family that had trusted God in everything. She felt afraid of the anger she felt at the terrible injustice of Paul's death.

Jim wished he could alleviate everyone's suffering, but quite frankly, he didn't know what to do. He *did* know that talking things out was a good way to ease pain and so he invited Matt and Sarah and Ann and Caleb to their home for dinner. Because he understood that Barbara was suffering, he told Barbara that he would handle everything for their fellowship.

He visited the fancy deli in town and bought cold, thinly sliced London broil, potato salad, macaroni salad, a tossed green salad with feta cheese, a couple of loaves of crisp Cuban bread, and some sweet Irish butter he knew they all liked. He also bought ice cream, hot fudge, walnuts, and whipped cream because they also liked ice cream sundaes. To make everything easy, Jim purchased some fancy heavy-duty throwaway dishes but used real cutlery as he set the table.

Barbara was grateful for the thought and effort Jim had placed into the fellowship and for saving her from doing the work attached to having everyone over. Marrying him was the best thing she'd ever done. He was so good, so loving, and considerate; and whether he believed it or not, he was a godly man. His courage to stand up for his principles was amazing!

She was grateful for the fellowship Jim had organized because she was still in a fog over Paul's sudden death and had, like Matt and Sarah, lost the energy she usually had for such tasks. It would be good for the family to be together. She *wanted* to talk about what had happened. And it was going to take place because of Jim.

Everyone was glad that it was a no-fuss meal. They weren't ready for fuss since they were still grieving and burdened by the questions they had about why Paul had to go through so much pain and then die so young. They ate with very little conversation. The food was good, hearty, and plain. When the table was cleared and they were ready for dessert, Jim heated the hot fudge and began to dish out the ice cream. Then slowly, tentatively, they began to talk about Paul. Paul's life had been incredibly difficult and none of it was his fault; none of it was something he had brought on by his own errors.

When Paul was only seven years old, he was sent to military school because both parents had to work to pay off their parents' astronomical medical bills. Paul had loved the school and done well scholastically. He'd joined the football team and met a coach who was concerned only with winning, thereby boosting his career, a coach who did unconscionable things to make a name for himself.

This coach wanted to win every game they played. He believed that if the team did well under his leadership, he would obtain a position at a bigger and better school and eventually move to the big leagues. Therefore, winning was all-important. He'd wanted to make the best of his team, but he did so in the most unscrupulous, damaging, and unconscionable way possible. He gave amphetamines to the little seven—to twelve-year-old children on his athletic teams, telling them they were vitamins. He believed that this would enable them to win. He was never caught. No one knew what he had done until years later.

By the time the coach left this school for a larger one, he'd arranged for the children to obtain "stronger" vitamins from someone off the campus. He hoped to move the blame elsewhere should it ever be noticed that the children had been compromised. No one realized what was happening. And now, almost thirty years later, few were aware that this had occurred. In those days, few parents knew what signs to watch for, so there was virtually no one to help these boys.

As far as Jim was concerned, this coach should have been prosecuted, then drawn and quartered. If so many years had not gone by, Jim would have tried to tell this story to Bill O'Reilly who still fought for the underdog through his television show, *The O'Reilly Factor*, and still didn't seem to worry about whose toes he stepped on. Jim hoped he'd always continue to do this.

But this coach got away with what he'd done because no one figured out what had happened to these boys until so many years later. Thus, Paul became a drug addict without his knowledge, without his consent, without his understanding, and fought against it for the rest of his life, finally succeeding against all odds.

Paul had been attending Mariners School between workboat runs, and as he moved through his instruction, he was given greater responsibilities aboard his vessel. At first, he simply wanted to provide a better life for his family. But later, he found that he loved learning and enjoyed the added responsibilities at work. He gained the respect of other men by his willingness to work hard, and never asked anyone to do something he wasn't willing to do himself. He was promoted from hand to second mate to first mate.

Just before he'd died, he obtained the coveted captain's license he'd always dreamed of. Finally, everything was going his way. His company had promised him his own boat! He just had to wait until one was available. He was happy again. He was over the pain his wife had continually brought him, and he'd found his children.

Paul had arranged to fly to Texas to meet with his children after so many years apart, and he was ecstatic. He'd bought new clothes, gotten a chic haircut that managed his thick, curly blond locks, and bought lots of gifts for his daughters. He had long conversations with the family about what ten—and eleven-year-old girls were like, what he should talk about, and whether or not they would like him, accept him after all these years, allow him into their life. He was terribly nervous yet deliciously happy at the same time.

Just a few months before he'd learned where the children were living, he'd asked his minister if he could become a deacon in the church. He'd wanted to go to the streets to bring God's words to the many places where those using drugs might be found. He wanted to help others as he had been helped. He felt that he might be able to strengthen some who were struggling to free themselves of the terrible curse of addiction. He understood that Satan was the power behind addiction. Satan targeted innocent children hoping they would become his victims.

Matt and Paul had often discussed one of the Bible verses that had helped Paul when he was struggling through the tough times. Matt read the verse from Matthew 12:45 which said, *"Then goeth he, and taketh with himself seven other spirits more wicked than himself, and they enter in and dwell there: and the last state of that man is worse than the first. Even so shall it be also unto this wicked generation."*

Paul always said that if an addict could accept the fact, believe the fact that it was a spirit or many spirits sent by Satan that kept an addict bound, they would understand that they had an enemy. They would have something tangible to fight. He felt that it was easier to fight back if one knew what you were fighting. If you knew where to direct your anger, you had a better chance of winning.

Paul knew that many addicts vacillated between blaming God and blaming themselves for their weakness, but he felt that this only made them feel more powerless. It opened the door to depression and self-doubt.

Paul said, "If you understand what is happening to you and why, you can fight back. You know what it is you are fighting. You need to know you can ask God for help, and in His power, you can order that spirit to leave. The Bible teaches us to discern the spirits, recognize them, and use the power that Christ has over them to make them leave."

He said that God knew Satan's power and how difficult it was for an addict to be free of the hold those spirits had over them. Paul would teach them Grandma's trick of yelling the word *no* aloud whenever a thought came that would not be good for them to entertain.

Paul felt that discerning the spirits was an important part of recovery. The Bible clearly stated that man was not stronger than Satan or the spirits Satan used. Only Christ and His angels were stronger. He recited a verse from Ezekiel 44:23 which said, *"And they shall teach my people the difference between the holy and profane, and cause them to discern between the unclean and the clean."*

Paul wanted to share his experiences and what had helped him and what he believed. He felt that there was so much to learn from the Bible about discerning the spirits, about understanding them, recognizing them when they came for you.

"You can try to visualize putting your hands around the spirit's neck and throwing it out. With the help of God, if you understand what you fight, if you understand the power and work of Satan and believe in and know how to employ the greater power of God, you will defeat that spirit," he'd say.

Paul also believed that Satan went after children so he could prevent them from ever becoming a child of God. Children and young adults were the most vulnerable. Satan would use drugs and alcohol to imprison them so as they grew into adulthood they would no longer have the ability to discern the spirits or choose the path God wanted for them.

Satan knew that if God obtained a certain number of souls for the First Resurrection, it would signify Satan's end. Satan was in a fight for his life but so were these children whom Satan sought to trap, and they needed to know this. Paul desperately wanted to help them. "You can't fight an enemy when you don't know who he is, why he does what he does, or how he works!" Paul said.

He also spoke about the various cultures during the time of Christ and of the many religions and many gods. He'd explained that the priests of these pagan religions employed occult and magic to convince their followers of their power. He'd quoted a verse from Exodus 7:22, saying, *"And the magicians of Egypt did so with their enchantments."* He said that they also used hallucinogenic drugs, as did the medicine men and shamans of many cultures to follow.

Paul had been impressed by a passage in the book of Luke that he felt could be a description of a drug addict. It was a story about a man who hid from society and lived in caves. Paul explained that living in caves could be likened to living on the streets, homeless. The Bible account said that this man was not in his right mind, was driven to rip off his clothing, and could become violent to the point where he had to be restrained, which Paul felt could describe the state one might be in from the use or sudden absence of drugs.

When Christ approached this man, Christ found him possessed of many devils, many spirits, which drove the man to this behavior. Christ ordered these spirits to leave the man, and they did, freeing him of their influence. Immediately, the man became himself and could then sit at the foot of Christ, clothed, healed and thankful to be free of the spirits that bound him. Paul pointed out that this story could be found in Luke 8:27-36 and says in verse 29, *"For he had commanded the unclean spirit to come out of the man. For oftentimes it had caught him: and he was kept bound with chains and in fetters; and he brake the bands, and was driven of the devil into the wilderness."*

Paul studied all the parts of the Bible that addressed evil or unclean spirits. These spirits were also known as powers and principalities and were associated with the fallen angels that Satan ruled. He explained that in Matthew 10:1, the Bible describes Christ giving not only the instructions but also the power to his disciples to cast out unclean spirits from those they would encounter so they would be healed. It said, *"And when he had called unto him his twelve disciples, he gave them power against unclean spirits, to cast them out, and to heal all manner of sickness and all manner of disease."*

Paul went on to say that Matthew 8:16 explains that there were *many* possessed by evil spirits in Christ's time and that He cast them out by his word and they were healed: *"When the even was come, they brought unto him many that were possessed with devils: and he cast out the spirits with his word, and healed all that were sick."*

Paul had once been asked by a recovering addict why he thought it possible that drugs or alcohol were used in those days, and Paul answered him by explaining that evil spirits caused many disturbances, which included physical and mental problems, not only drug and alcohol addiction. He reminded him of the accounts of hallucinogenic drugs used by sorcerers, healers, witch doctors, even by certain tribes of people.

He went on to explain that drunkenness and erratic and malevolent behavior and many mental illnesses could be caused and governed by these spirits and were mentioned often in the Bible. Ephesians 6:12 warns, *"For we wrestle not against flesh and blood, but against principalities, against powers, against the rulers of the darkness of this world, against spiritual wickedness in high places."*

Paul often spoke about the end-times when many evil spirits would live in men and provoke them to terrible acts. He'd read in Revelation 16:14 that God warned, *"For they are the spirits of devils, working miracles, which go forth unto the kings of the earth and of the whole world, to gather them to the battle of that great day of God Almighty."* Paul felt that this was happening today and evident in the reports we hear of suicide bombers, terrorists, the murders of children, and the increasing prevalence of drug and alcohol addiction that made men unable to recognize, thus fight, evil.

They remembered Paul and his goodness. They realized that when they listened to Paul speak, they'd felt his passion for doing good in the world and could see that the faith he had in God was a tender, gentle, strong, and beautiful faith. Sometimes they thought he was whispering when he spoke, but he wasn't. It was just the way he delivered what he said—so lovingly, so sure, so gently.

He'd been through so much pain in his life and yet he'd never complained. He never blamed God. In fact, he never asked for material or personal things, only that he could provide for his family and stay faithful to God. He'd been content in that. He'd been able to accept and trust God's will for his life. *Why couldn't they?*

They were all silent for a moment. Then Sarah spoke, and even she could hear the anger in her voice, an anger that came from bewilderment, from not being able to understand God. She wondered if her faith was being tested. She wondered why all the really good people had to suffer or die young and the rotten ones prospered and lived a long life.

When she said this, Caleb rose from his chair to retrieve the Bible from the coffee table in the adjacent living room. He brought it to the dining room table where they sat and opened it to Psalm 73: 2-3 so he could read to them about the prosperity of those who were evil: *"But as for me, my feet were almost gone; my steps had well nigh slipped. For I was envious at the foolish, when I saw the prosperity of the wicked."*

And then he read from Psalm 73:17 which said, *"Until I went into the sanctuary of God; then understood I their end,"* and then from Psalm 73:19, *"How are they brought into desolation, as in a moment! they are utterly consumed with terrors."*

"You must remember, Sarah, God clearly tells us that the faithful will suffer but also promises that we will never be given more than we can carry. God also tells us that in the end, there will be no more sorrow and no more tears. We can find this in Revelation 21:4, *'And God shall wipe away all tears from their eyes; and there shall be no more death, neither sorrow, nor crying, neither shall there be any more pain: for the former things are passed away.'*

"Our Heavenly Father also promises us in Revelation 21:7-8 that the evil that caused us so much heartache will be cast into the lake of fire forever. *'He that overcometh shall inherit all things; and I will be his God, and he shall be my son. But the fearful, and unbelieving, and the abominable, and murderers, and whoremongers, and sorcerers, and idolaters, and all liars, shall have their part in the lake which burneth with fire and brimstone: which is the second death.'*

"God explains that as we go through our difficult times, we are being tried in the fire and that we will come out unscathed and pure. He says in Zechariah 13:9, *'And I will bring forth the third part through the fire, and I will refine them as silver is refined, and I will try them as gold is tried,'* and in Revelations 3:18-19, *'I counsel thee to buy of me gold tried in the fire, that thou mayest be rich; and white raiment, that thou mayest be clothed, and that the shame of thy nakedness do not appear; and anoint thine eyes with eyesalve, that thou mayest see. As many as I love, I rebuke and chasten: be zealous therefore, and repent.'"*

Then Sarah remembered that Grandma had shown her where God had spoken of the "mysteries" of the Bible and had promised to open their understanding if they sought that understanding with a pure heart. Sarah took the Bible from Caleb and found Luke 24:45 and read, *"Then opened he their understanding, that they might understand the scriptures."*

"There is another verse that always helped me," Sarah told them. "It's in Jeremiah 33:3 and says, '*Call unto Me, and I will answer thee, and show thee great and mighty things, which thou knowest not.*'"

Caleb said that Grandma taught him to have the courage to speak up about the Bible and what God wanted of us and for us, and about what He had done for him. "Before Paul's example, I'd been shy about speaking up, wondering if what I said would cause others to scoff at me, but Paul never hesitated. He always had that courage. And he once read from Ephesians 6:19 the words '*And for me, that utterance may be given unto me, that I may open my mouth boldly, to make known the mystery of the gospel.*' God wants all of us to do this."

Barbara began to cry and asked if anyone could tell her about Paul *now. Where is he, what is he thinking, what is he doing?* Matt said that Barbara's questions had also been in his and Sarah's minds and they had just made the agreement with one another that for the next few weeks, they would search the Bible to see if they could find the answer to that question. When they found it—and they were sure they would—they would share it with all of them. They reminded everyone that Grandma had always said that when they needed a question answered or they faced a difficult circumstance, they'd find what they needed in the Bible.

Sarah reminded them that Grandma used to comfort them with the words she'd found in Romans 8:28 where God said, *"And we know that all things work together for good to them that love God, to them who are the called according to his purpose."*

So they concluded their evening with plans to meet again in three weeks at Caleb's house when Matt and Sarah would tell them what they learned about where Paul might be and what happened in and after death. Jim had listened carefully to their conversation. He'd heard only sincerity and trust and love. He'd seen integrity in their discussion and a united front in terms of their faith; he learned from listening to them and wanted to learn more. He did not let the others know of his interest; he remained quiet. He wanted to know more about death. And he doubted, telling himself, *They will never find what they are looking for.*

Jim heard the cynicism in his voice and enjoyed it, feeling that he'd never be caught up in the disappointment in God that the family would soon encounter. *They will not find their answers in the Bible.* He felt guilty because he knew he would not share these thoughts with Barbara. Somehow this didn't sit well with his conscience.

As they began clearing the dessert dishes from the table, Barbara confessed that she had had an argument with Paul a few days before he died and that it weighed heavily on her heart. She and Paul always had a very special relationship. Paul would hug her and tell her how proud he was of her and of her excellent education and how smart she was. He would tell her that he loved her very much and remind her that she'd been the one who had always given him the very best of holidays because of all the love and all the preparations she put forth.

She said that she loved him very much and was proud of him and of what he had finally been able to do with his life. Despite how unfair life had been to him, he was kind and gentle and loving. He was protective and had wanted to meet Jim to make sure he approved.

Barbara went on to tell the family that she had noticed how nervous Paul was about meeting his children because they had been apart for so many years and also because he would have to face the woman who he had loved so much and who had hurt him so deeply. Barbara told them that she'd suggested he ask if the children could come to him instead of going to them. If he did this, then the whole family could help him in the reacquainting process. She had said that for too long Paul had let his ex-wife push him around. Her words had hurt Paul, and he'd responded by saying he was handling everything as best he could and then had abruptly left her house.

She wished she could have retracted her words. She knew that he'd been hurt by what she'd said. She'd called him and left a message saying she was sorry for what she'd said, but then—and Barbara began to sob—he'd died, and she never knew if everything was okay between them. Barbara said that it still weighed heavily on her heart.

Matt wanted to comfort his little sister and so he reminded her that Paul knew how the devil worked. "Remember, Barbara, Paul knew who the devil was. He knew about the spirits that look for ways to bring us down by separating us from one another and from God. Paul understood that the words Satan used in the Garden of Eden he also uses on us today. Satan causes our children to 'eat' of a substance that brings them harm, saying as he did then, 'Go ahead, surely God says it won't harm you. It will only open your understanding!' I mean, it's amazing how the temptation of drug addiction is so similar to the temptation Satan brought Adam and Eve! Listen to this from Genesis 3:13: '*The serpent beguiled me, and I did eat.*' And from Revelation 12:9, '*Called the Devil, and Satan, which deceiveth the whole world.*' So remember, Barbara, Paul understood Satan and also understood that you were just trying to do your best. He knew that you said what you did out of concern for him."

Jim went to her side and took her in his arms, and she sobbed for a while as the family continued to clean up, not knowing what else to do. When Barbara stopping crying, she went to the powder room to wash her face, and the others gave her a hug when she came back to the living room.

They reminded her that Paul had never held a grudge and always came back smiling, forgiving, forgetting, teasing about their silly antics. And Barbara, remembering Paul's loving heart, knew they were right and was comforted. "After all," they added, "Paul had been very nervous about the upcoming visit to see his children."

Barbara told Sarah that she would look forward to learning what she and Matt would find in their studies about life after death, and with Jim's arm across her shoulder to comfort her, they said their goodbyes and marveled at how many subjects they had covered in one night and how it had been so good to talk about Paul.

When everyone left, Jim and Barbara got ready for bed, deciding to lie in bed and talk for a while before they went to sleep. Barbara told Jim that she appreciated his support and all he had done to make the evening such a success. She told him how glad she was that she had married him, that God had worked out such a wonderful quirky way to get them to marry before they had time to worry that it might *not* work! Jim said that he thought he was the luckiest guy in the world that Barbara had accepted him. Inside, he still felt guilty about his private thoughts that Matt and Sarah's expedition into the Bible would never bring them the answers they sought. *Well, maybe it's about time they see reality*, he thought.

They spoke for a while about Satan and how he came to earth to try to get mankind to follow him instead of God. Barbara reminded Jim of the story they heard in church last week about Satan's separation from God. She reached to the nightstand and opened their bedside Bible to Isaiah 14: 12-15 and read, *"How art thou fallen from heaven, O Lucifer, son of the morning! how art thou cut down to the ground, which didst weaken the nations! For thou hast said in thine heart, I will ascend into heaven, I will exalt my throne above the stars of God: I will sit also upon the mount of the congregation, in the sides of the north: I will ascend above the heights of the clouds; I will be like the most High. Yet thou shalt be brought down to hell, to the sides of the pit."*

"What a waste," Jim said. "Here he had everything . . . sitting on one side of God and wanting the other side, so he ended up losing it all because of his jealousy."

"Yeah, but he will lose even more in the end and we will gain so much if we stand firm in our faith by doing as God asks us to do," Barbara said.

They settled into their pillows and under the huge comforter with Jim's arm across Barbara's shoulders. Because Barbara had been so despondent over Paul's death, every other concern she had also surfaced to cause her worry. She longed to hear Jim say that his heart was beginning to open, that God had touched his heart and that he was beginning to believe again. Jim had already said that since he'd met Barbara and her family, he'd seen only integrity and honesty in how they lived. He saw pain eased by their understanding of the larger picture God had taught them. He'd even said that he saw hearts striving to do the right thing and trying to make restitution if they harmed one or the other.

Barbara's heart had overflowed with gratitude that her Heavenly Father had brought about this miracle, but now she commiserated over the fact that Jim simply could not connect his heart to the heart of God. And so they fell asleep, each loving the other while secretly harbouring concerns for one another yet content in the hope that all would be okay in the end.

A few weeks later, Matt telephoned Jim and asked him if he and Barbara would join them at Caleb's house that Friday evening. He and Sarah wanted to share some of what they'd found in the Bible concerning life after death. When they met at Caleb's, everyone saw the notes that Matt and Sarah developed and learned that in addition to the journal Sarah had written about Grandma's life, they were now putting together a journal about Paul's life and death.

Matt and Sarah were excited by their findings. Jim was curious, but skeptical. Matt began his description of what they had learned by reciting the Apostle's Creed, reiterating the words *"And He descended into hell, and on the third day He rose again and ascended into heaven"* and reciting from Luke 24:46 *"And to rise from the dead the third day."* Then Matt asked one question: "Can anyone negate these words that say after Christ died, He spent three days in hell before ascending to God?"

There was silence. In fact, Jim even gasped in amazement, wondering why he'd never put that together before. Then Matt went on to say, "So the next question is what did Christ *do* in hell for three days? We found a passage in 1 Peter 3:19 that said, *'By which also he went and preached unto the spirits in prison.'* This indicates what Christ *did*. And another in 1 Peter 4:6 explains *why* Christ went to hell, for it says, *'For this cause was the gospel preached also to them that are dead, that they might be judged according to men in the flesh, but live according to God in the spirit.'*

"Then we found this in John 5:25, *'Verily, verily, I say unto you, The hour is coming, and now is, when the dead shall hear the voice of the Son of God: and they that hear shall live.'* This tells us the outcome of what Christ did in hell! He brought testimony of the gospel to all who had died. Therefore, those who died in their sins could now choose to accept Christ, understand His sacrifice, and receive the gift of the forgiveness of sin if they were repentant! We found in John 8:56 that Abraham, who died righteous, saw Christ when He was bringing this testimony in hell, and he was glad! *'Your father Abraham rejoiced to see my day: and he saw it, and was glad.'*

"In Ephesians 4:9-10, it says, *'Now that he ascended, what is it but that he also descended first into the lower parts of the earth? He that descended is the same also that ascended up far above all heavens, that he might fill all things,'* and wait, there's more. In Romans 14:9, God tells us, *'For to this end Christ both died, and rose, and revived, that he might be Lord both of the dead and the living.'*

"What can we learn from this? Well, when we remember the story of the rich man and the beggar named Lazarus that we all know from Luke 16: 19-31 we know that when they died, the rich man went into a place of torments, and Lazarus the beggar went into the place where he was welcomed into the comfort of Abraham's bosom. Thus, we know there are at least two different places. From this story, we also know that those in both realms of the dead seem perfectly aware of what goes on in the other realm and to some extent what occurs on earth. Luke 16:23 says, *'And in hell he lift up his eyes, being in torments, and seeth Abraham afar off, and Lazarus in his bosom.'*

"We know that Christ's perfect death opened the way for His gospel to be brought to all men, and this meant that even those who died had the opportunity to receive the forgiveness of sin. However, it is also evident that not everyone in eternity, just as not everyone here on earth, avails themselves of the opportunity to partake of what God offers. Therefore, what can we conclude?"

Caleb said, "First of all, if you are trying to put this into the perspective of Paul, I would have to say that Paul is in the realm where Abraham is and that everyone in that realm today are those who accept Christ and have obtained the forgiveness of their sins. Paul worked hard to practice what Christ asked of him, he believed in Him, and always sought the forgiveness of his sins while he was here on earth, so we can conclude that Paul went where Abraham is."

They all knew about the experience of faith that Matt had had in church the previous Sunday. Following an animated and excited discussion, they concluded that Paul, whom Matt had seen dressed in a black deacon's suit, had wanted them to know that he was bringing testimony in eternity to all the souls who had died in their addictions without ever having known God and therefore died without the forgiveness of their sins. Paul brought them the testimony that taught them of God and of how they could now obtain the forgiveness of their sins while in eternity and while grace still was available. Exactly what Paul had wanted to do here on earth! They felt that Paul, in eternity, had the freedom to circulate from one realm to the other and back again.

Everyone was choked up—even Jim. He'd never heard anything so beautiful in his life. Matt and Sarah had told them that in church last week, Matt felt a tap on his shoulder when the congregation bowed their heads and folded their hands for the opening prayer. The tap seemed to convey the words "It's okay." Matt turned to see who tapped him on the shoulder and saw Paul dressed in a black suit and white shirt even though Paul had died the previous week. Then suddenly Paul was gone.

Matt had been shocked by what happened, and when he told his minister of his experience, the minister explained that the black suit and white shirt was symbolic of Paul working as a minister in eternity, probably doing the very same work he'd wanted to do on earth, testifying to those who had been under the influence of drugs.

For a moment, Jim thought that these words made him believe it could be possible that there was a god so perfect, so all-loving, one with a plan that was all-encompassing. If so, here was truly a god Jim could worship, a god who was just, would reach *all* mankind, and would eventually deal with *all* injustice. But how could Jim believe such a story? Surely what Matt called an experience of faith had been Matt's imagination. *Yeah, how ridiculous to think otherwise!*

There was silence in the room for quite a while as they pondered what they had just heard about life after death and related it to Matt's experience. All but Jim believed every word that had been said, and it impacted their hearts with the spirit of truth and the awareness that one of the mysteries of the Bible had just been unveiled. They were filled with thankfulness and awe.

Also planted into their hearts was the awareness that God needed Paul to do this work in eternity more than He needed him to do that same work here on earth. That thought touched their hearts too. As they pondered this, they all, even Jim, silently thought, *Wow, how incredible!* Jim's thoughts added *'if it were true'* and he couldn't make the leap of faith that would require his commitment—his total acceptance.

From what they had learned, they developed a greater understanding of why a service for the departed was held every three months at church. It wasn't just to pray for their relatives or those they loved or those they worried about, it was to also help those who were working in realms that held people who had been lost to God while on this earth. And it was to pray for those who *were* lost.

Jim thought of the soldiers in Iraq, the anger that those who died may have felt for those who harmed them. Surely, God would forgive these soldiers if they carried such well-founded hatred. He also thought of the Iraqi people who didn't believe in Christ, and suddenly he knew that if he believed, he'd have to take on a big responsibility—to pray for all these people only he might understand. That is, if he believed that stuff. But then Jim wondered who would pray for those who never learned of Christ...wouldn't it have to be those who did know? And who would pray for people and circumstances that so few people were exposed to, if not those who witnessed it? Maybe, there *was* something he needed to understand here, something he was being told. *Nah, that's a lot of baloney, I'm getting carried away in some crazy fantasy. I'm lucky that I don't believe in that stuff . . . if I ever did, I'd have a massive undertaking to pray for all the terrible circumstances I've seen in Iraq.* And so Jim closed his mind and closed his heart even though his conscience seemed to tell him that he was taking the easy way out. *Too much to think about.*

He saw Barbara looking at him and saw the joy on her face and on the faces of the others. What he saw told him that they were now more accepting of Paul's death. They felt that God had explained why He took Paul into eternity and knew that Paul would be happy with God's decision. They also felt that they now had a deeper understanding that even in death God was in control. They were able to believe that Paul was happy and that they would all have a future together some day.

Their conversation left a lot for them to think about and a lot for them to do. They now realized that God had taught them that they too had been given a commission. They were to pray for those who had died without knowing God. And they were to help Paul in his work in eternity by praying for those who, because of their drug addiction, may not have known God or obtained the forgiveness of sin. And so with thoughtful hearts, now content to let Paul go, content to trust God with Paul's soul, their pain eased. God had helped them; God had soothed them and held them in His arms. Paul was okay. Once again, God, through scripture, had answered their questions. Once again God had planted something special in Jim's heart to mull over. But God had also given Jim free will and Jim would have to decide whether or not what he was learning was important enough for him to give his heart to God. Only Jim could decide to take that first leap of faith to give his yes word, and become a child of God.

Chapter Seven

AND ALL WAS WELL

Matt and Sarah finally found time to sit together and talk. "So much has happened in such a short time that it's hard to keep track of everything," Matt was saying. "We've already been married six months, and I can't believe that it's been two years since Paul died. We were so blessed that God helped us through that difficult period in our life and helped us strengthen our relationship as we went through it. I had a terrible time accepting what happened to Paul, but now I feel that he is doing what he wanted to do and that one day we'll learn that he touched many souls with his testimony."

"Well, we sure have prayed diligently for all the souls who entered into eternity under the influence of any type of addiction, especially those who never knew God because of it. How sad to think of how many have died and how much they suffered because of their addiction. Those who loved them suffered a great deal too. Sometimes it is difficult for me to contain the anger I feel toward those who trap young people just to make a profit . . . children who aren't mature enough to understand the danger, who are not yet equipped to recognize the jeopardy they put themselves in. There are so many children whose parents have not taught them about God, or about Satan, and that too is so sad. But, Matt, isn't it absolutely incredible that God's plan has provided for *everyone* . . . even those who have gone through these terrible circumstances? I now recognize that there is so much more to God's plan of salvation than I ever realized and how truly miraculous it is.

"Because of the limitations of our human mind, we're locked into our inability to comprehend what is spiritual and thus different than what we know. There is so much we don't know. For instance, time moves slowly when we are in pain and quickly when we are filled with joy. And while we don't know much about the depths of the sea or the outer limits of space, yet accept that these exist, we balk at the concept of a long-term, all-encompassing, finely engineered plan for mankind that is placed into the physics of this world. We limit ourselves by our preconceptions, and by that, we limit what we believe God can or will do."

"You're right, we do. I think there are two parts to this. One is that we think in short-term, not long-term, results. Some people can't imagine eternity, therefore cannot give this life over to making that future life better. It's kinda like choosing not to finish high school because you were offered a full-time but mediocre job. It's what you're going to miss in the future that counts. The second part is that we don't recognize or appreciate what we have been given or that it all comes from God . . . at least not until we lose it. Matt, do you think it's a form of arrogance and a sense of entitlement that makes us put aside what we can't or won't understand? Like faith and God, even like Satan? God is real, faith is real, and Satan, well, he's real . . . and quite formidable, yet many people cannot or will not believe that he exists, is a real entity who has power over us."

"Sarah, I think that what you just said about thinking long term or short term is very important. I mean, for us. For the short term, we are in a home we love, a home filled with the warmth of Grandma's furnishings, filled with our love for one another, and filled with God's blessing. We also have a great family and wonderful friends. For the long term, because we love God, Satan is bound to attack at some point. This worries me. I guess I want to prepare for the long term . . . somehow obtain the assurance that we will stand through an attack and come out of it with our faith stronger, not weaker. I guess I wonder if we have what it takes during the bad times to continue to please God. God tells us that when we go through heartache, we are being 'tried in the fire' and that if we stand firm, we will come out *better* than when we went in. I think of the words in Job 23:10 where Job said, '*But he knoweth the way that I take: when he hath tried me, I shall come forth as gold.*' I sure hope we will say what Job said as he endured the attack Satan made on him. When I start to worry, I keep telling myself over and over again the words we found in Hebrews 13:5 where God promises '*I will never leave thee, nor forsake thee,*' and this eases some of my concerns."

"Matt, I believe that as long as our long-term goal is to stay faithful to the end and our actions support our achieving this goal, we'll be okay no matter what comes. It is already January of a new year, and in just the last few months, we've experienced so many blessings. The carriage house renovation began for Elizabeth and Rebecca; Heza arrived from Iraq, making Wade the dad of *two* children; Lorraine was born to Caleb and Ann, joining little Andrew, making them parents of two also; and Mary and Kevin have had their son, Teddie! Have you seen how Rebecca and Elizabeth are with him? It's a *joy* to watch. All of a sudden our family circle has exploded, and we've *lots* of kids around.

Let's see, Rebecca and Teddie, Andrew and Lorraine, Heza and Bara, and don't forget Jayden . . . That's seven children! And we *are* keeping our focus on the long-term goal of our faith. By publishing Grandma's story about God's plan of salvation we are helping not only the children *we* know, but *everyone* who will read the story. Ohh, Matt, all the children will love Grandma's story. I want them to learn that Satan is a real danger to them and also learn what God plans for their future."

"I hope they do, Sarah. I've just had these worries lately that things are going too well! But speaking of Grandma's story, Grandma's book has finally been sent to the publisher. It was a bear getting all that text into the computer, *amazing* how Grandma wrote it all longhand. So when the book is launched, you'll be able to fulfill your dream of telling Grandma's story to *lots* of children . . . . in fact, lots of people of all ages. The publisher still has to complete the final layout and then we'll have the galley editing to do, so it will still be a little while before we have the actual book in our hands. But I love how that story explains God's plan of salvation. It will help many understand God and what He wants and what we have to do to be a part of the wonderful future He's planned. How patient God is with us, and how kind He is to give us so much time to learn. He must get terribly frustrated with all the hardened hearts and hardheads He encounters. I'm not sure about the title of the book though . . . *Grandma's Little Book of Poetry: The Story of God's Plan of Salvation* . . . It's a little long and sort of sounds like a book of poetry rather than a story. But the rest of the family liked it, so . . ."

"Yeah, the title is a little bit long and doesn't describe the premise of the book as well as I would like, but we couldn't come up with a name we liked better, Matt. Since that was the title that Grandma placed on her manuscript, it just seemed right somehow to use it."

"Oh, Matt, did you know that Lorraine was released from the hospital yesterday? Ann and Caleb are looking forward to having her home again. I've never seen Caleb so worried, never seen him pace the floor like he did at the hospital. He said that every step he took was a prayer asking God to help Lorraine. It was touch and go for a while, and I was so worried that we would lose her. Children seem to be more resilient than I'd thought . . . yet look at what happened to that little child whose parents we met in the waiting room. He had a severe lung infection. The doctor thought that an inoculation was ultimately the cause of the infection. Evidently, he had an allergy to one of the components in the inoculation and the allergic reaction was so severe that it broke down his immune system. The weakened immune system then allowed the infection to take hold. Is that possible? I mean, this is stuff every parent should know. Grandma was allergic to eggs. After years of getting the flu following a flu shot and the doctors telling her that it was impossible to get the flu from the flu shot, finally, an alternative medicine doctor explained how the egg allergy broke down her immune system and that she did indeed get the flu because of the shot. It was that IgG Standard Food Family Sensitivity Assay from Immuno Laboratories that pinpointed her allergies, and most doctors don't do or believe in that test. And would you believe that it's not covered by insurance?"

"I was surprised to learn that. Grandma even wrote to the insurance companies, documenting how much money they saved . . . thousands of dollars . . . by her learning what was causing her to get sick so often. However, they never responded, never changed course or policy. Sarah, parents *do* need to know about these things to protect their kids. I wonder if *all* the ingredients of inoculations and flu shots and the like are listed on the Internet. Can you imagine the *barrage* of shots that Bara and Heza probably had in order to come to the United States? We ought to ask Wade about that. Poor Wade, he's really got his hands full! What a loving, giving heart he has! And what adorable kids. I'm so happy to see Bara running and jumping with his prosthesis. He's amazing. It doesn't slow him down a bit. Wade's got him running for that little football when they play together in the backyard, and he catches that ball 90 percent of the time! Heza, though, is still so shy. I guess it's because she is still getting to know Bara and Wade and Hildegard. She's kind of quiet, but like Bara, she'll open up quickly as soon as she has time to adjust and know she is safe. Aren't the kids just one year apart in age?"

"Yes, Bara was born on June 12, and Heza was born on May 30, a little less than one year later. That makes Heza three and one-half years old and Bara four and one-half years old. But don't forget, Matt, Heza has only been here for two and one-half months, so she watches right now rather than participates. But she is learning as she watches, and she is getting used to all the changes in her life. That's why she's still so quiet. Spending three years in an orphanage must not have been much fun. Wade tried so hard to speed up the adoption process, but there was so much paperwork, so much red tape that even though he tried, he couldn't make it happen any faster.

"Have you seen Hildegard in action with the three of them? Hildegard is a riot, trying to discipline them, trying to mother them, trying to get the kids ready for our school system by making sure they read well. She has been wonderful for Wade and the children."

"Speaking of Hildegard, Sarah, have you ever told her the story that Grandma used to tell you and Caleb and Josh to keep you in line? The one where Grandma named the housekeeper Hildegard?"

"Nooooooo . . . I'd be afraid I'd hurt her feelings! While the Hildegard of Grandma's story turns out to be an absolute *gem* by the *end* of the story, in the beginning, one gets a completely different idea about what she's like. I wouldn't want

Hildegard to think I consider her too strict. Although I guess if I told her the end of the story before I told her the beginning she might not jump to that conclusion."

"Sarah! Shame on you. Why, you're *afraid* of a little ole nanny. You're still afraid of the Hildegard in Grandma's story! Oh, honey, I'm only teasing you. It's a *great* story, and I think you *should* tell it to the kids someday, and you won't be able to unless you *first* tell it to Hildegard."

"Ohh, so I should use the German accent Grandma employed when she pretended to be Hildegard? Like 'Vas is loss . . . Zis roooom issss not picked up . . . Undt das is nicht goot!'"

"Yes! Our real Hildegard has a *great* sense of humor. I think she'd absolutely *love* the story *and* the accent!"

"Hmmm, I guess you're right, Matt. I probably *should* tell her. We've all become so close. But how? How can I tell her and not make her think I'm talking about the impression she made on us rather than just repeating a story that Grandma once told?"

"Good question, Sarah. I guess we could have a fellowship and invite Hildegard to come and then we can *all* tell her. In fact, maybe we can *each* tell a part of the story that Grandma used to tell. And if each of us employed the accent Grandma used, she'd probably laugh at how much we butchered it! She'll know we weren't singling her out, and I really do think she will enjoy the story. The kids will love it just as much as you and Josh and Caleb once did when Grandma told you the story."

"Okay, Matt, maybe we can have a storytelling evening. But speaking of having a fellowship, Matt, I wanted to talk to you about that. I'd like to have one in a week or so and invite everyone! And it's because, . . . well, . . . I have some really super news for everyone."

Sarah rose from her chair, walked over to Matt, and sat on his lap. She was grinning. She gave him a hug and he returned it. Then she said, "Matt, do you think 'Little Matt' is a good name for a boy or maybe 'Baby Sarah' is a good name for a girl?"

It took a moment for what Sarah said to register in Matt's mind. Then suddenly, Matt's mouth dropped open and he stared at Sarah for a moment and then tried to speak. The first sound was merely a croak. He closed his mouth and swallowed and then he whooped just as loud as he could. "What?" he asked. "We are going to have a *baby*? *Are* we going to have a baby? We are going to have a *baby*!"

And Sarah smiled and nodded her head. Then she hugged him again and said, "Yeah, Matt, we are. In July!"

"Let's see now . . . ummmmm . . . in seven months? *Seven* months? We only have seven months to get the room ready . . . and we'll have to buy a swing set. We'll have to get a gate for the top of the stairs and maybe one for the bottom of the stairs too. And we have to get a crib . . . oh, and a stroller . . . oh yeah, bottles and formula and diapers, lots of diapers. Boy, am I glad that we did some basic landscaping last fall after all . . . We can finish up this spring . . . so we can have a really nice yard for the baby. Oh, I almost forgot . . . we'll have to get a car seat for the baby too . . . In fact, we probably ought to purchase two car seats . . . one for each of our cars so we don't have to keep moving them. I'd better increase my life insurance. Oh, Sarah, we have so much to do!"

"Matt, I think you just uttered one hundred words in about three seconds! Slow down! Whoa! Now! Okay then. Now . . . aside from all we have to do, are you happy?"

"Happy? Happy? . . . I'm thrilled . . . excited, delighted . . . ecstatic, joyful . . . amazed, tickled pink, . . . and . . . exhilarated! And I'm jumping for joy! I can't believe that I'm really gonna be a dad! When did you find out, Sarah?"

"I'm just two months along, Matt. We have been so busy getting the book ready for the publisher and both working and studying for school that I just sort of ignored the first signs. But then last week, I checked the calendar and suspected something was going on, so I bought one of those pregnancy kits and it was positive, so I made an appointment with the doctor, which was today, and sure enough, he said I am pregnant. So I really only found out today. I didn't want to say anything at first because I wasn't sure. But now—"

"Oh, Sarah, here, let me get up so you can sit on the chair, not on my lap . . . Can I get you something, maybe a cup of herb tea? Should I get you a blanket or a pillow? Are you feeling okay, I mean, aren't you supposed to be nauseous or light-headed or something?"

Sarah laughed, secretly loving how solicitous Matt was being, and said, "Matt, I am not an invalid. I feel great and *I* will get us both tea, and *you* will stay right where you are! But seriously, are you happy? . . . Because I know that we had sort of planned that we'd complete our doctorate degrees before we had children . . . although maybe we could sit for them before the baby arrives if we work hard. Are you *really* okay with this?"

"Sarah, nothing could be better than this. A child is a gift from God, and everything else we have to think about can move to the back burner. All we do is shift our priorities, see what we can fit in, and it will all work out. Gosh . . . a baby! I can hardly believe it. It's incredible!"

"Wouldn't it be great fun to share our wonderful news with the others when they least expect it? Everyone thinks we'll wait another year to have a baby so if we have a fellowship where we can announce our wonderful news, it will be great to see the expressions on their faces since they will not expect it! Oh, Matt, I am so happy, and if you are happy too, then today is one of the happiest days of my life!"

"Honey, me too. I am thrilled with your news, and I love your idea of the fellowship for our announcement. Wow! Are you gonna be mom or mommy or momma? I guess I will be dada first, then daddy, then dad, or maybe later on, you know, in those 'cool' teenage years I might be called...Pop! I hope it's never "old man" like I've heard some kids say—isn't that how it works? Gosh, Sarah, this sure is one of our happiest days!"

"Well, let's get the calendar and check it and then phone everyone to set up our fellowship, a time when we will be making a wonderful new memory for *everyone*!" And so they checked the calendar and chose a date. They could hardly wait to make their big announcement. For now, it would remain their secret.

Then Sarah said slowly, "Matt, I've been thinking—" And Matt interjected, "Uhh-ohh, I know that tone of voice. You are gonna run something by me that you want me to agree to, huh? And now that you've softened me up—okay, out with it!"

"Well, Jayden said something a while ago that keeps popping into my mind. He said that he felt that his mother was lonely and wished she had friends like us. He also mentioned that he and his grandfather were the only people she was close to. I've felt badly about that and have been meaning to ask her to join one of our fellowships. Jayden and John are such super people that I'm sure Ruth is surely just as super. Do you remember when we bumped into all three of them at the supermarket and chatted for a while? Ruth seemed so sweet . . . and she was adorable too. What do you think of asking her to come with Jayden and John?"

"I think that's a *great* idea. If you want John and Jayden to come, then it's hardly fair to leave Ruth at home alone, so I definitely think you should invite her. She will know you *really* want her to come if you call her yourself and not just ask John and Jayden to bring her. She will feel better to know that the invitation to her isn't just coming because John and Jayden have been invited."

"Good idea, Matt. I will do that. I'm glad you agree that she should join us. And there's another part, . . . well, . . . ummmm, . . . I know you don't like people to interfere in other people's lives, but . . . well . . ."

"Out with it. What's the other part? . . . You look like the cat who swallowed the canary. What's this about interfering in other people's lives, *but*?"

"Well, . . . I'd kind of like to arrange the seating so Ruth will sit next to Wade. Do you think that would be appropriate?

"Wow, what a great idea! Oh, what a *really* good idea it is to try to bring them together, . . . but no, . . . wait. That would be too obvious. Let them think that meeting one another is just a fluke. I mean, if they felt that their meeting was just, you know, a 'natural' meeting, not prearranged, they can carry it further if they want to . . . or not if there's no, well, chemistry. Seating them next to each seems as if we are pushing them at each other. Just let nature take its course, and let's pray about it. I think they'd make a *great* couple. I know that I only met her that once at the supermarket, but I do remember that she was very pretty . . . and very nice!"

"Wouldn't it be super if Ruth and Wade liked each other? Jim would be happy about it too because he worries about Wade. He's always telling us that Wade gives so much of himself to others yet asks so little for himself. Should we alert Jim to our shenanigans?"

"I don't think so. Jim will definitely pick up on what could emerge from this, so all we have to do is to very casually let Jim know that both Wade and Ruth are coming to the fellowship. If I know Jim, he'll be planning a little strategy of his own."

"Oh, this will be fun, Matt! I can hardly wait. Next to our personal news about the baby, this is going to make the fellowship really special! It might be a good idea to play one of Grandma's wonderful little party games to draw everyone closer together too! What do you think?"

"That's a good idea. Everyone knows we often do this so it wouldn't be out of the ordinary, and those games do pull people together. We'll have to think of something special, something that will bring Wade and Ruth together too."

And thus, Sarah and Matt entered into their exciting conspiracy to introduce Ruth and Wade to one another, and Sarah prepared her guest list and began to make her phone calls. Soon everyone received their invitations and agreed to come. Sarah decided to make a turkey for that evening because there would be a large group and then created a list of who would be coming so they could determine what they might need in terms of additional food items and develop the seating arrangements that would work best for Ruth and Wade.

Sarah wanted to tell Barbara about her plans for Wade and Ruth but decided to follow Matt's advice and simply let nature take its course. It would be her and Matt's big secret. Well, of course not the biggest secret since the new baby would be their biggest secret, but it would at least be their next biggest secret to spring on the family. And, if they didn't tell anyone their plans to try to bring Wade and Ruth together, then no one would be disappointed if nothing came of it.

Guest List for February 15, 2009

Matt and Sarah
Caleb and Ann and two children, Andrew and Lorraine
Jim and Barbara
Josh and Debbie
Wade and Hildegard and two children, Bara and Heza
Kevin and Mary and one child, Teddie
John and Elizabeth
Jayden and Rebecca (great babysitters!)
Ruth (Jayden's mother)

Sarah's list added up to seventeen adults, and five children for a total of twenty-two! And Sarah couldn't help but think of the words in Malachi 3:10 that said, *"Prove me now herewith, saith the LORD of hosts, if I will not open you the windows of heaven, and pour you out a blessing, that there shall not be room enough to receive it."*

The phone rang, and Sarah answered to find Mary on the other end, asking Sarah to meet her for coffee the next morning for a quick get-together. It had been a few weeks since last they'd been able to sit and talk together. Mary explained that she needed to get out of the house for an hour or so just to change the routine she'd fallen into with the new baby.

The next morning Mary honked her horn outside of Sarah's house and immediately Sarah ran out, climbed into Mary's car and they happily hugged one another. They shared their joy at being together and finally having an opportunity to talk after such a long time. They drove to their favorite breakfast spot, chose a booth in a far corner and settled in for their long-awaited and welcome chat. Mary told Sarah that Kevin was watching the baby and had encouraged her to call Sarah. He'd said that it was time for them to get back to seeing their friends after finally getting accustomed to the routines a new baby brought into their lives.

"What are you up to, Sarah?" whispered Mary. "I know you, and you're holding something back from me!"

"What do you mean, Mary? What makes you think I'm holding anything back?"

"Well, you've got a Cheshire cat grin on your face, and I know you well enough to know something's up!"

"Oh, Mary, come on. Do you really think I could hold anything back from you?" Sarah replied with a wink.

"Yes, I do! So fess up!"

"Let's eat first!"

They splurged and ordered bacon and pancakes with boysenberry syrup and remembered when Rebecca had ordered bacon and pancakes and boysenberry syrup just about seven months ago when all the gals had gone for the fittings of their gowns for Sarah and Matt's wedding.

"Remember how Josh came into the restaurant when we were having lunch and just about tripped over himself when he saw Deb? That was such fun, and Deb handled him so well. Now their engagement is back on, and probably we'll be hearing wedding bells in a year or two!" They giggled to remember that day and how special it had been for all of them.

"Yeah, Mary, I do and I also remember how wonderful it has been to watch the blossoming of Josh's faith and also his relationship with Debbie. What a beautiful couple they make. And through all that, we have also watched your relationship with Rebecca blossom. Now the work on the carriage house is well under way and soon you'll have Rebecca and Elizabeth living there! I'm so glad that we found Grandma's manuscript about feng shui for you, and through that, Grandma chased the spirits right out of your house and out of your life! Isn't that a neat play on words?"

"Yes, that was an *excellent* play on words! But you are right, every time I think of how frightened I was about life, how my panic attacks held me hostage, and what I put Kevin through because of my fear, I am grateful to you and Matt and so glad that you showed us the path to God. Now look at us today. We have Elizabeth, Rebecca, and Teddie in our lives to love. We have the most terrific friends in you and Matt, and you have even brought us into the wonderful fellowship of your whole family . . . and we also have our loving congregation . . . Wow!"

"Mary, have you finalized the plans for the carriage house? Did you use Grandma's theory about the monkey swing? Was Elizabeth okay with all that?"

"Yeah, you were, once again, our beacon for what to do and how to gain God's blessing on our home. We used the math of divine proportion all throughout the carriage house and also for decorating Teddie's room in the main house. I teased Elizabeth about having a tape measure glued to her hip, and it was priceless to see Rebecca join in as they tried to obtain 'divine proportion' for their rooms and work the math. They ought to teach that method in school because it not only decorates a home beautifully but it also teaches math in a fun way and for a fun reason . . . especially the yucky stuff of fractions and ratios. Elizabeth and Rebecca even created a checklist for how each piece of furniture could fulfill one of the items Grandma spoke of, such as a taller and firmer chair for someone elderly. They really worked for the blessing this would bring."

"That's wonderful, Mary. I'll have to come over and see if I can sense the perfect proportions, see if I feel 'balanced'! Speaking of balanced and naming all our journals, Grandma's description of a monkey swing might be what we should call her method for balancing rooms properly. Now tell me, how are you managing with Teddie? Does he sleep through the night yet?"

"No, he's up once or twice, wanting to be fed. But Kevin is wonderful about it, and he will always get up if Teddie wakes up a second time, and he often gets up when he thinks I've had a rough day. Kevin is happier than I've ever seen him, and that makes me happy too. Oh, Sarah, God has been so good to us, especially when you think of all the terrible things I was doing before we met you and Matt. We are so blessed that you moved in right across the street from us! Now, Sarah," Mary scolded, wagging her index finger at Sarah, "you have successfully ducked my question . . . I know when the cat has swallowed the canary . . . So what's up?"

"Oh, Mary, dag nab it . . . You can always read me so *well*. Okay, here's what I *will* tell you and it's *all* I'm gonna tell you. Next Saturday, when you and Kevin, Teddie and Rebecca and Elizabeth come to our house, there will be two things going on . . . *two*! But you are going to have to wait to find out what they are just like everyone else . . . so there!"

"Sarah! Come on! At least give me a hint! Just a teeny-weeny, itsy-bitsy hint!"

"Okay, Mary, I'll even give you two hints, ready? One has to do with Wade, and one has to do with Matt! That's all I'll say."

"Sarah, this is so difficult . . . Now I'm going to be imagining all kinds of things trying to put it together. Is Matt going into business with Wade?"

"Nope."

"Are Wade and Matt up for some community award like 'best renovation' or something?"

"Nope. And that's all the questions that this little press secretary will take and all the answers you are going to get. Sooooo . . . let's change the subject. I want to know how John and Jayden are . . . I haven't seen them for ages."

"Well, Rebecca and Jayden are still great friends, and Rebecca has learned so much about the Bible from that boy. They go to the youth group together and have such fun. Remember when Jayden scared Rebecca about Halloween when he told her its real meaning? Well, last Halloween, Rebecca almost jumped out of her skin when the doorbell rang early . . . maybe four o'clock in the afternoon . . . and it was some trick-or-treaters. You should have heard her tell them the story Jayden told her, . . . wow, . . . and then she couldn't wait to leave the house for the fellowship the youth group had at the minister's house. She told me in no uncertain terms to keep the lights out. I felt as if she was my commanding officer for a moment and almost saluted her! When she decided to discard her old Halloween costumes, she cut them into pieces before tossing them in the trash so others wouldn't use them. She is one amazing girl, and I am so proud of her."

"You know, Mary, all of us have been so blessed to have found Elizabeth too. She did such a good job raising Rebecca and then she really demonstrated the self-sacrificing love that lives in her heart when she decided that Rebecca should meet you. I'll never forget the story we heard in church just before you got that phone call about Rebecca. It was a story of a mother and child taken by the soldiers in a jungle in Africa and the search to find them. Do you remember that? That was really a miracle of faith for you."

"Yes it was. How could I forget? It's hard to believe how close God is to us and how often He provides little miracles for us. And then of course, the biggest miracle ever was given to us . . . finding Rebecca! I love the song that has the words 'I was lost and now I'm found' because they sure do fit my experience like a glove. Sarah, we are looking forward to your fellowship. Thanks so much for including us. Because of all the things that have been going on—Ann and Caleb's baby, working on the carriage house, Teddie's arrival—we have all been so busy running around, and while we've seen each other, we have not had fellowship in a while. It will be great to get together and really talk and share and hug and pray together. How lucky we are! And speaking of luck, do you realize how many great babysitters we have on hand in Jayden and Rebecca and Elizabeth and even in Debbie, huh? Huh? We have so many children now in our circle of love—Andrew and Lorraine, Teddie, and Heza and Bara, and of course, the grown-up ones, Jayden and Rebecca!"

"That's for sure. Debbie is always in seventh heaven when she can hold a baby. She was born to be a mom, and Josh is lucky to have saved their engagement. Of course, it was because of a little help from us—a little female conspiracy! And of course, John, Elizabeth, and Caleb helped a lot too."

"Oh, wasn't that time period exciting! Elizabeth loved every minute of it, but Caleb really saved the day with his man-to-man with Josh. We have to give Josh credit. He sure did finally step up to the plate. And, of course, we do have to give credit to God for working it all out as He did and using us in the process!"

Mary nodded in agreement then pushed her chair away from the table and patted her stomach, leaned back in her chair and said, "Well, that was so good. I haven't had pancakes in ages . . . nor have I had a really good chitchat, so thanks so much, Sarah, for meeting me. Now I'd better get back home so Kevin can have a break from Teddie. Probably in another week or two, Teddie will be sleeping at night and we won't be so tired. Maybe then we'll get together more often again . . . Hey, we're just across the street!"

"That will be great. Ohh, Mary, it was so good to have this time together. I love you, ya know. We'll look forward to a great time at the big fellowship. We'll see you in church tomorrow. Ohhhh, Mary, I wanted to tell you that I love the way Kevin placed the quarter into Teddie's little fist last Sunday and helped him drop it into the offertory box as they entered the sanctuary. Starting young, that's perfect, you'll never go wrong doing that!"

When Sarah arrived home, there was a note on the counter from Matt. He'd gone across the street to visit with Kevin and would be back when Mary came home, which would be about now! As she waited for Matt to return, Sarah went into the library and sat in her favorite wing chair to leaf through the original of the manuscript they'd recently sent to the publisher. She began to think of their new baby and was glad she kept the news from Mary. She wanted to cherish the joy privately for a little while. She wanted to keep it just for her and Matt for the next week, then when they'd had time to ponder their wonderful gift from God, they'd share it with everyone else.

Sarah began to think of names for their baby. She had such a large circle of friends and family that many of the names she liked were already taken. She thought of some of the newly popular names of TV and movie characters but thought that she wanted something—well, something less worldly somehow. She seemed only to be thinking about boy's names, so maybe she was going to have a little boy. And then she thought of asking Matt about choosing the name Robert.

It seemed as if everyone was happy at this moment. Everything was going so well for all of them, and for an instant, fear struck Sarah's heart as she remembered Matt's words about Satan attacking when things went well or when they dedicated their efforts to God. All of them were vulnerable. And quickly, Sarah picked up her Bible and found the words in Isaiah 43:2 with which she'd once comforted Mary: *"When thou passest through the waters, I will be with thee; and through the rivers, they shall not overflow thee: when thou walkest through the fire, thou shalt not be burned; neither shall the flame kindle upon thee."* And she found another in Zechariah 13:9 that read, *"They shall call on My name, and I will hear them: I will say, It is my people: and they shall say, The LORD is my God."*

And then Sarah thought of the words to her favorite song, one they often sang in the choir. The words had been taken from Psalm 27:1 and said, *"The LORD is my light and my salvation; whom shall I fear? the LORD is the strength of my life; of whom shall I be afraid?"* And she realized that no matter what came their way, God would walk beside them and He would bring them through it and out of it, and her fear left and she was content.

Chapter Eight

THE ASSAULT

Saturday arrived, and Matt and Sarah were looking forward to seeing everyone and excited about the evening to come. Good food, watching what happened between Wade and Ruth, and their surprise announcement should make their fellowship quite exciting!

Early that morning they'd gone to the market together, the one that Mary had introduced to them when they first bought the house. The market's main feature was a huge brick building that took up an entire square block. Inside were booths filled with vendors selling everything from fresh fish to homemade sausage and from aged steak to freshly baked breads and pastries.

Enticing aromas wafted through the air. The aromas differed in each aisle, arising from the type of foods being offered. There were the strong, pungent smells of pickles, red cabbage, and sauerkraut competing with the sweet aromas of chocolate, ice cream, and candy, which in turn competed with the aromas of sizzling garlic, caramelized onions, and pizza.

The noise was overwhelming and was caused by the myriad of vendors hawking their wares, people calling out their orders, and others walking and talking their way through the aisles. Friends shared comments about the various delicacies before choosing what they wanted, and children clamoured to be heard as their mouths watered in the hope of convincing their parents to purchase their favorite food.

Outside, vendors filled the entire perimeter of the building and were also hawking their wares. There were unique pieces of handmade furniture, freshly cut flowers, potted ivy, beautifully fashioned ceramics, one-of-a-kind pieces of jewelry, books, and antiques. Other vendors offered various gourmet food items that were individually wrapped and ready to eat or bring home.

Tiny outdoor cafes hiding narrow specialty restaurants behind their patios filled the sidewalks across the street. Here too the aromas circled, looking for someone to entice toward a particular café. People of all ages, different ethnic groups, varying income brackets gathered to shop and enjoy the atmosphere and share a greeting with one another. People said hello to one another, and everyone was courteous because they had all come for a common purpose and shared a common enjoyment. Whether the weather was hot or cold, blustery or calm, even raining, people came. And today, so had Matt and Sarah come to participate in this incredible experience.

Sarah was dressed in a warm navy blue peacoat and a red beret, and Matt had worn a brown leather bomber jacket that left his hips exposed to the cold with only his thin jeans for warmth. Sarah slipped her arm into the crook of Matt's elbow and leaned in close to him. Matt felt her warmth and leaned to her with equal force so she would know that he appreciated her gesture of intimacy.

Matching their pace to one another, they first walked around the perimeter of the building to get some exercise and fresh air. When Sarah saw a heated booth filled with flowers, she asked Matt if on their way back to the car they could buy some flowers for their dining room table and also for the console in their entryway. Matt teased her, asking, "Why do you need flowers when you will be the prettiest blossom there?"

When they had almost completed their circle of the building and moved toward the front entrance, Sarah saw a vendor displaying two tables filled with little dollar items, each quite unique, and was reminded of Grandma's games. "Matt," she exclaimed, "let's look over here for a moment and see if there is anything we could use in a game for everyone to play tonight . . . one that perhaps the kids can enjoy too." Matt thought it was a great idea but couldn't imagine what to look for. He was quite sure that his imagination wasn't as wonderfully astute as was Sarah's.

But Matt was wrong. As they perused both tables, Matt's imagination soared as he discovered packages containing three mini notepads and pencils that might work if they played a game where everyone had to write down their scores or answers. Eight packages would be more than enough for all of them.

Then he found a package containing four tiny cups on handles, each cup sporting a rubber band with one end attached to the cup and the other to a tiny rubber ball. They weren't more than five inches high. Matt thought that getting the balls into the cups would create a great competition for the group. Sarah found some ponytail rings that were made of wisps of fake spiked hair and felt that they could think of something clever and funny to do with these.

But then Sarah squealed with delight as she and Matt saw a plastic bag filled with flexible rubber facial parts. There were eyes, noses, lips, ears, eyeglasses, eyebrows, and even mustaches. They were green and red and yellow and orange and purple! They reminded Sarah of a Mr. Potato Head game she once had. But these soft rubbery parts could be placed on a real face and had little stickums or rubber bands to help them stay in place.

"*Matt*, look at this," Sarah exclaimed. "This would be a *riot*! We could buy a *bunch* of packages, empty them into a punch bowl, mix them up, then we could draw straws to see who would go first to close their eyes and reach into the bowl and put on whatever they drew. And we'll take pictures once everyone has applied four or five of the face parts!"

"Sarah, you are incorrigible, but it would be funny and harmless and the kids would love seeing the grown-ups doing something like this, and they can join in. Hey, Sarah, we'll be," and in unison, both Matt and Sarah said, "making memories!" And they roared with laughter, delighted with their find.

The vendor sold them every one of her packaged rubber face parts and most of her balls and cups and pads and pencils too! The vendor was pleased by such a good sale so early in the day and to such a nice couple too. Matt ran back to the car with the packages so his hands would be free to carry whatever they later purchased when they moved inside the huge building.

With parking at a premium, he'd had to disappoint other drivers looking for a parking space who, seeing Matt put his packages into the trunk of the car, hoped to get his parking space. But Matt just shook his head, held his hands palms up as if to say sorry, closed the trunk, and ran back to join Sarah.

When Matt returned, Sarah suggested that they have a hearty lunch at one of the cafes so when they got back home, they wouldn't have to eat until dinner and could tackle the work they planned for the fellowship right away. First on the agenda would be to get the turkey into the oven as quickly as possible. Matt liked the idea of eating out and wanted bacon and eggs, toast and coffee, and maybe some hash browns. Sarah ordered the same.

Sitting at one of the tables on the outside patio of one of the restaurants enjoying the refreshing cold air, they smiled at one another to convey the sheer joy they felt at participating in such a unique experience. They admired the multicoloured awnings stretched across each café's narrow fronts and the coordinated colours of their brick facades and hand painted signs. When they finished their meal, and Matt had a second cup of coffee while Sarah finished her herbal tea, they walked across the street to the market.

They entered the huge brick building that held the vendors they sought for their food purchases and were immediately accosted by the heat and the sounds produced by huge ceiling blowers. As they struggled out of their coats, they saw a mini shopping cart that someone had just emptied; and since there weren't many carts available because space was at a premium, they were glad to get one. They loaded the cart with their jackets and, with their first stop the bread vendor, purchased four loaves of still warm, crisp Italian bread.

Sarah squealed with delight when she saw cookies decorated to look like Mr. Potato Head! They purchased the cookies amidst their giggles, agreeing that their Heavenly Father had a wonderful sense of humor to provide them with cookies that matched the game parts they had just purchased.

As they moved through the aisles, they purchased red potatoes, planning to mash them with the skins. They purchased a huge turkey, a package of turkey dressing that the woman said she'd homemade at five o'clock that morning, and then let her talk them into buying two pints of her homemade gravy. They decided that they would "doctor" up the gravy when they got home by adding some of the ingredients Grandma had always put into her gravy.

Just as they moved away from the counter, the vendor told them that she had placed some cranberry jam, also freshly made that morning, into their bag as a gift. They thanked her and moved to another counter where they purchased green beans and then to yet another vendor where they purchased some freshly made apple cider the vendor insisted they sample.

Mary and Kevin had offered to bring the desserts, and Ann was making the family's special mashed squash dish that they liked so much. Josh and Deb were bringing a new coffee called Bananas Foster, which they mixed in a certain proportion with another robust flavored coffee from Brazil. They were also bringing a quart of cream for the coffee and a box of Stevia packets, which was the no-calorie sweetener they all used because it was the most natural sweetener, therefore the healthiest. Debbie said that she would purchase some jars of red cabbage to which she would add brown sugar, the hard to find more beneficial vera cinnamon rather than the more common cassia cinnamon, and raw diced onions.

Elizabeth had offered to make trays of finger foods that they would use as an appetizer. They would serve these as soon as everyone arrived to stave off the craving for food that would be stirred by the aromas of a cooking turkey. Barbara and Jim were bringing chilled bottles of Asti Spumante and some table wine. John said he would bring a huge box of candy, telling them that he would bet they'd never seen such a large box of chocolates.

They would be surprised when Wade and Hildegard arrived with additional appetizers. Ruth had asked if she could bring something; but since it was to be her first visit to their home, they told her no, that everything was taken care of. Nevertheless, Ruth would bring a huge and an incredibly beautiful bouquet of flowers and a gift for Sarah and Matt's home.

When they arrived home from the market, they turned on the oven so it would preheat, hung their coats in the closet, and then began to put away their purchases. Their first job was to prepare the turkey, and when it was ready, they popped it into the preheated oven. Matt washed and diced the potatoes and placed them in a large pot filled with cold water. They would leave these in the refrigerator until they were ready to cook them. They cut up some onions and sautéed them in butter until they were caramelized, then they placed the onions and gravy together in a pot, covered it, and placed it into the refrigerator until time to reheat it for dinner.

Finally, they moved into the den where they began to open the packages of balls and cups and the packages of the colourful face parts. They placed these items into large crystal bowls and left them on the console in the den where they could retrieve them when they began to play their games.

When they completed these preparations, Matt walked to where Sarah sat in one of the wing chairs and sat on the floor at Sarah's feet, saying, "Sarah, I am overwhelmed by how much we have been given: our wonderful relationship, our loving family and friends, our comfortable home which we could renovate to fit us so well, our good health, and now the baby. I just wanted to say thank you to you, and I want to thank our Heavenly Father. Can we pray together, first me then you aloud?"

"Oh, Matt, you are so special. I am blessed to have such a wonderful role model in you. It is so right, so fitting that we should pray. Go ahead."

"Dear Heavenly Father, thank You.
Thank You for the incredible blessings You have bestowed upon us.
We are so grateful. We love You so much and long for the day that we can be
together in eternity and have the privilege of sitting at Your feet.
Father, please help us continue to learn Your words, to follow Your instructions,
to seek forgiveness for our mistakes, and to make restitution where we fail.
Help us to forgive others who also make mistakes.
Father, let us be Your instrument, so wherever we go, whatever we do,
we remain a child of God, and we conduct ourselves as Your child
and can be a help to others. Bless us and protect us, Father,

with the armour You provide for us and with the angel protection.
Give us godly wisdom in every choice we must make.
Bless and protect our friends and family and especially the little one that Sarah
carries under her heart . . . Thank You so much for such a precious gift.
Thank You for sending Your Son and for the great sacrifice He made for us.
Let us never be a disappointment to You.
Move the heart of those in eternity so they can accept the testimony brought to
them, especially those who suffered under the cross of drug addiction.
Strengthen Paul so he can continue to bring that testimony and let him know he
is carried on hands of prayer.
And, Father, please lay Thy blessing upon our fellowship tonight.
In Jesus's name, we pray. Amen."

And Sarah continued,

"Dear Heavenly Father,
everything that Matt just said, I say too,
and I ask You to help us be a beacon of Your light,
not only here on earth where we encounter children of God
and those who may not have found You, but also to those who are in eternity
and might have entered eternity never knowing You, never professing the Lord
Jesus. Let us be and become all that You want us to be,
and help us teach our children wisely that they too may be faithful.
Thank you for my wonderful Matt and all the family and friends we have.
Keep us all safe and in the palm of Your hand,
and thank You so much for this precious baby.
We want to bring joy to Your heart and never be a disappointment to You.
All this we pray in Jesus's name. Amen."

They sat for a moment in silence, their hearts gladdened by their prayer and humbled by God's love. They held hands for a moment, both hearts in unison. Then Matt stood and groaned from the effort to stand after kneeling for so long. Stretching his legs and laughing, he said, "I'm gettin' old, honey. Okay, let's get our chores done so we can hit the pillows for a quick nap before everyone arrives." Sarah smiled up at him and extended her hands for him to grab to pull her up too, knowing that the nap business was really for her, for the baby! He was so thoughtful!

The doorbell started ringing about four thirty, and little by little, everyone drifted in. The appetizers were slowly disappearing, and the conversation flowed as the aroma of turkey and dressing and gravy filled the air and made everyone salivate with the anticipation of a wonderful meal. Ruth arrived with John and Jayden, and as usual, John was exactly on time, not a minute late. But true to form, Elizabeth had arrived before him. "After all," she said, "I had an obligation to bring the appetizers before anyone arrived—hungry!"

Elizabeth, Matt, and Sarah had a few minutes to greet Ruth and engage her in conversation before the house filled with the others. Ruth was shy, but they could immediately recognize that she was also sweet and loving. Matt winked at Sarah as if to say, "Our little conspiracy should work just fine, and I can't wait until Wade gets here!"

Jim and Barbara, next to arrive, also took time with Ruth so she would remember their names and would feel welcomed by them. Then Jim busied himself with the coffeemaker so when Deb and Josh arrived with the coffee, it would only take a moment to get it started. He filled Sarah's thirty-cup automatic coffeemaker with the right amount of water and carried it to the buffet ready to plug in. He'd already placed the Asti Spumante in the fridge. Suddenly, a thought occurred to him and he asked himself, *Who is this Ruth? She is adorable . . . I wonder if she's single because if so, I'll have to make sure Wade meets her.* And his quick brain jumped to the realization that she was Jayden's mom and she was *single*, but he'd better get some facts before he said or did something dumb!

He drew Matt aside and asked him about Ruth and learned that she was indeed single and seemingly completely unattached. "Ahhhhh, she's the gal who finally divorced the egregious gambling alcoholic deadbeat so fond of ruckus?"

"Now, Jim, don't be sarcastic, don't use your Bill O'Reilly pithy-isms on me and don't judge! Yeah, you're right! That guy's got a lot of problems, but she is a really nice person and has gone through a lot because of that guy."

"Matt, do I smell a little plot here? A little matchmaking? If so, I want to help because I think it would be great to get that great bear of a man with a big heart a little personal joy . . . maybe even a helpmate in life, and from the sound of it, Ruth might also need a little personal joy! You know, . . . Wade and Ruth . . . Ruth and Wade?"

"Hmmm . . . a plot? Hmmmm, could be more like just bringing two people together to see what happens, don't you think? I mean, . . . gee whiz, Jim, would I be capable of any plot, of any subterfuge? Huh, Jim, . . . me?"

And Jim burst out laughing, saying, "Yeah you! Well, you might not have thought of it, but I am sure that if it wasn't you, then it was Sarah. And I have to tell you that I am really pleased. I can't wait to watch, . . . you know, like a fly on the wall . . . knowing what I know and knowing that poor Wade is the only one who doesn't have a clue! I can't wait to catch Wade, once he learns that Ruth is single, trying to sneak a peek at Ruth's pretty face when no one is looking!"

"No no, you're getting it wrong. Ruth doesn't have a clue either. In fact, no one does except me and Sarah . . . and now you. Believe me, Ruth's so gun-shy that she wouldn't have come to the fellowship at all if she knew of such a 'plot.' So if you are going to watch, then you'll have to watch *both* of them and maybe even plot yourself to find a way to bring them together without them suspecting *anything*!"

Jim grinned and wrung his hands with glee, saying, "Oh, this is going to be *fun.* Let's see now, okay, here's what I'm gonna do. I'll grab Ruth by the hand and drag her over to Wade and tell Wade to be nice to her because we have planned that he should marry her! I shall simply *pervestigate a petitory* or in your simple language, find by research what can be gained."

"Sarah, come here, honey, you have to hear this! Jim, tell Sarah just what you've just told me." And when Jim did, all the time winking and pretending to hold a cigar and twirl a mustache in the manner of Groucho Marx, the old TV comedian, when he was being risqué, Sarah laughed so hard her ribs hurt.

"No," she teased back, saying, "here's the *real* plan, Jim. I purchased a powerful love potion from the local pharmacy, and it is *your* job to pour it into their glasses. Got it?" And Jim replied, "Yeah, got it. Now let me go and get my supplies ready . . . Ahh, I'll need an eyedropper, right? Where is the bottle of love potion? Heeheehee, they won't stand a chance against us. By the way, do you have a minister coming today so he can perform the wedding? Hey, do you guys have a shotgun, and oh, Matt, . . . you willing to be a bridesmaid?"

Matt and Sarah were still giggling from Jim's antics when Wade walked in with Hildegard and four-and-one-half-year-old Bara and three-and-one-half-year-old Heza. Sarah made the introductions, and Hildegard went off to spend some time with her buddy, Elizabeth. Jayden grabbed Bara, and they went to play checkers. Heza, feeling shy, clung to Wade, and he held her lovingly so she would have time to get used to the number of people milling around. Jim went to stand near Wade so he'd feel comfortable.

Caleb and Ann arrived with two-and-one-half-year-old Andrew who ran to join Bara and Jayden. Three-month-old Lorraine was back in the hospital, and Ann and Caleb had left Sarah's phone number and their cell phone numbers with the hospital, telling the hospital staff that they would be back later that evening.

Then, Mary and Kevin arrived with one-month-old Teddie and also with Rebecca who would soon be fifteen.

Mary was carrying Teddie, and Kevin was carrying Teddie's bassinet, which he quickly set up in the turret room den within hearing distance of the living and dining room. Teddie was asleep, having just had his diaper changed and been fed his bottle. Kevin took him from Mary and laid him into the bassinet. Teddie continued to sleep, giving Kevin and Mary the opportunity to greet everyone.

Elizabeth had given Mary and Kevin the bassinet as a gift. She had sewn a beautiful skirt and hood from white organza lined with white satin as a cover for the body of the bassinet. Rebecca, quite a good little seamstress herself because of Elizabeth's patient teaching throughout her life, also helped. They had sewn tiny brightly coloured buttons in a random pattern all over the skirt and hood cover. Peeping beneath the bottom edge of the skirt and the bottom edge of the hood was a ruffle made of red satin that they had attached to the white satin underskirt. This made all the red buttons on the white organza stand out from the other brightly coloured buttons.

It was such a clever idea since the design neither spoke to a boy or a girl. Ribbons and bows for instance might have hinted that the baby was a girl. Elizabeth also made coordinating sheets for the bassinet's tiny mattress and a lightweight comforter to match. She'd made a padded bumper to cover the walls of the bassinet where it met the mattress so if the baby moved its little hands and feet, they would not touch any hard surface. The bassinet was absolutely beautiful, and how it had been dressed was truly a labor of love!

Jim took Barbara aside for a moment and whispered to her of the great secret "plot" that was brewing to bring Wade and Ruth together. "Shame on you, Jim, you'll ruin it. These things have to appear natural. If they find out what you're doing, they'll back away from each other, especially if you tease them about it! Please don't."

"Oh, honey, I wouldn't say anything. I'm just having fun. In fact, I'm tickled pink to think that Wade might make a friend in Ruth. He deserves to meet someone nice. Come with me to the table. I want to circle the table so I can read the name cards indicating where we will each be sitting."

"Okay, Jim, I'm sorry I jumped down your throat. I didn't realize you were teasing. I agree though that it would be so great for Ruth and Wade to become friends. I just didn't want us to mess it up in any way."

They circled the table, pretending to admire the way the table was set with its beautiful centerpiece. Jim noticed that Wade and Ruth were assigned to seats on the same side of the table but about four people apart. Jim immediately pointed out to Barbara that this arrangement wouldn't work to bring Ruth and Wade together because they needed to be able to see one another as they spoke so their interest might be piqued.

So with Barbara as a co-conspirator, Jim switched the names of Hildegard who was sitting next to Elizabeth and Ruth who was assigned to sit next to John so Ruth would be across from Wade and down one. This would work well. Wringing his hands and pretending to twirl a mustache and a cigar he didn't have, Jim smiled with his part as a co-conspirator and took Barbara by the arm to walk back to the living room and join in the conversation. Soon they were all called to dinner.

After everyone had taken their seats, Caleb said grace, and added a request that God would grant wisdom and expertise to the nurses, technicians and physicians caring for little Lorraine and provide her with everything she needed so she would soon be well. As Sarah glanced around the table, at first she was confused by the change in the seating arrangements, then she suddenly understood. She looked at Jim who winked at her and drew two fingers up toward his eyes and, using his fingers to point to his eyes, indicated that Wade and Ruth could make eye contact if they sat across from each other. Sarah smiled, understanding his signal and nodding her head in agreement with his assessment. She hadn't thought of that. Then she laughed at now having been drawn into Jim's conspiracy while unwittingly sharing hers with him!

Caleb began carving, and Matt filled the glasses with Asti Spumante for their toast. Matt gave the toast, thanking them all for coming and for the gift of their love and friendship, and asked God to bless them always. Sarah had quietly filled her glass with apple juice. Then they dove into the food and savored every bite. Comments flew back and forth about how good everything tasted and how much they had missed being together. When they began their second helping of food, Matt tapped his spoon against his glass and told everyone to listen up because Sarah had a few words to say.

Sarah stood. Her eyes went around the room, and she mentioned each person by name. Then she said, "As you all know, it's just six months since Matt and I were married and moved into this house which most of you helped us renovate. You *also* know that we are currently working furiously on our doctorates so we can sit for them this spring. We can hardly find the words to let you know how much we appreciate your prayers, your love, your example, your friendship, your help in so many ways. We have all known and believed that it takes a village to raise a child. Each of you are a part of our little village. We hope we've held up our end too and made a contribution to our friendship and the faith we share. So *now*, my wonderful little village of people, there will be one more for you to care for. Matt and I are having a *baby* in July!"

After a split second of silence, cheers filled the room, then everyone jumped up at once to hug Sarah and shake hands with Matt. Everyone was overjoyed.

Rebecca and Jayden were jumping up and down, yelling, "Another baby, another baby!" Bara and Heza and Andrew, to imitate Rebecca and Jayden, also jumped up and down and they too chanted, "Baybee, baybee." It was *wonderful*, and ever-thoughtful Ann snapped pictures of everyone for here again was the making of yet another memory for each of them!

With tummies well satisfied, Elizabeth and Hildegard went quietly into the kitchen to tidy a bit for Sarah while Matt announced that it was game time. Everyone gathered in the living room and overflowed into the parlour. Chairs were pulled from the dining room so everyone could sit in a circle that spanned both rooms. Matt led them in the cup-and-ball competition, and after a few minutes for a practice session, they each took their turn trying to get the ball into the cup and failed.

Jim had seen Wade watching Ruth when it was her turn to try to get the ball into the cup, and to make things perfectly clear to Wade, Jim walked over to Ruth and said, "Ruth, you only have two men in your life—one is John, the elder in his golden years, and the other is Jayden, the youngster in his formative years. So let a *real* man, a roborant man in his *prime*, show you how it's done. Notice the word, folks, *roborant*, meaning 'producing physical, mental, or emotional vigor.' Take note, Bill O'Reilly, . . . not that I'm being a rodomontade, boasting to ye of little word study!" *Where did Jim get these words?* they wondered.

Of course, Jim failed miserably, perhaps on purpose, to get the ball into the cup and everyone laughed. They teased him by asking, "That's an example of a *real* man? What was the word . . . a *roborant* one?" Jim just grinned; he'd accomplished his goal. Wade now knew that Ruth was available. Sarah and Matt had also realized what he'd done, how his little conspiracy was on a roll, and gave him a thumbs up!

Jayden mastered the ball-and-cup technique first. He'd figured out that if he shortened the rubber band by knotting it, he could maneuver the ball into the cup more easily. He teased Jim by saying, "Hey, Uncle Jim, maybe the 'youngster in his formative years' just outdid the guy 'in his prime'?" Jim laughed and totally agreed with Jayden, applauding the innovative manner in which Jayden had mastered the game.

Then came the potato face game, and the children gathered around. Only Heza and Andrew were too shy to play but both wanted to watch. Teddie was still asleep, and Mary planned to wake him after the game so he'd sleep during the night. Matt showed everyone the bowl of face parts and put one on to demonstrate how it was done and explained that they would pick a number from another bowl which would tell them when it was their turn to play. Whoever chose number one would go first, and whoever chose number two would be the second person to play, etc.

When they had all taken a number, with some squealing because their number was right up front, they settled down for the game. Rebecca had drawn number one and, reaching into the bowl with her eyes closed, came up with an eyebrow which she quickly secured to her own eyebrow. She ran over to the hall mirror to see what she looked like.

The next person to go, the one who'd drawn the number two, was Barbara, and she, with eyes closed, drew a huge set of orange lips. When she put these over her own lips, Rebecca and Jayden laughed so hard they cried, then Heza and Bara and Andrew laughed. The adults, the *village* as Sarah had called them, felt happy that the children enjoyed being with the adults and that they too were making memories. Round and round they went until everyone had drawn and everyone was wearing a face part.

"Now," Matt said, "number one draws again and has three choices. He can either draw from the pot to add to his face or he can take from another person, or he can draw from the pot and add that new part to someone else." Rebecca drew from the bowl and asked Jayden to stand. She walked to Jayden and applied the nose to Jayden's face near the ear he'd drawn. Then Barbara walked up to the jar and drew an eyebrow, a green eyebrow, and she too asked Jayden to stand and walked to him to apply the eyebrow. He really looked silly now. Heza and Bara and Andrew were laughing and loving the game!

When it was Jayden's turn, he decided not to draw. Instead, he removed the ear from his face and looked around the room, debating aloud whose natural ear would best match the ear he held in his hand. Everyone already had a rubber face part on their face, and as Jayden looked around the room he chose Wade, asked Wade to stand, and now Wade had two parts adorning his face. When it was Jim's turn, he too chose Wade. Now Wade wore three face parts.

Thus, when it was Ruth's turn, it was quite natural that she too ask that Wade stand and give him yet another face part. As she stood in front of him and reached up to apply it, Wade looked down at her, and their eyes met for the first time. They were both stunned by the jolt of electricity that seemed to pass between them. Flustered by what she'd felt, unaware that Wade had felt the same shock, Ruth broke her gaze first, applied the part to Wade's face, and sat down again.

But Wade too had been stunned, shaken. Never in all these years since his wife had died had he *really* seen another woman, and certainly he'd never been so moved by one. Wade's face reddened, and Jim, with his astute powers of observation, recognized what had occurred between them during their exchange. Jim had all he could do not to grin or dance a jig or jump up and pound Wade on the back, just as Wade had done to Jim when he'd proposed to Barbara.

The game came to a close and had been a huge success. Everyone had loved it, and Sarah gathered up the face parts to save for another fellowship. They'd play *this* game again! They went back into the dining room for dessert. Wade and Ruth had been talking together when the call came for everyone to move back to the dining room, so it was natural that they drifted into seats next to each other in the dining room.

Bara was on Wade's lap, and when Heza wanted to sit on Wade's lap as well, Ruth offered her arms to Heza and shy little Heza accepted and cuddled deep into Ruth's arms. Because it was so unusual for Heza to allow someone other than Wade, Hildegard, Jayden, or Rebecca to hold her, everyone noticed and they were touched.

Now because of the exchange they saw between Heza and Ruth, everyone suddenly had the thought that perhaps Wade and Ruth should become a couple. They hoped that something would bloom between them. John too noticed and his immediate thought was concern that his daughter could be hurt, but he quickly sent a silent prayer to God to watch over them both, and if God wanted something to work out between them, to bless that union. Only Rebecca and Jayden and of course, Andrew, Heza, and Teddie didn't have a clue about what was happening between Wade and Ruth or about the little matchmaking conspiracy that Jim and Barbara and Matt and Sarah had devised.

So the fellowship turned out to be a great success. Caleb asked Matt to pray with them before they all left, asking especially that he pray for Lorraine again, for godly wisdom in her physicians, accuracy in all her lab tests, kindness in her nurses, and also for safety in Ann and Caleb's trip to and from the hospital. They all stood in a circle as Matt prayed, and everyone decided to carry a constant prayer in their hearts for Lorraine.

Mary, always sensitive to troubles to come, didn't know why, but she felt uneasy for some reason. Elizabeth too had an uneasy feeling as if something bad was looming on the horizon. As Ann and Caleb turned to leave, John reminded them of the words from Isaiah 25:4: *"For thou hast been a . . . strength to the needy in his distress, a refuge from the storm, a shadow from the heat."*

The next day at the hospital, Ann and Caleb were told that Lorraine required surgery. They were assured that there was an excellent chance, barring complications, that Lorraine would then be fine. Their minister told them to cling to the words from Psalm 62:8 for comfort: *"Trust in him at all times; ye people, pour out your heart before him: God is a refuge for us."* They needed to trust God now more than ever before, and they needed to adjust their hearts to His decision in this matter. Lorraine had been diagnosed with ventricular septal defect, also known as VSD.

Time flew for the whole family because of how busy they were with hospital visits and their efforts to help Ann and Caleb. They all took turns looking after Andrew when Ann and Caleb went to the hospital and when Ann and Caleb flew to the larger children's hospital two hours away.

Everyone agreed on a selected time to pray in addition to their regular prayers so their group prayer for Lorraine would hit heaven at the same time. They also prayed in the sacristy with their minister, and everyone also placed something extra into the offertory at the back of the sanctuary for Lorraine. Time moved on, and slowly, Lorraine began to improve.

Jim and Barbara learned in March that they were also expecting a child and were overjoyed. Their baby was due to arrive by the end of November. They decided to name the baby Paul after Barbara and Matt's brother. At first, they did not tell the family their good news, waiting for a better moment. They felt that it would be difficult to rejoice when everyone was so worried about Lorraine.

As they moved through April, *Grandma's Little Book of Poetry: The Story of God's Plan of Salvation* was launched, and John took it upon himself to market the book to the local bookstores and church bookstores. He believed that the story would help others find God by better understanding the plan He had for them. With Sarah's permission, he also distributed books free of charge to some people they'd met whom he felt would benefit from the book. He also offered the book's royalties to fund-raisers organized by churches, community organizations, and youth groups.

They felt that this would help teach others about God's loving plan of salvation, the sacrifice God made for mankind, and the future He wanted for them. The novel also taught about mankind's mortal enemy and why he did not want God's plan to succeed.

Tragedy struck in May. Sarah lost the baby they had expected to arrive in July. She'd been seven months pregnant, and though she went into labor two months early and delivered with no complications to her health, the doctors could not save the baby. Matt and Sarah had been planning to name their baby Robert. Sarah experienced a heartache deeper than anything she'd ever felt before. She'd asked God why Matt's brother had to die so young and had thought she would never ask God that question again. But she found herself plagued by the same questions and by her desire to understand once again.

Mary visited Sarah often. Sarah lived just across the street so it was easy for Mary to call and visit often. She understood how despondent Sarah was and wished she could say or do something that would ease Sarah's pain. Sarah had always been Mary's rock of strength, and had always helped her keep her own fears and sadness at bay. She thought of how the words in Romans 8:14 fit Sarah so well: *"For as many as are led by the Spirit of God, they are the sons of God."*

Sarah needed to find peace, and just as Sarah had once given Mary a Bible verse to hold on to, Mary brought Sarah the words from John 16:33 that said, *"These things I have spoken unto you, that in me ye might have peace. In the world ye shall have tribulation: but be of good cheer; I have overcome the world."*

After Mary left Sarah, she wished with all her heart to find a way to comfort Sarah as Sarah had once comforted her. As she sat in her garden with the children to watch them play, she decided to pray once again for Matt and Sarah and Ann and Caleb. When she finished praying and saw Rebecca and Teddie together in such a pastoral scene, she felt that God was comforting her, telling her that all would be all right for the two couples. The garden was quiet, perfect, peaceful—and Mary's heart overflowed with the sense that God was with them.

On a personal level, Mary had everything now, everything she could ever want. It had been a long time coming, but now at last Mary was happy and now was the time to give something back to those who had helped her. Mary no longer harboured the terrible fear that had lived in her heart for so long. Now she needed to help her friends through their difficult times.

She looked at Teddie and saw his coal black hair and pale blue eyes, so like hers, and she saw Kevin's contagious smile and outgoing personality. He was a happy child who brought so much joy to everyone, and being in their circle of family and friends, he always had someone to hold him and meet his every need. They'd chosen the name Theodore because it meant "gift of God," and that was exactly what Teddie was.

How happy my life is now! Mary thought. *And now I can understand how living through those terribly difficult times had been the means by which God could reach me and change me.* Mary was grateful, thankful now for the experiences she once thought would destroy her. *It made me ready for this moment,* she thought, *prepared me so I could accept what God wanted to offer me.*

Her mind flew back to how her life had changed since Matt and Sarah had purchased the house across the street sixteen months ago. She had been so fearful then. She'd searched for any means that would bring her good luck. She had suffered from panic attacks, had been unable to sleep, and had felt alone and isolated, unable to relate well to others. She had also become obsessed with trying to find good fortune through the use of the ancient decorating art of feng shui. She'd almost lost Kevin over it.

When she refused to allow Kevin to bring into their home the beautiful hand-painted chest his sister sent them, fearing bad luck from "poisoned arrows" purported to emanate from sharp corners, Kevin balked. She was glad now that he had. How foolish she had been!

As Mary thought back to life just sixteen months earlier, she realized that her life had been like Grandma's monkey swing: everything she encountered, every effort she made tipped the foundation of her life, causing what was good to slip away and fall apart. She'd tried to build a life on the wrong foundation. She hadn't recognized the one thing that would bring balance into her life and had searched in the wrong places for security.

But now, thanks to the help of Matt and Sarah, she and Kevin had been able to find that precious commodity that could change their life and bring them the protection Mary had longed for since she was fourteen years old.

It had been a slow and painful process for Mary, but when she and Kevin finally turned to God, one by one their prayers were answered, and their understanding was opened. Mary's courage to trust God brought her a miracle of faith that reunited her with Rebecca. God had given her Elizabeth as part of that wonderful package; and Elizabeth became a friend, a sister, and a mother all rolled into one.

At last, with Matt and Sarah, their brothers, sisters, and friends, and Elizabeth and Rebecca becoming the "family" Mary had always longed for, she was happier than she had ever been. These people became the aunts and uncles for Rebecca and Teddie. These wonderful people filled what had been a terrible void in her life, and their fellowships were precious gifts from God.

It is wonderful to share your faith with others, to strive together toward the same goal, and to stand shoulder to shoulder with one another through every adversity. This thought still brought tears of thankfulness to Mary's eyes. These inspiring people were truly the children of God who not only came under God's blessing but also taught her every day how to seek His blessing in everything she did.

As Mary looked past the children and down the path to the carriage house, she was pleased by how nice everything looked. It had taken almost eleven months to complete. The outside of the carriage house boasted new double doors with a curved wood transom above and two sidelights on the outside of each door. A used brick stoop at the end of a winding brick path brought visitors to the doors. The arched wood panels over the windows and all the other exterior trim had been painted a soft turquoise colour and glowed with its satin finish in the dappled sunlight of the afternoon.

Elizabeth had planted dozens of shade-loving flowers along the brick path. The natural wood shakes on the roof and walls had aged to a soft brown patina that complemented the turquoise beautifully.

Mary was also grateful for Sarah's grandma. She had left them such a wonderful legacy about God's promises. Even in decorating, God had provided them with direction. This still amazed her. *Who would have thought,* Mary wondered, *that God would teach us what to do in our homes to gain His blessing and protection? Who would have thought that even this would be in scripture?* Now she understood that here was yet another way they could touch God's heart.

How wonderful that Sarah found her grandmother's decorating manual at just the right moment. *Grandma's journals were a legacy of love, a gift from a heart that sought God and found Him. How wonderful that Grandma desired to pass this gift of all she had learned to those she loved. Grandma would be so happy if she could see how many people she had reached and to see that Sarah was the instrument God used to do it.*

The inside of the carriage house was just as lovely as the outside. Elizabeth had laid out the rooms as close to divine proportion as she could and had made decorating plans to continue to improve these proportions through her furnishings. Divine proportion and the monkey-swing concept had been such an incredible gift! *Sarah's grandma was a gem in her knowledge of the Bible,* Mary thought to herself. They were so blessed.

Mary and Sarah had just spoken yesterday about their many blessings, but they also spoke of the trials and tribulations they were facing, especially Sarah's sadness about losing the baby. Everything had gone so well for them for so long now, and they knew that in this life, Satan would not leave them alone for too long. Evil was a part of life, and when it struck, it was a time for them to prevail in their faith and trust God to bring them through those circumstances. They had spoken of the journey ahead of them to reach the goal of their faith: to become a part of the First Resurrection and to learn and do what God asked of them.

Sarah had recited from memory a poem Grandma wrote. It was a part of the book that had just been launched called *Grandma's Little Book of Poetry: The Story of God's Plan of Salvation* and was based on another of Grandma's manuscripts, this one about God's plan for mankind and how to defeat the enemy who wants us to fail. The story was also interspersed with poems similar to the one that Sarah had recited.

Sarah said that the poem she recited spoke of how God would help them on their life's journey and had been based on the essay about how footprints in the sand indicated that we never walked alone, that God always carried us through our difficulties. Sarah brought Mary a copy of the poem, and Mary brought this poem to the garden so she could read it a few times and keep it in her heart.

Grandma had written the poem many years earlier. Mary decided to read the poem again and read it aloud so Rebecca and Teddie would hear it too.

Where Were You?

Lord, I saw some footprints
impressed upon the ground,

And recognized one pair was mine;
the other, Yours, I found.

I saw then that You walked so close
and shared my joyous days.

I felt assured of kinship
and of all Your loving ways.

But then there came another day,
one filled with great despair,

And I asked, "Oh God, Where are You?"
for the footprints were one pair.

"Do I really walk this path alone?
Where are You in my pain?

"What did I do to make You leave?
How can my soul make gain?"

And, gently then, the Lord said,
"I never left you, child,

I carried you safely in My arms,
those are My prints through the wild."

As she finished reading, Mary's eyes filled with tears. Her thankful heart spilled over, too full to be contained, and she sent a silent prayer to God to let Him know how much she appreciated the treasures he placed in her life. Rebecca, Elizabeth, Matt, and Sarah, and their family and friends were God-given treasures to nurture and protect. *Please, God, help me always appreciate these wonderful people whom You have sent into my life. Help me to show them how much I appreciate them. Keep us all safe and in Your word always. Please help all of us bear the sadness that comes with life,* Mary prayed silently.

Then Mary prayed aloud for Sarah and Lorraine. "Oh, Father, please help Sarah. Please help me to find a way to comfort her as she once comforted me. And please help Lorraine recover so Ann and Caleb's worry can be lifted."

Mary suddenly recalled something Sarah once told her about miracles. She'd said, "You know, Mary, we are so spoiled . . . like the child who asks for a doll for her birthday then later sees roller skates and then demands them both, never satisfied. We ask God to answer our prayers and He does, and He even provides little miracles to prove that He responds to our needs. Yet the sly devil comes to us, like he did with Eve and says, 'Did that one little answer *really* mean God hears your prayers? Better ask for confirmation.' And so we ask for confirmation, then another confirmation, as doubt comes to make us forget the miracles God wrought for us. But it *is* the little everyday miracles that we should listen to, believe with all our heart, even write down, not the doubt. When we keep remembering what God does for us, we can *stay* thankful, *stay* in the assurance that God is with us every minute. I know this, and yet I can't stop myself from wanting to know why God had to take my baby. And then I feel guilty because I am not trusting that all His decisions are perfect."

Mary could only tell Sarah what Sarah had once told her. "Sarah, it's okay to seek understanding. In fact, God says in Malachi 3:10 that we can try Him, and He will prove Himself to us. Remember the words '*And prove me now herewith, saith the LORD of hosts, if I will not open you the windows of heaven, and pour out for you a blessing, that there shall not be room enough to receive it.*' God tells us that we can 'prove Him' because He understands our needs and our fears. You yourself told me that."

Mary had been thankful for that advice from Sarah, and Sarah too had been thankful to hear these words from Mary. It helped her remember all the little things as well as the big things that God had done for her. She and Mary prayed together and asked God to never let any of them stray from Him, to help them remain faithful always, to allow them to keep in their minds as well as their hearts all He had taught them and all He had done for them. They both wanted to trust, to love, to be good wives, and to be true and faithful friends to everyone.

And God heard, and He moved their hearts with the promise that He would never let them go even through the tests that lay ahead, the trials and cares and worries they would experience in life. They knew that God would be there for them. What they didn't yet know was that God had also provided that Grandma's abiding faith and hidden treasure of love and wisdom would also be there for them, even after death.

But despite their good intentions, difficult times had arrived for Caleb and Ann and Sarah and Matt and would, at some time, arrive for the others as well. Each couple might face a different circumstance, one that would test their faith, and they might struggle through it, but they had each other and more importantly they had their Heavenly Father to see them through. They would have an opportunity to stand in faith and touch God's heart by that faith.

But Mary knew that Sarah, despite knowing this, still heard an inner scream asking, demanding to know, *Why? You took my mother, then my grandmother, then my brother-in-law, and now my baby . . . why?* and her pain would not lessen.

Mary, always of a sensitive nature, was acutely aware that Sarah was suffering. Loving Sarah as she did, she too suffered and wished she could do something to alleviate Sarah's pain. She knew that praying for Sarah would help, but she also knew that letting Sarah know she loved her and constantly reminding her of God's promises was also very important. On one occasion, after Mary had comforted Sarah, they prayed together and afterward, Sarah opened the Bible, looking for a word that they could hang on to as the end-times made itself known.

Sarah read aloud the words God gave them in 2 Peter 3:9 where Peter reminded the congregations: *"The Lord is not slack concerning his promise, as some men count slackness; but is longsuffering to us-ward, not willing that any should perish, but that all should come to repentance."* And she continued reading in 2 Peter 3:17-18: *"Ye therefore, beloved, seeing ye know these things before, beware lest ye also, being led away with the error of the wicked, fall from your own stedfastness. But grow in grace, and in the knowledge of our Lord and Saviour Jesus Christ. To him be glory both now and for ever."*

Sarah and Mary recognized that God had given them not only a promise, but also a warning about what was to come. Each hoped they would stand faithful through the difficult times, and each worried about their ability to do so. They knew that it was during the tough times that they would need to be reminded that God was still with them and was never wrong to allow what came. But they also knew that they might falter and would need their loved ones to remind them that God would lead them through their difficulties. And now those tough times had come for Sarah. They needed to remember that Satan was real, that God would allow him to test them, try to break their faith in God. And that if they stood firm, if they held on, the testing time would pass and they would come out of it better, more faithful, stronger, and better able to help others deal with their own time of testing. They may have awakened a sleeping giant, but that "giant" would one day be bound and one day cast forever away from the children of God.

Matt and Sarah had discussed with Kevin and Mary their concern over publishing Grandma's story about God's plan of salvation. They'd all read the story and loved it and knew that it certainly wasn't something that would make Satan happy since the story warned the reader about Satan's activities and taught the reader so easily and beautifully about God's plan. They worried that their faith would be tested and that evil was stronger than ever. They understood that Satan was now making his presence known through the depression and disappointment that Sarah couldn't seem to overcome and that now was their difficult time of testing.

Chapter Nine

HEZA AND LORRAINE, RUTH AND WADE

Lorraine did well in surgery and, in due time, was able to return home. The ventricular septal defect was repaired when the doctors performed a cardiopulmonary bypass on Lorraine's heart. However, Lorraine was still frail from all she had been through, and their newest fear had come because after the surgery, Lorraine had unexpectedly spiked a fever. Their physician told Ann and Caleb that even after Lorraine was sent home, if she ever had a fever that lasted more than twenty-four hours, they should bring her directly to the hospital.

He alerted his staff and his answering service that calls from Ann or Caleb should be put through to him, advising them that in Lorraine's case, a fever lasting more than a day could be a sign of a more serious problem that needed to be addressed.

The family continued in their prayers and continued to place a special offering for Lorraine into the offertory box in the back of the church. They kept in touch with Ann and Caleb to see if there was anything they could do for them.

During the first few weeks following Lorraine's release from the hospital, one appointed person in their circle of family and friends would take Andrew home with them for two hours. It was an opportunity for everyone to develop an even closer bond with Andrew and a time when Caleb and Ann could be together to devote their attention solely to each other and to Lorraine. Andrew, now three years old, looked forward to these excursions and would often ask if he could play with Bara and Heza who were now four and five years old.

Grandma had always warned her family to be cautious about the use of antibiotics and preferred natural remedies and the various supplements that support good nutrition, which in turn supports the immune system. Ann and

Caleb spoke with their physician about their concern; and though he wasn't pleased with their approach, he agreed to a consultation with an alternative medicine physician and together they came up with a plan that would support, in fact strengthen, Lorraine's immune system and thus allow them to use antibiotics only as a last resort.

The consulting physician had also recommended Sinupret Syrup for Lorraine's cough, which was the same cough syrup Grandma recommended to the family. It contained only natural ingredients such as cowslip, European elder, and European vervain. It seemed to work for both children and adults, and it had no side effects.

As Andrew bonded with Heza and Bara, who clamoured for Jayden and Rebecca's company, it came to pass that Wade and Ruth also came in contact with one another. Most often, it was Jayden and Rebecca who went to Wade's house because the Jungle Jim and the games and toys were there. When Ruth arrived home from work, she, rather than John, usually picked Jayden and Rebecca up from Wade's house to drive them home. Thus, Wade and Ruth met often.

When Jim became aware of this, he wondered if John asked Ruth to pick up the older children and, if so, wondered if John was also plotting to bring Wade and Ruth together. He also wondered if Hildegard might have been engaging in this subterfuge.

"Vell, cum inside, cum, vee eat!" Hildegard would say. "I heff chili mitt lots of meat undt big crusty brrrrread undt da goot sveet butter, cumen zee, cum." Wade would hear Hildegard, come to the door, and gently take Ruth's elbow, saying, "You have to stay so I can stay sane in the midst of all these children." Wade and Ruth would sit around the huge kitchen table to eat with Jayden and Rebecca and Heza, Bara and Andrew while Hildegard fussed over them.

Wade noticed that when Heza finished eating, she would slip from her chair and climb onto Ruth's lap. Ruth would reach down to Heza and lift her onto her lap, giving her a big smile and usually a hug. Heza sat quietly, happily in Ruth's lap while the rest of them continued to talk and to eat. Wade liked seeing them together, liked seeing Heza, the timid child who watched everyone so carefully, become so relaxed and trusting with Ruth.

As Lorraine continued to improve and her fever disappeared, she also began to put on some weight. Thus, Andrew's evening excursions were reduced to twice a week and then to once a week. Jim could see that Wade was in a slump and knew it was because without Andrew visiting, Ruth did not visit. Ruth occasionally phoned and asked if she could pick Heza and Bara up and bring them to Mary's because Elizabeth had made something the children especially liked for dinner and because the older children clamoured for a change of venue. When this occurred, Wade hoped for an invitation to join them, assuming Ruth would also be there.

In time, a routine developed; and when Ruth came either to pick up or drop off any of the children, Wade would meet her at the door and sigh deeply from a heavy heart when she did not stay or when they left for Elizabeth's house. He'd mope until he saw Ruth again, then gladly, hopefully invite her in; but it so seldom seemed to work out that she could stay.

When Jim finally understood what was happening, he figured that a little more interference on his part was necessary. He phoned Elizabeth and alerted her to his little "plot" to bring Wade and Ruth together. Elizabeth was delighted by the idea. She'd heard John say that he wished Wade and Ruth would hit it off. So Elizabeth jumped right on Jim's suggestion, telling Bara and Heza to invite poppa to come with them the next time they visited and also telling Jayden to make sure Ruth stayed for dinner too.

Then she phoned Hildegard, now her close friend, and alerted her to the "exciting works of Cupid's plot," and Hildegard now more firmly insisted Ruth stay when she came to their house. From that point on, neither Ruth nor Wade stood a chance. He and Ruth were thrown together "accidently" at least once a week.

Wade lived for the one night he could be sure that Heza and Bara would spend time with Jayden and Rebecca and for any other fellowships the family had, just so he could see Ruth. He also planned a fellowship in his own home every few months and became known as the master of the backyard barbeque. He'd installed a wonderful Jungle Jim in the yard for the children, which was not only practical and safe but also beautiful. It blended perfectly with the trees and foliage he'd planted to make the yard attractive and provided the children with shade on a hot day. Wade had also built two large picnic tables with matching benches and a half wall to hide the back of his huge stainless steel barbeque. All these structures were stained a deep reddish brown similar in color to the Jungle Jim, so everything matched. The yard was impressive. Wade was a thoughtful, hardworking, talented man.

One afternoon, as Jim and Wade were at work and found themselves in the conference room awaiting the arrival of another contractor, Jim could sense that Wade was very contemplative, not his jovial self. "What's wrong, buddy?" Jim asked.

"Nothing, Jim, just thinking."

"Listen, Wade, I've been watching you for a long time. You've done such amazing things—your career, your home, your friends, and best of all, providing Heza and Bara not only with a home but also with someone who loves them, cares for them, and is more than any father could be. You've so many accomplishments . . . and . . . *still*, you need to be hit over the head with a baseball bat! What's wrong with you?"

"Whadda ya mean, Jim, why do you say that?"

"Wade, there is a woman who is head over heels in love with you . . . and who even loves your *kids!* You are head over heels in love with her, and what do you do? *Nothing!* You mope, you have this woebegone look on your face, like a teenage boy . . . like a . . . a . . . a . . . a wimp, ya dumbkoff!"

"What the heck are you talking about, Jim? You don't understand—well, . . . did you say . . . I mean . . . what? . . . You mean you think she *loves* me? That's ridiculous!"

"Really? What makes you think it's ridiculous?"

"Why? I mean, geez, Jim, she's *gorgeous*, I mean, she's set for life—a grown kid soon to be off to college and . . . I mean, she can do what she wants, go where she wants, get any guy she wants. Why would she want to be tied down all over again with me? A potbellied, crabby old man with two kids and one that might need special assistance during his life. *Come on, Jim,* . . . get real!"

"What's the matter with you, Wade? Are you so self-centered that you think it's only *you* who cares about other people? Don't you see that Ruth and Heza *love* each other? Or that you have a heart so big it's easy to fall in love with you? You are so, . . . well, the old-world kind of guy. I mean, you know, gallant. You have manners when it comes to women, you're gentle with kids, a great handyman, and—I hate to give you a swelled head—but you are a good-lookin' guy. I mean, women dig tall and strong and able to carry the weight of the world. Gee, Wade, you sure sell yourself short. Where's that old chutzpah? Are you going to be, as Bill O'Reilly might say, a squinch?"

"Give me a break on the fancy words. Come on, Jim. This is serious. There is no way someone like Ruth would, as you so crudely put it, 'dig' me! I sure wish she did! But now, level with me, Jim. Tell it to me straight, no BS, you're just teasing again. You don't *really* think I have a chance, do you?"

"A chance? You ask her to marry you, and it will happen. She *loves* you. We all see it, why can't you? Everyone of us can see how much in love both of you are, and we've waited and waited and waited for you to make a move. Did you know that the word pusillanimity means ignobly lacking in courage? What the heck are you waiting for, Wade? Are *you* filled with pusillanimity Wade?"

Wade's jaws clenched. He stood. Thinking, quiet, not moving. Jim had seen this side of Wade before. In Iraq, he did the same thing when confronted with a problem. He'd clench his jaw, stand unmoving, think, then seem to make a sudden decision, and act upon it immediately. The sudden quiet in the room became a roar in Jim's ears as he too waited, unmoving, just watching Wade, hoping.

Wade repeated, Jim's words, "ignobly lacking in courage", huh? Oh yeah . . . well we'll see about that!" Suddenly, Wade turned and reached for his cell phone. He pushed one button, and shortly thereafter Jim heard him say, "Ruth? Wade. I hope it's okay that I phone you at work, but I will just take a minute. Are you free tonight for dinner? I mean, . . . just you and me . . . going to a restaurant?"

There was silence for a moment, and Jim's heart sank. Then, after what seemed such a *long* pause to Jim, Wade repeated, "Yeah, just you and me. I could pick you up at seven if that's okay, and I'll have you home by ten and we can go anywhere you'd like." Silence again and Jim wondered what Ruth was saying. He could hardly stand the suspense. Wade would kill him if he'd been wrong. Then after what seemed an eternity, he heard Wade say, "Okay then, it's a date. See you at seven." And Jim breathed again, unaware that he'd been holding his breath or that his heart was pounding in fear and anticipation of Ruth's reply.

Wade turned to Jim and literally bellowed, "Are you satisfied now?" and mumbling under his breath, "ignobly lacking in courage, my foot!"

"Yeah, you big clumsy bear, I'm satisfied. How about you?"

Then Wade grinned and slapped Jim on the back, saying, "Geez, Jim, thanks. I am the happiest guy in the world right now. I could dance a jig, in fact, I could even yell from the rooftop. Gee thanks, Jim . . . Gee, I don't know what to say." And he grabbed Jim in a bear hug, then clapped him hard on the back again. Jim's poor body was saved from further pummeling by the intercom announcing the arrival of the contractor they were expecting.

And thus began the courtship of Wade and Ruth. John was ecstatic and so was Jayden. They had both prayed for so long that God would send someone wonderful into Ruth's life. When John and Jayden, Ruth and Wade, and Bara and Heza were together, it just seemed so right, so natural, as if they had all been together forever.

Under Wade's love, the bitterness and loss of trust brought on by her first marriage began to dissipate, and Ruth felt the desire to attend church more often than she had in the past. She hadn't realized how angry she had been about what came of her first marriage. But during the last few weeks, she seemed to grow in the understanding that sometimes one has to endure heartache in order to appreciate what God wanted to bring into one's life; what wonders he had in store for one's future.

As Ruth's heart melted and her fear and anger subsided, she finally understood that she had subconsciously blamed God for her heartache, often feeling that she'd done all the right things to obtain God's blessings. Therefore she felt entitled to demand that God remove the heartache He had allowed into her life. She'd been angry at the injustice she'd experienced. She hadn't acknowledged her bitterness before but now was able to rest in and open up to the constancy of Wade's loving kindness. She recognized that it was her bitterness that had been holding back her blessing.

Ruth and Wade had many deep conversations about God. Ruth told him of her anger with God and of her father's steadfastness through her difficulties. She told him how her father had kept Jayden in Sunday school and in his youth group and had helped Jayden by being a wonderful role model. She'd been given so much by her father over the years and knew she'd always been in his prayers.

Often, she hadn't appreciated all he did for her because she'd been so defensive and bitter about her life. She realized that subconsciously she had blamed her father for everything that went wrong rather than taking a good look at herself or sending her anger where it belonged because it might not be safe to render her anger in that direction. It was a strange phenomena that because she could trust her fathers unconditional love for her, she could make him the brunt of her anger, blaming him for things he never caused, holding back her expression of love. She would have had to turn her anger elsewhere if she had not understood on a subconscious level that he would never abandon her even when she treated him so indifferently and did not give him the appreciation he deserved. Now she needed to step up to the plate, make restitution. Ruth said that she'd never acknowledged the terrible pain her father had been through in his own life even though he must have longed for someone to comfort him.

Wade told Ruth that he too had been angry over his circumstances. But he said that now they had been given the opportunity to change and to become role models themselves, not only for Heza, Bara, and Jayden but also for her Dad and all those around them. Perhaps both of them could take some of the responsibility off John's shoulders and give him the thanks and love he needed and deserved too.

They spoke about the qualities they saw in Matt and Sarah, in Barbara and Jim, in Ann and Caleb and how fine and good those qualities were. They spoke of how Mary and Kevin had been drawn to the friendship of Matt and Sarah by these very attributes. Wade told Ruth that he too would like to be a part of whatever it was that made these people so special. He said he thought that their faith seemed to be the driving factor.

From that day on, Wade, Heza, and Bara joined Ruth, John, and Jayden at church. Soon, Wade decided to join the church and to enroll Heza and Bara in the Sunday school that would teach his children about God. When Wade told Ruth that Jim had not yet joined their church but that he always attended the services and fellowships because of the promise he'd made to Barbara when they married, she was surprised. Wade also told her that he was present when Jim had made that promise. He was glad that Jim had kept his promise but disappointed that Jim hadn't joined the church. They both wondered why.

One evening, Barbara and Jim stopped in to visit Wade. Ruth was there, and so were John, Jayden, and Rebecca. When they decided to spend the evening together, they ordered a couple of pizzas, which made the children ecstatic. Wade told them that he and Ruth had set a date to be married in May. This would give them time to make some changes to Wade's house that would accommodate the needs of Ruth and Jayden as well, and to get her house sold and everyone prepared for their wedding.

Then Wade told them that he had asked to join the church and had asked Bara and Heza if they wanted this too. Barbara was thrilled, and so were John and Jayden. Jim was silent. Heza and Bara had heard Jayden speak of the fun he had in Sunday school, in confirmation classes, at the youth functions and were anxious to begin their own journey into these experiences. With Wade's decision out in the open and settled, Wade turned to Jim and asked him point-blank why he hadn't joined the church. Jim was startled by the question and didn't quite know what to say.

But Jim thought about Wade's blunt question. He knew that he trusted these ministers, these people, their faith. He'd seen them practice what they preached, but he was still hung up on committing to any particular doctrine since so many religions argued a different philosophy. Jim realized that he still had some unanswered questions. *Was it wrong to question?*

He knew he was a fence-sitter and he knew that the Bible warned about continuing to occupy that position, so maybe now was the time for him to let everyone know that he was not ever going to join the church. Period. He had many doubts and many unanswered questions, or at least many things that he couldn't quite understand and accept. Maybe that was why he was still sitting on the fence.

"I guess I still have some unanswered questions," Jim began, and John asked him what his questions were. "Well, I guess I can't quite get my mind wrapped around an . . . entity . . . that you claim can control me or control anyone else at whim and make them cause harm. I blame people for their actions, not some . . . entity. I mean, like I remember what happened to my mom, how her neighbor seemed so intent on doing her harm for no reason and I blame that woman for her actions. I feel that she was a mean-spirited, vindictive, jealous woman by choice, maybe by nature. She didn't want to change. She *liked* to do what she did even though she went to church and professed to believe in Christ!

"But then again, I begin to think on the other hand that it would make sense to think that she was controlled by an evil . . . entity. However, I find it hard to believe that someone can go to church, profess their faith, and *still* be controlled that way. Don't they feel guilty for their acts? Isn't the way they act a slap in the face to God? When someone can do that and claim to believe in God, it just doesn't make sense to me that they would even go to church. Is there any way to know whether this would be a person who is simply a person who gives in to their sinful human nature or that this is someone controlled by evil?"

Barbara, who had remained quiet up to now, hoping that this might be a turning point for Jim, said that perhaps Jim needed to start with the premise that there was indeed both a good and an evil force at work here on earth and that this force also existed in all people. She felt that perhaps it was the *degree* of accessibility each person allowed that force to work within them that made the difference between succumbing occasionally to evil and *being* evil. She said that a perfect example of this force *at its worst* might be the inhumane cruelties perpetrated by a child molester who inflicts such terrible harm on an innocent child. They have given in to evil and have become evil themselves.

"But remember," she said, "either way they won't go unpunished. God remembers every kind act we do, and He remembers every cruel act. God covers them both in Matthew 25:40 where He says, '*Inasmuch as ye have done it unto one of the least of these my brethren, ye have done it unto me.*' And remember too that God says that He will take vengeance on them."

Jim, those who deliberately choose not to learn and follow God's words, in other words, those who are lukewarm, are also being influenced by Satan. Their complacency is a satanic influence. Even though this influence seems less horrific than the influence over a child molester, it serves the same purpose of keeping them from becoming a child of God. God says even of these people, "*I will spue them out of my mouth.*" "The scary thing is Jim, that perhaps it's easier to disengage and repent from *obvious* evil than from a *subtle* evil."

"That's scary . . . in fact, . . . that's really interesting, maybe even profound, Barb, because that's probably very, very true."

Jayden said, "Grandpa, can you tell Uncle Jim all the stuff about Satan, . . . you know, . . . what he is capable of doing, why he can do it, you know . . . all that stuff that the Bible says? Do you have your notebooks in the car from that Bible study that you and Aunt Elizabeth had with Aunt Debbie? If you do, you can show them to Uncle Jim. Maybe Uncle Wade has a copier."

Wade said, "Yeah, I do have a copier, Jayden, . . . and I'd like a copy too if you make one for Jim because while I do believe that there is evil in the world, I don't think I've understood much about it being, . . . you know, . . . like a person or having powers over us or something."

John did have his notebooks in the car and hoped he'd be able to find what he wanted quickly. He went to his car and brought the books back to the house along with his Bible and concordance. Soon he found what he was looking for and was glad that he'd placed this info into a concise list when he and Elizabeth held the Bible study with Jayden, Rebecca, and Debbie. It would be easy to copy and easy to discuss. John and Wade went into Wade's office and made a copy of John's list for each of them so they could all follow along.

"Maybe, Wade, since you haven't been informed of the history of evil, we should start with that part, you know, like why evil is here and what it needs to do. Okay?" When Wade and Jim readily agreed, John said, "Okay, so I'll start with how it all began.

"In the beginning, God longed to fill His kingdom with souls who would truly love one another and love His Son and Him as well. He wanted these souls to understand the value of love, trust, and loyalty, and to choose to practice these attributes voluntarily. God began His plan by creating the earth in its limited universe. Then He created Adam and Eve to live happily in the Garden of Eden, walking and talking with Him.

"But the angel Lucifer, later known as Satan, rebelled against God because he was jealous of Christ and of the new being, man, that God wanted to bring to a higher position than Lucifer was. As a result of his rebellion, Lucifer was thrown to earth with the angels who chose to follow him and had thus also disobeyed God. These numbered one-third of all the angels. Lucifer became known as Satan. Satan knew God's plan and understood that when the plan was completed and God had obtained the number of faithful, loving souls He longed for, he would be thrown into hell for what he had done. To prevent God's plan from moving forward and thus forestall his own destruction, he destroyed God's relationship of trust and loyalty with Adam and Eve by enticing them to sin through disobedience. God, because He is bound by His righteousness, had no choice but to banish Adam and Eve as he had banished Satan.

"But God, knowing what Satan would do, provided a way for Adam and Eve and the generations to follow to escape the captivity Satan proposed for them and return to God. Christ offered Himself as the perfect sacrifice by which the sins of man could be forgiven.

"At every turn, Satan interfered with God's plan, trying to break those who would follow God. He had to because when God collected the number of souls He wanted for His new creation, Satan would be bound forever . . . so Satan is actually fighting for his life when he is discouraging us from our faith. But many of those tested by Satan's attacks are strengthened through these attacks, becoming like gold refined in the fires of tribulation. From these faithful, God is building what the Bible calls the bride of Christ.

"God even provided for those who died in sin by creating a means of testimony in eternity while grace is still available on earth. Christ entered hell after His death to give testimony of His triumph to those who had died in their sins before He could bring His perfect sacrifice. He told them that now they too could find forgiveness.

"God has allotted a certain amount of time for His chosen ones to be made ready, and when that time is up, His Son will return to earth for the First Resurrection when He will take to heaven both those from eternity who have obtained forgiveness and those alive who are faithful. When they are gone, grace will also be gone, and a great destruction will begin where one-third of all the people on earth will die. When the destruction ends, God will send His Son back to earth with those He had taken at the First Resurrection. These will have celestial (perfect) bodies and will reign as kings and priests for one thousand years of peace to bring testimony to everyone living or dead who was not taken in the First Resurrection. Satan will be bound during this time, unable to influence mankind, so all mankind will learn of and accept God."

"But after the one thousand years of peace, Satan will be loosed again for a little while so those who have now accepted God can be tried. Satan will wreak havoc on those not firm in their faith. Then will come the Day of Judgment when everyone, except those taken by Christ for the First Resurrection, will be judged. Some, which the Bible calls the goats, will be cast into hell with Satan forever while others, called the lambs, will inhabit God's new kingdom where there will be no sorrow and no tears. Those taken for the First Resurrection will continue to reign as kings and priests in the new kingdom. They will never have to be judged because their sins had been forgiven and entirely wiped away by God.

"Our desire is to work toward the completion of God's work here on earth, try to make ourselves worthy to be a child of God, and wait patiently for the return of His Son. We pray that those we love will be together in this new kingdom. We carry the hope in our hearts that soon God will find those who will become the bride for His Son. We are told in Romans 8:25, '*But if we hope for that we see not, then do we with patience wait for it.*'

"Okay, that's the basic plan, and scripture explains it all. Now to support what I've said, for instance, in Revelation 12:9, we learn that Satan was cast out of heaven. '*And the great dragon was cast out, that old serpent, called the Devil, and Satan, which deceiveth the whole world: he was cast out into the earth, and his angels were cast out with him.*'

"God warns us what will happen when this evil spreads and causes men to bring harm to one another. In Acts 20:29-31, we are told, '*For I know this, that after my departing shall grievous wolves enter in among you, not sparing the flock. Also of your own selves shall men arise, speaking perverse things, to draw away the disciples after them. Therefore watch.*'

"Then as we read further, we learn what Satan is like. For instance, in John 8:44 we are told, '*For he is a liar, and the father of it.*' And also in John 8:44, '*He was a murderer from the beginning, and abode not in the truth, because there is no truth in him.*' Then in Genesis 3:1, we can read, '*The serpent was more subtil than any beast.*' So in these few verses, we learn that Satan is a liar, a murderer, and is subtle in his attacks. Now in Matthew 4:1, it is important for us to note that Satan also tempts us. He is actually called the tempter. '*Then was Jesus led . . . to be tempted of the devil.*' And in *Matthew 4:3* '*And when the tempter came to him, he said.*'

"Additionally, Satan can move men to do his bidding (1 Chronicles 21:1), can walk back and forth on the earth (Job 1:7), can cause illness (Job 2:7), can take God's word from men's hearts (Mark 4:15), can enter man (Luke 22:3 and John 13:27), can blind the minds of them which believe not (2 Corinthians 4:4), can transform himself (2 Corinthians 11:14), can send messengers to hurt man (2 Corinthians 12:7), can hinder people (1 Thessalonians 2:18), and can produce signs and has powers (2 Thessalonians 2:9). It is important for us to know that Satan is capable of producing signs and has supernatural powers, '*Even him, whose coming is after the working of Satan with all power and signs and lying wonders.*'

"This verse in Thessalonians tells us that Satan is capable of producing signs and wonders. Signs and wonders support a belief in certain practices, symbols, or people. To safeguard us from being misled in this manner, God warns us not to embrace the practices of astrology, divining, numerology, and other occult practices. Signs and wonders from Satan can mislead us into believing false religions, especially those that say we don't have to *do* anything or overcome anything or need to act in a certain manner to become one of God's children. That's particularly frightening because our human nature encourages us to be complacent and lazy, and we are comfortable with our little daily sins. We can actually *like* them! Like the woman who hurt your mom. She probably thoroughly enjoyed her actions and had no remorse because she had either been convinced by a false doctrine that it was okay for her to behave that way or had justified her actions to herself!"

Suddenly, Bara spoke up and surprised everyone with the depth of his understanding. "I know when Satan is trying to make me do things that aren't right . . . It's when I hit Heza or when I get mad if Momma Ruth holds her and not me." Ruth had a rude awakening with those words and determined to give Bara more love and never cause him to think she preferred Heza over him. She'd thought he was so self-sufficient that he didn't want her to hug him. *Ohhh, out of the mouths of babes,* she thought!

John saved the moment by saying, "That's right, Bara. Wow, you sure do understand what that ole Satan wants to do, so from now on, you tell Mama Ruth how you feel because she *always* wants to hug you! But it's good that you understand where your angry feelings come from so you can get rid of them. God said in Matthew 5:6, '*Blessed are they which do hunger and thirst after righteousness: for they shall be filled.*'"

The evening flew by, and soon Wade told Heza and Bara that they should give everyone a kiss and say good night since it was long past their bedtime. He and Ruth took the children to their rooms after they said good night to everyone and got them ready for bed. The four of them said their prayers together, and then after a final hug from momma and poppa, they turned on their sides, ready to sleep.

When Ruth and Wade returned to the living room, the discussion had turned to the troubles that the family seemed to be currently experiencing. They were talking about how these troubles could be the result of an attack by Satan and his cohorts and if so, why.

Barbara was saying, "I've found in my life that as we grow in our faith and are about to take yet another step toward a greater trust in God and the acceptance of His will, something happens that causes us to waver in that faith or not accept His will but question it. This always happens with new believers. So I do believe that it *is* an assault on us and that God allows certain things to occur so we can be tested. We are not only tested so God or even Satan knows where our commitment lies, but also so *we* can see our commitment. I find that when I am tested, I grow in faith because it is through that heartache that I work harder to recognize God's plan and Satan's role. I also look more closely at my own actions and see where I haven't acted correctly or where I made a bad decision. I also recognize how much stronger in faith I've become after each difficulty has passed. This gives me confidence, and it shows me that I *am* developing in my faith. It becomes a sort of gift God's given me even though it hurts to go through the pain of its discovery. I've also learned not to let certain things bother me because I see from whence it comes. And best of all, I've learned to see God in all of it."

Ruth responded to what Barbara said with the words, "Wow, Barb, that's pretty deep, but it's also profoundly astute. What you've said makes me wonder if my faith is that strong. I mean, good for you, you have understood what God asks of you and you have made me say to myself I wanna be there too . . . I wanna be where you are in faith and understanding!"

"Well, don't forget, Ruth, I haven't had too many bitter moments, and I think that makes it easier to hang on to your faith. It's when the tests come. It's when we are so hurt that we ask ourselves where God is and that's when we are really tested. So I believe that it's the most *hurtful* circumstances we go through that holds us back the longest . . . but also provides us with the most *incredible* learning process. And you know, I really do believe in the generational thing . . . you know, the sins of the forefathers will be visited upon the third and fourth generation stuff. I mean, it kinda makes sense when we see some people really suffering time and again and others having it pretty good, hardly ever suffering. I have also seen that Satan doesn't bother the people he already has in his pocket. They seem to get off scot-free, yet I wouldn't want what they'll have in the end."

John interjected his thoughts. "From what we have gleaned from the Bible, there appears to be two categories of suffering—one is when we need to be tested, and the other is when we labor under the sins of our forefathers. Job, for instance, was simply tested. Job 1:11 tells us, *'But put forth thine hand now, and touch all that he hath, and he will curse thee to thy face.'* This shows that God was willing to prove that Job would remain faithful to Him. And in Job 42:10, we are told, *'And the LORD turned the captivity of Job.'* This verse shows us that Job had become a captive of Satan and that in time God freed Job from that captivity."

"This is why we need to pray for protection. Trust God. Learn. Put on the armour He offers us. These things work for our benefit whether we are being tested or whether Satan had an additional claim on us through the sins of our forefathers," Barbara added.

"This," Wade asked, "this sins of the forefathers or generational stuff is confusing to me. Can you go into more detail about it for me?"

John began to explain that when Adam and Eve ate the apple, thereby disobeying God, they opened the door to the curse that required mankind to learn about evil. But God arranged that through learning about evil, mankind could also learn to appreciate what is good. He explained that the requirement to learn of evil is the inheritance that resulted from the disobedience of Adam and Eve, and this is why it is called inherited sin.

"God gave us the sacrament of Baptism to help us overcome this influence. The sins of our forefathers is a little different although it works in a similar manner by being passed along from generation to generation. For want of a more precise explanation, I guess I can say that it is sort of like something that gets stuck in our DNA that must be dealt with. This is why some people never escape certain patterns. Alcoholism is one example I can give you. You often see this same tendency in a grandfather, a father, and a son. Only when we ask and allow God to cleanse us and then we take on the fight to overcome those patterns or tendencies or spirits can we break free. This is why God speaks over and over again in scripture about being an overcomer, fighting the good fight, watching for our enemy, praying for those who died in their sins, turning the other cheek, loving one another. He wouldn't keep repeating these things if it were not ongoing and important for us to do!"

John continued, saying, "It can even be seen with our country today. We've always been blessed as a country because we've kept God in everything, from school prayer to the décor of our government buildings to our currency. Now we are losing that blessing because a few are banning this form of thankfulness to, and acknowledgment of God. What had been passed down as a blessing from our ancestors is turning into a curse to future generations because we are taking God out of the equation. We also see the generational thing quite clearly as we witness the loss of faith, abuse, alcoholism, and a myriad of other problems going from grandfather to father to child. They call it a disease nowadays, but it is the generational thing. I mean, if you think about it, probably none of us here know what our ancestor four generations ago might have done, and if it was pretty bad, we might inherit the tendency toward that same sin or become the target of someone else who is driven to commit that sin. Without God's protection and what we have learned to help us fight this evil, we might be in some terrible circumstances. Conversely, we might have inherited the *blessings* we have and must be careful not to damage them for our own future generations."

"Geez, this is heavy stuff, John. I haven't been exposed to your church for very long and have to admit I never really studied the Bible, so I'm lost here," said Wade. "Yet what you say seems to make so much sense. I mean, as we see people harming one another for no apparent reason except some hate in their heart . . . I . . . well . . . I could never understand it. But if this is the nature they have inherited and they don't wish to change . . ."

Barbara pointed out that the troubles we cause or experience all come from Satan but could take one of three different paths—an inherited tendency caused by our ancestors which may never end, or directly from Satan or one of his evil spirits to specifically break our faith which usually ends and then starts up again, or allowed as a testing process we must endure which our faithfulness can bring to an end.

"Look at what's happened in our own circle in past years. My brother Paul met up with that terrible coach and was trapped, while still an innocent child, into the evil of addiction. Ruth, look at Satan's influence on your ex-husband and the suffering you and Jayden had to endure as a result. Wade, what about your wife's terrible illness, and Sarah's miscarriage, and Lorraine's surgery? Jim, look what happened to your mom because of that awful neighbor and the evil priest, and look how that damaged your faith. And remember Mary's foray into feng shui and what happened to her as a child? Oh, and what about the suicide bomber and how that person caused Bara's pain?"

"We've all been through a lot, and like Jim, each of us could have had all hope of trusting God taken from us. And all because of Satan or the actions of someone who was inspired by Satan. We are so blessed that God hung on to us and gave us the ministers and even role models like Grandma so we could be helped and we could understand. Through these means and through the Bible and the words of God we find in the Bible, we have been given the tools with which to fight evil. Without this wisdom, we wouldn't have known what to do or how to fight back, and we'd have been unable to be found worthy to become the bride of Christ. God seems to choose when we will receive this information. Then once we understand it, once we've been shown, it's up to us. It's our own free will to decide to serve God and overcome evil . . . . or not."

John added, "In a nutshell however, it's so simple. We can ask ourselves this: if we had a child we loved and that child and their new spouse would be coming to live with us, wouldn't we want that spouse to be the kind of person who would be honest, loving, self-sacrificing, loyal, forgiving, communicative—all those things and more? Sure we would! So does God. He wants the bride for His Son to have these attributes—to be someone with integrity and good character, to be loyal and willing to fight for and beside Him, and someone who learns of Him and is loving. Just understanding *this* shows us that we have to grow up and into these attributes as well."

"God describes that development in the bride of Christ in Revelation 19:7, *'Let us be glad and rejoice, and give honour to him: for the marriage of the Lamb is come, and his wife hath made herself ready.'* This tells us that *we*, if we want to become that bride, have to make *ourselves* ready. And in Revelation 18:23, God tells us that the bride had developed so beautifully that she was like a light that shone on earth and that when she left, others would notice because that light left with her. *'And the light of a candle shall shine no more at all in thee; and the voice of the bridegroom and of the bride shall be heard no more.'* This means that those who bring testimony will no longer be here on earth to bring it."

Then Jim added, "So you are saying that we are blessed because we are hearing all this stuff. That we'd better get on track so we can be a part of the bride. You're saying that we might not have another chance to be worthy for the first go-round, which is the First Resurrection, and thus will have to suffer and then be judged. Well, you said it's simple, but it's not. I am appreciative of what God has given me, but I don't buy into God allowing evil to hurt us. Why would He do that? Hey, Wade, I guess you think you'll be way ahead of me to become a bride in the church and leave me out! Some friend you are. Capitulating without even a fight or a question. Don't be a beleaguered bedlamite." Jim's sarcasm had surfaced again, and it was hurtful to everyone.

Barbara felt her heart sink and wondered if Jim was hiding his own fear of not fulfilling what God asked of him. She sent a prayer to ask God to intervene and bring about a change of heart in Jim. The words from Proverbs 24:3 popped into her head which said, *"Through wisdom is an house builded; and by understanding it is established."*

She had waited a long time for Jim's understanding to be opened. Would God reward her patience and answer her prayers? If He would, then she wouldn't have to worry about Jim anymore for God would carry Jim in the palm of His hand as He did all His children. And what about the baby that would soon arrive? Would Jim influence the child negatively? They would have to talk. Right now she felt discouraged and angry.

Wade was also shocked by what Jim said, and he knew that Barbara had been deeply hurt. So he quietly said, "Okay then, Jim, I'll do this without you, but I have to say I'm disappointed that your heart is so closed. I think you are dead wrong. I have questioned and my questions have been answered and *my* heart *has* been touched. Beware that *you* don't end up being the beleaguered bedlamite."

"Yeah, Wade, well, so I have a closed heart . . . Maybe I am brassbound, meaning firmly immovable in purpose or will. But I'm happy for you, and I wish you well as you find out what you've gotta do and do it! But . . . uhhh . . . you really ready to don a wedding dress? You're gonna look downright hilarious!"

There was silence in the room for a moment as everyone digested Jim's obvious and angry shutdown. They were disappointed in him but knew there was nothing they could do. This was going to be a choice that Jim would have to make for himself. But their patience with Jim was wearing thin.

Wade was angry too but decided that it was best to let it go. He knew Jim and knew that when he behaved this way, it was to defend himself from something. Maybe that was a good thing, maybe Jim *was* feeling God working in him. So Wade laughed to lighten the moment and replied, "Well, Jim, I think you're just jealous! I do look a lot better than you do even in a wedding dress!" And everyone laughed, happy that Wade understood and had let it go. If God could still be patient with Jim, they should be as well, but they were all concerned by what Jim had said and by his tone.

Barbara was heartbroken by Jim's behavior and silently thought, *No, Wade, right now Jim looks downright ugly to me by the way he spoke, but maybe it's just that he's scared. The commitment is too great for him. I wish Jim's behavior hadn't hurt me so much and hadn't made me feel so lost.*

While everyone laughed at what Wade said, in their hearts, they worried about Jim. His attitude was actually rebellious, not simply defensive. That wasn't good. Then one by one, they each said that it was getting late and they'd better be leaving for home. They carried the remaining dishes and glasses to the kitchen and stood in a circle while John prayed for their safe journey home, and finally having thoroughly enjoyed what they had shared about the work of God, they left. Who would have guessed that in one night, they'd learn that Wade, Bara, and Heza would join the church and that Wade and Ruth would set a date to be married!

But as Barbara gathered her things to leave Wade's house and go home, she couldn't help but remember the words that God had said to Job to encourage him to remember who he was. The words she recalled came from Job 40:7-8 and said, *Gird up thy loins now like a man: I will demand of thee, and declare thou unto me. Wilt thou also disannul my judgment? Wilt thou condemn me, that thou mayest be righteous?*

Chapter Ten

MATT AND SARAH:
CHALLENGES OF FAITH

Sarah was crying when Matt walked into the house. She'd been across the street talking with Mary. Being with Teddie, hugging him, watching him smile, listening to the precious sounds of a happy healthy baby brought the pain of losing Robert into her heart once again. Sarah *wanted* to accept God's will for her life; she even wanted to accept it with a cheerful heart as God wished, but she couldn't.

She was struggling with what had happened. She wanted to understand why Robert had to die, and she wanted to know that Robert, in death, was okay. Because he was just a baby, Sarah couldn't imagine how he might function in eternity, how he would be cared for, or who would care for him. She felt an uncontrollable fear for him, wondering if he too was afraid. She needed to *know* he was okay.

Once again, just as when Matt's brother died, she'd been thrown into a circumstance where she needed comfort; she needed to understand. If only she knew that God had a reason for Robert's death. Sarah struggled with these thoughts—on the one hand feeling guilty for not accepting God's will and, on the other hand knowing that in the past God had always answered her questions and opened her understanding.

That understanding had given her the ability to accept, to trust. Sarah knew what the Bible said, and she believed what the Bible said, so perhaps she should do as Grandma had always advised and turn to God's words for her comfort. If she prayed fervently for help, she believed that God would talk to her through scripture.

She wasn't looking for empirical evidence, for infallible scientific proof that Robert was okay, just something that would comfort her. She wanted something she could take on faith, some little word or phrase or story that she could apply to her situation that would calm her fears. She wanted the assurance that God still loved her, that He was totally in control of *everything* that happened to them. She wanted something that supported her need to believe that there was a good reason for what happened and that God had *ordained* it to happen. Then she would know that Robert was safe, that God would look after him. If she could just find this assurance, she would be okay.

Sarah's mind had been engaging so many difficult questions that this exercise left her exhausted, and finally, she could no longer find the strength even to pretend to be okay and gave in to her sadness. Only crying seemed to release the pressure, the frustration, and the terrible pain. It was as if she could hold only so much pain, and when she was full of it, then only crying would empty just enough of it to allow it to begin filling her once again. The worry in her heart for her baby was so paramount that she could hardly bear to think anymore and wished she could sleep to escape her thoughts. Grandma's little trick of yelling no to unkind or disturbing thoughts wasn't working the way it usually did.

It was at one of the moments when crying was necessary that Matt walked into the house. He felt terrible when he heard her sobs and recognized how much pain she felt. He understood why Sarah cried; he cried too in his own way. But he was confident that God knew that what He brought into their lives was right and that even though they didn't like it or understand it, it was necessary or God would use it in some way for the benefit of them all.

Maybe he was more pragmatic than Sarah, or maybe it was that Sarah had been the one to carry Robert so close to her heart for seven months and her bond was stronger. Maybe, as the doctor said, her depression was, in part, due to hormonal levels seeking to adjust once more. Nevertheless, Sarah suffered and Matt wished that he could give her comfort. Deep concern for Sarah filled his heart, and his desire to find a way to comfort her became of utmost importance to him.

Robert was special to both of them; he was and always would be their first child. They had felt his little kicks against Sarah's skin. They had talked to him and embraced him through Sarah's tummy. They had prayed with him by each placing one hand on Sarah's stomach as they prayed aloud. They had made so many plans for his future and, in fact, had ordered a crib, dresser, rocking chair, and changing table for his room just the week before they lost him.

They had both asked for and received the confinement blessing from their minister and had followed what he suggested to protect their child and to provide him with what they could to support his spiritual life. They did not watch a television show that contained violence or horror. Sarah did not read any books, magazines, or newspaper articles containing violence, terror, or gossip. They did not listen to loud vibrating music, songs with improper words, blasphemy or demeaning innuendo, but rather soothing music, perhaps classical or gospel music. Their favorite music was in fact the CDs created by their own church choirs, some of the most beautiful from the South Africa congregations.

They were careful about what their baby heard because they'd read that scientists had discovered that babies could hear through the womb. Their doctor had also told them of the incredible phenomena this seemed to be. Even the ministers of their church explained this to all expectant mothers and incorporated this into the confinement blessing when mothers-to-be asked them to pray for the child they carried and for their own well-being throughout the pregnancy.

Matt and Sarah followed this advice because they loved their baby. They wanted the best for him, and most of all, they wanted a godly environment for him. They'd wanted his environment, even in the womb, to be peaceful and happy. They'd wanted God's blessing for their baby. And they believed that every baby, every fetus, every embryo was a child that God knew and that God loved. Never before had Sarah had the need to be assured that God would look after all these children born or not.

Matt remembered Sarah asking him for a quarter so she could add this to her own offering when they went to church. As Sarah dropped the quarter along with her own offering into the box at the back of the sanctuary, she placed one hand on her tummy and whispered, "This is your offering, sweetheart, and soon you will be able to give it to God yourself." Matt was touched by Sarah's actions, and his heart had filled with the wonder of how special Sarah was to do this.

They had learned that their baby was a boy when the doctor ordered a sonogram. They had been to the doctor for Sarah's six-month checkup, and when Sarah mentioned that the baby seemed to be sleeping more because he seemed to kick less, the doctor wanted to be sure there was no problem. Nothing unusual showed up on the sonogram to indicate a problem, so they returned to their routine and tentatively chose the name Robert for their son.

Then at seven months, Sarah went into labor and delivered the baby. While the delivery was quick and easy, Robert was born never to take a breath. The doctors did not know what had happened, but said that they had not been able to hear a heartbeat when Sarah went into labor and suspected that something had happened perhaps a few hours or days earlier.

Matt's first instinct was to reassure Sarah that there would be other children, but as he considered this approach, he realized that another child would not be Robert. Sarah needed to mourn Robert first. She needed to give the pain of her loss over to God and begin to heal.

Matt realized that what he'd first thought to say would have been inconsiderate, not only toward Sarah, but also toward Robert. Such an approach would appear to take away how important Robert was to them. He understood that now. Therefore, for the moment, all Matt could think to do was to try to comfort Sarah, hold her, maybe even distract her in some way, and pray, asking God to comfort her.

Sarah had been very quiet when they came home from the hospital. She was sweet and responsive when a reply was necessary but only spoke to be polite. She was not her usual bubbly self. Matt was worried. He'd finally asked Sarah if she would agree to speak with their minister again and ask him to pray with them. But it hadn't seemed to help.

Now Sarah was asking him to help her search the Bible for a better understanding of why God had taken Robert, just as they had when Paul died. They had put aside a number of days after Paul died to search the Bible for answers as to why God had allowed Paul to suffer so much and die so young. Their search had been incredibly productive. Thus, Matt understood how important this new undertaking was to Sarah and that this was something they would have to do, do soon, and do together.

Matt didn't have a clue about what they should look for in the Bible or how they should begin their search. They already understood not only life after death but also understood that Christ had brought testimony about grace to the dead in eternity. They understood their obligation to pray for those in eternity to help them and support the work of salvation that took place there. But now Matt only knew that there was a question that haunted not only Sarah but also many who lost a child, and as far as he knew, no one had ever found the answer to that question in scripture. So he was worried about the outcome of Sarah's search.

But Matt's faith also gave him the assurance that somehow, someway, God would lead them to the words that would comfort them, show them that He never made a mistake and would reassure them that He was with them . . . . and Robert. Matt was determined to do his best to help Sarah find those words, the words God would provide. They set a date and time to bring their Bibles, concordances, notepads, and pencils to their cocktail table for a concerted effort to find what they needed in scripture.

The next day, Matt and Sarah heard the wonderful news about Ruth and Wade's engagement. When they heard that Wade, along with Heza and Bara, were to be adopted by the congregation and then a few weeks later, when the apostle arrived, receive the Holy Sealing, they were thrilled! Jim and Barbara said they would hold a special engagement fellowship for Wade and Ruth, and Wade had specifically asked if they could all engage in a conversation about the things of faith that Wade still wanted to learn.

When they spoke with Wade, he also told them about the conversation he'd had a week ago during which John had shown them his notes about Satan and the power of evil. Wade told them that he'd been fascinated by what he learned. He realized how little he knew about God, God's plan for mankind, and certainly about evil. He was anxious to learn more and looked forward to the next fellowship they would have.

Knowing that Sarah needed those who loved her to gather around her at this time and perhaps even a distraction, Matt had been delighted to place the date for the fellowship on their calendar and to have something so pleasing to talk to Sarah about.

But after their conversation with Wade, Matt could see that Sarah was still despondent and terribly anxious to study the Bible to find her answers. Matt worried for Sarah's sake, wondering if her questions even could be answered and silently asked God to direct their way. He was glad that he believed, because he knew that nowadays so many people had no knowledge of God.

Even today's political movement pulled away from God and scripture; debates raged about godly matters and even went against the foundations of American democracy. There was a constant and heated battle about when life began, and politicians were engaged in the questions of whether or not using embryos for research was murder, whether abortion was a sin, whether evolution negated creation, even whether or not God existed. It seemed that no one had the courage to stand up and make a definitive pro-God, pro-life statement anymore. It seemed as if few politicians upheld God's statutes at all.

With unbelief or erroneous belief so rampant in the world and growing every day, Matt did not want to do anything that might lead to a lack of trust in God in their own lives. Matt accepted that, as the husband, he was considered the "house priest" entrusted by God to look after his family's spiritual life. He was responsible for this, and as such, he needed to be careful to uphold the standard that God asked of him. He was responsible for Sarah's spiritual life too, so he needed to make sure this wouldn't derail her faith but strengthen it. And so Matt asked himself, *How can I help Sarah?*

Matt realized that their upcoming fellowship would cheer Sarah. It was usually great fun to be with Jim when the subject of politics came up. Jim's quick wit and cutting sarcasm, coupled with his incredible knowledge of what was happening in the world, always gave everyone food for thought and brought his point clearly to the forefront. Jim had strong conservative values and wasn't afraid to voice them or fight for them.

They'd often talk of politics at their fellowships, and seldom was anyone offended by differing opinions, but at heart they were all conservative, engaged in religious pursuits and desirous of equal opportunity for everyone. They wanted their politicians and government to have integrity and to follow what God asked of them. So usually they rooted for the same people, hoped for what was best for their country, and most of the time, they agreed on who the bad guys were. Sometimes they were afraid for those who stood up for God on television and radio talk shows; they worried that someone driven by hatred would assassinate one of them for what they stood for. They prayed for their country, its leaders, and all who had the courage to defend biblical standards.

But right now, Sarah had only one focus. She wasn't interested in politics, debates, or discussions. She was only interested in when they could tackle the questions she had and find the comfort and reassurance she needed. And Matt was going to have to make that commitment of time for Sarah.

But just as they began to discuss their plan of action, Deb and Josh dropped in and hit them with a bombshell: Deb and Josh were getting married in early November, only a few months away! They hadn't expected them to tie the knot so soon. Nevertheless, they were happy for them, knowing that Deb and Josh had been through a testing of their relationship and had come through it still in love and dedicated to doing what it took to keep the relationship strong. Josh had really turned his life around, and Debbie thrived under his love.

The wedding was going to be a small one. Debbie had commiserated over her raucous, non-religious family—who to invite, where they would stay, how long they would stay—and almost had decided to elope because of these problems. But Debbie wanted a real wedding in the church with the blessing that went with it. So they decided to have a small wedding and a small reception in the back of the church with no alcohol, simple food, and a wonderful wedding cake.

They told Matt and Sarah that they planned to ask Ann and Caleb, Mary and Kevin and Ruth and Wade to bring a crock-pot filled with something they all enjoyed. They asked Matt and Sarah if they would also be willing to bring their favorite dish. Josh told them that they wanted the wedding and reception to be a genteel and spiritual gathering and that they had warned Deb's parents that there would be no liquor served and that they could bring none with them. They had also found the courage to ask them sweetly not to drink before they came to the ceremony, to be kind and not to tease or use cruel barbs, just try to be nice to everyone.

At first, Deb had been afraid to say anything at all to her parents but told Matt and Sarah that she was proud of herself for letting them know that she wanted the blessing on her marriage and didn't want any spirits attached to the past to ruin the day. Debbie asked her minister to pray with her and to ask God to give her the courage to stand up to her parents, let them know what she wanted, yet help her be kind and loving to them.

Josh too spoke with her parents to explain that he and Debbie were asking God for a special blessing on their union and that they were asking everyone to treat the entire day as a holy day, a special moment with God. Her parents had been dumbfounded. They felt that weddings were supposed to be filled with music and dancing and conga lines, drinking and laughing, finding the garter on the bride, telling embarrassing stories about the bride and groom and teasing them about the wedding night. They didn't understand the importance of a marriage blessing.

It had been a tense moment, but then, having met Josh and seeing what a gentleman he was and assuming his whole family would be that way, they grumbled at Debbie and Josh's nerve to lecture them but then reluctantly agreed to abide by their rules. Matt and Sarah assured Debbie that she had done the right thing, that the blessing was the most important element, and it needed to be protected.

Only Elizabeth and their minister knew that Debbie and Josh were to have a child in February. The four of them met to discuss how this problem should be handled. They began their discussion by praying and asking God to guide them. Debbie requested the confinement blessing, wanting everything that God so graciously offered them for this special time and incredible gift. The result of their discussion was, with the approval of their minister, that they should not say anything about the pregnancy until after the wedding.

When the minister gave them the confinement blessing in the sacristy, they were told to be sure that everything they did and said and saw and heard would be something they believed would be good for their child. And so with their secret held close to their hearts and a concerted effort to do what was right, the wedding plans went forward. Elizabeth helped Debbie with the things a mother usually provided a daughter in terms of advice and assistance. Deb expected her baby in mid-February. Their wedding was to take place on November 7, so Deb would be close to six months pregnant. Deb and Josh were afraid. Their fear came from knowing they had broken the trust of those who loved them, including their Heavenly Father.

It wasn't that Debbie and Josh were ashamed of the pregnancy or wanted to hide the pregnancy. Yes, she and Josh should have waited or at least been more careful, but they were both thrilled to be having a child. They had completed college, had great jobs, and planned to purchase a house before the baby arrived. The only reason that they decided to hide the pregnancy was to avoid the terrible things she knew her parents would say at the wedding if they knew about it. Her parents would rob her of the blessing she so desperately sought. They would judge; they would be pleased to point out Debbie's fall from grace as they'd put it. They would want everyone to think that Josh was not all he was purported to be. This was just the way they were, the way they had always been. They loved to judge and condemn others. It wasn't something they did consciously, they just didn't know any other way.

And when Josh and Debbie discussed their concerns with their minister, he'd agreed that it would do no harm to wait until after the wedding to announce the pregnancy. While Debbie would have been content not to invite her parents at all, she and Josh had finally decided that by not mentioning the pregnancy until after the wedding, they could still do what they thought was the right thing to do which was to include her parents in their wedding plans.

Josh's family, on the other hand, never judged; they just loved and understood, and this made Debbie and Josh feel even worse that they had broken the trust the family placed in them. But when they talked it over—Josh, their minister, Elizabeth, who would run interference for them, and her—it was decided not to mention the pregnancy to either family until her parents went back home. Then later, if her parents realized that Deb had been pregnant at the wedding, they could no longer do any harm.

Debbie had already spoken with the dressmaker who had fashioned Sarah's wedding gown and had also made Sarah's bridesmaid's gowns. Mary had been one of Sarah's bridesmaids and had been about seven months pregnant with Teddie at that time. The dressmaker advised Debbie to select a gown with an empire waistline with lots of fabric flowing both in the front and in the back from the bustline and perhaps a series of small hoops to keep the skirt away from her body. If Debbie remained as slim as she normally was except for the bulge of the baby and didn't hold her flowers under her waist, she might be able to hide her pregnancy up to and including that day.

But for now, all Matt and Sarah knew was that Josh and Deb had a wedding coming up and that they wanted to do whatever they could to help. They told Debbie that they would be happy to bring something scrumptious to eat at the reception. Debbie told Sarah that she planned to ask Sarah, Ann, Ruth, Mary and Rebecca if they would be willing to purchase dresses for the wedding that coordinated well with one another. Perhaps each dress could all have the same-length skirt, the same-length sleeve, similar in cut and style, but that each would be of a different color. This would make the bridal party somewhat matched, very festive, and yet it would not put such a burden of expense or time on anyone that bridesmaid's gowns would and everyone would be wearing their favorite colors. And, they could all use the dresses again, anytime.

Sarah thought it was a great idea and that they would all be thrilled with the concept and the ease. In fact, she thought it would be a great idea if the gals went out together to shop and really coordinated their dresses so Debbie would be pleasantly surprised by what a nice combination of colors they could create. Sarah was excited by the prospect of doing this, and this pleased Matt. Debbie told Sarah that Barbara had asked if she could simply sit on the sidelines since her baby was due only two weeks after the wedding and could actually come early.

When Josh and Deb left, Matt commented about how amazing it was to think that in just a few years the family had grown to include not only the "big" brother and sister that Jayden and Rebecca represented, but also Bara, Heza, Andrew, Lorraine, Teddie, and soon another from Barbara and Jim. The count amounted to nine children ranging in age from fifteen years old down! Then he immediately wondered if what he'd said would bring Sarah's pain back to the forefront again. But Sarah, so happy for the others, was okay with their conversation and Matt was relieved.

Nevertheless, Matt recommitted himself to comforting Sarah as best he could. They talked for a while of all the upcoming events. He could see that Sarah was feeling better and asked her if she would like to go out to dinner and suggested that over dinner they could talk about what plans they needed to arrange for their Bible study.

He suggested they bring their calendar and choose when they would devote time to their project. He added that they could also discuss the upcoming fellowship when Wade planned to ask his questions and they would all be scrambling to answer them coherently! They could also talk about Deb and Josh's wedding. Matt wanted to help Sarah think about happy times and the joy the family had in one another's company.

But just before they left for the restaurant, Jim phoned to ask if Matt and Sarah would be willing to hold the fellowship for Wade and Ruth because Barbara was struggling with bouts of nausea at all times of the day and evening. Barbara had already lost ten pounds from being unable to eat and was too exhausted to hold the fellowship. They would, however, attend the fellowship if Matt and Sarah would hold it for them. He assured Matt and Sarah that otherwise, all was well with Barbara. Matt and Sarah readily agreed, and Matt was pleased knowing this would keep Sarah busy and help take her mind off their loss.

Sarah knew that Matt wanted to go out to dinner because he wanted to do something she might enjoy and take her mind off her worries. She didn't have the energy to cook so she gladly agreed to go. She washed her face, grabbed her jacket, and they left for the little Bavarian restaurant where they had once laughed about the fish shaped cutting board that had held the steaks they'd ordered. They remembered that day when they burst out laughing at the same time the moment their food was served. Their steaks rested in a wooden fish fitted into a metal plate.

They were reminded of the cutting board that had hung on the wall of Grandpa's mother's home. The fish reminded them of the story Grandma told of her first meeting with Grandpa's family. His family had played a joke on Grandma using a fish cutting board and later Grandma and Grandpa purchased a similar cutting board for every member of the family so they would not forget what they had done to her. It was such a great story and had created special memories for them.

Matt and Sarah ordered steaks once again, smothered with caramelized onions. They also ordered mashed potatoes and gravy and broccoli. It was delicious! And Sarah felt better. Over an ice cream sundae with hot fudge sauce, they made their plans. Every Tuesday and Thursday evening and every Saturday morning, they would spend two hours searching for the answers to Sarah's questions until they were satisfied. And they would telephone everyone when they got home tonight to make sure they knew that the fellowship would be held at their house instead of at Barbara and Jim's house.

When they arrived home, Matt called some of the family on his cell phone while Sarah called the others on the house line and it was all settled; they would all be there for the fellowship on Saturday, and they would all bring something scrumptious to eat. Everyone would be bringing a casserole, a Crock-Pot, or a salad, and really, it didn't matter what was brought because it was the fellowship that counted. Matt and Sarah would take care of coffee, soda, wine, dessert, and appetizers. Sarah became animated again, and Matt was pleased.

When Sarah phoned Mary about the change in the location of where their fellowship would be held, she learned of the recent activities at Mary's house. Since the carriage house had been completed and Elizabeth had sold her house, the movers were scheduled to arrive with the possessions that Elizabeth and Rebecca wanted from the house that had been sold. Most of the furniture for the carriage house was new, so there would not be too many items for the movers to bring. Elizabeth and Rebecca had already packed the few things they had kept at Mary's house so these too could be moved easily into the carriage house. They were excited about their move.

Rebecca would finally have a "grown-up room." She had followed the advice the gals had given her when they'd gotten together to be fitted for the gowns for Matt and Sarah's wedding. What a fun day that had been! Of course, the reason that Rebecca didn't bring any of the furniture from her room in the old house was because she considered it too childish for her new teenage sophistication! Elizabeth also purchased quite a few new pieces of furniture for the carriage house so she could create the divine proportion she wanted. She also considered the ideas Grandma listed in her manuscript that would please God and used all of the ideas on Grandma's list that she could possibly incorporate.

Mary told Sarah that most likely everyone would be popping into the carriage house in the next few days to offer help and to check everything out. The rooms had been either built to divine proportion or they had been furnished in a way that created divine proportion, and they all wanted to see it and "feel" it. Everyone had a copy of Grandma's divine proportion math-method of decorating, and Sarah had created yet another journal from the manuscript that told the story of divine proportion, a monkey swing and God's blessing. Everyone who read it couldn't help but wonder about divine proportion and quickly locate a tape measure so they could see how their rooms fared.

Matt and Sarah also planned to offer a helping hand at the carriage house and agreed that they too would pop in tomorrow. If they felt that they could help in any way, they would put aside their study and lend themselves to doing what they could. If they were needed, they'd get back to their study another day. If they were not needed, they would begin their study as scheduled.

The next day, after visiting the carriage house, taking a tour of the rooms, and seeing people already unpacking towels and sheets, knickknacks, and kitchen utensils, they could see that they would not be needed. They returned home and began their Bible study by first praying for guidance. Then they began making a list of what they hoped to find during their study. This proved difficult because they knew there were no direct questions nor direct answers about their circumstance. They would have to watch for the guidance and love they knew God would provide for them through scripture. Sarah needed comfort, reassurance that everything would be okay. Matt had already prayed that they would find what God wanted them to know.

At that moment, their doorbell rang. Barbara and Jim, having completed their tour of the carriage house and also deciding that there were enough people helping Elizabeth already, decided to visit Matt and Sarah for a little while. Matt told them that he and Sarah were about to embark on a Bible study, and Barbara excitedly asked if they could join them. Sarah was delighted, explaining that she wanted to see if she could find anything in the Bible that would address her concerns about Robert.

They sat together on the couch in the living room to create a list of words to look up in the concordance. Although they already knew that God had said that studying the Bible was like a mystery that would unfold, Sarah suggested they look up the word *mystery* once again in the concordance. Reading those words yet again might give them a clue. They found five references to scripture which contained the word *mysteries*. They were in Matthew 13:11; Luke 8:10; 1 Corinthians 4:1, 13:2, and 14:2. They also found twenty-two references to scriptures containing the word *mystery*. Not all of these pertained to what they were looking for, but they checked all of them for clues.

They read in Matthew 13:11 "*He answered and said unto them, Because it is given unto you to know the mysteries of the kingdom of heaven, but to them it is not given*" and remarked about how blessed they were that God helped them understand and, through that understanding, be comforted by His words. It was humbling for all of them. Then they read in Luke 8:10: "*And he said, Unto you it is given to know the mysteries of the kingdom of God.*"

They looked also at some of the verses that used the word *mystery* and found in Romans 11:25 "*For I would not, brethren, that ye should be ignorant of this mystery*" and in Romans 16:25 "*Now to him that is of power to stablish you according to my gospel, and the preaching of Jesus Christ, according to the revelation of the mystery, which was kept secret since the world began.*" Then they decided to see what was written in the book of Revelation since it was the last book of the Bible. What had been recorded there might bring a conclusion to the words they read previously. Revelation 10:7 said, "*But in the days of the voice of the seventh angel, when he shall begin to sound, the mystery of God should be finished.*"

"Matt, I can't believe there are people in this world who continue to function well yet know none of these things of God. Do you think it makes a distinct impact on their current life or only on their eternal life?"

"Not on their current life. And the reason I say that is because Satan wants them happy and unaware of their end. He knows that if people don't know what God says, they won't do what God asks, and if they don't do what God asks, Satan can pretty much ask anything of them that their moral system will allow. While even their moral system can eventually be corrupted, complacency about God is easy for Satan to obtain and less easily spotted by his victims! We think of evil as murder, torture, abuse and things that are blatantly wrong. But there is much more to evil than that. We let things *slide* when they are subtle even if they keep us from God. Things such as being lukewarm which encompasses being complacent; missing church services which encompasses the potential to miss the sacraments of Baptism, Holy Communion, absolution and Holy Sealing. It is also easy to neglect learning God's words, or what evil is, or what our future will be, or even the power of prayer. Satan loves to engage in these subtleties because he can accomplish so much without us realizing what is happening."

Barbara added, "That's sad. My heart really goes out to the people who don't know God or how Satan works. And if they had the opportunity to do so and turned it down, someday they will be so sorry."

"Well, I too feel badly for them. But we also have to remember that God is constantly working to bring His word to everyone. Whether testimony is brought through a relative, a friend, a book, a television broadcast, a minister, even a movie, everyone is brought God's word. But many will *not* listen, and of this group, some will be those whom Satan uses to persecute God's children. God's children are striving to learn His words and to follow them even when they have to grit their teeth to do it. God provides over and over again the means by which people can learn if they want to. But remember, God spoke of those who hear yet won't budge in Acts 7:51, '*Ye stiffnecked . . . in heart and ears, ye do always resist the Holy Ghost: as your fathers did, so do ye.*'"

Then Jim asked quietly, "Does Satan really have that much power over whether someone responds to God's words or not? Is this what happened . . . I mean, is this what you're saying happened . . . with me . . . are you aiming those words at me?"

Matt answered him, "Well, not necessarily, Jim, but let's look at that more carefully. Some people are lazy, you are not. They *know*, but they choose not to *do* simply because they are lazy. Some feel that they have too many other things to do, you don't fall into this category because you come to church. Then there are the complainers, those who 'murmur' as the Bible puts it, and you are not a complainer either. Then there are those who are evil, or led by evil who would never consider a relationship with God, and that's not you either.

But then Jim, there are also those who—like you, Jim—have been disillusioned, and yes, Satan did that although now, *knowing* what you do, you *are* allowing Satan and the bitterness and disillusionment he instilled in you to keep you back. Have you ever prayed that God would open your eyes, your understanding, and your heart to what He wants you to do? Have you ever asked yourself if you are not fighting back because it's easier for you not to. Or if the commitment you'd have to make in your heart is too great, and so you choose to harden your heart and sadly you choose not to do anything ? I don't know, and maybe you don't either . . . . but these are good questions to ask."

Jim was completely taken back by what Matt had just said. He was hurt. What Matt had said was . . . personal. He was surprised, shocked. He thought, *How dare he say that to me! He's judging me!* Then he thought, *I should be angry, really angry at Matt, but I'm not. I should call him on this . . . Why aren't I? Is it because he's right and I should ask these questions?*

Barbara, glad that Matt had had the courage to let Jim know what he felt, added, "Matt, maybe it's important to ask ourselves what God would want or not want in a bride for His Son. Would God want His Son's bride to have a hardened heart, or be unable to give his heart to his bride?

Sarah interjected, "Can you imagine the bride of the Lord Jesus doing something mean-spirited? For instance, like what Jim's mom had to go through with the woman and the bench. Or can you imagine the bride of Christ being sarcastic or cutting in her speech or plotting behind closed doors? Or one that would not want to talk to Him, listen to Him, learn of Him, believe Him? I don't think God would choose a spouse like that for His Son. In fact, that's how we all should think. We should all ask ourselves, would I want my spouse to act toward me as he does toward God?"

Jim remained quiet, still stinging from Matt's words. He was hurt by Barbara's words and devastated to hear the sadness in her voice. He wasn't pleased with Sarah's remarks either.

Matt's words had been like a knife entering his chest. And now, he was feeling berated *again* by Sarah's remarks. *Who would want a spouse like that?* Boy, that stung. Jim wanted to come up with a witty, sarcastic reply, but he'd lost the will and energy for it.

Then Sarah, Barbara, and Matt, unaware of Jim's thoughts, began to discuss how what God arranged for those in eternity was a mystery to many who didn't know what the Bible taught. They remembered what they had learned about death when Paul died. They remembered the journal Sarah had written about death and, through that research, understood why God asked them to pray for the dead.

Matt suggested they also review what they learned about inherited sin. He said that the thought had been nagging at him that perhaps—and this was only his scientific mind presenting a possibility they could explore—perhaps God allows some people to die young because they have reached the pinnacle of the development they can achieve on earth. Maybe there's something in some people's DNA or something that shuts down at a certain time or, worse yet, something that is not good for them that will become active and so it is actually a blessing to be taken early. Maybe it has something to do with inherited sin.

"Sarah, we know that God is love. Pure, perfect love. He loves everyone who was ever born, or conceived, or died and wants *everyone* to be found worthy. He gives everyone equal opportunity to do so. Yeah, He's provided the First Resurrection. But look, He's also provided a second chance by providing Judgment Day too! So it could be that one of the reasons someone dies young is because of the love God has for them. Rather than let a soul live a life where at a certain point sin will increase in their lives for some reason, God takes them—as a blessing. With Paul, I think this was true, but it was also because God could use Paul to bring testimony in eternity. But for others, it could be to stop sin from overwhelming them."

At first, Sarah was horrified by this idea. Jim was nervous about this train of thought as well but still said nothing. Then Sarah spoke her thoughts aloud, saying, "Are you saying it is possible that either someone could become steeped in sin because the sins of many forefathers come together in that person, or because God sees them slipping and acts to save them? Are you saying that because God would never want someone to suffer from either the sins they will succumb to or from the inherited sin they have to battle, He has made special provisions for them? Or are you just saying that because something traumatic might happen in their lives that would cause their loss of faith or even cause them to have hatred toward God, He has to take them?"

"Well, I'm not sure, Sarah. I'm just throwing out some possibilities. We know that inherited sin and the sins of our forefathers affect us. We also know that God made provisions through Holy Baptism, Holy Communion, and Holy Sealing and the Holy Spirit as well as through learning His words so we can be protected from these circumstances. But while we do not understand the whole picture, we do know that God's plan covers everything that pertains to His children and to all of mankind as well. We know that God wants *all* men to be saved."

As they mulled the idea of an accumulation of inherited sin over in their mind, they began to realize how little any of them knew about their ancestors from many generations ago. Then after a few minutes of silence, Jim, intrigued by this conversation enough to forget his hurt said, "Matt, I realize that no one knows what their ancestors from hundreds of years ago were involved in, just as no one knows what provides some people with genius levels of a particular talent. It's true that anyone's ancestors, especially those living hundreds of years or even a thousand years ago, could have done anything . . . good or bad. There may have been fathers and sons who murdered people and conversely there could have been fathers and sons who diligently studied piano, and either of these—the curse *or* the blessing—could have found their way into us. I guess it also follows that those good or bad actions could have been repeated over the many generations that followed as well. And this generation would never know from whence it came."

Jim's words made sense. They sat and thought for a moment about the repercussions of this conjecture, and then Sarah added, "You know, there are still many mysteries about why God decides someone will live and another will not, and somehow, . . . well, perhaps some things—maybe even this which we are talking about—needs to *remain* a mystery for some reason. But as we have been talking, one verse in the Bible keeps jumping into my mind. I remember a verse that spoke about the instructions given to the Israelites who were conquering a particular city. They were told not to allow anyone in that city to live, not men or women or children either. Not even the animals. And that instruction wasn't given just for one city, but for many. I remember now that I couldn't understand why the Israelites were given instructions to kill everyone. In one city they could live, but in another, either some or all had to die. Do you remember that? Oh, I don't know if I want to know this. Maybe there are some things that God feels we are not equipped to understand. Barbara, what do you think?"

"Maybe knowing would hurt too much, make us worry all the time, or maybe we'd have too many additional questions if we knew certain things. Or maybe we'd always be afraid . . . Or use what we know to distract from the Gospel. In fact, we know that God doesn't open the understanding of some because they would use their knowledge improperly, use it to debate or distract from the major goal of our faith."

"But do you remember that verse I'm talking about, something about the Israelites being told to kill every living thing, women and children too? Matt?"

"Sarah, I think Barbara is right about the danger of knowing too much. It's kind of like going to the dentist. The first time we have a dental procedure we might simply be afraid of the unknown, but the second time we need a procedure, we remember every detail of the things we didn't like. We recall the sound of the drill, the pain, the uncomfortable position of the jaw, the sudden jab of the needle—all the stuff we experienced the first time. God is so very gentle with His children that it's almost as if He too goes through what we do, so I think He tries to spare us. He knows we are unable to comprehend everything . . . *properly*. That's the key . . . *properly*.

"But Matt—and I'm just thinking this now—another new thought I just had. If our child asked us something, we'd probably try to tell him the truth, not hide anything. We might try to prepare him first, make sure he would be safe with that truth, but we wouldn't lie. Maybe God feels the same about us. Maybe He will always tell us the truth . . . and this is why He wants to teach us so much through the Bible so we can be prepared spiritually to handle all truths. He wants us to trust Him above all, and He wants to show us how to avoid certain pitfalls in life. And you're right in believing that God would not want us to pervert His truth or allow it to distract from the real goal of our faith.

"That's true, but getting back to your question about those verses in the Bible, yeah, I do remember the one you are referring to, and if you thought of it, maybe we should look at it. But I don't know where in the Bible to look for it. How can we find it?"

Barbara suggested that they look in the concordance under the word *children* and then said, "To narrow down what is probably a pretty long list, let's narrow *that* search to the parts where the Israelites were at war. In fact, wasn't Joshua one of the generals who conquered these cities?"

"Hmmm, yeah . . . here it is . . . the list of verses containing the word *children* in this concordance is over five pages long. Well, I can skim the list and call out to you the words in the verse description that might seem to refer to our subject. Okay? And if you think one might fit what we are looking for, we can look them up in the Bible and then we'll know if they actually are applicable. Here's one in Numbers . . . got your pencil? Numbers 24:17, '*And destroy all the children of Sheth.*' And here's one that gives the authority to do this, Numbers 31:15 '*And Moses said.*' And then in Numbers 31:17, it says, '*Kill every male among the little ones.*'"

"Wow, here's something in Deuteronomy 20:16-17. Let me look it up in the Bible . . . '*But of the cities of these people, which the LORD thy God doth give thee for an inheritance, thou shalt save alive nothing that breatheth: But thou shalt utterly destroy them; namely, the Hittites . . . Amorites . . . Canaanites . . . Perizzites . . . Hivites . . . Jebusites.*' Boy, that seems like a lot of people, and it seems that the instruction was very clear. And here's another in Joshua 6:21, '*And they utterly destroyed all that was in the city, both man and woman, young and old . . . with the edge of the sword,*' and Joshua 6:27 reiterates that in this action, God was with them: '*So the LORD was with Joshua.*'"

"Matt," Barbara added, "I remember reading that section of the Bible, and I think near these verses which you just read, there were places where God told the Israelites to spare the women and children. But in other cities, God told the Israelites quite specifically that they were allowed to marry the women and to have children with them. So what could be the reason that these instructions were so different, why some people were spared and others weren't?"

"Well, we mustn't forget that God did not *want* to destroy the people and said in 2 Peter 3:9, '*The Lord is . . . not willing that any should perish, but that all should come to repentance,*' and earlier in 1 Peter 3:19-20 explained that Christ preached the gospel to those who had died in the flood because of their sins, saying, '*By which also he went and preached unto the spirits in prison; Which sometime were disobedient, when once the longsuffering of God waited in the days of Noah.*'"

"Yes," Sarah replied, "that's why we have the rainbow. It was the sign of the covenant that God made after the flood, promising never to destroy all the people again until the very end. So maybe Joshua's time and instruction are similar to the times of the flood, but rather than kill everyone, God spared every soul He possibly could. Maybe He gave those instructions because He saw that there were some He just couldn't spare and still retain the spiritual safety of His children, retain goodness in the line of people that would eventually become the bride for His Son. I don't know, but that makes sense. It is difficult to understand. But maybe we can find an explanation somewhere in this same area of text. But let's continue through Joshua first and see where it brings us. Okay?"

"Hmmm, look at this, Sarah, wow, there's more. Joshua 10:39 says, '*And they smote them . . . and utterly destroyed all the souls that were therein; he left none remaining: as he had done to Hebron . . . Debir . . . Libnah.*' Then in Joshua 10:40, '*He left none remaining . . . destroyed all that breathed, as the LORD God of Israel commanded.*' It says, 'Destroy all that breathed as God commanded.' That's powerful. I wish I knew why they were told to do this."

"Ohh, look at this, Matt. Here's an instance where the Israelites didn't obey God . . . They didn't kill everyone as they were told . . . Listen to this. In Judges 1:28, it says, '*And it came to pass, when Israel was strong, that they . . . did not utterly drive them out,*' then in Judges 2:2, '*But ye have not obeyed.*'"

"Listen to this, Sarah, this might answer some of our questions. God tells them what will happen to them because they did not follow his instructions to kill all the inhabitants, listen, from Judges 2:3, '*They shall be as thorns in your sides . . . their gods shall be a snare unto you.*' And the result is mentioned in Judges 2:11: '*And the children of Israel did evil.*' And in Judges 2:13, '*And they forsook the LORD.*' 'They,' meaning the Israelites."

"I think this means that because they did not do as God told them, when they allowed the people to live, they ended up with sin having the power to overwhelm them. Sarah, that's it! Remember now . . . this happened before Christ brought mankind the forgiveness of sin. Later of course, God sent Christ so those who fell to sin could repent and come back to Him, and don't forget that when God sent Christ, He also provided the sacrament of Baptism to keep inherited sin at bay. But for these guys, there *was* no forgiveness, and there *was* no baptism, so they had to *avoid* sin entirely."

Jim, with a second concordance on his lap, still in awe over Matt and Sarah's observations as he followed along in the concordance, finally spoke up. "This is amazing, but wait a minute. If we jump down to Isaiah here in the concordance, there are more instructions about children inheriting the iniquities of the forefathers. Listen to this verse in Isaiah 14:21, '*Prepare slaughter for his children for the iniquity of their fathers; that they do not rise, nor possess the land, nor fill the face of the world with cities.*' Then in Isaiah 14: 25, God begins to speak of how sin, (Satan), will be dealt with and says, '*I will . . . tread him under foot: then shall his yoke depart from off them, and his burden depart from off their shoulders.*' And then God reminds us that He Himself either ordained or allowed this to occur because He says in Isaiah 14:27, '*For the LORD of hosts hath purposed.*' But then God tells us that we should trust Him in this because He says in Isaiah 14:32, '*And the poor of his people shall trust in it.*' Gosh this is incredible."

"Jim, I remember too that in 1 Peter 4:6, the apostles said, '*For for this cause was the gospel preached also to them that are dead.*'"

"That's right! And here in Isaiah 25:8, God also begins to provide some comforting thoughts about all these deaths. The people are told, '*He will swallow up death in victory; and the Lord GOD will wipe away tears,*' and in Isaiah 26:19, '*Thy dead men shall live . . . shall they arise.*' Then after all this bloodshed, all the harsh episodes connected to these invasions, Isaiah 30:19 says, '*He will be very gracious unto thee at the voice of thy cry; when he shall hear it, he will answer thee.*' And in Isaiah 30:26, we read, '*The LORD . . . healeth the stroke of their wound.*'"

Matt turned to Sarah and said, "Sarah, this insight into God's work is something we must hold on to."

"You know, Matt, I can remember how those passages were pretty boring to me when I read them within their own context years ago. I think I sort of glossed over the fact that for some cities the Israelites were instructed to kill every breathing thing and for other cities they were instructed to spare the people. But as we look at this scripture now as a means to understand why some die and others don't, it has lots of *potential* meanings, incredible, possible, potential *interpretations.* I mean, I'm not saying that these verses apply to our situation, but they certainly show us that there is a reason why some have such a different fate than others, and that God will make it right. It makes me think—well, wonder anyway—if perhaps something in the lineage or the sinful nature of some people is passed along in our—well, for want of a better word—our DNA. This could be why only certain people were to be killed . . . had to be killed . . . had to die, and others didn't."

"Sarah honey, don't despair . . . wait . . . let's continue to study. I mean, what you say is very possible. You and I know, I mean, we *really* know, really believe . . . we have actually *experienced* . . . that God has created an incredible instrument in the Bible. We've often marvel at how words written thousands of years ago apply to life today! It is as if each word ever written was written to answer our personal questions and whenever we ask them! The Bible is a true miracle. It is an incredible engineering feat! God doesn't want you saddened by His plan. He wants you gladdened!"

To distract Sarah Jim interrupted, saying, "Sarah, look up Isaiah. I think in chapter 54, there is something else about Noah. Yeah, here it is. It's in Isaiah 54:9-11 and says, *'For this is as the waters of Noah unto me: for as I have sworn that the waters of Noah should no more go over the earth . . . . O thou afflicted, tossed with tempest, and not comforted.'*

Jim went on to say, "You already believe in life after death, Sarah. You already believe in the resurrection of the dead. You already believe in the forgiveness of sin. And you already know that God wants all men to be saved and has created a plan that gives everyone the same opportunity. Additionally, we already recognize the power of prayer, and God has taught us that our prayers for those who have died are important and make a difference. So, Sarah, we know that Robert will be okay and that God did what He did for a reason, right? Sarah, I think that God was protecting him by taking him now."

Barbara noticed Jim's change of pronoun from "you" to "we" and was pleased, but she didn't mention it for fear Jim would negate his statement. But inside she was pleased and sent a quick Thank You to God that she had noticed. And Sarah, who hadn't noticed the change went on to say, "Gosh, Jim, I don't know what to say. If God was protecting Robert, it certainly goes with the kindness and gentle heartedness of God that we have experienced time after time, and how He looks after us and wants us all to be a part of the bride for His son. If what you say is true, then what we have just learned . . . again . . . is that I need to work on my trust, my trust in God to believe that He will always provide exactly what is right for us as He was doing for Joshua and his people to protect them. I must try harder to trust God explicitly to do that. And I do feel badly that I haven't done that in this situation. But ohh, it is so difficult . . . The pain is so great."

"Maybe sometimes death is necessary, Sarah," Barbara added, happy with Jim's obvious interest. "Maybe we need to think that Robert, like Paul, was rescued from something terrible and that now, in the hands of angels and others who bring testimony in eternity, he will be taught and guided in godly matters. Paul was rescued and even given a *great and important* commission, something he had asked to do. Maybe even babies who are aborted are actually rescued from a life that would have been too difficult for them. We don't know this, but we do know that God has made provisions for every injustice, every concern, and wants all men to be saved. Maybe if we focus on the future, that someday when we see Paul and Robert again, it will be wonderful and they will have prospered because God will have made sure that they did. When we trust God as we should, I believe that He will lead us to learning what He wants us to know so our hearts will rest easy. And what we still don't know for sure, we don't need to know because we know and trust the heart of God."

"Sarah, wait," Jim said. "I just found something spectacular in a verse farther along in Isaiah where we were just reading, and it follows what we just said about

God speaking of the flood and the afflicted taken in that flood. In Isaiah 54:13-14, it says, '*And all thy children shall be taught of the LORD; and great shall be the peace of thy children . . . . for thou shalt not fear: and from terror; for it shall not come near thee.*' Sarah, it says thy children shall be taught . . . . that's such a comfort! And before we moved to Isaiah, I had also seen back in 1 Peter 3:13-14 where God offers us comfort by saying, '*And who is he that will harm you, if ye be followers of that which is good? But and if ye suffer for righteousness' sake, happy are ye: and be not afraid of their terror, neither be troubled.*'"

They could see Sarah's expression change from despair to hope, then to conviction, and Sarah repeated what Barbara and Jim stated, "Yes, we *do* know the *heart* of God, don't we? And thus we need not be afraid or troubled by *anything* that happens." What we have learned is that the heart of God is loving and caring and He commiserates over those who suffer, even those who die in their sins. Despite what mankind does, because of His loving heart, He wants them to repent, and be saved.

And Sarah, beaming, repeated her words, "Oh yes, that's it! We *do* know the heart of God, and it is so kind and loving and because we *know* His heart, we can trust Him with what is most precious to us, as Abraham trusted God with Isaac. We can believe that God had to take Robert for his good and for ours, and we must trust God in this. I'd forgotten about Abraham and Isaac. Yes, we do have to trust God. Abraham was the most trusting and most obedient of all men, and that's why God said that his obedience would be considered righteousness in the eyes of God and because of that obedience he could enter heaven."

Sarah, do you remember the story we heard from one of the ministers about a child who was dying? Remember he said that there once were parents who called their apostle to the bedside of their twelve-year-old child who was dying and asked him to pray that God would spare the child. The apostle told them that he must first explain something to them. He could either pray to God to ask that He spare the child, or he could pray to God to ask that He exercise *His* will upon that child. The apostle told them that they would never go wrong if they prayed 'Thy will be done,' but when they asked for something, they might get what they asked for and it might not be the better path for them. Well, they asked that the apostle pray that their child would live. That child lived, and when he was twenty, he got in with the wrong crowd and did some pretty terrible things culminating in shooting someone to death and spending the rest of his life in prison."

"Yes, I do remember that story, and it is true that God knows so much better than we do what the future holds and what is best for us. Matt, what we have just understood is profound; it is a gift we have been given by God. He gave us this gift because of how much He loves us and how much He wants our suffering to be alleviated. We are *now* where He wanted to lead us. And our journey has been incredible. We must always remember these words: *it is because we know the heart of God, that we can trust Him implicitly.* This is our truth, this is our personal and profound truth and it is what supports our abiding faith."

And Jim too was suddenly assured that God had led Matt and Sarah to this moment to help them accept His will. For just a moment, Jim felt that here was the truth, here were the true children of God, and herein would lie his own blessing. But Jim did not voice these thoughts.

So Sarah came to accept Robert's death and to be content. All of them came to experience yet another of God's magnificent gifts. They knew that He had comforted them, opened their understanding, and taught them. He had brought them to where they needed to be through scripture. He taught them that they didn't need every answer if they could but trust Him. And that if they *knew* Him, *understood* Him and the plan He had for them, and if they could recognize the incredible love in God's heart for them, they would easily be able to trust Him with everything in their life.

Matt read one final Bible verse to them because the Bible on his lap fell open to the page and the words jumped into his consciousness as if God had one final thing to say to them. Matt read from Revelation 19:9, "*And he saith unto me, Write, Blessed are they which are called unto the marriage supper of the Lamb. And he saith unto me, These are the true sayings of God.*"

And Sarah responded to what Matt read by quoting from Jeremiah 33:3: "*Call unto me, and I will answer thee, and show thee great and mighty things.*" And then Sarah said, "Now that we have learned these things, we have a responsibility to pray for those who grieve here on earth from the loss of a child, because so many do not understand or accept God's will. We also need to pray for those parents who chose to have an abortion, for they have a terrible burden to carry. And we need to pray for all the *children* that have and will enter into eternity, *especially* those who were aborted. Our prayers can help them find the altar of grace and with God's help they too will be shown great and mighty things.

Chapter Eleven

WORRIES, WEDDINGS, AND WONDERS

Everyone gathered at Matt and Sarah's for the fellowship. They we so pleased to see the change in Sarah. She didn't seem sad anymore, and in fact, her entire countenance seemed joyful. Everyone wondered what had brought this wonderful and welcome change. While no one wanted to ask, they all secretly hoped they would learn what had happened to bring Sarah so suddenly and miraculously out of her depression.

The house bustled with the activity of many people. The smaller children ran to find games and settled themselves on the floor on one of Grandma's thick oriental carpets to play with Rebecca and Jayden who took charge of teaching them the rules of the games they chose. The adults busied themselves at the buffet table to set out the food they brought.

The house overflowed with the enticing aromas that emanated from Crock-Pots filled to the brim with something wonderful to eat. Matt had placed a series of safety outlets along the back of the buffet so the Crock-Pots and the coffeemaker could be plugged in and everything kept warm. The dining room table on one end held the small plates and napkins and the bite-sized hors d'oeuvres. The center of the table on both sides held the utensils and the larger plates and napkins for dinner. The opposite end of the table held the desserts, small dessert plates, and the smaller napkins and forks. Once everything was set up, there was no work to do because everything was buffet-style, a help-yourself evening.

Matt and Sarah had placed the dining room chairs in the living room and in the parlor adjacent to the living room. These rooms opened to one another by means of a huge set of darkly stained and beautifully varnished double doors that would slide into the walls and disappear when open. This combined space offered a large great room effect. They placed the dining room chairs around these rooms so all the seating in both rooms would form a sort of circle to allow for better group conversations.

Roasted garlic, marsala wine and mushroom sauce, thick caramelized onion gravies, rosemary, and basil filled the house with their mouthwatering aromas; and soon the fellowship was in full swing. Usually, whoever lived in the home where they gathered provided the opening prayer, but they could defer it to someone else, often either a minister in their church or the elder of the group. Today, Matt asked Caleb to pray. They all looked to Caleb as the patriarch of the family and their role model.

They stood in a circle, the children knowing to stand quietly, bow their heads and fold their hands. When total quiet descended upon the group, Caleb began by thanking God. He thanked Him for loving them, for providing such a wonderful future for them, for sending His Son so they could have their sins forgiven. Then he thanked God for their family circle and their friends and for His blessing on their striving to learn and follow His words. He asked for the angel protection for all of them and asked that the Holy Spirit would abide with them and teach them. Then he asked God to provide Lorraine with the healing she needed and to look after Robert and provide healing to Matt and Sarah.

Caleb asked God to let those in eternity know that they were prayed for and invited to the altar of grace. He asked for the blessing that would allow them to remain close to Him and to keep their conversations filled with godly wisdom and be of such substance that it would be pleasing to Him. Finally, he asked for the blessing on their food and on those who had prepared the food with loving hands. Then they all said amen in close unison. Even the children piped in at the end of the prayer with their loud amens. Caleb had prayed with such passion that each of them had been moved.

The adults helped the children fill their plates and settle comfortably to eat. Then the adults filled their plates and dug into the food as if they had starved themselves for days. They ate with gusto, some remarking that anything that tasted so good surely carried a huge number of calories, others laughingly claiming that there weren't any calories in the food. But at that moment, no one cared about calories; they just enjoyed every bite.

When they completed their first round at the buffet table and began their second helping more slowly, Elizabeth and Rebecca told them of their day and their move into the carriage house. Rebecca was excited about her new "grown-up" room and invited everyone to come see it when they could. Jayden remarked that even he thought her room was "really cool." Elizabeth raved about the benefits of the sense of balance that employing divine proportion had created.

Those who'd already visited agreed that the cozy atmosphere did seem to be a result of the perfect proportions in each room's architecture and furnishings.

They also spoke of Deb and Josh's upcoming wedding, and Debbie told them that she and Josh had made an appointment with a realtor to look for a starter home for them. She assured them that they had instructed the realtor to show them homes within a five—or ten-mile radius of where the rest of the family lived. Everyone was pleased by this news and pleased to see Debbie's joy.

Wade and Ruth's engagement became the next topic of conversation, and everyone offered their best wishes and told them how happy they were for them and what a beautiful couple they made. They asked Jayden how he felt about becoming a big brother to Heza and Bara and enjoyed Jayden's enthusiastic reply: "I always wanted a brother or sister and now I've got both, and they really need me too because I have to teach them so much, ya know, about church, about this country, about all the games we play . . . ya know . . . *everything!*"

As usual, Matt and Sarah's home looked beautiful and was the perfect setting for Grandma's beautiful antiques. And when Grandma's many clocks started their chimes for the hour, Sarah told them that Rebecca and Jayden had taken Heza, Bara, and Andrew on a tour of the house to see the clocks and had taught them how to listen for the silence and then listen for the ticking of the clocks.

With that, little Heza laid her finger against her lips and said, "Shhhhh." Everyone was delighted with her response, so Bara, not to be outdone, said, "I know how to do it too, look." And he too laid his finger across his lips and said, "Shhhh" and cocked his head from side to side as if listening and then added, "Ticktock, ticktock." And Andrew said, "Me too!" They congratulated the children on what they had learned, and the children beamed under their praise.

Caleb told Wade how pleased he was that he was joining the church; and Wade began to tell them of the incredible experiences he'd had when Barbara, Jim, and John had come to his home for a quick visit and ended up teaching him about Satan. "I'd never heard that stuff before. I still find it almost a little creepy. I mean, . . . to think of Satan as being right beside me, waiting to pounce is . . . Well, it's like a movie where the bad guy is an invisible alien with supernatural abilities."

"Well, it is like that, Wade! That's why some people have such a hard time understanding the threat, understanding that it's a never-ending battle every day to stay safe. Because it's so different than what they are willing to believe, many don't take it seriously. Most people think, assume, or even expect—yeah, *expect* is the better word—that life is supposed to be good and that there are no supernatural forces. But in reality, life is a training camp, like boot camp, where we can be put through the wringer. But like boot camp, once we toughen up, once we know what to expect and are aware of what each day could bring, we can handle it. It's when we selfishly keep *expecting* happiness without putting in our work to gain God's protection or to recognize the subtleties of evil that we are disappointed . . . and can become a disappointment. The really sad thing is that those who don't have troubles may be those who are of no threat to Satan, so beware, for *not* having troubles could suggest that you may not be a child of God."

"Caleb, I don't know why I never knew all these things before. I went to church as a kid, but I never heard this stuff. *Why*? Yeah, I saw pictures of this devil in a Halloween costume—all red, with horns and a tail, maybe a pitchfork—but certainly never knew he'd been a beautiful angel sitting next to God or was such a threat to me and everyone I love. I had absolutely no idea!"

"I know, Wade. Over time, Satan has been able to create misconceptions and misinterpretations of God's word and has brought complacency and irresponsibility into our religion, our churches, into our leaders, and even our families and neighborhoods. Today's generation is the end product of years of slow disintegration of our reliance on the word of God and our awareness of the work of Satan. Hardly anyone knows what the Bible says anymore, and some who do know misinterpret God's words, saying there is nothing anyone has to do to be a part of the First Resurrection except believe that Jesus has saved him! But can you imagine God choosing a bride for His Son who never followed any rules, never worked at being a good wife to Christ and good child to God? Can you imagine a disloyal bride unwilling to stand by her husband? Or one that knew nothing about her husband? No! And it breaks my heart to see so many misled."

"Caleb, last week, when we were discussing Satan and his capabilities, I was really taken by surprise. I'd never given one thought to what the devil can do. Never even gave a thought to the possibility that everything we do in life, every action we take passes along to our family either the curse of sin or the gift of a blessing. It's mind-boggling, and yet it makes *sense*! Knowing this has made me worry more about the kids. I want to learn what I can do for them so they won't suffer, won't walk into those traps that evil will lay for them. I feel, . . . well, . . . like my hands are tied. I don't know enough about spiritual matters to know what I can do to help them. So I need help to learn how to protect Heza and Bara, and don't forget, we don't know *anything* about *their* ancestors."

Matt spoke up and asked Wade if they'd talked of the "armour" God told them to wear. When Wade looked befuddled and then said "Armour?" Matt began to explain.

"Well, when we read the Bible, we have to remember that it was written during a specific period of time and used words applicable to those times so the people would understand. When a warrior put on his armour, it was to protect him while he fought. Thus, God's word *armour* means that He has provided us with ways that we can be protected during an attack by Satan or his evil spirits or from a person whom Satan inspires to attack us. Our job is to learn God's words and incorporate them into use in our lives. We must learn *what* protection God offers, how to use it, and teach this to our children. The primary way we learn God's words is by studying the Bible."

"And it's fascinating to learn! When we understand what action we need to take when we are attacked, we automatically know what to do and thus we are protected. Best of all, we are also blessed. For instance, when we use what God has provided and we resist an attack by Satan, God refers to us as an overcomer and in Revelation 3:21 tells us '*To him that overcometh will I grant to sit with me in my throne.*' God often describes an overcomer as someone who put on a clean robe or washed his robe, meaning that they washed sin away by following what God asked of them. Revelation 7:13-14 teaches this: '*What are these which are arrayed in white robes? . . . These are they which came out of great tribulation, and have washed their robes, and made them white in the blood of the Lamb.*'

"God also lets us know that to be an overcomer isn't easy. We know this because He tells us in Revelation 7:17, '*And God shall wipe away all tears from their eyes.*' When we understand this, then God goes on to explain that to be able to stand against evil and grow into the overcomer He wants us to be, we have to 'wear,' not just know, the protection of the armour He offers. In Ephesians 6:11, He says, '*Put on the whole armour of God, that ye may be able to stand against the wiles of the devil.*' And in Ephesians 6:13, He says, '*Wherefore take unto you the whole armour of God, that ye may be able to withstand in the evil day, and having done all, to stand.*'

"I think you heard in the service at church last Sunday that Christ is often referred to as light like in 'the light of the world' and that evil or Satan is darkness. Thus, we can understand what God means in Romans 13:12 where we read, '*The night is far spent, the day is at hand: let us therefore cast off the works of darkness, and let us put on the armour of light.*' Complacency is similar to darkness and so subtle that many people remain in that state, believing that everything is okay spiritually with them. Sadly, they're wrong. Satan has blinded them.

"So to boil it all down, the armour or protection God offers is found in His words, and we find these in the Bible, in our churches, in our fellowships with one another. The armour, God's words, covers all things. This is why we always try to speak of God's words during our fellowships . . . so we can learn, be reminded, have things clarified, stay on the path to our goal.

The words of our Heavenly Father teach us that this armour comes to us through the sacraments of Holy Baptism, Holy Sealing, and Holy Communion and through prayer, keeping the Sabbath holy, tithing, fellowship, trust, and doing our best to put others first. In other words, love our neighbors and teach the gospel to others. But the key words, however, are that God's protection lies 'in His words.' If we don't immerse ourselves in God's words, we cannot protect ourselves. If we don't know His words and keep them foremost in our minds and in our hearts, we can't be protected, and if we are not overcomers, we can't be a part of the bride of Christ.

"The armour of God can protect the children of God so well that even Satan cannot penetrate that armour unless God allows Satan this access, and God does this only to work a particular circumstance to our benefit! And our part—our role, Wade—is to keep learning God's words so they are what governs our thoughts and actions!"

"That's a great explanation, Matt, but from what you say, it seems as if the learning process is not easy to absorb and I bet that it takes a lifetime to learn. If our basic nature is a sinful nature and causes us to become angry, vindictive, defensive and forget or ignore God's words or we become lazy or don't stay alert and watch for what's wrong, don't pray, how do we rise above it? What adds to this vulnerability is that somehow we don't think of the end-times as being *now*, being an imminent occurrence. I think that few people understand the importance of being a part of the First Resurrection or understand the consequences of not doing God's will. And it's our human nature to put things off. So how can we stop these patterns of behavior?"

"Well, unless we learn what we are supposed to do, we can't change. That's the kicker. And then when we do learn, we have to make the commitment to incorporate God's instructions into our lives. That takes work. And then we have to take a good look at ourselves from time to time because there are also those who simply ignore their failures. I mean, God forgives our failures but only when we feel genuine remorse and are willing to keep striving to overcome them."

Mary spoke then and told Wade and Ruth how she had overcome her debilitating panic attacks and a fear so strong that she'd spent her entire life searching for ways to obtain good luck. "If it wasn't for God sending Matt and Sarah to us by having them purchase this house right across the street from us, we never would be where we are today. In fact, I might even have died without ever having known God as I do today . . . My doctors kept increasing my medications because of my symptoms, and the medications became stronger and stronger . . . and became a crutch. But God went right to the cause, showed me where I was acting against His direction even while receiving the help of Matt and Sarah. When I finally had the courage to break away from what I was doing to follow and trust God, He healed me!"

"And I got my wonderful wife back!" Kevin added.

Sarah spoke of the depression she and Matt had experienced when both Grandma and Paul died less than a year apart and then began to tell the group about their recent foray into the study of God's words because of the loss of Robert. She and Matt described what they learned about the instructions God gave to Joshua when he was about to invade a city.

Matt retrieved the notes Sarah had made from their study and explained how in one case Joshua was instructed to kill all the inhabitants in one city but spare those in another. He asked the group if anyone knew why. No one understood the significance of the instructions to the Israelites. They were perplexed by these instructions. Matt and Sarah asked if they felt there must be some significance to what God had asked Joshua to do, and they all felt that there must be even if they could not see it. Matt went on to tell them that he and Sarah, Barbara and Jim had drawn some conclusions and one was that for some reason, certain people *had* to die and that as they read further, they discovered that it might have been because of sin and to protect those God loved.

Matt explained that when the Israelites had not followed God's instructions by killing all the inhabitants of a city, a series of events followed that caused them to forsake God. He quoted from Judges 1:28, reading, *"It came to pass . . . they . . . did not,"* and in Judges 2:2, *"Ye have not obeyed."* And in Judges 2:3, *"They shall be as thorns in your sides . . . their gods shall be a snare unto you."* And finally from Judges 2:13, *"They forsook the LORD."*

Everyone audibly gasped, never having understood these words before. Wade was speechless and secretly thanked God for sparing Heza and Bara the way He did. Jim, always ready to play devil's advocate, said that the only argument he could offer was that God told them to kill the inhabitants because He knew they would never bow to the rule of the Israelites and would rise up against them. Once again, they all agreed that this could also be a possible explanation.

But Sarah told them how her heart was moved as they studied this word of God and how something inside her believed that God was telling her that some things were necessary, that He had a reason for what He did. She felt that God was trying to comfort her, tell her why she did not have to worry, why He did what He did, let her know that what He did was necessary for them. She said that for her, it was a miracle of faith and that she was truly satisfied.

"But," she said, "it was when we realized that we *knew and trusted* the heart of God, and we realized how loving and gentle His heart is that the study changed course. That was when my faith could finally take over."

Everyone sat in rapt silence, their minds going a mile a minute to absorb this information. It was disturbing because they realized that they had never before had *any* definitive explanation for why God ordered Joshua to kill an entire city of people and spare the people in other cities. "Whenever I read this accounting in the past," Sarah said, "I glossed over it, accepting it as a fact, not asking questions about why Joshua's instructions might be different for each city he invaded. In fact, I did wonder why there had to be so much killing, such mass killing, and it disturbed me quite a bit. Those acts of killing were not the acts of the God I know, and so I did not understand those verses and just let them slide at the time. I read on, accepting that this was how it was in those days."

"Sometimes when we read the Bible, we don't really take it in, and we don't take certain parts of it literally. But then at another time, we are directed back to that part of scripture and see it in a wholly different light, and we learn something we never knew before. In this case, we learned that in some cases, certain people had to die, and just as in Noah's day, that reason appears to have been to prevent sin from spreading . . . almost like someone whose DNA carries a sickness that could be passed to their children so they opt to adopt."

Barbara added, "I think this is why scripture and God's plan are called mysteries. Do you remember the scripture where God refers to us as having a veil over our eyes and thus unable to see clearly? It's in 2 Corinthians 3:14-16 and tells us, *'But their minds were blinded: for until this day remaineth the same vail untaken away in the reading of the old testament; which vail is done away in Christ. But even unto this day, when Moses is read, the vail is upon their heart. Nevertheless when it shall turn to the Lord, the vail shall be taken away.'*

"Sometimes I feel as if I'm in a world of incredible enlightenment, of pure wisdom . . . it swirls around me. But then as I reach for it, a fog so thick begins to hide it and I can't see it. It's too much for me to absorb, too complex for me to understand. While I see it and accept it and *almost* grasp it, I can't quite get there. I do know however that it is incredibly perfect, and I commiserate over my inability to comprehend its totality. But on other occasions, I do see clearly and I'm overwhelmed by how profound *and complete* God's words are."

Sarah added, "*Profound* is the *perfect* word. What happened to us as we read the account of God's instructions to Joshua was that we somehow felt the love of God and had an incredible glimpse into God's beautiful heart. And *this* was our truth, this was what we'd needed to learn—that God's heart is *so* loving, *so* beautiful, *so* perfect that just knowing this, just having this reaffirmed, allowed us to trust Him completely and *that was all we had to know*. And I remembered the words in Jeremiah 33:3: '*Call unto me, and I will answer thee, and show thee great and mighty things.*'" God showed us that *everything* He does is to help us, to protect us, to keep sin from spreading to His children, to give us what we need to be a part of the bride for His Son."

Ruth added, "Sarah, I have learned something similar. I had not trusted God sufficiently and wasted years being angry about what happened in my life. My Dad has always been the biblical scholar in our family, and I rebelled against what he said. I left everything, even Jayden's spiritual education, up to him. Now I feel that God is asking me to wrap myself around His words, really learn them so I can appreciate my Dad and his faith and stop being so bitter about the past. Now God's words have become so important to me that I want to keep hearing, keep placing myself where God's words will be spoken. That's why it's so wonderful and such a privilege to spend time with all of you. Now with Wade and Bara and Heza coming into the church, I think God is asking me to step up to the plate too and gain the same level of conviction that Dad has. I couldn't climb out of my troubles because I didn't commit myself to God. God couldn't bless me when I wasn't doing as He asked, when I was so bitter, and when I even took my troubles out on my Dad because I was so wrapped up in myself and my own concerns."

If anyone had looked over to where John was sitting, they would have seen John beaming with the joy of hearing his daughter's words. His prayers for his daughter had been answered! And Jayden, appearing engrossed in the game the children were playing on the floor, had also heard his mother and his heart sang too. They both knew that Ruth had finally rejoined life, finally was her old self again, finally had the strength and energy because of the love she received from Wade to draw closer to God.

Barbara reminded them that when Paul died, they'd all challenged God's will, but it was again God's words that gave them the understanding about why God might have taken Paul and even how his suffering had prepared him for the great work he would do for God in eternity, in the realms where so *many* young addicts were amassed.

"This knowledge allowed us to be comforted. There is always comfort and instruction and safety in God's words. Whether we hear them from the altar of grace or we read them or we have these family discussions, we not only learn from His words but we are changed by them because we begin to see the bigger picture. We also learn that we can trust God and trust in His kindness and the incredible plan He has for every soul that ever lived or died. But we also learned that we must pray for the dead and especially for those with whom we might have something in common or in some way understand."

"One of the things that impressed me," Jim continued, "is that God isn't angry with us if we question. He's actually glad that we ask questions because then He can show us His plan, show us why things are the way they are, and show us how to live in the best way possible to reach the goal of our faith. There's a part of scripture that really hit home with me where God tells us that we can ask Him to prove Himself to us. I'll never forget the book and chapter. It's in Malachi 3:10 and says, '*And prove me now herewith, saith the LORD of hosts, if I will not open you the windows of heaven, and pour out for you a blessing, that there shall not be room enough to receive it.*'"

"You're right, Jim," Caleb said. "But there is a difference between challenging God and seeking to understand His words. He can see what lives in our hearts, and He will not reveal himself to those who want to take this wisdom and twist it to their own purposes or those who challenge Him because they want to prove Him *wrong*. In fact, to these people, all I can say is beware. Remember the verse at the very end of the Bible, Revelation 22:19 where it warns, '*And if any man shall take away from the words of the book of this prophecy, God shall take away his part out of the book of life, and out of the holy city, and from the things which are written in this book.*' This means that every word is to be taken literally, taken seriously. It is *us* who may not understand, not interpret correctly . . . and not that there is something wrong with what is written. We have been exceptionally blessed in that we all have sought to understand, and God has revealed what we sought. But remember that to whom much is given, much is expected, and we'd better not take what He has given us lightly. We too can fall. And pretty quickly."

Matt added, "It's important to recognize that once we have been given this understanding through *any* means, we no longer have an excuse not to do what God asks."

Ann added that sometimes she felt afraid. "We've all learned so much. In fact, everyone in our congregation learns if they go to church regularly. But my fear is whether or not we've recognized that having been given this wisdom translates into being given a great responsibility. We know so we have no excuse if we flub it. We can't hide behind the excuse that we did not know, that no one told us, or that we didn't understand . . . so we have to perform. God has trusted us with so much so we have to honor that trust."

"Geeeeee," Kevin replied, "everything you say is true, Ann. But now, I'm nervous about my failures. I mean, maybe not everyone knows all the things that we do. Not everyone has a church and ministers and friends and family who all work toward the same goal and understand what serving God entails. But we have been given this wisdom, so maybe we need to ask ourselves, how can we know that we are doing all that we are supposed to be doing? I have to admit that sometimes I get tired, I get angry, I do what I shouldn't rather than what I should. Sometimes I am even aware that I'm not doing what's right and still I don't stop—that's the scary part!"

Elizabeth responded to Kevin's words beautifully, "We will never know whether we have done all we could have done and we will slip up often, but what we need to remember is that God knows that we are imperfect and He knows that while evil exists, we will always be sinners. So it's the *striving* that counts. It's our loyalty to God and to His children, it's our desire to learn and do God's will that counts. It's the level of our remorse when we fail. It's our desire to make restitution for any harm we have caused. While you were talking, Kevin, I looked up a couple of verses that tell us this. In 1 Kings 8:46, we are told, '*For there is no man that sinneth not,*' and in 1 John 1:8, we are told, '*If we say that we have no sin, we deceive ourselves, and the truth is not in us.'* And in Romans 5:8-9, we are comforted by the words, *'But God commendeth his love toward us, in that, while we were yet sinners, Christ died for us . . . we shall be saved . . . through him.'* So our job is to do as King Josiah in 2 Kings 23:3 did: *'And the king . . . made a covenant before the LORD . . . to keep his commandments and his testimonies and his statutes with all their heart and all their soul.'"*

"Elizabeth, that was beautifully put, thank you," John said. "We were all getting a little nervous there. And let me just add that prayer works. Prayer keeps us in a close relationship with God, and in 1 Peter 3:12, He tells us, *'For the eyes of the Lord are over the righteous, and his ears are open unto their prayers.'* God forgives our mistakes when we are truly repentant, and great rejoicing takes place in heaven when a sinner repents. Luke 15:7 tells us, *'I say unto you, that likewise joy shall be in heaven over one sinner that repenteth, more than over the ninety and nine . . . which need no repentance.'"*

Debbie said that she wished with all her heart that her parents could believe and would desire to attend church. She said that even though they were as different as night and day, she loved them and knew that if they understood and could accept what God wanted them to know, they would make some changes in their life, and they would understand her so much better than they did now.

They would also be able to understand why she was compelled to do what would bring God's blessing into her own life. She said that she longed for a family that conversed about God as they were now doing and shared the difficulties that life brought them and also spoke of their efforts to do what God wanted and of how much they loved God. "That's why I am so grateful for all of you."

Debbie spoke also of the upcoming wedding and asked the family to rally round them to make sure that everything that took place allowed them to hold fast to the blessing, the sacrament of marriage that they cherished. "If Josh and I can have God's blessing on our marriage, we can withstand the days of trouble that will inevitably come, and I want that with all my heart so I want to protect that blessing and not let anything interfere with it."

Debbie told them that she hoped the example the family always was to others would move her parents' hearts. Everyone could see that she was worried about her parents, about their soul life, about their future, about how she could share what she had been given with them.

Debbie explained that none of her family members had grown up with relatives or friends who actually knew God, who searched His words, or understood His plan. She wanted this for them so badly but knew that not everyone *wanted* to know, *wanted* to listen or learn, and that it was very difficult to change the ways and habits of a lifetime. She told them that she wasn't sure that she could walk between the two families because she only wanted the one direction for her life and for her husband and her children.

She worried because she knew that she wanted to run away from her relatives so she would not witness their disinterest nor experience the heartache this brought her. Yet she felt it was her job to be an example, a role model to them and to pray that they too would be led to God.

As Debbie spoke, Jim realized that Barbara must have often had the same thoughts about him, and it hurt him to learn that he might have inadvertently hurt the person he loved so much. Jim continued to listen quietly, and his heart was filled with a mixture of guilt, rebellion, a new awareness, an old perverseness, the wish for a sarcastic remark to come to mind, and the need to act. But he held his tongue and kept his inner turmoil to himself.

Barbara told Debbie that she understood Debbie's feelings. It *was* a hard line to walk when families differed in their understanding of God. She described how her brother Paul had to walk that line because his wife had hated the church. Barbara said that perhaps Debbie should place her parents in God's hands and let everything take its own course, not forcing anything unless the opportunity to speak of God arose. "However," Barbara said, "Do not feel obligated to spend time in an ungodly environment. Just keep praying, and above all, remain a beacon of loyalty to God."

"We will all pray for you, Debbie, and ask God to guide you in your words and actions. When you do speak in the presence of your relatives, just remember the words in Matthew 10:19-20, '*Take no thought how or what ye shall speak: for it shall be given you in that same hour what ye shall speak. For it is not ye that speak, but the Spirit of your Father which speaketh in you.*'"

Then Debbie turned to Jim and said, "No offense, Jim, but I've wondered how Barbara remains so calm with your . . . your . . . distance from spiritual things. I mean, you play devil's advocate with the family's Bible searches and add what you love to call your pithy comments about their Kool-Aid faith or their noncombatant approach when others hurt them, and Barbara just accepts it. I think I'd get angry. Although I do think it's great that the two of you found that middle ground to accept your differences and realize I need to find that with my parents. But I'm not so sure I can do that. Right now, it makes me angry that they are the way they are. How have you and Barbara managed to stay so close when you are so far apart in your beliefs?"

Jim was stung by Debbie's words but didn't know why. She was right. Everything she said was true. But for some reason, it had hurt his ego . . . maybe because he sensed that she might not think highly of him because he had shown himself to be so resistant to spiritual matters. To save face, however, he needed to act as if her comments *hadn't* bothered him. "Let me answer that, Deb. We've managed because Barbara is one in a million. Not many people in her circumstance would have been so loving and patient. I know that long ago, she placed me into God's hands and decided to let God work on me rather than all of you. But let me tell you something. All of you *have* worked on me even though you thought I wasn't aware of it. Not forcefully but subtly through your personal commitment of loyalty to one another and to God. I've seen it. I've watched you through good times and through bad, and I've watched you turn the other cheek and grit your teeth to do what God wanted rather than what your own human nature wanted you to do. I would've gone in there punching, but watching you, I've been amazed at how it always seems that God fights the battle for you and in time it all works out for you. And I respect you all for that. But I don't like being pushed, and neither do most people. So my advice to you, Deb, is to just be an example to your parents like all of you are to me. It works in most cases—mine, maybe not—but I believe that in your case, it will work."

Jim continued, saying, "You have all been trying to get me to admit that I've been a jerk to sit so long in the congregation and not become active, not join, not participate. You can't pull the wool over my eyes. I didn't just fall off the turnip truck, you know! Believe me when I say that I've noticed all your subtle conniving and all the arm-twisting you've done where I am concerned! And sometimes I hate it! But as much as I don't like to admit it, you've made an impact, and I've had to admire your conviction. But as for me, well, . . . I've been me . . . but I've been honest with you. I don't know where I'll end up in this, but I do wish you'd let me make the decision myself and stop pressuring me. So to help you all repent—and to put an end to all your finagling—let's make a deal to wait awhile and let me think about all this stuff. How about cutting me some slack!"

There was total silence in the room for a moment. Then realizing that while Jim was stating his case, he hadn't said what he usually did about *never* believing, so they were placated. They told Jim that they had to admit that they did try to push him; and they were very pleased that he *was*, after all these years, still coming to church, praying with them, listening and participating in their discussions. And they thanked him for doing that.

Secretly, however, they worried about Jim's lack of commitment. They knew that Jim was angry and while he acknowledged many points they made, he rarely admitted it had touched his heart. Privately however, they all felt that Jim was ready for God and thought of the old saying "Methinks thou doth protest too much" when he acted as if he did not believe! But Barbara railed with impatience and asked God to take her fear for Jim away and help Jim be drawn to Him.

Deb was relieved by what Jim had said about drawing others to God. She wanted God's blessing for Josh and for her child, but as she grew in her own faith, she also wanted it for her mom and dad. Her glimpse into Jim's heart, unlike listening to his words, helped her see what was possible for her parents. She too was aware that Jim's heart was melting even if he couldn't see it himself. She would ask Josh if they could begin to pray every day for Jim, for her parents, and all her relatives.

It was time for everyone to say good night. The time had gone quickly, and the conversations had been so lively that there had been no time for the game Sarah had planned. They rejoiced however in their conversation, in Wade's greater understanding, in Sarah's peace, in Debbie's concern for her parents, and miracle of miracles, in Jim's words that had shown them he'd been listening and absorbing all they'd discussed. It couldn't have been a more perfect evening.

Chapter Twelve

ABIDING FAITH,
HIDDEN TREASURE

As Caleb and Ann were leaving Matt and Sarah's house on Saturday night, they asked Josh, Deb, Matt, Sarah, Barbara, and Jim to come to their home on Tuesday evening. They said that they had something to share with them. The three couples were terribly curious about what Caleb had to tell them, and although they talked about it every day, none of the couples had a clue about why Ann and Caleb wanted to see them.

On Monday morning, when Sarah phoned Ann to ask what she could bring, Ann told her that she had just spoken with Debbie and they decided to purchase Chinese food for everyone. They planned that Josh and Deb would stop at the Chinese restaurant on their way to Ann and Caleb's to purchase everyone's favorites dishes. They would eat together as they talked. Josh and Deb knew that Sarah and Ann both liked orange peel shrimp, Matt's favorite was shrimp in lobster sauce, and Caleb's favorite was moo goo guy pan. Deb and Josh's favorites were fried rice and also beef in mushroom sauce. Barbara and Jim's favorite dish was lemon chicken.

Ann made apple cobbler for dessert, which she knew everyone liked. Caleb purchased vanilla ice cream in case they wanted to splurge and add that to the top of the apple cobbler. Ann always added raisins and walnuts to her apple cobbler along with lots of brown sugar and cinnamon and would serve the cobbler piping hot since everyone liked it best that way.

Andrew and Lorraine, tired from a busy day, had been fed earlier and had been put to bed before everyone began to arrive. Right after Matt and Sarah were settled in the living room, Ann checked the children and, finding them fast asleep, joined the conversation between Matt and Sarah and Caleb. As the four of them talked while awaiting the arrival of Barbara, Jim, Josh, and Deb, they spoke of the previous Saturday's fellowship and how informative their conversations had been. They again voiced their amazement about how scripture could be read one day and not understood and become crystal clear when read another day as God opened their understanding to the magic in His words.

When Deb and Josh arrived, they went directly to the dining room where Ann had placed two large teapots of Chinese tea along with plates, cups, napkins, and the serving and eating utensils. Deb and Josh carried in three large bags filled with the white cardboard containers of food and unloaded them into the center of the dining room table.

The aromas of garlic and mushroom sauce, orange and lemon, and spices they could not name floated from the table, and they were glad that there seemed to be plenty to eat. Within minutes, Barbara and Jim arrived and, after greeting one another everyone took their places at the dining room table. Caleb said grace, and they all dove into the boxes, claiming their favorites and eating with relish.

Deb filled them in on their wedding plans, providing details about the wedding cake they'd chosen. The baker was going to add ribbons of icing around the perimeter of the various layers and also at the base. This icing would change color every two or three inches to match the different colors of the bridesmaid dresses. "Isn't that neat, unique?" Debbie exclaimed. "And the cake is huge because they raise the levels onto sticks and platforms or something!" Debbie's excitement and pleasure was so evident that everyone smiled, enjoying her enjoyment.

When they had eaten, Caleb suggested they wait for dessert since everyone felt full. He thought that they could talk first and then finish the evening off with the dessert. Everyone agreed, patting full stomachs. They quickly cleared the table and sat down once again, looking expectantly at Caleb. Caleb had returned to the table with a stack of thick important-looking envelopes, and their curiosity soared.

Caleb began by telling them that when Grandma died, the lawyer had asked Caleb to visit his office. When Caleb met with him, he presented Caleb with four envelopes and the instructions that they were not to be opened until circumstances occurred that were very difficult to bear. There was a letter for him, another for Sarah, and one for Josh. There was also a letter for Paul, and this, Caleb explained, was why he had asked Barbara and Jim to join them tonight.

The lawyer told Caleb that each letter was to be given to the addressee only when they were dealing with a difficult circumstance and that no one else should be given their envelope.

After the attorney had given the envelopes to him along with the instructions, Caleb had placed them in his safety-deposit box at the bank. He asked God to help him correctly determine when he should distribute each letter, including the letter addressed to him. He went on to explain that when he and Ann were told that Lorraine required surgery and that she was very ill, he felt it was the right time to open his letter.

Caleb's voice faltered at that moment, and after he gained control of the emotion he was feeling, he cleared his throat and said, "Grandma always knew when we needed her and knew what we needed to bear a difficult circumstance. I sure wish she were here now." Then Caleb told them that he wanted to read them a small part of the letter Grandma had left for him and Ann.

Caleb explained that when the lawyer read Grandma's instructions to him, he stated that these were handwritten letters fashioned in Grandma's elegant old-fashioned script. The first page of each letter was the same for everyone, but the pages that followed were just for the addressee of the letter and therefore different than the others. The lawyer also said that Grandma had instructed the lawyer to tell Caleb that it would be up to him to decide when these letters should be dispersed as long as the addressee was dealing with a difficult circumstance.

Caleb reached across the table to hold Ann's hand as he described his thoughts when he read his letter and admitted to breaking down in tears to think of what Grandma had put into this thoughtful deed. She had wanted to provide comfort to her grandchildren even after she died. She wanted to teach them, help them.

She knew that they would definitely encounter difficult times. It was a part of life, a part of Satan's work and God's refining process. Difficult times were part of God's plan of salvation. Grandma wanted to be sure they understood this and would hold fast, trust God, and be comforted by the love He had for them. By knowing how much God loved them, they would be able to trust Him throughout their difficult circumstance. And so she wrote these letters to help them accomplish this.

Caleb reminded them that Grandma, of course, could have had no idea what would come their way, but she had prayed for them, and she spoke to God about what she wanted to do for them. She asked Him to help her choose the right words, words that would fit their circumstances at the time they opened her letter. She also asked God to show her which scripture she could include in her letter that would address their particular circumstance, their particular need at the time they opened her letter to them. As Caleb explained this, again his voice broke with the emotion he felt and from the love he had once again experienced from Grandma.

Caleb told them that he and Ann read their letter together and had cried together. But they cried tears of gratitude, of thankfulness because they felt the love that had gone into the letter. They also felt the incredible love between God and Grandma that was evident when He answered her prayer to inspire her with exactly what they would need. He said that he and Ann wanted to share the scripture with them that Grandma had provided for them. The scripture that, unbeknownst to Grandma, would be applied to their fear for Lorraine. He said they felt that by sharing this with them, they too would see the miracle of God, the miracle He provided for them through Grandma.

Caleb reminded them that each of them knew God, knew what incredible experiences of faith He provided for them, but when these were reinforced time and time again, it renewed their strength and the conviction of their faith. Caleb said that God gave them the gift of abiding faith through His words because He loved them so much. But he also wanted them to be reminded of the treasure they'd always had in Grandma by *her* example of faith. To most, what Grandma did and thought, her prayers and her faith, were hidden; but for them it was very different. They'd been there, they'd seen it, they'd experienced it, so it was not a hidden treasure but a treasure they had been privileged to witness every day of her life and to share with one another.

Caleb explained that as he and Ann sat in Lorraine's hospital room waiting for her fever to break . . . . or spike again, he suddenly remembered the letters. Their minister had just visited them at the hospital and had prayed with them at Lorraine's bedside. Every day, sometimes twice a day, they received such a visit and the prayers of one or two of their ministers. They knew that everyone in their congregation prayed for Lorraine as well. Earlier in the day the doctors told them that this night would be a decisive night for Lorraine because the infection she'd acquired needed to turn around that night or they might lose her.

When Caleb remembered the letters, he looked at his watch and saw that he still had time to get to the bank to retrieve his letter if he hurried. Reminding Ann about the letters, he asked her if she would mind staying at the hospital while he ran to the bank to retrieve their letter and that he would return with it immediately so they could open it together. When he returned to the hospital, he and Ann went into the sanctuary of the little chapel at the hospital and opened Grandma's letter.

Once again, Caleb needed a moment to control the emotion he felt and then began to speak again. "The scripture Grandma left for us, the scripture she chose and wrote down almost three and one-half years ago, is from Exodus 33:22 and says, '*I will put thee in a clift of the rock, and will cover thee with my hand.*'" The others gasped, understanding the significance of those words. The name of the hospital, which had only been built last year, was Rockcliff General Hospital.

They understood why Ann and Caleb were incredibly strengthened by those words and knew, as Ann and Caleb knew when they read those words, that God would heal Lorraine. If God said that He would "cover thee with My hand" they knew nothing could harm them. Caleb went on to tell them that sitting in that tiny sanctuary, having read these words and recognized their special significance, they thanked God and they were comforted. The next morning, Lorraine's fever broke, and the doctors pronounced that they believed little Lorraine would make a full recovery.

Grandma's letter was a miracle of faith for them and demonstrated how closely God cared for every detail of their lives. Because Grandma loved and trusted God, this experience was made possible. Grandma was the vessel through which God could work. Grandma had left another verse, which was for all of them. It was in each letter, but the one Caleb had just read to them had been for Caleb and Ann and their particular circumstance.

Caleb said he could actually feel the connection their little family had with God, and he was grateful; his heart overflowed with thankfulness for what had been laid into their hearts by their mother and grandmother. Their abiding faith had directed them to God's perfect love and thus to uncover the precious treasure that God's words, His love and their faith would be in their lives. He told them to never lose sight of the fact that parents and grandparents had a strong influence on their children and could create a magnificent blessing for their family if they lived their life and taught their children as God asked them to. Grandma had certainly done this for them.

Caleb told Sarah that with the loss of her baby Robert, he felt that it was the right time for her to have her letter. As Caleb handed Sarah her letter, she told him that she was touched by his willingness to share his letter from Grandma, something so personal, and that she wanted to do the same after she and Matt read theirs. She asked if she and Matt could use Caleb's study to read their letter and that after they had done so, they would come back to the dining room so they could share what they would with the others.

Matt and Sarah entered Caleb and Ann's beautiful study and sat together to open Grandma's letter. As Sarah read aloud, she began sobbing as she felt Grandma's presence through the love in her words; and she handed the letter to Matt, telling him that she longed to have Grandma here right beside her and couldn't help the wishing of it that filled her.

Matt began to read aloud the first page of the letter, which Caleb had explained was the same for each of them, and they read the words from Grandma that Caleb had so aptly described as a hidden treasure of faith. Grandma had reminded each of them that God had the power to do anything and did so through the truth and treasure of His words reminding them that Jeremiah

32:17 said, *"Thou hast made the heaven and the earth by thy great power and stretched out arm, and there is nothing too hard for thee."*

As Matt began the second page, the page that was just for them, they smiled at the words Grandma had chosen to open the letter, words that had always been so special to Sarah. Grandma opened her letter with "My Dearest, Darling, Sweetheart, Love" and Sarah's eyes filled with tears. As Matt continued to read, they felt not only Grandma's presence but also God's presence because the scripture not only fit so aptly what they had just been through when they lost Robert but also fit so perfectly what their recent Bible study had uncovered for them: the knowledge that Robert was okay and that they would be united with him someday.

They were in awe that Grandma would have chosen these words and even more so that God would have led Grandma to these particular words. The scripture Grandma had chosen for them was from Isaiah 60:20 and told them, *"Thy sun shall no more go down; neither shall thy moon withdraw itself: for the LORD shall be thine everlasting light, and the days of thy mourning shall be ended."*

They sat in silence for a few minutes, both digesting the words in the scripture. Amazed by how perfect they were for them. Sarah knew that she would no longer mourn Robert, that God's love was complete, and His kindness perfect. Words chosen by Grandma over three and one-half years ago just for Sarah, just for her terribly painful circumstance, were truly miraculous. They could recognize that Grandma's words were truly inspired by God who already knew what would have happened by the time Matt and Sarah read those words. "Ohh Matt, God says that He will be our everlasting light and our mourning shall be ended."

They were beaming when they walked back to the dining room. The others, worried that Matt and Sarah might be overwhelmed by the same sadness Sarah had felt a few weeks ago, were overjoyed to see them smiling. Knowing Matt and Sarah's pain, knowing how difficult things had been for them when Robert died, they were anxious to hear what Grandma had written.

As Matt and Sarah shared what they had just read, again they were all struck by the miracle of what God had given them, the miracle of the connection Grandma had with God and with them. They were in wonder over the total and absolute goodness of God, by His all-encompassing love for them, and by the miracle of faith He had given them through the abiding faith of Grandma and through the treasure His words had become to them. The treasure Grandma wanted them to find was no longer hidden.

Then Caleb asked Josh if he felt that he should have Grandma's letter now. Caleb said that he knew how much Debbie had been worrying about her parents and about the wedding plans but wasn't sure if this was sufficient to open a letter of such importance. Therefore he would leave the decision up to Josh. Caleb said that he would be glad to continue to hold the letter for them if this was what they wanted.

Josh responded with a great deal of emotion in his voice. He told Caleb that he did, indeed, want to open Grandma's letter now because there was a circumstance that he and Deb were experiencing that weighed heavily on their hearts and was something they could not currently share. Matt and Sarah, Ann and Caleb assured Josh and Deb that they would respect their privacy and his decision to read Grandma's letter. Caleb handed Josh the letter, and he and Deb went into Caleb's study to read the letter Grandma had written for them.

Deb and Josh also sat close together to open Grandma's letter, and Josh first prayed that the words they were about to read would bring them comfort not only about the wedding and about Deb's parents but also about the baby that no one knew about, except for Elizabeth and their minister. They were afraid that keeping the news from those they loved, would disappoint them, make them feel shut out. They were desperately afraid that they would lose the respect of those they loved. So, both Josh and Deb were thankful to have a word from Grandma to sustain them because they were feeling overwhelmed with fear.

They were also struggling with a sense of guilt, struggling with their decision to keep the pregnancy a secret, and struggling to do what would be best for everyone, including the child they wanted to protect. They understood that life would inevitably dish out some tough times but also knew that in this circumstance, they'd been the cause of their struggle. As they acknowledged the part they had played in bringing about their concerns, they had to acknowledge that despite this, God was telling them that He loved them.

As Josh began to read, he was overwhelmed by his feelings, openly crying. He stopped reading and explained to Deb that he'd never taken the time to tell Grandma how much she'd meant to him. He'd been rebellious after his mother died and at times hadn't been kind to Grandma. He hadn't realized that he'd been angry that God took his mother, and he hadn't appreciated what a gift his faith was or how hard it had been for Grandma not only to lose her daughter but in some way to also lose Josh. Now he realized how hurt she must have been and how she hid her own pain to love him, pray for him, and never give up on him. She'd written to him, Emailed him, and phoned him to stay in touch with him when he left for college and always let him know that she loved him and that God loved him.

When Josh had composed himself, he read Grandma's words aloud and read the same verse Caleb and Sarah had been given from Jeremiah 32:17 that said,

"Thou hast made the heaven and the earth by thy great power and stretched out arm, and there is nothing too hard for thee." Then he turned to the second page and read the scripture that Grandma had left just for them. And he and Deb, just like Sarah and Matt and Ann and Caleb before them, were amazed by the words. They were exactly what he and Deb needed to hear.

Their scripture was taken from John 14:27 and said, *"Peace I leave with you, my peace I give unto you . . . . Let not your heart be troubled, neither let it be afraid."* Debbie gasped. She couldn't believe that these words had been chosen years ago by someone who had no idea what her parents were like, no idea about her concerns, about the baby, about the guilt that ate at them, no idea that they were both afraid. She and Josh were struck by the words telling them *not* to be troubled, not to be afraid and even giving them the promise of peace! And they too knew that they had had an experience of faith, a gift from Grandma too, the gift of Grandma's hidden treasure: her faith and her love for them that transcended death.

Not knowing what was truly troubling Debbie and Josh, the family looked up expectantly as they returned to the dining room, and they were relieved to see them smiling. They could see that Josh had been crying and realized that whatever it was he carried, it was not a light burden. But when they saw their smiles, they knew that all would be well. As Josh and Debbie shared their scripture with Sarah and Matt, Caleb and Ann, they all recognized that whatever burden they carried would work out okay in the end because the words in the scripture were so comforting. God's words helped them recognize Grandma's abiding faith and the treasure of her love.

They spoke for a while about what Grandma had left for them, how thoughtful she was, how much she loved them, all that she had laid into their hearts. They vowed to try to provide these gifts to one another and their children. "Grandma's love was a godly love. Her incredible relationship with God is evident in the words she left for us . . . . it's a miracle!"

Caleb told them that Grandma had also left a letter for Paul, not knowing, of course, that he would die so young. Caleb explained that Paul's letter was why they asked Jim and Barbara to join them this evening. They talked at length about what they should do about Paul's letter, and Barbara suggested that they all read it together.

"We all loved Paul. He was, for all of us, our brother in faith and for Matt and me, our blood brother, so let's share the letter to him and then talk some more." Matt agreed, adding that once they read the letter, they could determine if it would be something they should save for Paul's children in case there would be a time when the children would seek them out. Either Matt or Barbara could hold the letter for that eventuality.

Grandma had left two scriptures for Paul. The first was from Matthew 25:21 and read, *"Well done, thou good and faithful servant: thou hast been faithful over a few things, I will make thee ruler over many things: enter thou into the joy of thy lord."*

They looked at one another, awestruck by the words "enter thou into the joy of the Lord," wondering if each of them interpreted the words to mean enter into eternity. And as they began to speak, they realized that each had indeed interpreted the words this way and could hardly believe that Grandma would have left such a set of words.

Then they read the second scripture Grandma had left for Paul. It had come from Acts 20:35-38 and read, *"I have shewed you all things, how that so labouring ye ought to support the weak, and to remember the words of the Lord Jesus . . . It is more blessed to give than to receive. And when he had thus spoken, he kneeled down, and prayed with them all. And they all wept sore, and fell on Paul's neck, and kissed him, Sorrowing most of all for the words which he spake, that they should see his face no more. And they accompanied him unto the ship."*

Matt could hardly speak. They all sat for a moment in silence. Barbara was crying softly, and Jim had moved to put his arm around her shoulders. Barbara asked, "How did Grandma ever find a scripture so fitting . . . I mean, it speaks to Paul's work in eternity, it speaks to his death . . . by name, and it even mentions a ship! It's actually incredible! It really was inspired by God. I'm amazed."

Then Matt spoke with awe about the experience of faith he had after Paul died and recalled that Paul had been dressed in the black suit and white shirt of a minister in their church and had tapped Matt on the shoulder to let him know that he was okay. When he and Sarah had later described to their minister what had occurred, he explained that Paul's dress indicated the work he was doing in eternity, the work he'd wanted to do just before he died. Paul had asked to become a deacon and to work with those who seemed lost to drug addiction.

And then he'd died, and they were to "see his face no more." The words "I have shewed thee all things" and "He prayed with them all" spoke to their hearts that Paul was indeed doing the work he wanted to do for God. They felt that the scriptures Grandma left for Paul were really for them to reinforce what they believed about why God took Paul and the work Paul did for those who died in their addictions never having known God.

Matt said that he was so glad they could all share in Grandma's letter to Paul and thanked Caleb for his wisdom. It too had reinforced their faith, helped them recognize how God worked in those who loved Him to bring miracles into their lives. Once again, they were reassured that Paul was happy, had a job to do in eternity that he'd wanted to do on earth. Once again, they were reassured of life after death, of the incredibly loving nature of God, and of the all-encompassing nature of His plan of salvation. Sarah's joy at the thought of Paul and Robert being together in eternity was overwhelming and she too began to cry, but they were happy tears.

Then Jim began to speak slowly, quietly, and without the usual sarcasm in his voice. From the tone of his voice, they knew that what he had to say was important. "Well, I've listened to you talk for years now, and to tell you the truth, I've also watched all of you. Maybe even watched you, hoping you'd show me a reason to doubt you, to put you in the same category as many so-called believers who talk but don't walk God's teachings. I think that in some callous way, I looked for you to fail. But through all these years, what I have seen is your faith and I've seen that faith rewarded. I've also been quite amazed at what you've found in the Bible that answers so many questions . . . some that you've had, and many that I've had. Remember when you pointed out the scripture that indicates that evolution can be compatible with creation . . . remember that? Remember when you asked me what I believed caused us to have days and nights and seasons and I said it was the sun? That conversation showed me . . . I mean, . . . it *really* blew my mind because . . . well, it showed me that the Bible could be *real* . . . uhhh . . . coexist with most parts of science. What I read may not prove anything empirically, but it sure did *allow* science to live side by side with the Bible, and to me, that was amazing! But stubborn as I was, I pushed that aside, telling myself that one home run doesn't win a ball game.

"But the home runs kept coming, and even though I wanted you to be angry with me so I had an excuse to turn away from religion, from believing, you kept on loving me, kept living as God asked you. And you did that even when I was pushing you away. So . . . Well, I have been thinking about joining the church for a long time. Maybe it's been my pride that held me back . . . You're aware that I hate to be wrong. Maybe I also feel that it has taken me so long to make a commitment that I was embarrassed to admit to how I felt. But now it's time. In fact, it's long overdue for me to make a decision and ask you all to respect that decision.

"Today moved my heart like no other. Reminiscing about all that has happened and your responses to what has happened make me realize that none of you ever waver from loving one another or from loving God. The role God plays in your life is incredible. What happened today blows my mind. Suddenly, I feel ashamed by my stubborn attitude and ask you to forgive me. And . . . not to be outdone by all of you knowing scripture so well, let me lay one on you to show you that I too have been reading the Bible . . . It's from Psalm 18:28 and says, *"For thou wilt light my candle; the LORD my God will enlighten my darkness,"* and this is exactly what God has done with me. He worked with the darkness of my ways and didn't give up until a candle was lit inside my heart. So your prayers and your example have worked. God *does* answer the prayers you offer for those who do not believe, and He is willing to work on hearts even when it seems impossible to think that a hardened heart can be changed. I'm a prime example. What happened today really clinched the deal. What Grandma could have written so many years ago and have fit your circumstances so well is nothing short of a miracle, as you say, an experience of faith . . . and today, that's what God gave me—an experience of faith to see what He did so many years ago that fits today; the treasure of His love and the treasure of your love and your abiding faith. I am especially touched by what Grandma wrote about Paul, I almost cried . . . a grown man crying! But I always had a special place in my heart for Paul. It meant a lot to me to finally see what God provided for him. Well, and hold on to your hats—I will join the church the same day that Wade and Heza and Bara do . . . if you'll have me!"

Everyone congratulated Jim and went over to hug him, clap him on the back, shake his hand, and everyone's eyes sparkled from tears held back. Then Barbara walked over to Jim and looked up at him with her love for him shining in her eyes, and Jim put his arm across her shoulders and gave her a hug, knowing that what he was doing was not only a blessing for him, but also for Barbara and the little one that would soon be born. The whole family basked in that blessing too, and they were thrilled.

And so their evening ended, and their faith had once again been increased by what they shared. They clearly saw God's hand in their lives. They also saw that they wanted to live up to the example that Grandma had left them. They needed to get to work and become the kind of a role model for their children and grandchildren and for their congregation that Grandma had been for them. They needed to grow into becoming a beacon for everyone they came in contact with so the light of God's words would shine from them and be an invitation to all.

They decided to pray together and ask God to help them. They prayed for the souls who entered into eternity without knowing God and felt assured that God would not forsake them, and they thanked God for what He'd brought them. Caleb read them two Bible verses that he asked they all take into their hearts to help them be what God asked of them, what would make Grandma proud of them and help them become a blessing to those around them. He said he'd looked for these verses before they arrived this evening.

The first scripture was from Micah 4:2 and said, *"Come, and let us go up to the mountain of the LORD . . . he will teach us of his ways, and we will walk in his paths."* The second was from Isaiah 42:6 and read, *"I the LORD have called thee in righteousness, and will hold thine hand, and will keep thee."*

And God smiled, and the angels rejoiced, for these children of God would go out into the world to touch the hearts of many and as Acts 2:42 stated, *"And they continued stedfastly in the apostles' doctrine and fellowship, and in breaking of bread, and in prayers."*

These children of God had learned what a true treasure was. Grandma's hidden treasure was now no longer hidden but living as a beacon and testimony in their hearts for all to see, an abiding faith that had even transcended death. And the words they had been given through scripture were a treasure they could keep forever in their hearts and which would lead them to the goal of their faith: To be a part of the bride of Christ and to spend an eternity with God.

He shall call upon me, and I will answer him:
I will be with him in trouble; I will deliver him, and honour him.
With long life will I satisfy him, and shew him my salvation.
Psalm 91:15-16

Bibliography

Archer, Gleason. *Encyclopedia of Bible Difficulties*. Grand Rapids, Michigan: Zondervan, 1982, p. 161.

Barnhouse, Donald Grey. *The Invisible War*. Grand Rapids, Michigan: Zondervan Publishing House, 12th printing, 1976, copyright 1965.

Boyd, Robert. *Boyd's Bible Handbook*. Eugene, Oregon: Harvest House, 1983, pp. 122-124.

Halley, Henry H. *Halley's Bible Handbook*. 24th ed. Grand Rapids, Michigan: Zondervan Publishing House, Copyright 1965.

Merriam-Webster, *Webster's Ninth New Collegiate Dictionary*. Springfield, Massachusetts: Merriam-Webster Inc, Publishers, copyright 1986.

Morris, Henry M. *The Bible and Modern Science*. Chicago: Moody Press, 1951, 1968.

—*Many Infallible Proofs*. Chicago: Moody Press, 3rd printing, 1977.

New Apostolic Church. *The Holy Bible* (King James Version). Canada: Thomas Nelson, Inc., Camden, NJ, 1972.

O'Reilly, Bill. *A Bold Fresh Piece of Humanity*. Broadway Books, copyright 2008, pp. 194, 234, 239.

Rimmer, Harry. *The Harmony of Science and Scripture*. Grand Rapids: Eerdmans, 1936, p. 33.

Roget's II The New Thesaurus, by the editors of The American Heritage Dictionary. Houghton Miflin Company, copyright 1980.

www.blueletterbible.org/faq/don_stewart/stewart.cfm?ID=625.

Strong, James, LLD, STD. *Strong's Exhaustive Concordance of the Bible.* Abington, Nashville, thirty fourth printing 1996, copyright 1890.

Scriptural Index

Abiding Faith, Hidden Treasure

This following scriptural index is comprised of twelve subjects listed alphabetically and in the order they are found in the book. These are as follows:

- *Commitment* God Asks of Us

- *Devil*, Satan: His Power and Influence

- *Forgiveness* We Need to Obtain

- *Instruction* God Gives to Help Us

- Joining *Creation* and Evolution

- *Mystery* of God

- *Power* That Is God's Alone

- *Protection* God Freely Offers

- *Refining* Process We Must Endure

- *Sinful* Nature of All Men

- *Warnings* God Issues to Help Us

- Why *Death* Is Necessary

Index

F

Forgiveness We Need to Obtain

I

Instruction God Gives to Help Us

J

Joining *Creation* and Evolution

M

Mystery of God

Mystery of God

P

Power That Is God's Alone

Protection God Freely Offers

R

Refining Process We Must Endure

S

Sinful Nature of All Men

W

Warnings God Issues to Help Us

Why *Death* Is Necessary

Excerpt From:
And Then They
Asked God

Elizabeth had finally given in to John's request that she accompany him to the hospital. He wanted to show her what duties he performed as a hospital volunteer and the rewards it brought him. She hadn't wanted to go because hospitals held bad memories for her. She knew her thoughts to be irrational, so when John had been persistent in his request, assuring her that *his* hospital would bring her good memories, she had agreed to go. He'd told her that she could make a difference in the lives of others, and this statement had pushed her into agreeing to accompany him.

Rebecca and Jayden had been spending many hours perusing the college campus brochures they had either received in the mail or been given by their guidance counselor at school. They seemed to talk endlessly about this upcoming and exciting venture. Watching them, heads together, bent over the table in concentration and overhearing their conversations of the pros and cons of each curriculum finally convinced Elizabeth that they might really be leaving after all. She didn't want Rebecca to go.

Elizabeth cringed to think of waking up every morning to an empty house, of not having Becca's happy chatter and loving companionship give so much purpose to her days. While she fully understood that time marched on, that Becca eventually would leave her nest, Elizabeth was not yet at the point where she could accept it gracefully. She was however wise enough to understand that while emotionally she couldn't bear the thought of being separated from her daughter nor of her daughter out in a world filled with so much danger, intellectually, she wanted Becca to obtain a good education and prepare for her future. She also knew that as Rebecca became more independent and self-sufficient, Elizabeth would not worry as much about her own advancing age or the state of her health.

Elizabeth had been in her late forties when she and her husband adopted month-old Rebecca, and even then, she'd worried about being almost seventy when Rebecca graduated from college and could finally step out on her own. At that time, neither she nor her husband had seriously considered the consequences for Rebecca should either of them become ill. She shared these thoughts with her friend John, knowing that he too was experiencing the pangs of preparing for his grandson's departure to college.

John had practically raised Jayden, so Elizabeth understood that for John, it was more like letting a son go rather than a grandson. Always pragmatic, John assured both Elizabeth and himself that Rebecca and Jayden's foray into college life was important to their future and that he and Elizabeth *had* to support and encourage it. But Elizabeth knew that secretly, despite his words, John also suffered. Jayden had been the focus of John's life for so many years and when Jayden left, it would be John who felt the impact the most.

John's daughter had recently remarried, and though John was happy about her marriage and grateful for the good man her husband was, he missed the constant companionship they'd shared before his daughter had met her husband. Ruth's happiness was well worth whatever loss John felt. Before she remarried, Ruth had been despondent, worn down by the responsibilities of maintaining a home for Jayden and raising him alone. She'd been thankful that John had stepped in, had retired from his job so he could help by being home when Jayden came home from school.

John had also invested much of his time in Jayden's scholastic and spiritual life by checking his homework and tutoring him when needed. He brought him to Sunday school, then confirmation classes, and as he got older, John brought him to the youth events that the church provided. John had become Jayden's role model and Ruth's strength. He'd also helped financially because Jayden's father had stopped paying the child support ordered by the court. But now, in the space of only a few years, everything had changed. Ruth no longer needed him as she once had. And John was glad. That's how it should be.

Ruth had a wonderful new husband whom John liked immensely. Jayden would be going away to college, and John now had the opportunity to engage in a new purpose for his life, something that would benefit others. With the economy such a mess, John reasoned that while he could go back to work, he would not want to take a job away from someone more in need. Thus, he determined to increase the number of hours he worked as a volunteer at the hospital and to see where else he could be of use to others. *After all,* John thought, *Christ himself said in Matthew 25:45, "Verily I say unto you, Inasmuch as ye did it not to one of the least of these, ye did it not to me."* This means that if I do not help others, I do not help Christ.

Because John knew that Elizabeth was going to miss having Rebecca close, he wanted Elizabeth to join him in his volunteer work. Rebecca had been Elizabeth's only focus since her husband had died, and with no relatives, no family, she would be hard-hit by Rebecca's departure. He hoped that today's visit to the hospital and accompanying him on his "rounds" would pique Elizabeth's interest. Though he planned that they would only volunteer a few hours at present, once the children left, he and Elizabeth would be ready to take on additional responsibilities immediately.

Elizabeth appreciated John's efforts to help her find a way to be productive as Rebecca spread her wings for her flight into adulthood. But she wasn't sure that she would go along with John's plan. The smells of a hospital still conjured up the pain and fear she'd had to fight for so long to overcome. Antiseptics, anesthesia, the distinct odor emanating from the radiology department, even the general odor of sickness and death assaulted Elizabeth's sensibilities whenever she entered a hospital and brought the unpleasant memories back. A hospital was where her husband had been diagnosed, where he had undergone many surgeries to stop the progression of his cancer, where he'd later received his chemotherapy, and from where he'd finally been sent home to die.

But John had been persistent in his quest to have Elizabeth "give volunteering a try" that finally she had given in, but only after extracting a promise from John that if she still felt the same way about hospitals after one week of helping him, he would no longer expect her to volunteer. He'd agreed to her terms. He knew that hard work, serving others, being needed were all a balm for the soul.

When John's wife had died so many years ago, he'd gone through many of the same experiences that Elizabeth had when her husband had died. Every day that his wife had been ill, John had fought his anger at the injustices that life could bring to bear. He could deal with injustice for those who were unjust, but it was especially hard to bear when injustice kept coming at those who were so innocent, who deserved goodness and kindness.

His wife had contracted Lou Gehrig's disease. Watching her lose her ability to function, become totally debilitated, and struggle even to breathe wrought a tremendous anger in John. His wife had had her full mental acuity right up until the end, and because of this, she knew exactly what was happening to her, knew she was suffering in dying. Despite this, she had remained cheerful and loving. Her incredible attitude toward what was happening made John's anger even worse because he felt that what his wife had to go through was so unfair. His anger was directed toward the disease and the cruelty that this particular disease imposed upon its victims.

He knew that directing his anger in this manner was okay as he could channel the energy created by his anger toward helping others or toward helping to raise funds for research. But his anger was also directed toward God, and he felt guilty about this. John wondered why God allowed evil to live happily and unfettered, prosperous and fulfilled while good was beset by so much hardship. This anger had filled John's heart with bitterness and had taken him a very long time to resolve.

Elizabeth had had a similar experience. She had watched her husband die slowly in pain yet remain faithful and loving and accepting of God's will to the very end, and it had broken her heart. She and her husband had known each other since they were teenagers, and she had always loved him, even before he ever noticed her. He had been her role model, and their life together had been perfect. They never had children of their own but had adopted Rebecca when they were in their forties. Rebecca was a wonderful child and brought them much happiness. Her husband had died when Rebecca was just twelve years old.

Then two years later, as if the loss of her husband wasn't enough, Elizabeth began suffering some vague symptoms, which the doctors told her could be the onset of a serious and debilitating disease. After long discussions with Rebecca and finally agreeing on what they should do, they had set out to find Rebecca's birth mother so that if Elizabeth should die, Rebecca would still have a family. Elizabeth prayed fervently that if they found Rebecca's birth mother, she would be worthy of a daughter like Rebecca.

Their search brought spectacular results. They did find Rebecca's birth mother, and she had been overjoyed to find Rebecca. And with Rebecca's mom, Mary, came Kevin, Mary's husband. Then Rebecca and Elizabeth met their friends Matt and Sarah, Ann and Caleb, Josh and Debbie, and Jim and Barbara who also welcomed them. All these wonderful people became Elizabeth and Rebecca's extended family.

God had heard their prayers and had arranged everything perfectly. Mary too had been praying that someday, she could be reunited with Rebecca. Thus, Elizabeth and Rebecca gained a wonderful new family who were people who loved God and practiced what they preached! It was such a blessing to each of them, and as they exchanged their stories, they realized the incredible miracle God had wrought for them. It was through them that Elizabeth had met John.

Looking back, Elizabeth could recognize the many occurrences that had led them to meeting Mary, and she wondered at the complexity of the engineering feat that brought this miracle to them. So life was good; it was just this transition period that seemed difficult. It was this letting go, this empty nest thing that both she and John would have to cope with in the coming years.

The children still had another year of high school to finish before they left for college, so the worries that John and Elizabeth shared were even a bit premature. Maybe it was natural for parents when they recognized that each day, their children's lives filled with more and more outside interests and parents had to acknowledge that their position in their child's life would be changing forever.

Do all mothers experience these emotions? Elizabeth wondered. *Is it that there must be a gradual moving apart of a child and parent in order to come together again as friends?* She thought of a saying she'd once heard that said that if you let a bird fly away from you and it comes back to you, it will be yours forever, but if you imprison the bird, it will never be yours. Maybe it was in the letting go that the decision to hold on could be formed. Maybe an adult relationship could only be formed when *both* parties worked toward nurturing it, when both parties consciously decided to undertake the responsibilities that came with sustaining a trusting and eternal relationship.

Elizabeth had been an only child too, so she tried to remember how it was with her and her mother. She'd always been close to her mother and had always loved her and respected her, but then again, it was a different time, a different generation, a time when parents and children remained connected throughout life. There were fewer options then. *But,* she thought, *it's also different with each mother-and-daughter relationship, isn't it? . . . After all, look at Debbie and her mom. They are as far apart as can be.*

Maintaining a close relationship between any two people was a two-way street; one can't make a close relationship happen without the other wanting it to happen as well. Whether the relationship was between friends or relatives, between husband and wife, or parent and child, it needs nurturing from both parties and it needs trust between them as well. *I hope and pray that Rebecca and I will never lose those qualities because I would be devastated if our love could not be sustained, let alone flourish during our separation from one another.*

There are so many unknowns in life, so many different personalities, differing opinions, so many times when we are sure we are right only to find that we were wrong. There are so many circumstances that wield an influence on the way we think and act, Elizabeth thought. *What can we do? What should we do to keep safe, to keep our relationships as we want them, as God wants them?* Elizabeth realized that one needed to lay a foundation of love, honor, integrity, and respect in a child and do this spiritually as well. Then when rough times came or a separation occurred, prayer and love would eventually mend any broken parts. *With God, all things are possible,* Elizabeth thought. But she also knew that without God, good things broke down.

Elizabeth, like John, felt that faith in God was paramount to life and would bring them through all difficulties. Their faith led to their children's faith, and it brought them a source of strength and a beacon of light they could share.

She'd read in scripture that God wanted parents to teach their children of Him and wanted children to honor their parents. It was interesting that scripture demanded that children honor their parents and yet warned that in the end-times, they could turn one upon the other. What God was explaining was that one would be a child of God and the other would not.

Elizabeth ran to her concordance and found the scripture she wanted, then turned to Matthew 10:33 and read, "*But whosoever shall deny me before men, him will I also deny before my Father which is in heaven.*" Then in Matthew 10:35, she read that Christ explained, "*For I am come to set a man at variance against his father, and the daughter against her mother.*" Then in Matthew 10:37, Christ said, "*He that loveth father or mother more than me is not worthy of me: and he that loveth son or daughter more than me is not worthy of me.*"

She understood these words, understood that God asked children to honor their parents, and parents to teach their children of God and that doing this showed that they followed God's statutes and placed God first in their lives. But when either of these two parties did not do this, Satan had an opening through which he could destroy that relationship. If this occurred, sometimes the one who loved God and determined to follow God's statutes must choose God over the relationship.

As Elizabeth thought back over the past few years, she could identify the times when God's blessing was evident in their lives, and together, she and Rebecca had blossomed in joy and appreciation. But she could also identify the times when Satan struck, when pain and heartache filled them, and when they struggled to accept their circumstances.

Then they searched God's words for answers, for the comfort they needed, for the assurance that God was still in control. Elizabeth realized that she could identify those hard times, the time *after* the heartache. For it was indeed *after* the attack when God blessed them for their faith, gave them the comfort they needed. It was during the attack that God gave them the strength to endure. But often they didn't feel that strength while they lived through their trials. They felt weak and defeated. Yet these were indeed the times when their faith had grown. Elizabeth felt that if they learned from what had occurred, they would have less to go through in the future.

Thus, Elizabeth knew she would be able to endure as long as she remained faithful, as long as she trusted God in all things, as long as she kept God first in her life and her prayer life strong. She thanked God for her new friends, her newly extended family, the faith they too had in God, and the example they were to her. She thanked God for Rebecca and for Jayden. Jayden was such a good friend and wonderful role model for Rebecca, and his faith in God was strong.

So instead of thinking about the troubles that might appear in the future, Elizabeth determined to think only of the good things they had right now. Difficulties would come, Satan would attack, but they had God on their side. They had their faith to sustain them and a future to fight for. She needed to tell these things to Rebecca, warn her to stay faithful, to do as God asked even when it hurt so she would always have His blessing.

And with these thoughts, Elizabeth recalled a Bible verse that she'd always loved and decided to write it down and keep it with her so in troubling times she could read it and be reminded of God's presence. She opened her Bible and, with pen and paper, copied the words she found in John 14:1-2, "*Let not your heart be troubled: ye believe in God, believe also in me. In my Father's house are many mansions: if it were not so, I would have told you. I go to prepare a place for you,*" and in John 14:27, "*Let not your heart be troubled, neither let it be afraid.*"

But what John and Elizabeth hadn't expected was the role they would have to play in the lives of their newly extended family and friends when the evil one struck again.

About The Author

Helen Gumienny Glowacki is an interior designer, writer, teacher, and motivational speaker. She was the host, writer, and producer of the television series *The Contemporary Woman*, broadcast by UA-Columbia Cablevision, which addressed interior design and the health, relationship, parenting, and life issues of interest to women.

Helen also co-hosted a number of twenty-four-hour telethons featuring celebrity guests to raise funds for various community projects and was a guest co-host for a cable television game show.

Helen's writing credentials include an extensive background as a freelance feature writer and a staff writer for four newspapers; author of newsletter articles; developer of marketing manuals, most notably for the INOVA Hospital System; and designer and editor of a newsletter for the Martin/St. Lucie Chapter of the United States Amateur Ballroom Dancers Association.

A graduate of William Paterson University, Helen received her Bachelor of Arts degree in communications, magna cum laude. Helen also has an associate of science degree with honors and is a registered nurse. She has served on the boards of directors for two associations and taught interior design for adult school programs. Some of her larger design projects include Avon Headquarters in Morton Grove, Illinois, and Chilton Hospital in Pequannock, New Jersey and was listed in *Who's Who of American Women* and *Who's Who of Women Executives* in 1992.

As a popular speaker at ease with an audience, Helen addresses aspects of interior design and addresses the work of God and His word through scripture. Her venues have included women's groups, church groups, community service and religious organizations, high schools and colleges, libraries, cruise ships, and large adult—and assisted-living condominium complexes.

Helen appeared as a guest on a radio show and performed dance routines for theater groups, television, army camps, and veteran's hospitals. She held the title Mrs. Packanack Lake for five years and has received a number of community service awards.

Helen has donated her *"Grandmother Series"* novels, her *"Why God Why Series"* and her other non-fiction books to cancer centers, drug and alcohol rehabilitation centers, prisons and mission schools, most notably to *The Henwood Foundation* in Zambia, Africa to help bring testimony of God's plan of salvation to others. She also posts articles on her Facebook wall which address our relationship with God,

Helens greatest joys are her husband, two children, and four grandchildren, and singing in the choir of the New Apostolic Church. She and her husband enjoy ballroom dancing and have performed for various charitable functions. Her heart's desire is to help others find the love and comforting presence of God through her writing.

To learn more about Helen's novels and her non-fiction books, visit her website at www.helenglowacki.com.

To become a distributor or to purchase in quantity for a fund raising project or to provide testimony, please send an email to helen@helenglowacki.com.

Helen's readers can also visit the author on Face Book at http://www.facebook.com/pages/The-Grandmother-Series/155300907853909?ref=ts.

www.ingramcontent.com/pod-product-compliance
Lightning Source LLC
Chambersburg PA
CBHW031106260626
47172CB00001B/243